THE

The animal eyes [...]
side of the shed w[...]
on his back with [...]
Arnold. Arnold bou[...] [...]kal's
snout snap shut as [...] horrid slow-
ness, he turned his he[...] [...] his master, blinding
him with the lamps of [...] eyes.

Master? Arnold thought wildly as the twin cones of
light settled on his face. *Am I its master?*

Mongster stared at him. Arnold stared back with his
blood pumping thickly in his veins, blood suddenly
turned to sludge by those eyes. What could he read in
them? Hate? Compassion? Or a simple and mindless
desire to kill?

MONGSTER

Praise for Randall Boyll's *After Sundown*

"Absolutely terrific. It's a genuine pleasure encounter-
ing such an unanticipated talent from out of the blue.
What Randall Boyll has crafted is a Mormon parallel
to Stephen King's *The Shining* . . . A strange and en-
grossing tale. I'm predicting that his is a new career to
pay close attention to!"

—Edward Bryant, *Locus*

Randall Boyll Books From The Berkley Publishing Group

AFTER SUNDOWN
DARKMAN
SHOCKER
MONGSTER

MONGSTER

RANDALL BOYLL

BERKLEY BOOKS, NEW YORK

MONGSTER

A Berkley Book / published by arrangement with
the author

PRINTING HISTORY
Berkley edition / January 1991

ISBN: 0-425-12485-1

A BERKLEY BOOK®TM 757,375
Berkley Books are published by The Berkley Publishing Group,
200 Madison Avenue, New York, New York 10016.
The name ''Berkley'' and the ''B'' logo
are trademarks belonging to Berkley Publishing Corporation.

10 9 8 7 6 5 4 3 2 1

From time to time a writer likes to toss a word of thanks to the people who have influenced his career, and while I failed to do that with my first novel, I thought I'd give it a shot this time. So, then, my humble appreciation goes out to:

Nye Willden and John C. Fox of the Dugent Publishing Corporation, publishers of *Cavalier* and *Gent* magazines, who steadily bought my stuff when no one else was interested . . .

Stephen King, who makes frequent appearances in this book (probably grounds for a lawsuit there) . . .

Richard Surmacz, editor of my first novel, *After Sundown*, my man behind the scenes who made it all happen . . .

Ginjer Buchanan, my editor of this one, who knows her stuff . . .

and the people who are plowing through this extensive dedication, wondering if the rest of the book is any better.

Author's Note

There is no town in Indiana named Wabash Heights. There is no man named Weasel there, there are no Alfred and Jack Cumberland, no Norman Parker, no Spack and no Jimmy and no Jed. Sadly, Mike Taraday does not exist, and neither does Don Marston, though I wish it were so.

But there *is* a young boy named Arnold, and he *did* have a father named John, and the things in these pages very surely occurred, or soon will.

But there is no Wabash Heights, on any map, between Indianapolis and Terre Haute, in the Hoosier State known as Indiana.

But I have been there, and this is what I saw . . .

· 1 ·

The Incident at the Wabash Tavern

ON THE NIGHT that Frank "Weasel" Whipple beat the living shit out of his stepson Arnold, he stopped by the Wabash Tavern first in order to get drunk. This was normal behavior for Weasel Whipple, a large, pot-bellied man with a stubbly beard and eyes like beady, deep-set black buttons in his face—normal behavior to get drunk every night after work, that is. It was not his intent, as he entered the dim little tavern that stank of sour beer and stale cigarette smoke, to beat the living shit out of his stepson or anyone else. He just wanted to get plastered. It was April 19, 1990, five o'clock on a Thursday evening. He had been pounding dents out of car bodies all day at Hyman & Sons Body Shop, where he worked, and had built up a powerful thirst for beer.

The bartender, Mike Taraday, saw him come in, and sighed to himself resignedly. Weasel Whipple was like a clock, so punctual was he. A big mean clock, like Big Ben, all full of wound-up springs and huge clashing gears. For Weasel it was always thirteen o'clock, an unlucky time for everybody. He came in and took his usual seat by the door. The few patrons of the Wabash Tavern at this early hour glanced at him and quickly away.

"Beer," he grunted at Mike.

No shit, Mike thought, sliding open the cooler door and hauling out a bottle of Falls City. He popped the cap off and went over to the Weasel.

"Ninety cents, Weasie."

"On my tab."

"Your tab's up to eighty dollars already. Don't payday ever come?"

1

"You'll be the first to know when it does," Weasel growled, taking the bottle in one meaty hand. He tipped it to his lips and drank half of it in three swallows. A line of it trickled out the corner of his mouth and slid into his beard. He scuffed at it with his wrist.

"The owner says to cut you off at ninety bucks, Weasie," Mike Taraday said. "House rules."

Weasel fixed his black-button eyes on him. "Screw the owner. I can take my business some other place."

If God grants small favors, Mike thought, but did not say it. Instead he said, "Ten beers tonight, maybe eleven, and I have to cut you off. I want you to understand that now, while you're sober, so there'll be no trouble later on when you're tanked. Eleven beers tonight, and that's it." Mike looked at him speculatively. "Unless you've got some money, that is."

"You want money?" Weasel Whipple leaned back on his bar stool and dug in one pocket. He hauled out a handful of change and slapped it on the bar. Mike saw pennies, a few nickels. "Ever heard of a 'lectric bill, Mike? Ever heard of gas, and water, and sewage, house payments, car payments, kids' lunch money? Ever heard of three leeches sucking you dry?"

Mike knew well enough what this leech business was all about. Ever since last May, when Weasel had married Karen White, divorced mother of three, Weasel had taken to calling the kids leeches. God alone knew why Karen, at thirty-five still a pretty if somewhat sheepish woman, had married this beast, this Weasel. Mike had known Karen in high school. Mike knew everybody in Wabash Heights, Indiana, and everybody knew everybody else. Weasel was a relative newcomer, having roared into town two years ago in his battered '72 Malibu towing an orange U-haul with one flat tire. It was quickly rumored that he had left Terre Haute with the law on his heels. Something about knifing a man in a bar; no one knew if this was true, and no one was asking. One thing Weasel had let be known about himself early on: don't fuck with me, I won't fuck with you. And mind your own business while you're at it.

He usually drank alone. At times an old buddy from Terre Haute would be with him, and they would whoop it up until the tavern closed at three, get a case for the road, and drink it while bombing the backroads in Weasel's ruined Malibu. How

Weasel ever made it to work in the mornings was a mystery. Mike knew Elsius Hyman, his boss, and had heard tales of roaring hangovers, puking in the bathroom, broken Q-Tips stuffed in Weasel's ears to drown out the sound of his own hammer on auto-body sheet metal. With anybody else it would have been funny. With Weasel, it wasn't.

"I got kids," Mike said. "I make it."

"Yeah? You make minimum here, like I do? You kiss George Washington's ass on every dollar before it goes flying in the wind? You got finance companies hounding you day and night?"

"Everybody's got their troubles," Mike replied, and was glad to see a hand wave at the other end of the bar. He walked off to get the hand-waver his beer.

"Razzle-frazzle fuckhead," Weasel grumbled. He regarded his beer bottle for a moment, scraped at the label with one big thumbnail, and polished if off in another three swallows.

"Beer!" he shouted. He had not eaten breakfast, too hung over to stand the sight of food. He had not eaten lunch, though Karen had packed him one in his big black lunch box—braunschweiger sandwiches and a cheap pickle, for Christ's sake. His stomach had revolted at the sight of that, too. He had slipped out and gone to the Three-Penny Tavern, which was a block away from Hyman & Sons garage, and where his credit still had some merit. For lunch he had downed six beers and gone back to work smelling like an exploded brewery. Hyman's son, the garage foreman, had noticed but didn't care all that much. Weasel was a good body man, mean-assed dipshit or not.

"Beer down here!" Weasel shouted.

Mike trundled over with a fresh Falls City. "Two down," he said.

"Lick my balls," Weasel snapped. Mike was not a big man, and if he wanted to, Weasel could shove him head-first down that stinkhole they called a toilet at the other end of the tavern, and flush him away. The thought had occurred to him more than once when this business about no more credit popped up. Well, tomorrow was Friday, payday, and Weasel would hand over a ten or a twenty and re-establish his good standing with the owner, Sam Liddey, who never made an appearance here anymore, anyway. Sam had been suckered by some Jehovah's Witnesses a few months ago and now considered drinking a

sin. Owning the bar and selling forty-cent Falls City at ninety
cents a bottle wasn't, though. Weasel, if he had had a sense of
humor, would have chuckled at this. He didn't, so he didn't.
He just considered it another of the mysteries of the universe,
which he considered to be God's asshole anyway.

Weasel drank. The four hours since his lunchtime beer had
left him with a mild headache and a driving thirst for more
beer. As he drank this second beer, the eighth of the day, his
buzz began to be replaced and he relaxed a bit. Eleven beers
tonight, what the hell. Maybe he would surprise the old lady
later by getting a hard-on for a change. That thought set his
crotch to tingling. Karen didn't look too bad naked. Sure, her
tits were baggy and she had cellulite dimples all over her ass,
but in the dark she was as good as the next. He decided then
and there that he would bang her tonight. Screw the kids, let
them hear. She was always worried about that. The two-
bedroom shack they lived in had walls thin as plasterboard
could be. The Goodwill cast-off bed they slept in squeaked like
an old pickup on a gravel road when they screwed. Well, screw
that, too. Tonight old Weasel would have a surprise for the
whining bitch he had married.

He looked up at the Budweiser clock on the wall above the
rows of liquor bottles. Five-fifteen. Two down in fifteen minutes. That left nine to drink before Mike cut him off, and that
would take until about, about . . .

Weasel scratched his head. His thoughts were getting too
swimmy to perform feats of mathematical genius.

"Beer!" he shouted.

The tables were starting to fill up. Some floozy in a screaming red dress sailed over to the jukebox and dumped quarters
inside. Weasel turned to watch her. It was May Gimbel, the
wife of that drunk Harley Gimbel. He and Harley had almost
gotten into a fistfight here not two weeks ago, though Weasel
no longer remembered what it had been about or what had
started it. Harley didn't like guys looking at his wife, maybe
that had been it. Weasel looked over to the table Harley was
sitting at and got a cold, long stare from the man. Weasel
decided he would bed May down someday, just to show Harley
what was what.

He turned back to his beer as a country tune began to belch
out of the old juke. Somebody else came in and now the bar
began to fill up as bad as the tables were. Some pansy in a suit

was sucking Michelob out of a bottle at the other end, two guys were engaged in a conversation about the Indianapolis Colts beside him, and that left three empty bar stools between Weasel and them. He listened in for a while, then decided the Colts could go to hell.

He drank. He shouted for more.

"Four down," Mike said, bringing it.

"I don't need a fucking time clock. Especially not out of you."

"Don't get wise on me, Weasel," Mike said, and glared at him. Weasel glared back with his brooding black eyes, fumbling in his shirt pocket for a cigarette. Mike made a hasty departure, thinking of pocket knives and zip guns.

Weasel drank, smoked his cheap no-brand cigarettes, and thought. That's what it was like, that's exactly what it was like. A time clock. There was a time clock at work and now there was one here, too. A bit of anger blossomed in Weasel's brain, feeding on self-pity and self-righteous indignation. He had been a regular customer here for almost two years. He ought to get treated with some respect.

Two more guys wandered in, laughing and whooping, glad to be off work. They sat down on the bar stools next to the Colts fans, leaving only one empty space between Weasel and the rest of humanity. The jukebox thundered, playing Johnny Cash now. Weasel hated Johnny Cash worse than most people hate rats. The old shit couldn't sing a tune to save his life. Weasel thought about going over and smashing the jukebox in with his fist. Instead he drank, losing some of it out of the corners of his mouth. He cursed himself and armed the beer off his beard.

"Beer!"

Mike lollygagged for a while this time, pretending to be busy stacking warm bottles in the cooler. The clock above him said five-thirty. *Christ,* Weasel thought desperately, *at this rate he's gonna cut me off by seven. Cut me off like a bunch of green bananas out of a tree.*

"Beer down here, dammit!"

Mike relented and got him one. Weasel lit another cigarette, grimacing at the shitty menthol taste. Karen had picked up a whole carton of these cheapo bastards at the local Kroger last week, hoping to please him by saving some money. Weasel had cuffed her a good one for that. The bag had been married to him for eleven months and knew he smoked Marlboros, not pansy menthol cigs that came in yellow packages with a big red pair of Cost-Cutter scissors adorning the front.

His anger deepened with each drag off the cigarette. He wished to Christ he had not gotten married, wished to Christ he was a bachelor who could live off minimum wage without having to beg the government for food stamps and welfare. At times the government sent some fat hag of a social worker over to his house to check up on them; she had to make sure, for Uncle Sam's sake, that the Whipples were living in the poverty they deserved. She even inspected the kids' closet for clothes and shoes, and made sure Weasel had not pulled some trick on the welfare people by buying a newer car. On the days when she made her appearance Weasel made sure to get double drunk, just so he could go home and face the humiliation of knowing the social worker had been there snooping. What a life. At forty, Weasel had seen enough of life to know that it was a big steaming pile of shit. If it wasn't for beer and cigarettes there would be no reason at all to live.

He finished his beer and mashed out his cigarette. The Budweiser clock rolled inexorably on toward seven. Alcohol was streaming pleasantly through his veins now, making his head light and his face a bit numb, as it usually did. He leaned sideways on his stool and farted, a good smelly beer fart. Nobody noticed; the juke was blasting some modern tune that to Weasel's ears sounded like pure shit. He sniffed deeply of his own fart, wondering briefly how the inside of the human body could smell so rotten, and hoped some of it would drift downward to the pansy-ass sipping Michelob at the other end of the bar. Maybe he would look over at Weasel and there would be grounds for a fight.

"Beer!"

Beer was brought. Weasel was drinking it down when the door drifted open and some punk kid who looked like a weight lifter came in. He had incredibly short blond hair and monstrous biceps and thighs. He stood squinting through the gloom and smoke, then spied the empty stool beside Weasel and sat down. Their knees bumped briefly.

Rage flared in Weasel's brain, a bright white light. He assessed the kid out of the corner of his eye. Big fucker. Too bad. If it had been some skinny little shit Weasel would have coldcocked him for bumping his knee. Now the ultimate indignity: the bastard was bigger than him. Hate simmered in Weasel's heart at the injustices life dished out to him again and again.

Mike Taraday came over. "What'll it be?"

"Hell, whatever," the kid said. He made a face. "What smells so bad?"

Weasel grinned inside.

Mike sniffed. "Dead rat, old puke, dog shit on somebody's shoe, or Weasel. Take your pick."

Weasel started up from his chair. The bit of reason alcohol had not yet dissolved out of his brain made him relax again and sit back. You do not punch out the local bartender when that bartender is letting you run up a tab. You lick his ass and hope he relents when the magical eleven-beer limit comes. "Kiss my pecker," he snarled as nicely as he could, and dug out another cigarette. He got his Bic out and lit it, inhaling furiously, hating the taste, hating the world.

"That Falls City looks okay," the kid said.

"You got ID, partner?" Mike retorted. "You look kinda young."

"Uh, my wallet's in my car. Locked in the glove box. It's uh, jammed."

Mike sighed. "No ID, no beer. Sorry, son."

"Hey, I'm on leave from the Marines," the kid said. "Don't that count for nothing?"

"Not in this state."

"But I'm serving my country!"

"And I'm not serving you. Out."

Weasel had pricked up his ears at this bit about serving your country. If there was one thing Weasel could stand in this world, it was a man in uniform. At least he knew they were getting shit on as bad as he himself was. Weasel had seen service in the Air Force, rising to the rank of airman first class before getting demoted and discharged for punching a second lieutenant in the chops.

"Get him a beer, Mike," Weasel said. "I'll vouch for him."

Mike snorted. "You don't know him from Adam."

Weasel hooked an arm over the kid's beefy shoulders. "Mike, meet my nephew Joe Smith. He's twenty-one years old. Birthday's today, matter of fact." He grinned at the kid. "Ain't that a fact, Joe?"

The kid looked perplexed, but only momentarily. "Sure," he said. "That's right. Today's my birthday."

"Oh?" Mike's eyes got narrow. "Okay, Joe, what's your uncle's name?"

"He knows my goddamn name!" Weasel shouted. A few heads turned; the juke was between songs. "He knows my name's Frank Whipple," Weasel said somewhat more quietly. "Only, he don't know this town calls me Weasel. He calls me Uncle Frank."

"Yes, Uncle Frank," the kid said. "Yes indeed, Uncle Frank."

Mike spread his hands. "Falls City, then. The BATF comes in, I'm sunk. So what? Old man Liddey's got religion, Weasel has a nephew in the Marines, and I'm just the fucking bartender." He went off to get the beer.

"And get one for my Uncle Frank here," the kid shouted.

The two settled back more comfortably into their stools. "Thanks," the kid whispered, and dug out his wallet. He produced a twenty-dollar bill out of a large sheaf inside and laid it on the bar. Weasel's bleary eyes brightened. The military must be paying mighty fine wages nowadays. This kid could be milked all night. And Mike Taraday could shove his eleven beers up his ass.

"So, Joe, how you been?" Weasel asked.

"Okay, I guess." The kid offered him a grateful smile, then turned it into a frown. "If you can call being a Marine okay, that is."

"How much time you got left?"

"I'm just out of basic. Name's William King."

"You from around here, Bill? I don't think I've seen you."

"Naw, Indianapolis. I was headed for Terre Haute to visit my grandma and thought I'd stop by for a beer. No crime in that, huh? They serve us beer on base."

Weasel waved his hands. "You don't need to tell *me*. You're old enough to get shot to pieces but not old enough to drink. It's the fucking government. Society, you see. Society sucks."

The beers came. The kid, Bill, paid.

"Something still stinks," he said as the jukebox began blasting some ancient Elton John tune. Something about good-bye Norma Jean.

"You mean to tell me," Weasel said, looking at him as

levelly as his wobbling head would allow, "that you're twenty-one years old and still can't tell what a fart smells like?"

"Oh." Bill looked studious. "I thought maybe somebody died."

"In this joint, you could," Weasel said. "Die of fucking thirst." He laughed uproariously at this. Bill laughed with him.

"Were you in the service?" he asked after a bit, shouting above the noise.

"Air Force," Weasel replied. "Light colonel, retired."

Shock spread over Bill's face. "Jesus, sir," he blurted, stiffening. "I didn't know you were an *officer*!"

"Calm yourself," Weasel said, enjoying this. "When I retired I took off all my brass and ribbons. I was a pilot. Vietnam. Forty-two missions."

"Bomber?"

"B-52. We turned Hanoi into a parking lot."

"Wow."

Weasel worked on his beer, immensely self-satisfied. The kid was still stiff as a plank. It was the terror of officers, ingrained into young recruits by drill sergeants the world over. The treatment had not worked well on young Frank Whipple; he hated them worse than he hated snakes. Hence the lieutenant. Hence the discharge, dishonorable. Weasel had burned his disgraceful DD-214 the second he was free. From then on it had been downhill all the way.

He finished his beer. Bill hastily called for another, though his was barely touched.

"Better drink it before it boils," Weasel said, nodding toward his sweating bottle. As soon as the kid got loosened up that wallet of his would be making frequent appearances, Weasel knew that as fact.

"To the Air Force," Bill said, and drank up. He chugged the whole bottle down and let out a belch like a shotgun blast.

"To the Marine Corpse," Weasel said, and snatched away the beer Mike brought. He grinned at Mike maliciously, then downed his own bottle without a pause. His belch, when it came, rattled the liquor bottles under the clock.

"Two more!" Bill cried.

Mike scuttled away, shaking his head.

Weasel lit a cigarette, then as an afterthought offered one to Bill. The kid shook his head. "I work out. Weights."

"Thought so," Weasel said.

"I can bench press four-eighty."

"Good for you, son." Mike came back. Bill paid. Weasel shoveled his pile of pennies and nickels back into his pocket.

"Chug-a-lug, chug-a-lug," Bill said, and did just that.

"They teach you that in basic?" Weasel asked when he was done.

"Fucking-A," the kid said. Already he was getting tipsy. "The Marines are tough."

"Fucking-A," Weasel agreed, and tossed his beer down in six gulps. His throat went cold as ice and threatened to close up on him. For a terrifying second he thought it was all going to come back up onto the bar. How many had he had so far? Everything was becoming hazy.

"Beer down here!" Bill screamed. He hammered his fists on the bar, making ashtrays dance. "Beer down here!"

Mike came running. "Hold it down to a roar," he said, passing two bottles over. He extracted two dollars from the pile on the bar and went on his way.

"Chug-a-lug," Bill said. He stuck the spout of his tall bottle between his lips, tilted his head back, and Weasel watched in amazement as the beer slid down his throat without so much as a gurgle.

"Drink up, Colonel," Bill said. "Us military men, we know how to do it, huh?"

"Sure do," Weasel said. His eyesight was trying to double. Dammit, why hadn't he eaten those braunschweiger sandwiches? Then he could have drunk this kid under the table. As it was, he was ready to fall off his stool.

"Gotta piss first," he said, and got to his feet. The room canted sideways and he clutched the edge of the bar, finding his balance with an effort of will. He headed toward the back, lurching and stumbling. This wasn't going the way it was supposed to. The kid was making him drink too fast. It was barely six o'clock. Christ, by ten he'd be dead.

He found the rest room door and stepped into the minuscule, stinking room that contained only a toilet. Swaying on his feet, he pissed for an eternity, watching the graffiti on the walls fade in and out of focus. The floor was wet with some joker's piss and Weasel's work boots squished in it as he rocked.

He went out, forgetting to zip up, leaving tracks on the wooden floor. He found his stool and climbed up on it.

Two full beers were standing in front of him like brown soldiers at attention.

"Semper fi!" Bill screamed over the roar of the jukebox. "Chug, Colonel! The Air Force ain't as pussy as they say!"

Weasel chugged. His stomach was a bloated balloon in his belly. He could almost feel his abused kidneys manning the pumps in a frenzy to get rid of it. His throat ached, and he thought for a moment that he might be giving himself cancer at this rate, throat cancer, cancer of the stomach, cancer of the dick that had to spray all this stuff out.

"Bartender!" Bill shouted. "Bring us two more. Hell, make it four. My uncle and me are having a party, and my grandma can go to hell!"

Mike came over with two bottles stuck between the fingers of each hand. He plopped them on the bar, eyeing Weasel. "You're going glassy on me, Wease," he said gravely. "Maybe you ought to head home."

Weasel saw two Mikes. He snarled at them both, flipping a hand to make them go away.

"Hey, buddy," Bill said. "You got any of them little onions?"

Mike frowned. "Huh?"

"You know." Bill's young, round face was red with the high glow of too much alcohol taken too fast. "The little onions that come in olive jars. I got something to show my uncle."

"We got olives," Mike said, "pickled eggs, and jerky snacks."

"Do they have those little onions in them?"

"What, the jerky snacks?"

"Funny guy, for a civilian. Gimme some olives with the onions in them."

Mike rolled his eyes and went away. He came back with a tall jar of olives stuffed with pimentos. Small pearl onions floated among them.

"Yeah," Bill said. "I learned this trick at Quantico, Uncle Frank. It shows you're a tough Marine."

He opened the jar and dug through the olives with his fingers, coming out with an onion. Weasel watched him, intent on focusing his eyes, working furiously at it. Sweat stood out on his forehead.

Bill stuck the onion up his right nostril. He jammed it in tight with a finger. Tears sprang into his eyes.

"Okay, watch," he said, sounding like a man with a bad head cold. He tipped a beer back and chugged it all down as smoothly as before. Then he pinched his left nostril shut and made snorting noises. His chest heaved. Tears streamed down his cheeks. He gave one last huge inhalation, jerked as if slapped, then straightened, grinning.

"Huh?" Weasel said.

Bill bared his front teeth. The onion was perched between them. Weasel saw with revolted horror that there was a nasal hair stuck to its gleaming round surface. Bill bit down, squirting onion juice. He chewed it up and swallowed.

"Never seen that, huh?"

"Sure I have," Weasel lied. "In the Air Force we did it all the time. We did it before we took off for Hanoi."

Doubt flitted through Bill's young eyes. "Do it, then."

Weasel thought about it. His thoughts chased each other in useless circles. Already his bladder was thumping again. He reached for the olives and knocked them over. Juice sloshed across the bar, trailed by rolling olives and onions.

"Barkeep!" Bill shouted. "Get us a towel!"

Mike came over and sopped up the mess, growling. He set the olive jar upright and shoved it to Weasel. "Okay, Colonel, I seen it. You have a talented nephew."

"Fuck him," Weasel growled. The world was a tilt-a-whirl, spinning and rocking. Damn those six beers for lunch. What a stupid move that had been.

"You see, son," Mike said to Bill, "there are certain people in this world who will tell you anything you want to hear in order to get a free beer. There are people like Weasel here who wouldn't know Hanoi from Honolulu. They are known as bullshitters, and you are sitting beside one of the kings of the trade. In the past they were called freeloaders. Now we're kinder." He cast Weasel a sweet smile. "Go on home now, and sleep this off. Your head's gonna be a watermelon in the morning anyway. And you've got a family to support."

This information, and its load of insults, worked its slow way through Weasel's ears and into his spinning brain. Rage blossomed, flared, and suddenly roared alive like a blast from an open furnace. The world was being unkind to him again.

"Gimme them goddamn onions," he said, grabbing the olive jar and dragging it under his face. He stuck his fat fingers inside and managed to dredge an onion out. He stuck it up his nose and pushed the bottle away.

"Now you gotta chug-a-lug," Bill said. Mike watched all this with a satisfied half-grin on his face.

Weasel tipped his head back and chugged. The onion burned in his nose like lukewarm lava. The juice of it trickled into his sinuses, making him want to gag. He managed to get the beer down, but it threatened, as the last one had, to come roaring back up. He slammed the empty bottle back down on the bar, aware that his entire face felt aglow from the stench of the onion, which felt like a huge bulb in his nostril. He belched in Mike's face.

"Now suck her inside," Bill said, no longer seeming like the innocent kid, suddenly as threatening as Mike Taraday and his eleven-beer limit. Weasel squinted against the tears that were forming in his eyes. Damn, but that onion burned. It felt like a white-hot light bulb jammed up his nose. He pressed his other nostril shut and sucked. The onion slid deeper into his nasal passage. He paused for breath. Warm tears coursed down his cheeks.

"Maybe you have to be a weight-lifter," Bill said, winking at Mike.

"Or a bullshitter," Mike agreed sagely.

It was a trick, a dirty trick, Weasel realized with sudden and terrible surety. The kid had been playing him for a sucker all along, instead of vice-versa. It was like those stupid strong-man competitions on ESPN, where Arnold Schwarzenegger or Franco Colombu blew up hot water bottles until they burst. You had to have powerful lungs for this. Arnold and Franco were not three-pack-a-day men.

"God, my nose," Weasel bleated.

"Suck," Bill shouted, laughing.

Weasel sucked. The hideous burning onion squelched its way deeper into his head. His sinuses slammed shut against the intruder, swelling up to block it.

"By doze," he wailed. "God, by fuggig doze!"

"Suck it, Colonel! Suck it, and the beer's on me all night!"

Weasel jammed his finger up his free nostril, and sucked. His lungs ached from the effort. The onion seemed to have swollen to ten times its original size. And now a tremendous sneeze was building inside him.

"Cripes, just blow it back out," Mike said.

Weasel relented and blew. Nothing happened. His head thumped and hammered. His face went from red to purple.

"Stuck!" he cried, still sitting with one finger jammed up his nose. "The fugger's stuck!"

Bill doubled up with laughter. The juke was between songs again and now people were looking over. Weasel looked around, seeing the mirth in their eyes, the mirth that was always there but which they kept hidden for fear of their lives. Now Weasel was too deep in his own misery to knock heads together, too drunk and full of onion to do anything but sit there and cry.

The sneeze built. Weasel prayed for it. He unplugged his nose and waited.

"I think he's dying." Mike laughed, and a titter swept through the bar. Even Harley Gimbel was laughing. Him and his floozy wife with the red dress. Rage and pain sizzled in Weasel's brain. He would make them pay, make all of them pay, if only this fucking *onion* wasn't stuck in his head.

His chest began to swell. His eyes fluttered shut.

"Oh, shit," Mike breathed, and ducked away.

Kaplooey. Snot blew out of Weasel's left nostril in a long gray string. But the onion, Jesus God, the onion, it was still there. There was a fire in his skull, a lit match flaring in the depths of his head.

"You gotta suck it in," Bill said, laughing himself into hysterics.

Weasel sucked. He blew and sucked. The onion was as good as welded, as hot as freshly welded. He whimpered and gurgled.

"Help be," he moaned.

"Suck it," Bill said, and now it sounded strangely obscene. "Suck it, *Colonel!* Suck it suck it suck it!"

"Wad did I ever do do jou?" Weasel shouted. "I god jew id here, didn't I?"

"Hey, don't get steamed," Bill said. "You stuck the damn thing up your nose, not me. And you lied to me. Air Force my ass. Officer my ass. You tried to sucker me."

"Fuggig bunk!" Weasel screamed, standing up. His bar stool tipped over and hit the floor with a wooden thump. "Jew dricked be!"

This threw Bill into fresh hysterics. The whole bar was laughing at him now, mean old Weasel Whipple with an onion jammed permanently in his nose. Oh, he could see it on their laughing faces, the things they'd been hiding for so long. They hated him as much as he hated them. Now he was helpless and they were letting it all show.

He hauled back and punched the kid on the side of his head. This knocked him sideways, further knocking him against the Colts fans, who knocked against the pansy in the suit and made him spill his Michelob off the end of the bar. Dead silence fell over the little tavern like a black sheet.

"Come on," Weasel screamed, waving his fists. "Bunk! Bunk! Snod dozed bunk!"

"Lay off, Weasel," Mike shouted.

Bill recovered himself and stood up. A drunken grin of anticipation crossed his young features. "Okay, you phony fucking colonel," he said, breathing hard. "You won't believe what happens next."

"Out of my bar!" Mike shouted.

Bill threw a deft right-hand punch that landed square and hard on Weasel's ponderous belly. He let out a strangled whoof as the kid's fist drove itself nearly to his spine. In an instant beer was spurting out Weasel's gaping mouth, a golden, frothing fountain. Bill jumped back and watched while Weasel bent and puked all over the floor, his hands clamped to his stomach, retching and gasping. Weasel felt as if his eyeballs were ready to pop out.

Mike went to the cash register, which was perched beside the cooler, and drew a baseball bat out of the dim space there. He waved it back and forth like a flagpole. "Out, kid! You got no ID anyway! Out!"

The kid looked around haughtily. "No problem," he grunted, and scraped his remaining dollars off the bar.

"Leave two bucks for the olives," Mike said.

Bill snorted. He threw two dollars in the air. "Fucking hole in the wall," he mumbled. "Wabash Heights my ass. All of you go eat shit. I gotta see my grandma."

"Out!"

The kid stepped wide over the sparkling pool of vomit and went out.

The jukebox hummed to life. Waylon Jennings sang of love in thundering basso tones.

"See what kind of a frigging mess you made!" Mike screamed at Weasel, who was hauling himself upright by the edge of the bar like a swimmer trying to clamber into a boat. One clawing hand found the olive jar and sent it spinning away. A full beer got knocked over and wheeled across the bar, gushing foam.

"Jesus frigging Christ!" Mike screeched. "Somebody throw that drunken fucker out!"

The Colts fans, who had jumped away when the melee started and knew Weasel well enough to hate him, were only too glad to help. Weasel felt hands under his arms, saw the bar disappear to be replaced by floor. The tilt-a-whirl had gone utterly crazy now, was being driven by a capering madman who would let nobody off. Weasel groaned and thrashed. His work pants were wet with vomited beer and clung to his uselessly pedaling legs.

They tossed him out on the sidewalk. It was still light. Cars swept past with April sunlight winking cruelly off shiny paint and chrome bumpers. The sky was a dusky evening blue. Weasel crawled to his car, still retching. The beer, he was thinking dreamily. It was still cold when I puked it. And those fuckers are going to be laughing about this for fifty years.

He got the Malibu's rusting door open and hauled himself inside. It took an age to find his keys, another age to get one of them into the proper slot. The onion burned in his nose, bright fire. Weasel cranked the motor while the world outside spun and danced. The old Chevy started, died, belched, started. Oily smoke shot out the holes in the muffler, turning the world briefly into a churning blue cloud. He dropped the shift lever into reverse and cooked some rubber backing out. He cooked more rubber on the short trip home. By the grace of God, there were no cops about.

Hatred churned in his brain as he drove. The puking had helped clear his head a bit. Things were coming into focus for him again.

Somebody would pay for this. Somebody would pay for all of this. This shitpile of a life, the punk and his onion, the hands and the sidewalk and the laughter. Somebody would pay, you could bet your ass on that.

As it turned out, it was his stepson Arnold who paid the heaviest price.

At first.

· 2 ·

Arnold Pays

ARNOLD WHITE WAS lying on the couch reading a hardbound copy of *Mein Kampf* while his stepfather Weasel was driving home. In the tiny living room the TV was blaring "Wheel of Fortune"; his younger sister, Melissa, nine years old, was watching it avidly, trying to guess the words before the contestants did. She was pretty smart, like thirteen-year-old Arnold, and usually got the words right off the bat. The baby, Angie, was playing with old wooden blocks on the scarred and chipped hardwood floor. Karen, their mother, was ironing clothes, keeping an eye on the TV. No one expected Frank (none of them dared call him Weasel) home until eleven or twelve.

Adolf Hitler was a rambler. Arnold had decided that already, and he was only on page twenty-two. None of this *Mein Kampf* made any sense so far. Arnold had picked it up at the public library expecting a brilliant story of World War Two, a subject that fascinated him. Instead he was reading the meandering personal history of a young man who wandered the streets of Vienna without a penny in his pocket in 1922. What in the world did that have to do with WW2? Arnold was intensely disappointed so far. He put the book down on his chest and tried to make sense of what he had read up to now. He couldn't.

The library lady, old Mrs. McCormick, had certainly given him a curious glance when he brought *Mein Kampf* up to her for checkout. "I know you're a bookworm, Arnold," she had said in her grandmotherly voice, "but don't go getting strange ideas from this book. The author was an evil man."

Perhaps so. Arnold wanted to find out why. The only truly evil man he knew was his stepfather, and his stepfather was

17

certainly too stupid to ever write a book. How could you be evil, and write a book? Arnold had read all of Ray Bradbury, Poul Anderson, Isaac Asimov, and Stephen King. He loved all of them like brothers, especially Stephen King. His books were full of monsters and spooks and dirty words. Did that make him an evil man?

Arnold sighed, staring at the ceiling where the leaking roof had turned the plaster yellow. Thirteen was a tough age. It was made doubly tough for Arnold by his size (only four feet eleven), his weight (ninety-one pounds), his bookwormy appearance (his real father, who lived in Texas now, had been a bookworm, too), and by his stepfather, Weasel Whipple, the ugliest and meanest man Arnold had ever met. Arnold wore thick glasses, which had been held together with white tape in the middle since they'd been broken the last time Frank had punched Arnold out. New glasses were out of the question, of course, so the tape would have to do forever. Truth was, it didn't do at all, and the glasses sagged so pitifully that Arnold was forever readjusting them on his thin and mournful face.

"Catch as catch can!" his sister Melissa shrieked at the television.

Arnold glanced over. She was right. The contestants, however, were stumped. Arnold wondered if they advertised for stupid people for the dumb show. Surely they did. How else could they find such morons?

"Gah dah," baby Angie said, scattering blocks across the floor with her chubby baby hands. Arnold felt sure she was trying to say goddamn. Another influence from the most evil man ever to have lived, dear stepfather Frank, who in Arnold's eyes made Hitler look like Mister Rogers. He glanced over to his mother and saw a thin woman wearing a frayed green blouse and blue jeans gone pale with age. Her eyes were heavy-lidded and pouchy. Her brown hair was a ratty tangle. She was deteriorating pretty fast. Slowly it had been coming to Arnold just why she had married Frank eleven months ago. He had heard things said, paid attention when the two were fighting. Mommy had thought she was pregnant. Something then about a miscarriage. The result? Married for life to Hitler's horrible henchman, Frank Whipple.

He sighed. He picked up the book again and found his place. It was a fat book, the kind he liked, almost too heavy to hold up. But darn it, it wasn't like Stephen King's big fat books. At least they got interesting pretty quick. This *Mein Kampf* was a bore.

He flipped through the pages, hoping to spot an interesting line. Nothing caught his eye.

The front door burst open and there stood Hitler in wet brown work pants and a red T-shirt.

"*Jesus fuggig Ghrist!*" Weasel Whipple screamed. "Somebody ged this fuggig onion oud of by doze!"

Karen shrank back, startled. The iron she had been pushing over a pair of Frank's huge pants lay steaming and forgotten.

"What?" she asked.

"Fug you!" Frank screamed, and lurched through the room toward the bathroom. His knee caught the coffee table and sent it over with a crash. He was holding his huge head in his hands, and now one hand went down to clutch his knee. He looked to Arnold like he was crying. Drunker than a skunk, of course, but crying.

That was all right with Arnold. Let the big mean asshole cry. Since he had moved in, there had been a lot of crying going on.

"What do you suppose?" Karen said. She looked like a cornered mouse. In her eyes Arnold could see the fresh memory of recent beatings, drifting up like thin winter clouds. She started toward the bathroom, hesitated, came back, stood by the television wringing her hands. The baby caught the mood and began to cry. Karen swept her up automatically and deposited her on the couch between Arnold's legs. From the bathroom came gasps and slobbering noises. Then a tremendous sneeze. Another.

Melissa got up off the floor and went to Arnold. She sat beside him, stiff and unsure, "Wheel of Fortune" forgotten like the iron. In her school dress she was pretty, the way their mother Karen had been pretty before the divorce and Frank Whipple. Melissa's hand went out automatically and clutched at Arnold's. He put the book on the floor and held her hand.

"Damn!" Frank Whipple shouted. "Ow! Ow!"

"I guess I'd better . . ." Karen said, swaying back and forth like laundry caught in a vagrant breeze. "Maybe I should . . ."

"He's drunk," Arnold said.

"Well, yes," Karen replied. "Yes, yes . . ."

"Probably puking his guts up."

"No, I think he's hurt . . ."

Go kill him, Arnold thought with bitter hopelessness. *Take advantage of the moment and stick a knife in his back.*

But he knew she wouldn't. She needed a man. She was too hesitant, too indecisive, to ever live on her own. Perhaps Dad had dumped her for this very reason. Arnold felt a brief flash of hate for her, and for Dad. If only she would stand up for herself once in a while, stand up for them all! If only Dad had stayed! But she fluttered like laundry and did nothing for anybody, and Dad had found a new life in Texas.

"I'll go see what's wrong," Arnold said, getting up, careful not to knock the baby over. He gave Melissa's hand a parting squeeze and adjusted his broken glasses higher on his nose. He squared his shoulders, took a step, and stopped.

His stepfather was bellowing like a wounded bull now. The tiny house was full of his roars and his slobbering. New fear inched its way up Arnold's spine like a slow, cold snake, almost setting his teeth to chattering. It had never been this bad before, never. Maybe somebody had knifed Frank at the Wabash Tavern. Arnold had heard the rumors at school about his new stepfather. Something about fighting with knives in a tavern in Terre Haute.

Arnold had a vision then. It wasn't clairvoyant, and didn't exactly descend over his sight like a cloud. It played out in an instant on the screen of his inner mind: Frank comes out, knife in hand, and slays the whole family. Cuts everybody's throat. Even the baby's. Blood flows over the wooden floorboards like spilled red water. It makes the evening news, fills the headlines of the *Wabash Heights Observer* for a week. Deranged man kills family. Held without bond. I didn't know what I was doing, weeping man tells police. I'd been knifed in this tavern, see, and was out of my mind.

Arnold swallowed. His throat clicked dryly. He took another step, passing his mother, who still fluttered. The baby howled. A contestant on TV shrieked with joy at having solved the puzzle. The audience applauded madly. The world was all noise and mayhem.

Arnold dragged himself toward the bathroom. It was at the other side of the kitchen. He went through the kitchen, which was dark, and which contained a drawer that held knives. New headline: Frightened boy kills stepfather. I had to do it, boy explains to police. He was Hitler.

The bathroom door was half-open. Light spilled out. Frank was bent over the sink furiously blowing his nose, his chest and back heaving, tears squirting out his eyes, a string of snot hanging out one nostril into the drain. He roared and bellowed between blows. There were no apparent knife wounds on him.

"Dad?" Arnold squeaked with what tiny authority he could manage. "Are you hurt?"

Frank Whipple turned his head. His eyes were almost bloated shut, but what remained visible of them glittered with hate, sparkling dots in folds of flesh. Arnold saw with disgust that his ratty beard was full of snot and spit.

"Dad?"

"Don't gall be dad, jew liddle shid!" Frank shouted. "I ain'd your fuggig dad!"

I know, Arnold thought with bottomless despair. *My real dad took off a year ago without saying goodbye.*

"Can I help somehow? What's wrong?"

Frank straightened.

"Jew gan helb be by geddig the fug oud of by life!" Frank screamed. "Fuggig leech!"

Arnold took a step backward, but curiosity got the better of him. "What happened?"

Frank bared his teeth at him. "I've god a fuggig onion stug up by doze, that's whad."

Arnold gaped at him. "You've got an onion stuck up your nose?"

"Dell your bob to ged some dweezers or somedig. Dow!"

The smile that was digging at Arnold's facial muscles upon hearing this bit of news fought a bitter battle with his common sense. It was so comical: his idiot stepfather rendered helpless by an onion in his nose—probably somebody at the tavern had held him down and jammed it up there—and that brought visions of two men going at each other not with knives but with onions, big long green onions that the loser had to take up the nose. The image was too hilarious; there was a clawing cat of a smile behind his lips now, screeching to get out.

"You mean you've got a real *onion* up your nose?" Arnold asked with calm dignity.

"Jes, jew liddle dozy shid!"

The cat clawed its way out. But it was a horde of cats, a battalion of them. Arnold began to chuckle, then to chortle, then to laugh loudly and uproariously at this. He held his stomach with one hand and his ailing glasses with the other, nearly doubled over with a strange and dreadful kind of hysteria. It was the hysteria of a man strapped in an electric chair when the power suddenly fails; the killing machine is just a chair after all. And Weasel Whipple was a stupid, stupid man rendered harmless by an onion.

Arnold howled helplessly. It was the funniest thing he had ever seen, the funniest thing he had ever heard in his thirteen years. A man with an onion in his nose.

He laughed. He screamed with it. He nearly rolled on the floor.

And thus it was not unexpected, even in his feverishly laughing brain, that his stepfather should lunge at him like a maniac from one of the horror books, smashing the half-open door aside and sending it bonging into the wall, his face twisted with rage and hate and pain. Weasel Whipple threw a roundhouse punch that landed directly on Arnold's mouth, snapping teeth that had not yet done five years' service in his mouth, splitting his lips, bowling him over in a tremendous somersault. Pain screamed at him from the bleeding hole that had been his mouth. His glasses hung from one ear. He opened his eyes and saw a swimmy world where the kitchen ceiling and its network of plaster cracks and flaking yellow paint spun and whirled. His mouth was full of salty blood and hard chunks like bone splinters. He went up on his elbows and said dreamily, "Onions?"

"Jes, onions!" Frank Whipple screamed, laying hold of Arnold's shirt with both hands and yanking him upright. Karen appeared in the corner of Arnold's eye, his mother who could no more stop this than a cow can stop a train. She fluttered back and forth, making motions as if to come in the kitchen, other motions as if to go out, his fluttering mother, the cow in front of the train.

"I'll gill jew!" Frank screamed in Arnold's face, and in the dreamy world of pain Arnold now floated in he had a vision of a Jew with gills. The Creature from the Black Lagoon. We will not, however, feed him pork.

Pow. Side of the head, this time. Blood sprayed out Arnold's right ear, the one his white-taped glasses hung from. Mysterious noises whined there, there where his eardrum had burst. Pain came at him from new directions, sharp as tacks. He opened the hole of his mouth and screamed.

Distantly: "Frank, stop it!"

How now, brown cow? Arnold grinned a red and broken-toothed grin. He saw a fluttering cow-picture in front of a speeding locomotive, saw the locomotive punch through it and reduce it to multicolored tatters.

Thump. In the gut this time. Arnold was being held in the air by his shirt, a shirt his father had bought him before he disappeared, a birthday shirt that was a remnant of a happier time, a blue short-sleeve shirt with a tiny crocodile on the breast. Thank you, Daddy, Arnold had said, and his daddy had winked at him. Behind that wink there had been plans of leaving, secret betrayals. Daddy, oh Daddy! Did I fail you so miserably as a son that you had to leave me?

Splat. Eyeball, this time. Bony protector there, called a socket. Arnold was a boy of some intelligence. You cannot injure the human eyeball with a balled fist. You can, however, make it black and purple and red and blue and swell it up like a colorful beach ball, 80-20 vision defect requiring humiliating thick glasses or not.

Splat. Pow. Thump. More screams, Melissa this time, the sister in the photographs where Dad is proudly holding her on his shoulders at Shakamak State Park, erector-set lifeguard bench in the background, brown-green water behind it all. Happy times with Dad as safe and immovable as the Rock of Gibraltar, Dad who would someday drift away from the continent of his family and wind up in Texas, Texas of all places. Did Melissa fail you too, Dad? Did she fail you so bad that you had to give us Frank Whipple as your replacement?

Bong bong bong. Head against refrigerator. Woman screaming, girl screaming. And an onion up his nose, great God in heaven, the greatest gag of all time! Fool your friends! Mystify your neighbors! You can actually make an onion DISAPPEAR UP YOUR NOSE!!!

"I . . . hate . . . you . . . ," Arnold said between blows, but as the blows went on and on he was reduced to begging for his father, which only incited Frank "Weasel" Whipple to a new rage . . .

"Ringer's solution."
  "IV drip, Ringer's solution."
Ringing in his ears.

"Continue until he's conscious, and then we'll see what we're up against."

Ringing in his ears.

Arnold opened his eyes and saw that a huge white pillow was about to be draped over his face. He thought of smothering, of being smothered, that Frank Whipple was about to smother him with a white pillow . . .

"There's a sign," a woman said. She straightened. It was her breasts, not a pillow, then. She had been bending over him. She was wearing white. Something hurt on the back of his hand, and he realized he was being punctured there by a thick needle.

"Ow," Arnold said quite clearly.

"Another sign, Doctor. Wouldn't you say?"

A low chuckle. Arnold felt a warm big hand on his wrist. "Hold the solution for a moment, then," the man who had chuckled said. It was hard to hear him over this ringing in his ears, this Ringer's solution in his ears.

"Daddy?" Arnold said.

"I'm Dr. Price, son. Do you understand me?"

Arnold relaxed a bit. The pain on the back of his hand went away as his vein adjusted itself to the intrusion of the needle. Something cold was dabbed there. Arnold smelled alcohol.

"Can you hear me all right, son?"

"Yes," Arnold croaked. "You're Vincent Price."

Chuckle chuckle chuckle. "My, what a brave boy," the woman said. Arnold saw in this world of white that she was a fat nurse. He tried to turn his head to see the doctor, and pain rocketed up from the base of his skull into his ear. He cried out.

"Don't try to move just yet," the doctor said. "You have a fractured skull. Nasty . . . fall . . . you took."

Arnold digested this in weak silence.

"If your right arm feels heavy it is because it is in a cast. But then, we ought to talk later about this, eh?" Chuckle chuckle.

"My mouf," Arnold said.

"Seven stitches upper, three lower. Sorry about your teeth."

Arnold probed his lips with his tongue. Sharp ends of threads poked it, as if he had a harelip somebody had sewn up. His teeth were jagged stumps. They ached abominably. His vision was becoming more clear and he could see white walls. There was something like a white shower curtain hanging on a rod to his right. A dazzling overhead fluorescent bar threw harsh white light everywhere. To his left was a tall metal contraption like a hat rack. There was a plastic bag full of clear liquid hanging from it, and a few twists of plastic tubing dangling around it. The bag had "Ringer's Solution 0.05%" stamped on it in small black letters.

"My ear hurts."

"Burst eardrum, son. Nature will take care of that." The doctor and the fat nurse exchanged glances. They knew, and Arnold guessed, that nature might never take care of that. He might be deaf in that ear forever. That sent a shiver of fright through his veins, but it was oddly muted, seeming to come to a dead end when it hit his brain. He felt fuzzy all over. He was only vaguely aware of the hospital noises surrounding him—and they all came from the left. He closed his eyes.

"Go ahead and connect the drip," the doctor said. From his point of view this case was cut and dried. Worst example of child abuse he had ever seen, and he had seen more than a few. Wabash Heights was a mean little town, a hard-drinking, working man's town, and hard-drinking working men often tended to take out the frustrations of their dreary lives by pounding on the kiddies once in a while. And it would forever be the same story when the kiddie was brought to the hospital by the weeping, guilt-ridden mother: little Johnny fell down the basement steps. Wabash Heights was full of klutzy little Johnnies and basement steps half a mile long, Dr. Price often thought.

This little Johnny had fallen off the moon, by the looks of him. His chart read like the chart of a soldier who had been a little too close to an artillery blast. Dr. Price had seen enough of these in Vietnam; he was getting sick of seeing them here. Hairline skull fracture. Right arm snapped cleanly in two. Internal rupture of the stomach lining. Burst eardrum. Broken teeth. Enough fist-size bruises to paper a wall with. Classic case. The boy's father ought to be tied to a post and shot.

But that was a matter for the police. This was a delicate legal situation. Dr. Price had been on emergency staff of the County General Hospital at seven o'clock when the kid was brought in. His mother drove up to the entrance in a battered old Chevy. Staggering under her son's unconscious weight, barely looking any better herself, she had wobbled her way to the admitting desk and begged for a doctor. Price, passing by, had glanced out in the dark and seen two other children in the car, a girl and a baby. Both had their faces pressed to the grimy glass and were crying. The car was old and battered, like this ruined family. For a brief second Price had thought that if the father was in the car, Price himself would go out and stretch the bastard out like a Persian rug. But the father hadn't been in the car. They never were.

Delicate situation, then. Charges must be pressed here. Charges *must* be pressed here. A demon like this kid's father couldn't be allowed in the same house with children again. Even if he only got drunk and struck once a year, once a year was too much.

"Drip that a little slower," Price said, indicating the IV tube. He looked at his watch and saw with surprise that it was nearly ten. "Is the mother still out there?"

"In the hallway, when I wheeled Arnold out of emergency."

"Arnold?" Price passed his fingertips over his forehead. Arnold. Of course. Little Johnny. The kid had a name. Had the father cared when he nearly killed him?

"Arnold White."

"I want to talk to her myself," Price said.

"Daddy," Arnold murmured in his half-sleep.

An expression of weary exasperation passed over Price's face. Your daddy just pounded you to a pulp, son, and still you call for him. Why do you Johnnies always do it? To beg forgiveness for having been in the way of those pounding fists, those kicking, work-booted feet? Why?

He left the room frowning, and went into the hallway. There were benches against the lime-green walls, flanked by stubby ashtrays that looked like cannon tubes. A bedraggled woman was sitting in one of the benches with a sleeping baby on her lap. A little girl had curled up against her and gone to sleep with her thumb in her mouth. Price's heart went out to them. The woman was droopy with sleep. Misery surrounded this pitiful troupe like a fog.

"Mrs. White?"

She looked up with hope and expectation leaping onto her face like a quick mask thrust over her tired features. "Is Arnold all right?"

Price put his hands together, contemplating his thumbs.

"Alive, sure. The boy is alive." He looked up. "Have you called the police yet?"

Her mask dropped, to be replaced by one of suspicion. "No. Why?"

"Because of the terrific beating your son barely survived."

Her eyes got small. "He fell," she whispered.

"I know," Price snapped. He took a breath, reining his feelings in. He was a professional man and would remain that way, no matter how this went. "He fell down the basement steps, I would assume."

She nodded, this Mrs. White whose husband was almost a murderer.

"Long steps you have, Mrs. White."

"It's Mrs. Whipple, now."

Price nodded internally. Stepfather, then. It was too typical. "Shall we," he said conversationally, "drop the bullshit for now? Your husband beat your son almost to death. I want him prosecuted."

Alarm now, the mask. "Can you do that?"

"I cannot. You can."

"No."

Price swallowed. He toyed with the stethoscope that hung at his chest, the same one he had pressed to a ruined little boy's heart not three hours ago. Ker-thump, that heart had said. Help me, I am alive after this horror that has been visited upon me.

"Why not?"

"Because there's nobody to prosecute, Doctor. Arnold is a very . . . clumsy . . . type of boy. He wears glasses and doesn't see well. I told him to fetch me a jar of green beans out of the basement—I do home canning, you see—and he fell down the steps. I heard him fall and I picked him up and I brought him here."

She offered him a thin, tremulous smile. Are you buying it? that smile said. I have sat here practicing this for hours, it is for sale to anyone willing to buy, so will you buy it? Will you?

"Your son was beaten by your husband."

Doubt danced in her muddy brown eyes. She looked to Price as if she were ready to pick up her surviving children and run away, and then again, now, as if she were ready to stay here and tell the truth. She flutters, he thought. Here we have a fluttering woman.

"Well, actually . . . ," she said.

"Yes?"

"There is a lot of junk in our basement. Arnold landed on that junk."

Oh, so well practiced. Hell, she'd had three hours to sit here and concoct all this. Price took a measured breath, retaining his composure. "I will get a nurse's aide to watch after your children. You and I will go to the office at the end of the hallway and make a phone call. It will take less than a minute. You will inform the local police that you wish to file a complaint against your husband. They will arrive, and you will tell them the truth."

She started to rise, this Mrs. Whipple. She sat back down. Her children moaned in their sleep. She clutched them close. "Arnold fell," she said.

"Fell my ass!" Price nearly shouted.

"Don't!" Her hands fluttered up to cover her ears. "Don't scream at me!"

Dr. Price had witnessed terror in Vietnam, had experienced it himself during a rocket attack on his mobile surgical unit. Here it sat before him, a slight, rat-haired woman who looked old and sick and too terrified to do anything but sit there with her hands fluttering near her ears. Of course she didn't want to be screamed at. All the screaming was supposed to go on at home.

"If you let this continue, one of your children will die," he said evenly.

"Frank didn't mean it," she said, putting her hands down beside the baby. "He was out of control."

"Drunk, you mean?"

"No! He had . . . he had something wrong with him. A headache. An allergy. A sinus condition." She bared her teeth helplessly. "What do you want me to say? That he had an onion stuck up his nose?"

"Be serious," Price said. "Come with me and make that call."

"No." She drew herself up straighter. "I want to see Arnold."

"He's in no shape, to be quite honest."

"He can't stay. We don't have any money. We can't pay."

"And he can't leave. You'll have to take that up with the welfare people."

"No! Don't you see? Frank hates welfare. He'll come and

take Arnold out himself. If he hadn't been so busy I couldn't have brought Arnold at all. He doesn't know we left, see. He went back in the bathroom. He was hurting.''

Oh, the poor hurting bastard, Price thought. "No one takes Arnold out of here without my permission," he said. "I guarantee you that.''

"Oh, oh," she said, and began to cry. She covered her face with her hands. "You don't know Frank. He'll take Arnold back. The bills, he worries about the bills.''

A twinge of unexpected guilt sparked alive inside Dr. Price. As an M.D. he made an easy hundred grand a year before taxes even in a hick town of two thousand like Wabash Heights. What could he know or understand of bills and pressures and worries? It occurred to him that he was scheduled to play golf in the morning. How's that for the democracy he fought for in Vietnam? That life should be so unbalanced, that the poor should go on being poor while doctors and millionaires lived lives of incredible luxury?

"I'm sure the welfare department will handle all the bills, Mrs. Whipple," he said uneasily. "Also, the hospital can make easy payment arrangements. As for myself, there'll be no charge for the services I rendered. I'll even talk to the radiologist about it, see if we can't get those X-rays for free, too.''

She offered him a defeated shrug. "So? It probably cost a hundred dollars just to walk into the emergency room.''

Hundred and ten, Price thought. *For her, might as well be a million.* "About that phone call," he said, brushing the thoughts aside.

She shook her head emphatically. "No phone call, Doctor.''

"You realize you may be condemning your son to an early death. Or your daughter, or even that baby.''

"I need a man, don't you see?" she hissed at him fiercely. "A woman can't make it alone with three kids. Not even with you doctors offering free services. What will I do with my husband in jail? And how long would he stay there? How mad will he be when he gets out? What will happen to us then?''

Price ground his teeth helplessly. She was probably right. A man evil enough to do such damage to a skinny thirteen-year-old stepson would no doubt find new and inventive ways to vent his rage when the jails let him go. He might get three months, six months for child abuse. Then he would be back.

"Very well then," he said in his best professional tone.

"You may visit your son in the morning. Visiting hours are posted at the entrance. I'd expect we can release him in three to six days if no complications from the concussion develop. Then he'll need several weeks' bed rest. And he'll need to see an ear specialist. Also I want his eyes checked. There may be retinal damage."

"Okay," she mumbled, and he could see in her eyes that no eye or ear specialist would ever be seen at all. No money for it. And the beastly stepfather would probably be here in the morning when he sobered up, not to visit the boy but to take him out before the bills started adding up.

"Good-bye, Mrs. Whipple," he said.

"Good-bye," she replied. "And thank you."

Her tone was cold. Price stalked away, feeling a little cold inside himself. He had done what he could. He had worked on the boy for three hours free of charge. There was still plaster under his fingernails from making the cast. He could easily charge her seven hundred bucks and still consider himself a servant of humanity, true to his Hippocratic oath.

"Doctor?"

He turned, hoping for the best.

She had struggled to her feet with her burden of children, staggering under their weight, and was offering him her purse. "Arnold's glasses," she said. "Inside somewhere. Would you give them to him?"

Price came back and looked in her open purse. A twisted pair of thick spectacles had been shoved inside amongst the bric-a-brac. He pulled them out and found himself holding two pieces. A dirty twist of white tape was stuck to one of them.

Both lenses were splattered with dried brown smears of blood.

"He'll get them," he said, feeling hollow as well as chilled. He could not wait to meet this monster, this husband, Frank. He was pretty tough with little boys. How would he be against a grown man, and a doctor to boot?

He went back to Arnold's room to have the nurse retape the glasses and clean them up.

Karen Whipple staggered down the corridor with her two sleeping children in her arms.

At that moment Frank "Weasel" Whipple sneezed into the bathroom sink for the fortieth time. The onion blew out and lay there on the rusted chrome of the pop-up drain like a large wet pearl.

"Final-fucking-lee," he muttered, and went to his bedroom to pass out.

The episode with the onion was over.

The rest was yet to come.

· 3 ·

The Man in the Next Bed

ARNOLD'S SEDATIVE WORE off shortly after midnight, and he came out of his drowse with the sound of whispers gurgling in the dark. His eyes drifted open as far as their swollen condition would let them, which wasn't far. He perked up, listening for that noise, those gurgling whispers.

They were coming from his left. But no, that wasn't right. He was deaf in his right ear. He turned his head just the slightest bit to a flare of fresh pain and saw that on his left was only a white wall, ghostly and dim in this half-light. The hat rack with its Ringer's solution hulked at the side of his bed like a chrome skeleton. His hands were cold and his broken teeth ached and ached.

Gurgle. Whisper. Gurgle.

He frowned, creating fresh pain between his eyes. Everything was dark and blurry. The door was half-open and even the corridor outside was dim. He turned his head farther to the right and saw that his glasses were on a small table there. Somebody had taped them with fresh white tape. He tried to move his arm to reach them and remembered the cast. It looked like a ghost's white arm with pink fingers sticking out the end. Pain was thumping underneath it, keeping time to the beat of his heart.

He moved his left hand and the plastic tubing uncoiled itself from the rack like a snake dropping out of a tree. The needle in the back of his hand hurt, too. He raised it to his eyes and saw, foggily, that his hand was wound with tape to hold the needle in place. He wished it wasn't there. It made his wrist feel cold. He tested his face with his fingertips and found a strange moonscape of bumps and lumps. There was a turban on his head, winds and twists of gauze to hold his skull together.

He remembered crying out for his daddy. Daddy hadn't come.

Tears formed in his eyes, grew large, and slid down his temples into his ears.

Gurgle. Whisper. Gurgle.

What *was* that?

Gently, he moved his head again. Pain creaked at the base of his skull. The noise was coming from behind the shower curtain, which he now recognized as a room divider, the kind that could be thrown back with a single toss. Other people were here in this room, then, and one of them was gurgling and whispering.

Arnold strained to hear. It was hard with only one ear working, and his dead ear threw out a disturbing whine like distant whistling. But it was really there, that sound: gurgle hiss hiss gurgle. Whisper whisper whisper.

Curiosity gnawed at his brain. Was he dreaming? Drugged? Sure, he had been drugged, but that fuzzy feeling was wearing off quickly. He tapped his forehead to make sure he was awake. He was. Part of him wanted to go back to sleep, where pain did not exist, but part of him wanted to know who or what was whispering on the other side of the divider.

He tried to sit up. An involuntary groan escaped through his shattered teeth. His head felt like a lead bowling ball, and the cast weighed a ton. He used his good arm to push himself up. The snake of plastic tubing moved with him, hissing quietly across the crisp white sheets. He got upright and watched the dimly lighted room tilt and rock for a minute. Then it settled down.

There was a mirror set in the far wall by the door. A ghost reflection sat in it, an Arab with a fresh white turban and black pockmarks for eyes. Arnold bared his teeth at the reflection. A toothless Arab with a gigantic bruise for a face grinned back at him.

He moved his legs out of bed. He was wearing some kind of frock, a pale blue dress. Even in this light he could see dark slashes on his shins where Frank had kicked him with his heavy boots. They ached, too, now that he was looking at them.

Gurgle. Hiss. Gurgle.

He forgot about pain for a while and concentrated on standing up. Cool air drifted across his backside as his gown fell open. He could feel the strings that tied it together, scraping at his back. Somebody had stolen his underwear, and he felt hideously naked under this thin blue dress. But still, still . . . what was that noise? A machine? A respirator? Was somebody sick over there?

Of course, you dumb shit, Arnold told himself crossly. *This is a hospital.*

That thought brought new curiosity. Was he in a children's ward of some sort, a special place where all the beaten children of Wabash Heights were brought? And if so, was the kid over there behind the divider in worse shape than Arnold was? That would be neat to find out.

He had taken a shuffling step toward the divider when something yanked on his hand.

He gasped, looking back at his captured hand, full of wonder and terror, and saw that it was only the IV tube, which had now reached its limit. The bag swayed back and forth on its rack, gently rustling. It was almost empty.

Well, hell. That certainly ended *this* operation.

Gurgle. Whisper whisper.

Arnold skirted the foot of the bed, walking like a bent old woman in a nursing home, holding the bed for support. He came to the rack and saw that it stood on tiny black wheels.

Neat.

He dragged it along with him as he went back to the divider. The wheels squeaked softly. Plus it was a handy crutch, for Arnold was still not quite sure of his balance. His cast pulled at him, a new and unfamiliar weight. His skull felt like a dropped eggshell, full of cracks and dents. The turban was hot and he wished he could tear it off.

He came to the divider and slowly dragged it aside to take a peek.

Another bed, just like his own. White sheets were pulled up to the chin of someone, a dark head on the white pillow. One hand stuck out from under the sheets and was hooked into a claw that pawed at the air in mindless circles. In the air on this side there seemed to be a strange, thin odor, as though Arnold could smell someone dying. But that had to be in his mind.

Fright slithered into his belly like the uncoiling IV tube, spurting cold liquid into his bowels. Had they put him in the same room with a *dying* kid? Were there worse fathers in the world than Frank Whipple?

He moved closer, tugging his IV hanger with him. The wheels squeaked like little whispers in the dark. He came near to the bed and could see now by the size of the hand that this was no kid, this was a man, an old man. Wrinkles and veins stood out on his hand that clawed at the air in circles.

Gurgle. Whisper. Gurgle.

The old man was gurgling. Arnold had read enough horror novels to recognize a death rattle. It was the sound you made when you were kicking the bucket, a throaty gargle that meant your bucket was set up and about to be booted out from under you.

The old man raised his head. His eyes gleamed madly in the dark. His hair stuck up in tattered gray wisps.

Arnold scuttered backward and flung the curtain in front of himself to block out the scene. Dread gnawed at his mind. What horrible thing was happening here? Would the old man die? Would his ghost float out of his body, whispering and gurgling, and attack the little boy who had witnessed the private affair of his death? Or would he die and come back to life, totter out of bed, and eat Arnold like a corpse out of *Night of the Living Dead*?

You read too much, his mind told him with jittering rationality. *Everybody always says that about you. And you watch too many monster movies.*

"Hey," the old man whispered after a protracted gurgle. "Heyyyy!"

Arnold froze.

"Hey, kid. Kiiiiiddddd!"

Arnold moaned. The dying old geezer had spotted him. He tried to get back to his bed, but the IV rack had hung up on the curtain and was tugging him back.

"Kiiiidddd!"

Arnold flung the curtain aside again, disengaging it from the IV rack.

The old man had sat up. He was reaching out to Arnold with both claw-hands.

"Kid!"

Arnold whimpered. The old man seemed about to get out of bed. But he had an IV rack too, and a long snake of a coil that led to his wrist. That didn't matter to the living dead, though. The living dead didn't need IV tubes stuck in their hands.

"Kiiiddddddd!"

He had died and was seeking a victim.

"Nuh-nuh-nuh," Arnold moaned, rooted to the spot by the specter of a living corpse about to attack and satisfy its ghastly lust for human flesh.

"I'm dying, kid. Help me."

Hmm. Arnold scowled. Damn those books, those movies. The old guy wasn't dead at all.

The old man flopped back down. He gurgled. His hands paddled the air.

Arnold moved closer, leaning on his squeaking IV rack. The smell grew stronger; only it wasn't the smell of death, as Arnold's overactive imagination had presumed, but the smell of excrement. The old geezer had shit himself.

Well, so had Arnold. Just about.

"I never told," the old man said as Arnold drew close. "Never told."

"Told what?"

"Ah-ha!" He raised his head, eyes gleaming. "A young Arab! Secrets are best told to the young ones!"

"What?"

"I see the angel of death, kid. Don't try and fool me. But I never told, see, not even when they broke my legs. I crawled away when they wasn't looking."

Arnold looked at the old man's legs. They were large and stiff under the sheet. Why would an angel of death break his legs?

"Who broke your legs?" Arnold asked breathlessly.

"Cumberland," the old man said promptly. "Never forget that name." He took a labored, gurgling breath. Now Arnold could see bruises all over his face. There was a Band-Aid on his cheek. "Burnt me with cigarettes, the bastards. But I never told!"

"Told what?"

"The grave should hold this secret. Come closer, young Arab."

Arnold bent over him. That gurgling breath smelled awful.

"Tea bags and tannin. That'll bring him. Egyptian tea. Must have had a hell of a fondness for it!"

"What?"

"Forty million dollars at last pricing! They knew it, too

Cumberland, he's old like me. But his son, his son! He wants it as bad as the old man does. Never get it, kid! Never get it! I give it to you!''

''What?''

The paddling claw-hands found Arnold's left arm and gripped it tightly. The flesh of them was dry and horny. ''Are you real, sonny? I been seeing things.''

''I'm real,'' Arnold squeaked.

''Then he's yours, my Arab friend. Don't squander the riches! Protect his memory! He belongs to your people!''

Arnold frowned deeply. The old geezer's claws had sunk into his skinny arm like talons.

''He'll do as you want. 1932, don't tell me, I'll tell you. I seen him, older than ancient, older than time. The old Arab, he knew the secret. He gave it to me on his deathbed. Full circle, then. I give it to you.''

Confusion whirled in Arnold's mind. Had the man said forty million dollars? He immediately thought of treasure maps, and excitement worked its way through his veins. It was quite clear now, as clear as a book. This old man had been a pirate. He had a buried treasure somewhere. Cumberland and his son wanted the map. But the old man never told.

''Where's it buried?'' Arnold asked in a husky, excited whisper.

''Old Parker place. Under the shed. I beat Cumberland back to the mainland by four days. No airplanes back then. Steamers, we used. We snuck it past the port authority's noses in a crate marked machine parts. I kicked him off the gangplank before we sailed. He would have sold it, see. Sold it like a chunk of California gold. I dug all night to bury it, and then I hid out all these years. But it's priceless, and it's yours. Use it well.''

His skinny chest stopped heaving. His eyes slid shut. The gurgles stopped. The talons digging into Arnold's arm relaxed.

''Mister?''

Silence.

Gooseflesh broke out all over Arnold's body.

''Isis ki Osirus,'' the old man wheezed abruptly. ''Don't say it unless you mean it. And don't say it too often. Anything used too much loses its effect. Don't tell me, I'll tell you. I ought to know! Now say it!''

''Isis ki Osirus,'' Arnold repeated.

"Shhh!" The gleaming eyes flew open. "Let him rest for a while."

"Is that where the map is? Under the shed? Or is the treasure there?"

Those eyes grew waxy, staring at the ceiling. Arnold passed a hand over the old man's face. He never blinked. He tapped his forehead as he had tapped his own, to see if he was awake or dead. Arnold's IV snake moved with him.

The old man was dead.

The overhead light stuttered on. Arnold whirled, expecting to see Frank Whipple standing there with his hand on the light switch and an evil leer on his bearded face, but it was only a young man in orderly's whites. Beneath a cap of curly black hair was a thin, pinched face. He settled amazingly clear blue eyes on Arnold.

"Is that Atkinson?" he demanded, pointing to the bed.

Arnold could only shrug. The dead man had not mentioned his name, had only told a bizarre and wonderful tale.

The orderly eased the door shut. The latch clicked softly. *A mighty sneaky orderly,* Arnold thought immediately. Then he noticed his shoes. He was wearing work boots below his clean white cuffs, the same kind Frank Whipple favored, with hooks instead of eyeholes for the laces. The laces were bright red. The boots were caked with drying mud.

The orderly with the clear blue eyes and the red boot laces took another step toward the old man's bed. He looked over at him. "Atkinson," he breathed, nodding. A knowing grin spread across his thin face. "He almost got away from us again." He looked over at Arnold with a sudden expression of surprise, as if he had just noticed him. Arnold felt immediately guilty for not being where he was supposed to be.

The orderly moved past him, shoving him casually aside, nearly spilling him over. He bent over the dead old man and took hold of his shoulders. He shook him.

"Dead," Arnold said. "Just died."

"Bullshit," the orderly snapped. "I know his tricks."

He hauled back and slapped the dead man across the face. The sound of it was loud and fleshy. The old man's Band-Aid came off and fluttered down beside the bed. There was a round burn hole on his cheek where it had been.

"Where is it?" the orderly, who Arnold now assumed was no orderly at all, said in a whispered growl. He shook the old man like a man battling a large and uncooperative fish. "Snap out of it, Atkinson, and talk. Tell me where it is."

Arnold backed away with his creaking IV rack. "He's dead," he said again.

The young man snapped his head around. His curly hair fluffed up and settled itself lower down on his forehead. Arnold felt sure it had to be a wig. "He can't be dead. Can't be!"

He bent back to his work. "Your last chance, Atkinson. Talk now or you die."

He reached underneath his orderly's whites and dug at a hidden pocket. Now Arnold could picture the whole thing as it must have been: the man sneaks in, steals some whites from the laundry room, and puts them on over his regular clothes. The hospital is asleep for the night, only one drowsing nurse is on duty. The man is up to something bad. The man wants Atkinson's secret.

A small pocketknife was produced from that hidden pocket. The phony orderly snapped it open and held the blade over one of Atkinson's dead and staring eyes. "Stop the act now, Atkinson, unless you want to be minus an eyeball."

Atkinson, who could no more stop the act than Arnold could, stared at the ceiling with his unblinking eyes.

The young man stuck the blade straight into Atkinson's right eye. It made a thin wet popping noise. Clear fluid spurted out.

The young man straightened. He scratched his head and his wig moved again. "No," he whispered. "No!"

The knife protruding from Atkinson's dead eye gravitated slowly downward until it was resting on his cheek. His eyeball was pulled hideously far out of its socket. It seemed to be staring at Arnold, who was frozen with fear and disgust. *Isis ki Osirus,* that eyeball seemed to say. *Don't say it unless you mean it.*

The secret. Only one living person knew it now.

The young man shuffled slowly around to face Arnold. His blue eyes were nervous and darting, the eyes of a hunted criminal. "You!" he barked in a ferocious whisper.

"Muh-muh-muh?" Arnold stuttered.

"Did he say anything?"

"Nuh-nuh-nuh . . ."

In two giant steps the fake orderly was in front of Arnold. He grabbed a fistful of Arnold's gown under his throat and jerked him taller. Fresh air wafted across Arnold's naked buttocks. "Did he tell you where he hid it? Did he?"

"Uhmuh-uhmuh-uhmuh . . ."

"Did he?"

"No!"

"Not so loud! I saw you standing by him. What did he say?"

"Nothing! No buried treasure, nothing!"

Bright knowledge sprouted in those clear blue eyes.

Oh, Arnold, Arnold's mind yammered at him like a scolding mother. *You can be such a dope sometimes.*

"Talk, kid!"

Arnold shook his head in a blur, feeling the pain of his fractured skull and his own stupidity.

The young man slapped him. Arnold almost laughed. It was a love tap compared to what had happened to him barely six hours ago.

"You think it's funny, huh?" He let go of Arnold's gown and took hold of his left hand. He crunched the bones together. *Such an amateur,* Arnold thought, even though a scream was building behind his lips at this new atrocity so close on the heels of the last one. Dear stepfather Frank would pound them with a hammer, pro that he was, or grind them under his work boot like five cigarettes that needed putting out in a particularly bad way. This kid was a beginner in the art of child abuse.

"Make a sound and I'll knock all your teeth out," the young man with the slipping wig growled as he crunched Arnold's hand in his own.

"Too . . . late," Arnold gasped, and bared his teeth.

That threw him. "Well then," he said, frowning, "how about this?"

He jerked the IV out of Arnold's vein. The tape that held the needle in place ripped away from his skin with a damp tearing noise. Blood squirted across the room to the floor in small spurts. Ringer's solution bubbled out of the bloody needle, which hung from its tube on the rack, swaying back and forth, a disappointed snake that had lost its victim but still dripped clear venom.

"Now bleed to death, you little fucker!"

Okay, Arnold thought, feeling shocked and swoony. *You asked for it, bucko.*

He wrenched his mouth open and screamed.

After a moment, distant hurrying footsteps sounded in the hallway.

The young man ground his teeth. His head swiveled back and forth as he looked furiously from the dead Atkinson with the knife in his eye to the door that was about to burst open.

He put his face close to Arnold's. "You I'll get later," he snarled, then went to Atkinson and pulled the knife out of his eye. He wiped it on his stolen pants, clicked it shut, looked around a bit more as if examining the room for telltale clues, then went out. Arnold heard him say something to someone, no doubt lies upon lies to whoever had come running when Arnold screamed. The door was whipped open again.

"Young man!" the fat nurse with the pillows for breasts snapped. "You get back in that bed!"

Arnold did better than that.

He fainted on the spot.

And came to with rough hands shaking him.

"Go 'way," he murmured. There had been too much pain, too much excitement going on, too many attempts on his life. Sleep was the only escape from the reality and danger.

"Come on, you frigging leech. You ain't gonna lay here draining my pocketbook dry."

Arnold opened his eyes. Hitler, looking puffy from sleep, his hair a wild and greasy mess, was bent over his bed. His breath stank like the bottom of an old beer barrel. Weak morning light filtered through the room's single window, making everything gray and black shadows. Arnold closed his eyes against it all.

"I said come on!"

Thick arms wormed under him. He was hoisted off the bed. His head ached terribly, and under his cast his heart kept a slow and steady beat. "Daddy," he murmured.

"You daddy me again and I'll break your other arm, you skinny little shit."

The world spun as Frank Whipple jerked Arnold around and prepared to stomp out of the room. Something familiar tugged on Arnold's hand and he heard the IV rack crash over. Frank cursed and threw Arnold back down on the bed. "How do you unplug this fucking thing?" he muttered to himself.

Familiar footsteps thumped down the hallway. Arnold

cracked an eye open just as the door blew open and the fat nurse charged in. He noticed that the room divider had been swept open and that the old man had been taken away. Perhaps he had never been there at all; perhaps nothing had been there but a very peculiar specter in a very peculiar dream.

Then he remembered the knife in the eyeball. But he also remembered that he had a fractured skull, possibly a concussion, and that in such a state young boys can often do and dream strange things.

"You get your hands off that patient!" the nurse bellowed.

Frank Whipple turned to face her. "He's my boy and I'll do what I want to, fatso. Unplug him off this damn wire."

"I'll do no such thing. He won't be released until Dr. Price says so."

Frank squinted at her. "You tell that fancy-ass doctor I ain't paying him a cent. And you tell this fancy-ass hospital it ain't getting a dime. Nobody asked for your help."

She made a face indicating tremendous indignation. "The boy's mother brought him in, and in he'll stay. Now you get out of here."

"The boy's mother is a brainless bitch. If I hadn't've been tied up, I'd have killed her before I let her bring him here." He bared his teeth. "And if you don't unplug this damn tube I'm gonna unplug some of yours. Get me, fatty?"

"That does it," the nurse snapped. "I'm calling the police."

"Call away," Frank said, and ripped the IV tube out of Arnold's vein. Blood shot out in a thin red squirt. Arnold squeezed his eyes shut again. This was all just too much.

"You fool!" the nurse cried.

"Frank Whipple ain't nobody's fool, lady." He hoisted Arnold again. "Get out of my way or I'll run you down."

She turned and ran away. Arnold heard her footsteps receding down the corridor fast. He was jerked and tugged some more. The door frame banged against the side of his head, the side with his dead ear. It let out a little squeal of protest. Pain bracketed his skull like a torturer's love cap. He lay limply in Frank's big arms, too tired and full of misery to struggle. His eyes drifted open of their own accord, and he saw the lime-green walls of the hallway, the benches and the ashtrays. They swept past in a blur as Frank hurried him out of the County General hospital. At the entrance-exit Arnold saw the fat nurse through the windows of an office, speaking on the telephone. He could hear her voice, muffled. She was shouting.

They got through the doors and Arnold got his head banged again. He saw a sky gone orange-pink with sunrise, smelled cool fresh morning air. The door fell shut behind him. He flopped in Frank's arms like a large, understuffed doll, trailing blood from the hole in the back of his dangling hand. They went down steps. They crossed the parking lot. They came to the car, and Frank stood him on his feet while he opened the back door. Arnold swayed and rocked while blood dripped down in big red splotches on the tops of his bare feet. Frank pushed him inside and slammed the door before Arnold had a chance to get his feet fully inside. The door swung shut on his left foot, crunching it in a cold metal vise.

He screamed.

"Holy *Christ*!" Frank Whipple howled, opening the door long enough to let Arnold get his foot inside. Three of his toes were mashed and purpling. On one of them the toenail had been ripped halfway off. New pain to add to the old, new blood to flow from new places. Arnold chewed his lips to keep from crying. It was cold this April morning, and the remains of his teeth chattered while he shivered in pain and misery, skinny shoulders hunched up to his ears, arm and cast clutched to his chest.

Oh, Isis, he thought, remembering last night's dream. *Isis ki Osirus.* How had his mind dredged up such absurd little words? This world had no room for fantasy, no place for dreams. This world was real and cold and it hurt.

Frank got in up front. The car creaked on its ruined springs. He was about to slam his own door shut when someone shouted something from behind the car.

Frank snapped his head around. Arnold did too, but not as fast.

The phony orderly with the slippery wig was standing behind the car aiming a large .45-caliber pistol at Frank Whipple's head.

"What the shit?" Frank said.

The orderly edged around the car, holding the pistol in both extended hands. He was still wearing his stolen whites. He came to the open door and wagged the gun in Frank's face.

"Gimme the kid," he said.

Frank's black-button eyes grew large. "Who in the fuck are you?"

"None of your beeswax, that's who. I want the kid."

Frank's eyes got small again. "Welfare, huh? Not satisfied just to snoop in my house once a month, huh? Now you got to follow me around with a fucking *gun*!"

"What?"

"Well, welfare *this*!"

Frank knocked the gun aside, lunged up, and punched the thin-faced phony orderly in the mouth. The gun went off with a noise like a cannon. Arnold's deaf ear squealed. The car was filled with stinking blue gun smoke. Arnold stared at everything with his jaw hanging slack, every ache and pain he had ever had in his life forgotten, even his newly mashed toes. His evil stepfather and the man who had stuck a knife through a dead man's eye were having a fistfight in the hospital parking lot, going at each other like pit bull terriers on betting night. The skinny orderly took a shot straight to the nose. Blood spurted out his nostrils and his wig slipped down over his eyes. He swung blindly and caught Frank Whipple in the ear.

Bust it, Arnold thought, growing avidly interested in the outcome of this strange duel. *Bust his eardrum wide open like he did mine.*

Frank howled and clutched his ear. The orderly, who was not an orderly at all, who was, in fact, rather disorderly at this moment, used the opportunity to cast his wig totally aside, revealing a sweaty bald head that had a few solid bars of hair over the ears. Without the wig he looked much older. Like about thirty-five, Arnold guessed. But even more interesting than that, he looked like he knew karate all of a sudden. He went into a stance like Bruce Lee, ducked and dodged a few of Frank Whipple's clumsy swings, and karate-chopped Frank in the throat.

Arnold grinned. His stepfather was now walking around like a man who has gotten a chicken bone caught in his throat in a restaurant and is politely trying to inform his fellow diners that he is in the process of dying. His face had gone a wholly satisfying purple. Now the orderly kicked him in the balls. Frank dropped to his knees on the asphalt as if to pray.

"Hooray!" Arnold shouted, bouncing up and down on the Malibu's beat-to-death seat. "Kill him! Kill hi—"

Wait a minute. Frank Whipple was no angel, but neither

was a guy who would stick a knife in a dead man's eye. Arnold hesitated, no longer bouncing, no longer happy at all. Jesus Christ, the orderly wanted to *kidnap* him. Why should he cheer for that?

Frank staggered to his feet. He choked and spluttered. The disorderly orderly executed a lightning-fast series of punches to his ponderous belly. Frank whoofed and retched. A part of Arnold watched this with boundless glee, another part with growing concern. What would it be like to be kidnapped? Tortured, like the dead old man had been tortured? Get your legs broke, have a hole burned in your cheek with a cigarette—just how cool would that be?

So he sat quietly, not rooting for either team, while Frank Whipple got the holy bejesus pounded out of him. The smell of gun smoke was still thick in the air, and it reminded Arnold that perhaps there was a semblance of salvation to be found here after all. Neither man had the gun. That meant it was lying on the ground somewhere.

Or on the front seat.

He leaned forward and looked. Split foam rubber, the tatters of a seat cover. No gun. He opened his door and saw it lying on the asphalt just a few yards away. Ponderously, still moving like an old lady, he got out, managing to bang his head on the doorframe and make it scream at him some more. He hobbled over to the gun and picked it up. It weighed a good two pounds. There was a Colt emblem on the wooden grip. Stamped onto the side of the gun were the words Combat Commander, Colt Industries, Inc.

Awesome.

Now, who to shoot it at?

He aimed it at Frank Whipple, who was busily defending himself as best as his size would allow. Then he aimed it at the bald orderly.

He thought for a moment that it would be best for all if he aimed it at himself. End this misery, end it forever.

He was still debating when the blue Wabash Heights city police cruiser roared up the hospital's winding drive with its blue and red lights flashing. The fat nurse had done her work. The cops came to a screeching halt nearby and two of them tumbled out. They pulled their guns and aimed them at Arnold.

"Drop it, kid," one of them shouted.

Arnold gaped at them. He stared down into the barrel of the

gun, able to see the twists of rifling snaking inside, even able to see the silver tip of the bullet waiting to fly out at the touch of the trigger.

"Drop it *now*!"

Arnold dropped it. It went off, another cannon shot, and the bullet he had stared at so wonderingly soared harmlessly into the air. It would land, unnoticed, in a wheat field a mile away, near a farm run by Norman Parker, a farm known simply as the Parker place.

It was a place Arnold would be visiting quite often in the days to come.

There was a treasure buried there.

· 4 ·

Arnold at Home

"Now YOU JUST lie quietly and get some rest," Karen Whipple
said. She sat beside Arnold and smoothed his forehead with
one of her thin, pale hands. She looked too old to Arnold, too
full of cares and worries. There was a fresh lump on her cheek,
just starting to turn purple. They were in Arnold and Melissa's
bedroom, a tiny cubbyhole with two beds and a chest of drawers. The walls were cracked and pitted; in spots the wallpaper
hung down like giant tongues. It was wallpaper with cowboys
and Indians on the north and south walls, smiley flower faces
on the east and west walls. Arnold's father had put it up himself
back in those happier days before Texas stole him away, saying
that two of the walls were Arnold's and two of them were
Missy's. If a boy and a girl got to share a room, then we ought
to make it fair. Daddy had grinned when he was done, proud
that he was able to hang paper and make the cruddy little room
more acceptable. As it had turned out, he wasn't much of a
paper hanger. He had worked at the local Kroger as a checker,
minimum wage. Now he was doing something with oil rigs
and Arnold hoped he was getting rich.

"I brought you a cookie," Melissa said, putting one in Arnold's left hand. He smiled apologetically and handed it back,
indicating his broken teeth and stitched lips and grimacing to
show pain.

"Sorry," she said, looking crestfallen.

The baby squalled in the front room. Karen got up. "Now
get some sleep," she said, and went away.

Melissa and Arnold regarded each other. "Do you hurt
bad?" she asked.

Arnold rolled his eyes. His whole body felt like a rag that

47

had been wrung out and sent through a fast-action spin dryer. It was eight o'clock, an hour and a half since the fracas at the hospital parking lot. The cops had separated Frank and the fighting orderly and read them the riot act. The orderly denied any knowledge of the gun, claimed Frank had pulled it on him. Frank claimed otherwise, and loudly. The fat nurse had come out and demanded that Arnold be brought back inside, but Frank had jurisdiction over him and brought him home anyway. The cops had left, shaking their heads, not wanting to make any more out of the whole affair than was necessary.

Arnold had kept quiet about everything. He was learning that in such matters it was best to keep your mouth shut. Besides, there were secret things going on. A small matter of a buried treasure, to be precise.

"Wait till I tell you what happened," he whispered to his sister now, and motioned her closer.

"You're supposed to go to sleep," she said, but came closer anyway, taking a bite of cookie. She was still in her pajamas, hand-me-downs from Arnold with sailboats on them. School didn't start for an hour and she didn't seem to be in a hurry to get ready. There had been a lot of excitement around here. Arnold could only imagine the scene that had taken place when Frank woke up out of his drunken onion stupor and found out Arnold was in the hospital. It was a miracle Karen wasn't there, too. She knew she had taken her life in her hands by bringing Arnold to the hospital. And in the end, it hadn't done much good. He had gotten a cast and a turban out of the deal. Karen had gotten a fist to the face. And Arnold was back, just where Frank wanted him.

"This old dying man told me a secret. He told me about a . . . oh, come here!"

She edged closer.

"Bend down. This is a high-powered secret. Can you keep secrets?"

"Cross my heart," she said, taking a nonchalant bite out of her cookie but making no move to cross her heart. "What's the big deal?"

Arnold sighed. The biggest secret in all the world, and this dumb girl wouldn't even cross her heart. If Frank had been in the house, he wouldn't even tell it. But Frank was at work.

"Missy, if you breathe a word of this to anybody, I'll fracture you. Now do you want to be in on it, or not?"

"Do, I guess."

"Then bend down here so nobody hears."

She did. "You've got bad breath," she said after a moment, and wrinkled her nose.

"Forget that! What would you say if I told you I know where there's a buried treasure? Or at least a map that could lead us to one."

She considered it, chewing thoughtfully. "I'd say you were a nut."

"Am not! An old man told me where it was before he died. And a guy wearing a wig tried to kidnap me."

Missy's eyes grew large. "Wow," she said. "You really do have a broken head under all that gauze."

"You dummy!" He told her the story then. She ate her cookie and brushed the crumbs off the front of her pajamas, seeming enthralled. Arnold relaxed onto his pillow when he was done, waiting for her reaction.

She worked her tongue in her mouth, seeking out remnants of the cookie that would probably be today's entire breakfast. She sighed. "Did they give you drugs or something? You've cracked."

"No! I swear!"

"I have to get ready for school," she said. "Turn your head."

"Missy! Come on, believe me! Forty million dollars!"

"Turn your head so I can get dressed. I'm not getting dressed with you watching."

Arnold turned his head, growling inside. Dumb idea anyway, telling a stupid girl. Now she would blab it all to Mom and say Arnold's fractured skull had made him whacky. And if Frank got a whiff of this, he would be out at the old Parker place with a shovel if he believed it. He'd be out there with some of his drunken buddies from Terre Haute in a heartbeat, like a pack of grave diggers.

"Are you going to tell Mom?" Arnold asked the wall.

"Tell her what?"

"What I told you, stupid!"

"I might. Why?"

"Because it's a secret! And you crossed your heart."

"Did not."

"You said you would."

"Yeah, but I didn't."

"Then cross it now. Cross your heart and hope to die, stick a needle in your eye."

"That's dumb."

He turned his head, angrily and swiftly, so swiftly it hurt. "You've got to promise!"

"Hey!" She was in her panties, rummaging through a drawer. She threw her arms up to cover her skinny chest. "Turn your head!"

"Oh, you. You don't have anything to look at anyway."

"Do so. I'm getting breasts."

Arnold laughed. The idea of his little nine-year-old sister, Melissa, getting breasts was idiotic. "Show me, then."

"No! Mom!"

"Shhh! Okay, okay." He turned his head to the wall again. "Now promise you won't tell."

"I promise I won't tell," she said in a bored singsong voice.

"Now cross your heart and hope to die."

"I'm crossing it. Don't peek."

Arnold peeked. She was crossing her heart, and by God, she *was* getting lumps on her chest. Amazing.

"You creep! You peeked."

"I see titties," Arnold sang out happily. "Itty bitty titties."

"Mom!"

Distantly, from the front room: "You kids keep quiet and get along! Missy, get ready for school!"

"I am, but Arnold keeps looking at me!"

"Arnold, turn your head!"

Arnold groaned. "Oh, all right." He studied the wall again. A brown Indian was shooting an arrow at a galloping cowboy, frozen for eternity in that pose, or until the wallpaper finished its job of slowly unpeeling itself, in which case the Indian and cowboy would wind up in the wood-burning stove in the front room.

"So where's this buried treasure?" Missy asked as she got dressed.

"Think I'd tell you?"

"Don't care if you do."

That seemed to settle it. Missy was not to be included on the roster of grave diggers. It would be a one-boy operation.

"Okay," Missy said at last. "I'm done. See?"

Arnold looked at her, not caring if she had put on Oshkosh overalls and clown shoes six feet long. He saw that she had put on a faded blue dress tied at the waist with a wrinkly red ribbon.

"Puke city," Arnold muttered.

"Bite it," she replied nastily. "At least I'm not wearing a turban and a gown that shows your ass."

Arnold hastily pulled the sheet up to cover himself. "Get out of here."

"Gladly, you nuthead. Buried treasure my patootie. I think Frank smashed your brain in."

"Good. Now get out and leave me alone."

She stuck her tongue out at him and left.

Arnold lay there, hurting but slowly healing, thinking furiously about his buried treasure and what he would do with the forty million dollars once he dug it up.

Some other people were thinking about the treasure too. Thinking hard about it.

One of them was Jack Cumberland, known to Arnold as the phony orderly. Jack was thirty-seven, two years older than Arnold had guessed, a bald man with a fondness for wigs, women, and Wild Turkey whiskey. His wig was currently lying in a hospital parking lot like a dead mole, there were no women around, and he couldn't afford Wild Turkey, so he was drinking Ten High whiskey, which he had gotten at the local People's Drug for $5.99. That had about finished him financially. It had taken most of his available cash to buy the Colt .45, and the cops had confiscated that. Things were not going too well for Jack these days.

The other man was Alfred Cumberland, his father. He was thinking about the treasure too. He had spent every day of his life since 1932 thinking about the treasure, ever since he and Atkinson had found it in Egypt and Atkinson had kicked him off the gangplank of the *Mary Trieste* in order to keep the treasure for himself. The thought of it burned in his brain like a fever, had, in fact, driven him close to insanity. Sitting in a seedy rented trailer house on the outskirts of Wabash Heights, he was drinking Ten High with his son.

"Damn," Alfred Cumberland growled, and slurped at his whiskey. A hot morning sun beat down on the tin roof of the trailer, heating the place up degree by steady degree. By noon it would be unbearable inside and he would retire to his bent lawn chair outside. The lawn chair was bent because Jack had beat Atkinson over the head with it two nights ago.

"Double damn," Jack said, and drank. He was feeling decidedly lousy.

"How in the hell did we let him get away?" the elder Cumberland snarled. "I thought we'd knocked him clean out."

"Well Jesus," Jack said defensively. "Both of his legs was broke. Who'd expect the old fart to up and crawl to the road? Who'd expect somebody to pick him up and take him to the hospital?"

"You sure he's dead, are you?"

Jack snorted. "Tell you what, Pop. Let me stick my knife in your eye and see if you flinch."

"Don't get smart with me!" Alfred roared. He was almost eighty, but by God, no son of his was going to get mouthy. Alfred carried a wooden cane with a lion's head handle and could use it to great effect if he had to. The dead Atkinson could testify to that. Alfred had beat him silly with it in an effort to get him to tell where the treasure was.

"Fifty-eight years," he muttered. "Fifty-eight years to find that double-crossing shithead, and he goes and dies on us. Bastard!"

They drank in silent misery. All the curtains were drawn to shut out the sunlight, and it was semidark, and getting hot. The smell of cheap whiskey filled the trailer's little kitchen like a pungent gas. Beneath that was the odor of dusty carpets and a toilet that had been plugged up for three days, which was how long Cumberland and son had lived here. They had rented the trailer when the trail they had followed for so long led them to Wabash Heights, and it hadn't taken long to find Atkinson. They had spotted him strolling through the Wabash Heights City Park, a weed-infested acre with a rusty swing set and a slide, and a couple of benches for teenagers to screw on in the night. Yet Alfred Cumberland should have known Atkinson would be here in Wabash Heights, because it was where Atkinson had been born and raised. It was only natural that he would return here in his old age to die. If the thought had struck him a year or two earlier, they would have had Atkinson and the treasure long ago.

Now Atkinson was dead. And maybe, just maybe, he had told some smashed-up little kid where he had hidden it back in '32. Maybe not.

"Only one way to find out," Alfred muttered in his gravelly old-man's voice.

"Huh?"

"I said, only one way to find out. We have to find that kid."

"Shit, Pop, I don't even know his name. And his dad ain't the type to just let us borrow him for a while. He protected that kid like a tiger."

"Most dads would, I guess. How come you didn't use some of that fancy karate they taught you in the Army? That would have showed him."

Jack sighed. "I didn't learn karate in the Army, Pop. I went to school for it."

"Yeah?" The elder Cumberland fastened age-bleared eyes on his bald son. "Fat lot of good it did you, eh? You didn't get the kid did you? Pussy!"

Jack glared at him. "I told you the cops showed up. What was I supposed to do, kidnap him while they watched? Ain't you got no brains left, you old pecker head?"

"Don't smart-mouth me, boy." He wagged his cane at him. "Here, quit hogging that bottle."

Jack handed it over. Alfred poured himself a juice glass full with his shaking, gnarled hand. "It boils down to this," he said reflectively. "We find the kid, we find what I been looking for since Atkinson stole it in '32. We sell it like it should have been sold in '32 and make ourselves rich." His voice suddenly switched into a high, warbling falsetto. "It's a national treasure, Al. We can't melt it down and sell it in ingots. It's a priceless national treasure! And it has powers! I seen him get up and walk!"

His voice dropped back down into its normal, grating range. "Atkinson! Shit on him! The man was a fool who'd seen too many Boris Karloff movies."

"And now he's a dead fool," Jack said sullenly.

"And you let the kid get away, you dork."

Jack snatched the bottle back and poured his own glass full. "I told you the cops was there! Get off my ass!"

"I'll lay this across your ass, idiot!" Snarling, the old man waved his lion-headed cane, a treasure from his days wandering Egypt and delving into tombs with Atkinson. Most of the tombs had been grave-robbed centuries before. One of them hadn't. "You let him get away, you dumb fart!"

Jack gripped the bottle in his sweating hand almost hard

enough to break it, leaning forward across the wobbly kitchen table with all his teeth showing. "I told you the cops was there! Now let it drop!"

Alfred thumped the tip of his cane tiredly back down on the floor. Jack leaned back and took a drink. The two men regarded the ruined paneling of the walls with the anger fading from their eyes.

"We gotta find that kid," Alfred mumbled after a minute. "I could only afford a month's rent on this dump, and my next social security check doesn't come for two weeks, and I'll have to have it forwarded from home. What are we going to live on in this shitpile of a town?"

"I guess I could get a job," Jack said morosely.

The old man snorted. "The earth would crack in two if you ever held one for longer than a day or two. The sky would probably fall."

"Just shut your face. All my life you been telling me we got forty million dollars worth of gold hid someplace, only you don't know where. Why should a man work when he knows he's got that?"

Alfred shrugged. "Agreed. Who'd have thought it would take all this time to find it?"

"And it ain't found yet. Remember that."

"How could I forget? Don't think that just because I'm almost eighty I'm going senile on you." He tapped his forehead. "Fifty-eight years, boy. Fifty-eight years I been thinking about that sarcophagus, remembering the way we found it, how we dragged it out of Egypt right under the port authority's watchful eyes. Mules, boy! Back then we had to use mules!"

Jack leaned his face tiredly on his hands. "Don't tell me the story again, Pop. I've heard it a zillion times. You stamped the words 'machine parts' on the crate and covered the sarcophagus with burlap bags."

"And if they'd have caught us, we'd still be in an Egyptian jail, don't forget that."

"Jail. Yeah. I almost wound up there today myself."

They lapsed into unhappy silence once again. The heat in the trailer rose, degree by degree.

"The kid," Jack said, brightening as he swiped at the sweat that had trickled into his eyes. "They'd have his name at the hospital. I've still got those orderly clothes. I'll just sneak back in and check on him. They've probably got his name, address, everything.''

"Yeah?'' Alfred grunted. "Then what?''

"I pay him a little visit. A little shit like that, he'll talk.''

Old Cumberland hoisted his cane. "This'll make him talk. I won't give him such an easy treatment like I did Atkinson. I'll bust a few of his teeth out.''

Jack thought about the kid, and the blunt stubs and gaping holes in his mouth where his teeth had already undergone a bit of treatment, but said nothing.

"Well?'' Alfred barked. "When you gonna do it?''

Jack filled his glass again. "Soon as this bottle's gone. Just as soon as she's gone.''

She was gone ten minutes later. So was Jack, wobbling down the cement blocks that served as the trailer's front steps, squinting drunkenly into the late morning sun that hung in the hot gray sky. It was muggy outside, no fit day to call spring, more like steamy summer already, and his clothes, faded blue jeans and a T-shirt, were already pasted to him like a second skin. He swiped a skinny arm across his face as he lurched to his father's car, a decayed old Dodge Dart with California plates. The orderly's whites were wadded up in the back seat, and he let the notion of putting them on now pass. Just too damn hot. Besides, another idea was sprouting in his brain, and he might just forget about playing orderly again. Perhaps there was a better way to do this.

He got in the Dart, which was hotter than a steam bath, and rolled down all the windows, puffing and groaning from the contortion of rolling the back ones down from the front seat. Anybody stupid enough to live in Indiana deserved just what they got, he decided as he fired up the old car. This place had the lousiest weather he had ever encountered, and in his travels across the country with his father to find Atkinson he had visited nearly every state in the union. Colorado, Nevada, Maine, New Hampshire—God, he could hardly name them all. And always Atkinson stayed one step ahead of them, protecting the treasure for the moronically simple reason that he regretted having stolen it but didn't dare give it back. He had as little desire to go to prison as Jack did. The current penalty for grave robbing in Egypt was life in the slammer, or death if they felt like it, and there was no statute of limitations.

He backed out of the gravel drive and headed east toward

Wabash Heights' main drag, Highway 40, known to the locals as Maplewood Avenue. Wabash Heights was really little more than a speck on the map, a few stoplights on US 40, a few stores and a few falling-down houses. When the brick-making industry collapsed in the 1940s, Wabash Heights' death knell had sounded. The only people left behind were the ones too stupid to get out after the factories left. Jack guessed the average income in this dying little burg to be less than six grand a year. If it weren't for the taverns, Wabash Heights would cease to exist.

"Piss on you," he said to the town as he drove, unknowingly, past the Parker place and found the highway. He went right, weaving all over the road, feeling hot but very fine, courtesy of the half bottle of Ten High, thanks. The first light he encountered was red. He ran it, grinning, daring any of the cops in this pissant hole to stop him. In his present state, why, he just might punch out the local law, punch some fat-ass cop right in the chops. That would show them what they could do with their little town. But he realized in a drunken way that it wasn't the town he hated, or the cops, or even the heat. It was Atkinson, and the way he had told some nameless kid the secret that even torture and two broken legs could not force out of him. Some nameless (but soon to be named, if things at the hospital worked out) little kid, sitting on a prize worth forty million dollars. It wasn't right, and it wasn't fair. But it was the best break they'd had so far. Getting that kid to talk would be a piece of cake.

He found the hospital drive and went right, lumbering over the curb and giving the old Dart a tremendous bounce. He looked around for cops, remembering the events of this morning and growing a bit jittery. He had gotten off pretty easy, considering what could have happened. Perhaps if they nabbed him for drunk driving and happened to recognize him, the outcome wouldn't be so genial. They'd want to know why a man from California was making such a spectacle of himself in their little town. They'd want to know what he was doing here. They'd want to know a lot of things that Jack Cumberland wasn't especially anxious to tell.

Thus he took the winding drive at a slow and careful fifteen miles per hour, trying hard to avoid the curbs, squinting hard with the effort of seeing things straight through the blur of too much whiskey on an empty stomach. Like Frank Whipple,

Jack had been having a more than casual love affair with the bottle for many years, Jack needing it to keep at bay the gnawing dread that Atkinson and the treasure might never be found. He had grown up with the name Atkinson hurled through the house like a curse, grown up hearing his father tell in an ever more bitter voice the way he had been betrayed by his partner in 1932. His mother, never big on mysterious treasure, had gotten sick of her husband's obsession, gotten tired of bills from the faraway detective agencies Alfred was eternally hiring to track down Atkinson. She had left the scene in 1968, when Jack was sixteen, and secretly, Jack had been glad to see her go. He had inherited his father's obsession, had fallen into his father's habit of checking the price of gold every day, had gone almost berserk with joy when it shot up in the frenzied days of 1974 to nearly five hundred dollars an ounce. What had been worth slightly more than three million dollars in 1932 was suddenly worth forty. That's when the cross-country trips had started, the eternal trekking from state to state in search of Atkinson. Jack estimated he had held over two hundred jobs in the last fifteen years, always making just enough money to put a roof over his and his father's head, food in their mouths, and whiskey in their bellies. The jobs never lasted more than a month. Then the two would be off again, leaving behind unpaid phone bills, utility bills, detective bills. Jack considered it nothing short of miraculous that none of the detectives ever chased *them* down for payment the way they chased Atkinson down for the secret.

But now all that was ended. They had found Atkinson, Atkinson was dead, the search was over. Now it was a search for a little kid with missing teeth and a face that looked like a deep-space picture of the dark side of the moon.

It seemed almost too easy.

He pulled into a vacant parking space, killed the motor, and got out. Sweat ran off his bald head in small rivers, and he sopped at it with his sleeve. As he crossed the lot he spied his wig, a dead mole killed again and again now by having been run over countless times. He picked it up, shook the dust out, and stuck it in his back pocket. A run through a washer at a Laundromat and the thing might be presentable again. If not, he'd buy another, even if it meant getting a job pumping gas or some such. This business of being bald at thirty-seven did not sit well with Jack Cumberland.

He puffed up the steps, aware of the stench of alcohol on his breath, but not really caring all that much. It didn't matter. And the orderly's whites could stay in the car forever, could rot there. He would not need them again, because he was no longer the phony orderly. He was Ralph Jones, the worried uncle.

He adjusted his face as he swung the doors open. A frown of fatherly concern creased his brow. He pursed his lips into a bit of a pout. He hunched his shoulders slightly. He hoped like hell no one was on duty who would recognize him.

He stepped into the relative cool of the hallway and made his way to the admitting desk. It was surrounded by a waist-high wall, topped by greenish glass layered with wire mesh, with a hole at mouth level. A middle-aged lady wearing a lime-green dress that matched the walls was sitting there sorting through papers. He strode to her and pecked on the glass.

She looked up, frowning at being distracted. "Help you?" she said, holding her place in the papers with a finger.

"Yes," Jack said, wanting to swipe again at the sweat that was streaming off his naked head. "I'd like to see my nephew."

"Visiting hours are posted," she said, pointing to a black placard on the wall behind him. "You can see him now."

"He's in room 103, is that correct?"

She sighed. "What's his name?"

Jack maintained his composure. This was the rough part, the area where the ground sloped away to possibly rocky shores. "I received word he'd been in an accident of some sort," he said, making his face even more pinched and troubled. "I got here as fast as I could. I love that boy dearly, he's like my own son in a way."

She shook her papers. "His name?"

"My sister said he'd lost many of his teeth. Something about his head too. A fractured skull?"

"Sir, if you'd give me the patient's name . . ."

Jack covered his mouth with one hand. "Oh, the poor boy," he said through his fingers. "I'm so upset I can barely think straight."

She sighed again, placed her papers primly on her desk, and reached into a drawer. She withdrew a fanfold sheet of computer printout. "One-oh-three." She ran a finger down the list. "Currently empty."

Jack feigned surprise. "Empty? But my sister said he was in 103. Has he been let out so soon?"

"We had an Atkinson and a White. Atkinson is deceased. The White boy, Arnold, was removed by his father early this morning."

"Arnie was removed?" The name Arnold White burned itself into his brain, never to be forgotten. He grinned internally, stifling a shout of pure joy. He was barely aware that the front door had swung open to his right and that someone had come in and was about to breeze past him. "You know, I haven't kept in touch with the family much until I heard the news of Arnie's accident. Do you have his current address? So that I could see little Arnie?"

She sighed. *Lady,* Jack thought, *you sigh a lot. But I love you madly. Were it not for this glass I would reach out and hug you. Maybe even rape you for the hell of it, you miserable bitch.*

Someone grasped his elbow. He jerked as if a cattle prod had been slammed against his arm. He turned, expecting all manner of bad news, most likely the father of Arnold White, here to kick ass again. But it was only a large, genial-looking man in a white shirt and blue slacks.

"Are you a relative of Arnold White?" the man asked.

"Duh," Jack responded.

The man smiled apologetically. "Excuse me for startling you. I'm Dr. Price, on staff here at County General. I'm very concerned about Arnold White. In fact, I'm on my way to check on him as soon as I get my doctor clothes on." He shrugged. "Sometimes I think golf is one of my patients. My swing needs surgery, I'll admit to that." He extended a hand. "You say you're a relative?"

"Uncle Ralph Jones," Jack said robotically, and shook his hand.

"Then let's go take a look at your nephew, Mr. Jones."

"That'll be hard," the sighing lady sang out. "His father manhandled him out of here at sunrise."

"What? He did?"

"I tell no lies, Doctor. One of the nurses even called the police, but there was nothing we could do. The stepfather had jurisdiction."

"Oh, swell." Price looked immensely angry. Jack stared at him, totally befuddled.

"Now listen to me," Price said, drawing him away from the window. "I assume you're related to the real father. Is that correct?"

"Yes," Jack replied, nodding hugely.

"Then let me give you some advice, Mr. Jones. Get that boy away from his stepfather. It is a deadly situation. Unfortunately my hands are tied in this matter, but yours aren't. Perhaps you can talk the mother into filing charges. A man like that Whipple fellow is too dangerous to be allowed to run around loose."

"I'll, uh, see what I can do," Jack said, bewildered. "Do you know what their current address is? I live out of town, and they move around a lot. When, um, Arnie's mother called, I was in such a state of shock that I forgot to ask her."

"Sure. Hold on." Price moved to the window. "Jane, did we get an address on the White boy last night?"

She consulted her computer paper again. "524 South Kentucky Street. Really the Ritz, huh?"

Price snorted. "Seediest part of town. It figures. Did you get that, Mr. Jones?"

"Sure did," Jack said, and did he ever. It was nestled in his brain beside the flashing mental neon that was Arnold White's name, also never to be forgotten. He gave the doctor a big smile. "Thank you very much, sir. I'll see what I can do about this situation."

"Great. Get that boy out of there, if you can. Time may be running out for him."

Jack grinned inside. The dumbass doctor would never know just how right he was. "Gotcha," he said, tipped the sighing lady a wink, and went out into the heat of the day, humming a happy tune under his breath. He still had five or ten bucks in his wallet, he had found his wig, and he knew where to get hold of the kid. And that cheap drugstore was just down the street a bit, where Ten High could be had for five ninety-nine a bottle. He and Pop could have one swinging party this evening, get royally plastered, and then around midnight or so, whammo. The kid would never know what hit him after Jack Cumberland got through with his ass. Everything was working out just fine.

· 5 ·

Night Moves

MIDNIGHT.

The weatherman on station WTHI out of Terre Haute had predicted unseasonable heat, temperatures in the eighties, records being broken throughout the Midwest. Around midnight, he had predicted, viewers could expect a light rain that might bring some late-night relief from the heat. And tomorrow, folks, another record breaker. Now stay tuned for Johnny Carson, following these important commercial messages.

Arnold saw none of this, being stuck in bed, but he had heard the man's professional television voice drifting in from the living room. That had been about ten-twenty, around the time Missy came in to get ready for bed and he dozed off watching the wall while she undressed. His sleep was troubled by the pain in his head and mouth, but sleep he did, until Frank came staggering home shortly after twelve and shook him roughly awake.

Arnold opened his eyes, jerked out of a jumbly dream that was almost a nightmare, and saw in the dim light that filtered from the hallway the apparition of Hitler with wild and tangled hair, standing over him engulfed in beer fumes and stale tavern-smoke odors. He was rocking on his feet, grinning a secretive and mysterious grin.

"Guess I taught you one, didn't I?" Frank Whipple grunted.

Arnold nodded his aching head mutely.

"If you'd have blabbed to those cops this morning I would have throttled you on the spot, kid. You knew that, didn't you?"

Arnold nodded again. Melissa shifted and mumbled in her sleep on the bed across the room. Crickets chirped their song outside, and distantly Arnold was aware of the buzz of a light

61

plane crossing the dark sky. His hands tightened into helpless fists. Oh, to be on that plane and away from this monster.

Frank bent lower, his head wobbling on his neck. The stench of beer grew almost too thick to bear. "Why did that guy pull a gun on me, shithead? Why did he want you? I been thinking about it all day. That hospital's got no right to send some karate-fighting orderly after me just for taking you out of their shithole of a hospital, now do they? And with a gun, even. It just don't add up, but I think you can add it up for me. I think you know who he was, and what he wanted. At least, that's how I figure it."

Arnold stared at him, silent, filled with a sudden and desperate need to spit in his face and send him reeling across the room. But the punishment would not fit the crime, and Arnold was in no mood to die tonight.

"Tell me who he was, Arnold."

My, my, Arnold thought. *Hitler must be mighty puzzled to stoop to calling me Arnold instead of the usual shithead, dipshit, or leech boy. Drunk as he is, he is trying to be civil. But there are secret things going on, and not even a drunken Hitler can drag those secrets out.* So Arnold shrugged.

Frank formed one meaty hand into a fist and swiped it casually past Arnold's nose. "Slam bam, thank you, ma'am," he muttered. "I could kill you in a heartbeat. Want that, Arnold? Huh, Arrrrrrnold?"

Arnold shook his head, fighting that urge to spit at those gleaming black eyes and those tobacco-yellow teeth that shined like dirty ivory in the black hole of Frank's leering mouth.

"Talk to me, sonny. Tell me the things I want to know. Why was that guy after you?"

"He must have been cwazy," Arnold said, then blinked in surprise at himself. Cwazy? Had his broken teeth and swollen lips turned him into Elmer Fudd, the eternal hunter of that cwazy wabbit? "Cwazy," he said again, and there it was. Presto, folks. I now have a lisp. Or lithp, if you prefer. Another gift from loving stepfather Fwank.

"He had a wig on, you know," Frank said as if to himself. "Like a disguise. And that gun. Jesus. I must be the bravest fucker that was ever born, to knock it out of his hand like that. Like John Wayne, that's me." He laughed, belched, then hiccuped. "Duke Whipple. Hardy-har. Jesus."

Oh, go the frig away, Arnold thought savagely.

"So you don't know nothing, huh?" Frank said.

Arnold wagged his head back and forth. The tape that held the turban to his head pulled at his hair.

Frank took a handful of Arnold's gown in his fist and yanked him roughly up off the bed. He brought his face even lower, a twisted face from which the stench of beer came out like a fine and stinking mist on the outrush of his breath. "Lying little fucker." His eyes gleamed, insane and drunken. "How about some more of my specialty, the leech-boy knuckle sandwich? Want that?"

A cold, ugly flower of fear blossomed in Arnold's belly. Again? Tonight? So soon after the last massacre?

"Tell me!"

Arnold looked past Frank's head and in the light of the hallway saw a ghost image of his father, the fabled disappearing-to-Texas father, bidding him good night in a kind and gentle voice, the voice of a bookworm who had no business being within fifty yards of an oil rig. *Oh Dad, Dad,* Arnold's mind sang out, but it was an old tune too often played to no audience at all.

"Talk, shithead!"

"I . . . don't . . . know . . . anyfing . . ."

Frank shook him. Arnold's heavy arm jiggled and flopped, making his shoulder pop. Almost-forgotten aches ballooned all over his body in remembrance of last night's festivities.

"Liar!"

In this blurring world Arnold saw Melissa sit up in bed, hands clamped over her mouth, her eyes wide, white, and sleepy Os.

Frank hit him on the cheek. Arnold's head snapped sideways with a distinct click. He prayed for a broken neck, a quick and painless end to this agony.

"Tell me who he was!" Frank roared, and now the baby began to squall in her crib, which was parked in the other bedroom, beside Frank and Karen's bed. The world was a dim and blurry carnival ride, full of noise.

Karen appeared in the hallway. There was a skillet in her hands. She looked weak and sick, a shrunken scarecrow with a pasty face and a fresh bruise on one cheek. Arnold saw her and prayed she would metamorphose into his father, a tall and thin man who would be no match for Frank but would die in defense of his children if only he had not left for Texas and its oil rigs. Incredibly, she edged closer while Frank shook the dust out of Arnold, raising the skillet over her head. There was old bacon grease in it, a white mat. Some of it trickled down the skillet's handle. *Do it, Mom*, Arnold thought with wild desperation. *Do it before that grease starts dripping in your hair.*

"Why did he want you?" Frank screamed, and Arnold saw the skillet appear high over his head, heard his mother grunt. There was a faint whooshing sound and then the musical bong of the heavy metal crashing down on the crown of Frank's head. The grease flew out in a single round sheet, a grease Frisbee. It splatted on the cowboys and Indians with a moist thump.

Frank let out a grunt and dropped Arnold. He fell to his knees, eyes wide and mystified, his hands starting up toward his head. Arnold saw the shine of blood there, but it might have been grease. Eternity waited as Frank Whipple decided whether or not to fall over. Arnold held his breath. Even the baby, perhaps distracted by that single musical note, the song of Arnold's salvation, stopped squalling.

The crickets stopped chirping outside. Briefly, out of the corner of his eye, Arnold thought he saw something move outside the window, but whatever it was, it was not nearly as interesting as watching Frank sway on his knees like a Muslim holy man. *Will he bow down to Allah*, Arnold wondered, *or will he not?*

Karen let out a slow, wheezing sob. The smell of bacon was everywhere. The skillet dangled from her fists, dripping grease on the bare wooden floor. She looked as if some sneaky fool had come up behind her and administered a skillet to her own head.

"Oog," Frank said thickly. He clutched his head in his big dirty hands.

Bow down, Arnold thought wildly. *Bow down, you unholy holy man.*

Frank got up. He executed a stumbling turn to face his wife. She raised the skillet just as his fist shot out automatically. The skillet rang again, but this time it was his fist that had hit it. He howled in pain, then swung again. Karen blocked the swing with the skillet. Bong, the skillet said. But she was falling back, and Frank was advancing like a slow and clumsy dancer. His work boots found the puddle of grease, and he did an awkward jitter and jive, fighting for balance. This time he fell on his butt. The whole house shook.

Karen raised the skillet. *"Not my babies!"* she screamed, something pent up in her that let itself out now like a blast from a trumpet, and Arnold watched in utter glee as she began to pound Frank over the head again and again, making the skillet hammer and sing like a horseshoe on a blacksmith's anvil. She worked in a furious and hard-breathing frenzy. Her hair was in her eyes, and she paused for a minute to brush it away, a prizefighter taking a short break before going back to the business at hand.

Frank took the opportunity to slump to the floor, kayoed. Arnold could almost hear his skull crackle as multiple goose eggs sprouted up on his scalp. Blood ran down his face in dark wet zigzags. He began to snore.

Karen looked at her children with eyes glassy and shocked. The dark worry lines of her face grew deep, making her look even more old and bedraggled. Tears began to track down her cheeks. Melissa joined in, leaning against the wall behind her bed crying and shaking with her covers pooled around her waist.

"Arnold?" Karen sobbed, still holding the skillet between her knees, "did he hurt you again?"

Arnold sat up, groaning. "What are we going to do when he wakes up? He'll kill us."

"He won't remember," she replied. There was hope in her voice, but it wasn't very convincing. She stared at the wall, frowning. "He'll think he was in a fight at the bar. That's what I'll tell him."

"But it'll just go on and on. He's getting worse evewy day." Dammit, there it was again, that Elmer Fudd voice. Arnold licked his dry lips.

"I know," she said. "I never thought it would be . . . like this. I never thought." She looked suddenly at Arnold. "You have to leave for a while. He seems to hate you more than the rest of us. I don't know why, Arnold, I swear I don't. I thought there was some decency in him. I thought he could . . . love you after a while. That's what children need, a father. I thought, I thought . . ." And then she was crying too hard to speak, a pitiful specter in the dim light with a dripping iron skillet in her hands.

"I can stay at Joey's," Arnold said. "Spend the night like I used to. His mom likes me."

"Joey's," she said dreamily. "Such nice people."

Arnold got up. Now his neck ached, as if he had slept on it wrong. From the shoulders up he felt bent and deformed, the Elephant Man at thirteen. He stumbled across the room to the chest of drawers, steering wide of snoring Frank. He got some clothes out and sat on Melissa's bed.

"Untie this thing," he said to her, indicating the hospital gown.

Sniffing, she bent to the task.

"Now you turn *your* head," he said, getting up again. The gown slithered to the floor and he was naked. He got himself into his shorts, then put on socks and a pair of old and faded jeans. Frank snored in the silence.

"Mom? Help me with this shirt, huh?"

Karen placed the skillet carefully on the floor and came over to Arnold. Together they worked his cast into one of the sleeves. It was an old plaid shirt, a birthday present from better times. Karen buttoned it up for him. She placed her slim hands on his shoulders, then jerked away. Arnold saw that her hands were slick with grease. She rubbed them on her dress. "I'll drop by and see you," she said. "When this thing with Frank is straightened out, I'll bring you back."

She bent and kissed him. Arnold felt his eyes sting as tears tried to force their way out. This thing with Frank would never be straightened out, and he would never come back. Melissa began to cry again. She knew the facts. Until mom wised up and dumped the huge creature she had married, Arnold could never live at home again. Despair welled up inside him, cold and mean and hurting. He was leaving home for the last time. And at thirteen, for God's sake. Orphaned at thirteen.

In the other room, the baby began to cry again. Karen stood up. "I can't drive you, honey. I have to stay here in case Frank wakes up again. He might attack Missy this time."

Arnold looked into her tear-bright eyes. "I'll kill him," he said. "I'll kill him if he does."

"Aw, baby," she said, and now she hugged him, greasy hands forgotten. "Everything will work out. Just stay away for a few days. Only a few days. You'll have fun at Joey's."

"Sure I will," he said bitterly. The tears were trying to

come out on him again. He turned to his sister. "Find my shoes, okay, dork?"

She got out of bed, went to Arnold's bed, and got on her knees. Among the litter of toys and junk underneath she found his sneakers. She came back and handed them mutely over. Arnold saw without surprise that there were dark blotches on the tops. Old blood. About a day old, brown now, dead cells on battered canvas. He recalled that he had wanted a pair of Nikes for Christmas. What he got were these, cheap K-Mart specials made in Poland, of all places. They had been his only present.

His mother put them on his feet and tied them. Arnold got up. For a brief moment the world swam out of focus. *Concussion,* his mind told him calmly. *Blood clot on the brain.* Who really cared?

Frank shifted on the floor, slobbering unintelligible words in his stupor. Arnold took a breath, hating the smell of bacon that seemed to have embedded itself in the walls forever, and probably had. It came to him that he might never see this room again, the cowboys, the Indians, the smiley faces on the east and west walls. He was a boy on the run, the Elephant Boy on the run. He wondered if the circus would take him in. Marvel of the century, folks. Pay a quarter, only a quarter, and see this freak of nature, this orphan with the bulbous head and the cratered face. Yowza, yowza, step right this way.

"Bye, Mom," he said.

She kissed him again. "Joey's is only a few blocks away. Be careful, okay?"

A few blocks away? Try fourteen or fifteen. "Sure. And if he tries to get Missy or Angie, I want you to whap him with that skillet some more. Okay?"

She nodded. "He won't touch them."

Yes, yes, Arnold thought. *But he'll most certainly touch you.*

"Bye, Missy," he said.

"Bye," she muttered, and then flung herself down on the bed and began to cry into her pillow.

Arnold went down the hallway and through the kitchen, shuffling on his battered legs, bent slightly sideways against the pull of his heavy cast. *All I need now,* he thought, *is a hood with one eyehole, and I will be the Elephant Man reborn. And someday my ruined skeleton will hang in a museum.*

He went outside and pulled the door softly shut behind himself. The latch clicked, the last sound of home, he supposed, he would ever hear. He went down the crumbling cement steps to the sidewalk, aware of a slight warm breeze that carried the scent of distant rain. The crickets had started their chatter again, and overhead the new April leaves whispered against each other in the branches of the trees. There were no streetlights in Wabash Heights save for a few on Maplewood Avenue, but the way was clear enough to see by the intermittent light of the moon. Arnold looked up at it as he walked. Clouds scudded across the black sky, shining ghost white under the full moon. An involuntary chill worked its way up his spine. On a night like this, the werewolf would be about. Even when the rain started, the werewolf would be about. And what could be more horrible than to be attacked by a wet werewolf?

He shambled on, acutely aware of the breeze and the darkness, the darkened houses sliding past, the distant noise of cars on Maplewood Avenue. Several of the houses on this street were empty and condemned, rotted hulks like the ruins of war. He quickened his pace as he went past these, horror houses where rats and zombies lurked, where murder victims buried in cellars and crawl spaces sat up with dirt cascading down their rotting faces, dead eyes opening at the sound of a young meal hurrying past. They would come lurching out, arms outstretched, zombies whose fiendish need to feast on human flesh knew no limits, zombies who tottered in the dark and the rain in search of warm meat . . .

Stop it!

Dopey-ass. Sure it was starting to rain a bit, but that was okay, everything was okay, there were no such things as zombies or werewolves or Jason or Freddie, the dead stayed dead, Frank would stay zonkered all night. There was nothing to worry about except getting to Joey's house without having a nervous breakdown from all the frigging horror *books* he had read, the horror *movies* he had seen, the horrible *things* he had lived through since Frank Whipple came into his life . . .

Wait.

Arnold stopped, his heart thudding heavier in his chest. The breeze was gusting good now, but past the whoosh of wind in his ear hadn't he heard . . . footsteps . . . behind him? Sneaky footsteps, like someone walking on the weeds that lined the cracked and leaning sidewalk instead of walking on the cement?

Werewolf feet whispering through the grass and weeds?

No. Bullshit. There were no such things.

Were there?

Arnold turned his head on his aching neck, filled with a calm and drowsy terror, sure that under the on-again-off-again light of the moon he would see Lon Chaney sneaking up on him, perhaps hiding now behind a tree, wolf eyes glistening with dreadful hunger, dreadful intent, peering from behind a trunk with his sharp wolf claws clicking dryly over the bark as he prepared to lunge.

Something, some man-shape, seemed to duck behind a tree several yards away.

Arnold swallowed, his eyes bulging, his head filled with mad and horrible thoughts. Home and the pitiful refuge it offered were a block away now. There was only one thing left to do now, and that was to keep on walking as calmly and rationally as possible, think good thoughts, daydream about bikes and summers and the fun that life still had in store for him if he lived beyond this night.

He walked. It occurred to him to whistle, but he knew that through his stitched lips there would come only a strangled noise of fright. He concentrated on breathing slowly in an effort to make his heart stop hammering so. Had he seen a man duck behind that tree? Of course not. Had he heard wolf steps in the grass? Of course not.

The moon beamed down through an opening in the clouds, and Arnold glanced back under its ghostly light.

There was a man sneaking up behind him. No, not a man, but a werewolf indeed, one with a curly cap of hair and a snarling beast face that shone like a white ghost in the moonlight. His eyes, sparkling diamonds, glittered wickedly.

Arnold broke into a lumbering trot, whimpering, not wanting to be eaten on this balmy night or any other. Now the wolfman left the grass, and Arnold could hear his feet slapping on the cement as he hurried to follow.

A wolfman in shoes.

Hmm.

Arnold's gibbering mind tried to reason with him as his trot became a dead run. Wolfmen do not wear shoes, do not have white faces, do not run breathing silently but slobber and growl in anticipation of the kill. This was no wolfman, Dracula perhaps, a teenage Frankenstein maybe, but no wolfman. That

curly hair, that thin white face—something familiar there. The
scene in the hospital room loomed up on the darkly fearful
screen of Arnold's mind, an orderly in a curly wig sticking a
pocketknife in a dead man's eye. No, no monster here, folks.
Here we have a man in a wig, a man with a knife that didn't
hesitate to stick itself in places it ought not be stuck. Like in
eyeballs. Like in little kids.

Arnold crossed Twelfth Street, lurching and stumbling over
the decaying curbsides, dimly aware that the moon was gone
for good and that a fine mist of rain filled the air, cool against
his warm face, sheeting down out of the black sky, where the
moon was nothing more than a white hole ringed with rainbow
colors. He wanted to scream, to shout for help, but this was
Kentucky Street, a narrow thing no wider than an alley, a street
where empty houses leaned like old tombstones, a street where
the population had moved out in droves years before Arnold
was born, when the brick factories closed their doors and depression settled like a pall over what remained of Wabash
Heights. He could scream his throat to shreds here and not be
heard, except maybe by an old lady too stubborn to move and
too scared to do anything. So he kept his scream inside and
concentrated on pumping his made-in-Poland sneakers up
and down as fast as they would go.

The footfalls behind him drew inexorably closer. He could
hear the man puffing now. He heard him hiccup, then curse.
Arnold looked over his shoulder and saw that the famous phony
orderly was weaving all over the sidewalk as he ran. Drunk,
then.

Goody.

Arnold poured on the speed, holding his cast tight against
his chest, his left arm swinging a good steady rhythm. He knew
the remains of this neighborhood quite well. Up ahead on the
right was what was known as the old Jenkins place, a leaning
shack with a hole in the roof where firefighters had chopped
their way through when the attic burned in 1982. That was
when the Jenkins had collected their insurance money and
moved away, leaving the place to rot. Arnold had personally
shot out all of the windows with a BB gun when he was nine.
It was a dim and spooky place, and his mother had made it
quite clear he should never play there. The place was caving
in.

He veered right and cut through the knee-high weeds of the

front yard, then thundered up the wooden steps. The front door stood ajar, as it had for years, a black rectangle. Arnold plunged through fast enough to flutter the placard beside the doorway that proclaimed the house condemned. Before the Jenkins had moved, Arnold had played with little Arley Jenkins here, and knew the house as well as his own. It was what was known as a shotgun house, because the shot from the front door to the back was a straight one, with the rooms branching off to the left and right, a cheap bungalow, as cheap as Arnold's home. But he knew it by heart. He and Arley had raced toy cars down the twenty-foot hallway before the fire came and swept Arley out of town on the thankful wings of his dad's insurance check.

Arnold stumped down the hallway, slower now. Chunks of plaster the size of dinner plates had fallen in here, and boards from the sagging walls stuck out at dangerous head-high angles. The place still smelled like burnt-out firewood, even after all these years. Ducking and dodging, skidding on plaster chunks, Arnold maneuvered down the hall in utter blackness, his left hand tracing against the wall. He heard the man . . .

. . . *Cumberland. Don't ever forget that name. Cumberland* . . .

. . . the man named Cumberland clump up the steps, wheezing and blowing, and heard him stop at the doorway.

"Hey, kid!" he called out. The dead house swallowed his voice like the cry of a bat.

Arnold ducked under a jutting board, with no intention of answering. Beyond the back door was a small porch, and beyond that, the backyard. There was the small matter of a chain-link fence to negotiate, and that could be a problem, but certainly no bigger a problem than a man who would stick a knife in an eyeball as casually as you might stick your finger up your nose if no one was looking and a particularly pesky booger was lodged there.

"Kid! Kid! Arnold!"

Holy shit. Now Cumberland knew his name. Arnold came to the back door and hurled himself against it, scrabbling for the doorknob with his good hand. His fingers closed around the smooth, cool metal, and he gave it a tremendous clockwise twirl.

The knob came off in his fist. He blinked, stunned, amazed, outraged by this cruel turn of events. He stuck a finger in the knob-hole and felt for something, anything, some kind of hidden spring or latch. Nothing. Cumberland started down the hallway, thudding into the walls and the protruding burnt two-by-fours, crunching heavily over the plaster. Arnold tried to stick the doorknob back on, slamming it again and again against the spot where he hoped the hole was, turning it uselessly, grinding it into the soggy wood and scraping it against the square of moldy brass trim.

"Arnie! Hey, you little shit! Arnie!"

Arnold dropped the knob and started toward him. There was a door on the right that led to the remains of the Jenkins' bathroom. This one was open. Arnold slipped inside, trying not to breathe too loud, squinting with the effort of trying to remember what this room had looked like before the fire. Bathtub to the left, sink to the right, toilet beside it. Small window above the toilet, handily shot out with BBs by an Arnold who was nine and had a father who worked at Kroger's as a checker.

He moved to the toilet, his sneakers crunching on debris. He was able to stand on the rim of it by hauling himself up with a hand on the windowsill for balance. Now the window was about chest high. The thin framework that had held the panes in place was still there. Arnold took hold of the lower board and pulled. The rotten wood came away easily, and Arnold found himself holding what resembled a cross. Oh, if only it were Dracula bearing down on him. This would drive the monster away.

He shoved the cross through the window to the weeds outside. Cumberland was close now, moving cautiously but making a lot of noise as he smashed boards aside and cursed them for being there. Arnold jumped up and caught the windowsill with his good elbow. His feet pedaled against the wall, removing plaster as he clawed his way up and out. Face-first, he fell into the weeds, breaking his cross under his chest. He got up spluttering, his mouth full of grassy-tasting weeds, his head thudding. He heard Cumberland come to the back door, heard his fingers scratch as he hunted for the knob.

"Arnie! Where'd you go?"

Arnold struck off across the backyard, tall wet weeds slapping at his shins, the rain coming down pretty good now, a welcome coolness on his face. Cumberland hurled himself against the door behind him, shaking the house. A few shingles slid off the roof and slapped down on the cement of the back porch, which at one time had had a roof of its own but was now naked and crumbling. He smashed the door again, and this time Arnold heard the squeal of rusty hinges as it swung open, like the sound of crypt doors creaking open in Transylvanian castles.

"Kid!" Whispered, this time. "I ain't gonna hurt you!"

Oh, sure. Just like he wasn't going to hurt the dead man, Atkinson, when he stuck that knife in his eye. Arnold blundered into the chain-link fence, rattling it along its entire length. It was too dark to see now, too dark with the moon hidden behind a pile of clouds. Arnold scuttered sideways, feeling for a post. When he found one he grasped the knob on top and tried to swing himself over.

He almost made it. His right leg went over but his pants got hung up on the spiky tips of the chain link, and he found himself straddling the fence, sitting on those spikes, which punched through his jeans like cold, dull needles. He almost howled with pain, thinking wildly that if he ever got lucky enough to get over this stupid fence, he would leave his balls hanging on it.

Cumberland came off the porch. His footfalls became sneaky whispers as he left the cement and plowed through the weeds. Arnold struggled to get his other leg over, totally stuck now, hearing his pants tear in a dozen places, feeling those dull needles press hard into his scrotum and butt. He leaned his weight sideways and finally fell onto the other side, leaving tatters of his pants and chunks of his skin on the wire. He landed hard on his cast, shooting a hot bolt of pain through his arm, but it didn't matter. He got to his feet just as Cumberland crashed into the fence.

"Don't run, Arnie! I got a present for you."

Sure again. A present like a knife in the eye, or two broken legs like he had given old Atkinson. Arnold turned and ran, knowing that there was a line of trees here, thick maples crawling with ivy and nettles. At one time he and Arley had shinnied up these trees and thought of making a treehouse, but these trees belonged to the neighbors across the way, the neighbors into whose back yard Arnold now ran. He was heading toward Georgia Street, not quite such a dumpy area as Kentucky Street, but no Park Avenue. There were dead houses here, too, but also some live ones. To his left Arnold could see squares of light, windows in a house where somebody was still up. Rain

was running down his face in rivers, and his turban had become a weird and heavy hat. Stumbling like some strange
dwarf, he ran toward the light, cradling his cast with his other
arm, hearing Cumberland make his clumsy, jangling way over
the fence. A tree loomed up before him, and he dodged it,
charging through nettles and clinging ivy that tried to snag his
feet and send him sprawling again. One little fall, he knew,
one more slowdown in this desperate race, and he would be
caught.

The weeds and ivy became grass. Arnold picked up the
pace. He saw with a sinking heart that the lighted house was
surrounded by a chain-link fence of its own, even higher than
the Jenkins' had been. This time he ran pell-mell toward it,
clasped his arms together tight, and jumped with every ounce
of energy available in his legs. Something snagged at his shirt
and rasped across his cast, clipped his knees and the toes of
his Polish sneakers, and then he was tumbling in wet grass on
the other side, bonking his head on his cast as he rolled to a
stop.

He got to his feet, woozy and dazed. His turban was coming
unwound, and a long wet strip of gauze dangled in front of his
face. He brushed it back over his shoulder and ran around the
house to the front. There was a wooden porch there, lit by a
yellow bug-proof porch light mounted beside the front door.
Arnold raced up the steps with his breath pumping up and
down his throat, burning fire. There was only a screen door
there, and inside he could see a fat man in a recliner watching
television. There was a Chihuahua dozing in his lap. Arnold
beat on the door, slapping it against its frame. The dog came
alive and began to yap.

The fat man looked over. He had a can of Budweiser in his
hand. With the agonizing slowness of a man well into his cups,
he leaned his weight out of the recliner and tottered to his feet.
The Chihuahua beat him to the door, madly barking. "Watcha
want?" the man asked over the noise.

"Help me," Arnold squeaked. He tried to swallow, but his
throat was too dry. Distantly, around the side of the house, he
heard the fence rattle.

The man stood on his side of the door, making no move to
open it. In the pouch of his face two bleary eyes regarded
Arnold with drunken hostility. "Is it Halloween?" he asked.

"Or are you one of those kids who's been fucking with my dog?"

"A man is chasing me," Arnold gasped.

"Fucking kids," the man snarled. Then, to the dog: "Shaddup, Butch, or I'll kick you to the moon!"

"Pwease," Arnold said.

The man made an expression of drunken perplexity. "Pwease? What the fuck are you, a harelip or something?" His eyes grew narrow. "You the one who's been climbing my fence and chasing my dog around? Them Chihuahuas got weak hearts, you know. One good scare and wham, deader'n dog shit. Well?"

"Pwease hide me," Arnold begged. The fence had stopped rattling. Cumberland was coming around the house.

"How'd you bust your arm, kid? Climbing my fucking fence? Good for you!"

"Mister, pwease . . ."

"Pwease this, harelip." He showed Arnold the finger. "Stay off my fucking property!"

He grabbed hold of the main door and threw it shut. The porch light rattled. Dead bugs sifted out of the rusting fixture, victims of previous bulbs. Arnold hammered on the screen door in a frenzy.

"I got a fucking shotgun for you!" he heard the fat man roar. The dog barked and clawed at the door.

"Pwease!" Arnold screamed, and then a cold wet hand was clamped over his mouth from behind, blocking off his screams, blocking off his breath.

"Gotcha, Arnie," Jack Cumberland panted into his ear. He jerked Arnold's unbroken arm up between his shoulder blades. Arnold screamed into his hand.

Cumberland giggled. "Nice little chase, shithead. But you won't believe what happens next."

He hauled him off the porch.

· 6 ·

Arnold Captured

"Fifty-eight years," Alfred Cumberland snarled in Arnold's face. He waved his cane under his nose. "That's a damned long time to wait for something that rightfully belongs to you in the first place, don't you think?"

Arnold said nothing. He was looking into the face of Father Time himself, a wrinkled and age-ruined face made of seams and fissures and saggy skin. The old man's eyes were red-rimmed and watery. He had a single brown tooth in the front. The stench blowing in Arnold's face was like hot whiskey barrel scrapings, the same stink the old man's son carried about him like a fog. Jack Cumberland was currently leaning against the kitchen wall of the trailer sucking Ten High out of a bottle. He was grinning a drunk and leering grin, watching his father begin the interrogation of Arnold White in the cruddy little living room. It was just past one o'clock.

"How old are you, boy?" the old man asked.

Arnold clamped his lips tightly together, making his stitches hurt. He would say nothing, emit no sound at all. Tonight was the last night of his life. He would go out with dignity.

"Answer me, I say! Respect your elders!" He thumped Arnold's head with his lion-headed cane. Bing, a tiny thump, a tiny pain. Nothing compared to all the others.

Ooh, but Arnold, the broken legs. How do you break a leg? Hit it with a sledgehammer? Twist it till it snaps? Bend it backward at the knee until all the gristle tears and the kneecap pops out like a round bar of soap and you're staring at the bottom of your Polish sneaker with all your tendons hanging out like snapped wires? How?

76

"That ought to open your mouth a little, boy. Now, where's the sarcòphagus buried?"

A frown twitched at Arnold's eyebrows. Sarcophagus? That was a word he'd heard before, but not very often. Wasn't it an old-fashioned word for . . . coffin?

"Don't play dumb on me, sonny. The gold, dammit, the gold. Where did Atkinson tell you it was hid?"

Arnold held his tongue. Sweat ran down his face. The trailer was a stove with night rain ticking and hissing on the tin roof. The only light came from the bare bulb over the table in the kitchen ceiling. Sharp shadows lay everywhere, pointy and black, fuzzy to Arnold's eyes without his glasses.

"Make it easy on yourself boy. Tell us now and we'll let you go. None of this is your concern. Jack!"

Jack grunted.

"You sure this is the kid we've been looking for?"

Jack nodded. He took off his wig and wiped his forehead with it. "It's him."

"Well then, by God, he's going to have to talk. I'm too old for this tomfoolery. Tape his mouth shut so we can get to work."

Ooh, Arnold thought dreamily, *they are going to break my legs now. At last we shall find out how it is done.*

"Tape," Jack said. He pushed himself away from the wall, wobbling badly on his feet. He stuck his wig on his head. It was backward. He was as bombed as you please; during the drive from town out here to the trailer court he had spent more time off the road than on. Arnold had made the journey in the trunk, but even in there he knew a drunk was behind the wheel. Jack had been singing old Beatles songs way out of tune. The trunk had stunk so bad of exhaust fumes Arnold thought he was going to die if the singing didn't kill him first. No such luck, though. Before dying, he was to have his legs broken.

Jack made his way out of the light. Arnold heard a medicine cabinet screech open, distant rusty music. Things thumped and clattered. Jack came back with a roll of Johnson and Johnson white tape, the two-inch-wide variety used for especially nasty cuts and bruises, the same roll that had been used during the interrogation of Atkinson. He unrolled a strip, tore it with his teeth, and stuck it over Arnold's mouth. He slapped it down tight. Arnold's battered lips wailed in protest.

"All right," the old man said, breathing a little more heavily now, "jerk his pants down."

Arnold's eyes bulged from their sockets. Jerk his pants down? What in the name of Jesus and Mary and Joseph . . .

Jack unsnapped his pants, unzipped them, and raked them down to Arnold's ankles. He managed to fall over in the process.

Old Cumberland didn't like this. "Get the fuck up, you drunken ass!" he roared.

Jack got up. He had spilled a bit of whiskey out of the bottle onto his hands. He licked them clean, made a face indicating satisfaction, then went back to work on the bottle.

"His drawers too, goddammit!"

"Bitch, bitch, bitch," Jack muttered into the bottle, and yanked Arnold's Fruit of the Looms down with one hand.

"Okay." Alfred Cumberland looked down at Arnold with fatherly disapproval. "You've been a nasty, nasty little boy," he said. He slapped his cane down across his open palm. It made an unpleasant cracking sound. "Nasty little boys must be punished."

Jack went back to his favorite leaning spot on the wall. He grinned at Arnold. "Buck up, kiddo. The old fart used to cane me shitless all the time."

Arnold did not buck up. He felt a familiar weakness in his knees, a vague nausea at the prospect of unbearable pain to come.

"Bend over," the old man said, still slapping his hand with the cane.

Arnold did not move, even though his humiliation was final and complete. He could see himself as through someone else's eyes, a skinny short kid all beat to shit, a cast on one arm, the tatters of a turban on his head, his shirt soaking wet, his pants and underwear bunched around his ankles, his tiny genitals shriveling to nothing from fear while these two maniacs watched without caring. This ghost image of himself floated before his vision, Arnold White stripped of everything, his health, his mother, his sisters, his father. What was the use in any of this? Where was the sense?

"Bend over, I say!"

Arnold didn't move, enthralled by this vision of a life so utterly without worth or hope. What use did he have for forty million dollars? What use did he have for anything?

Old Cumberland swung out with the cane, roughly the way a one-armed man might swing a golf club. Its passage through the air was marked by a distinct hissing sound. The tip of it caught Arnold squarely in the testicles with a high, crackling snap.

"Oooj," Jack Cumberland said, wincing.

Arnold went down like a sapling in front of a bulldozer. He squirmed on the dusty, rutted carpet, eyes squeezed shut in supreme agony, pain a monster boa constrictor let loose in his belly, crushing and mangling every vital organ it touched. His breath left his lungs and his diaphragm locked up. Pain sizzled through his body, army ants in his veins, boiling turpentine in his arteries. His hands opened and clenched, finding rug, furniture legs, old Cumberland's baggy trouser cuffs. He coughed and retched against the tape, his cheeks bellowing in and out.

"Now, you nasty boy," Alfred said, "now you get your *whuppin!*"

He brought the cane up. The gold lion's head glittered between his fingers. His son Jack turned his head and sucked liquor into his mouth, giant swallows.

The cane swooshed. It cracked into Arnold's buttocks, raising a long purple stripe. Arnold's shadow crawled after him across the floor, twisting and winding. Cumberland followed him. The cane went up. It went down.

Crack!
Crack!
Crack!
Crack!
Crack!

Jack Cumberland looked over. His face, bleary and bloated from alcohol, was drawn up as if an unpleasant memory had just swept over him, one too keen to bear.

Crack!
"Uh, dad."
Crack!
"Dad."
Crack!
"Stop it, you old fucker, it hurts!"

Hurt, did he say? Oh God in heaven, the hurt was sharp and brittle and more killing than mere hurt, more killing than pain. Arnold squelched his way across the floor like an oversize worm until his head was butting the wall, his buttocks alive with agony, welts jumping out on the tender white skin there like long angry tattoos. This was a new torture, one he was not accustomed to. Frank only beat him and kicked him; his real father had only occasionally swatted him with his open hand. Nobody had ever caned him before. Nobody had ever laid the meat of his ass open as casually as a butcher might cleave a roast in two, or three, or four, or . . .

. . . *crack crack crack crack crack crack crack crack* . . .

. . . eight.

"What did you say, boy?" Alfred Cumberland roared, turning, breathing hard, his old man's lungs wheezing and rattling.

Jack pushed away from the wall, his bottle clenched tightly in one fist, his wig sliding and skating on his head. "I said to stop it, dammit. You're killing the kid."

"With this?" The old man hoisted up his cane and regarded it, seeming puzzled. "God, Jack, I used to cane you till the cows came home, and you never died on me. Where the hell's your common sense gone to?"

"I just don't like it, that's all."

"Then get the fuck out till I'm done."

"No, no, it don't work that way." Jack pushed his wig back in place, frowning. "Can't you see what this kid's been through? He's already been pounded to fuck and back. What does pain mean to him? See his arm? Busted. See his teeth? Gone. His stepdad did that to him. The doc at the hospital told me that. Does it to him all the time by the way he talked, and I believe it. You should have seen the fucker, all big and scruffy and looking like the devil himself. If I hadn't've knowed karate he'd've killed me dead as shit."

"So?"

"So we need to use brain power, Pop. Pain don't work with this kid, just like it didn't work with Atkinson. You can't pound forty million bucks out of somebody. Atkinson proved that. I snapped both his legs clean in two, and he still ate whatever he was going to say. We pounded him silly with that lawn chair, burned him with cigarettes, and he laughed at us."

Alfred's face twisted up. "No! He didn't laugh! He screamed! Hah! Through his nose!"

"Yeah, yeah, I remember. And then we came in for a drink and he shuffled off to Buffalo. I beat the weeds all night looking for his ass, tromped the swamps, everything. But what good would it have done to find him? He was dying, and still he wouldn't tell.''

"So?''

"Well, so, so, so. So I'm telling you this. I can reason with the kid. Fuck, promise him a fifty dollar bill, what kid wouldn't jump for that? Hey, Arnie!''

Arnold, eyes clamped shut, head pressed into the shoddy paneling of the east wall, immersed in a private night world lit only by the brilliant uncaring stars of pain, made no reply.

"He'll come out of it,'' Alfred grunted. "You always did.''

Jack winced. "Yeah. And I swore I'd kill you someday.''

"You did?'' Alfred frowned. Then his drooping features sagged deeper in a dark expression of anger. "Kill *me*, huh? *You'd* kill *me*? Hah!'' He swooped his cane through the air, making well-practiced circles with it, the nose of the lion's head spinning in his gnarled fist. "Lay a hand on me, boy! I dare you!''

"Aw, Pop.'' Jack rolled his eyes. "Turn the burner down, will ya? Here.'' He offered the bottle of Ten High. "Put out the flames.''

Alfred snatched it from his hand, glowered at him, and drank. The cane still spun. Jack had to give the old fart credit for one thing: he knew how to use that cane. God, did he know how.

Alfred finished. He armed a drool of whiskey off his chin. "All right, Jack,'' he said, and the cane stopped spinning. "Do what you have to with the kid. Just don't fuck it up.''

"Right. Now gimme that.'' He snatched the bottle back, which was about one-quarter full. "Kiss her good-bye, Pop. We're going to try a bit of truth serum on the lad.''

"Say what?''

"Truth serum, old man. Hydrogen peroxide, or whatever the fuck it is. Brain juice.''

Light sparked in Alfred's eyes. He looked at the bottle in Jack's hand sorrowfully, but the light of knowledge still burned there. "Hate to waste good—whoops, I mean lousy—whiskey on him, but what the hell? Forty million bucks will buy us all the whiskey we want.''

"That it will,'' Jack agreed. He stalked over to where Arnold lay, no longer twisting quite so furiously. "Arnie? Oh, Arnie-boy?''

He bent down and turned Arnold over on his back. His cast

slid across his chest and banged on the floor. It was streaked with green from the grass of the chase. The cottony part at both ends had bits of wet dirt in it.

"Arnie?"

"Aw, fuck you," Alfred snapped. "Let me cane the little bastard till his eyes pop out."

"Back off, old fart. Arnie?"

Arnold opened his eyes. As a semblance of focus came back he saw sagging ceiling tiles overhead gone yellow with age, warped and bulging walls, and the pinched and shiny face of a man driven to insanity and back by greed and whiskey. Colored stars shot across this whole scene, the remnant of his pain. He let his eyes slide shut again. The stars were almost pretty now.

Jack peeled the tape off his mouth, so gently it could have been a mother's touch. He stuck a fingernail between the stubs of Arnold's teeth and levered his jaw open. "Gonna give you some joy juice now, Arnie my boy. The world's oldest painkiller." He unscrewed the cap and tilted the bottle to Arnold's open mouth. He filled it like a teacup, recapped the bottle, and watched.

Nothing happened.

"Possum," the old man grunted. "The boy's playing possum. Trying to trick us by playing dead."

For once the old man was right, but only partially. The possum had crawled into Arnold long before the caning, long before the bumpy ride in the trunk of Jack's ancient Dart. The possum was named despair, and it had made itself at home inside Arnold as soon as Jack's hand was clamped over Arnold's mouth on the front porch of that idiot with the yapping Chihuahua. The fat man with the chatty dog and the Budweiser in his hand could have opened his door and saved Arnold this final indignity. He could have alerted the police. But all he cared about was his dog and his yard and his crappy chunk of property, and like Wabash Heights itself, he didn't give a damn about people in trouble. He was Arnold's last hope, and he didn't know it, and had he known it, he wouldn't have cared. It was the town, then, and the mean and shallow people who inhabited it. Wabash Heights was a misnomer. The place should have been named Hell.

"Swallow'r down, Arnie," Jack cooed. "Elsewise I twist your little dick out by the roots."

Arnold considered it from the distance his mind had obtained from reality. He was aware, over the burning square mile of skin that had been his butt, of a pungent and hot-tasting liquid in his mouth, a smell in his nose like gone-over pickles. He could feel his cheeks and tongue beginning to pucker the way they puckered when his mother made him take a tablespoonful of that rotten Formula 44-D when he had a cold. His stomach twisted itself shut at the thought of swallowing this stuff.

"Out by the roots. Arnie. Out by the roots."

Okay, Arnold thought. Sure, why not? All he wants you to do is swallow. You've swallowed a lot in your life. You're short and you're skinny and sometimes big kids pick on you. You swallow it. Your dad disappeared without so much as a good-bye or a puff of smoke, and you swallowed it. Your stepfather is a giant mulching machine with fists the size of wheelbarrows, and you've swallowed that too. You've even swallowed some of your own teeth. So why not swallow some of this guy's rotten-pickle-tasting Formula 44-D?

He swallowed. It was a big gulp, but he swallowed it all. The whiskey drove its way down his esophagus like a truckload of Tabasco sauce and parked itself uneasily in the knot of his stomach. He retched a bit, but only a bit.

"Open up, Arnie. Take-a you medicine, or I pull offa you dick."

Arnold opened. Stars swooped across the dark field of his closed eyelids, glowing comets. Ah, to be there, between the planets and far from the sun, where comets slip without sound through a black and endless space, to be in a spaceship, yes, one of Poul Anderson's spaceships, where the menace of danger is a thousand light-years away, and the hero always wins in the end for the simple fact that he was a hero all along. And Dad, dear Dad, will you be there too? You can bring your oil rig with me to Mars, but stay with me, stay with me until the end of time.

Glug-glug. Arnold let himself be filled. The glugging stopped, and he swallowed. The truck blew its horn on the way down, blew a song that went "through the lips and over the tongue, look out stomach 'cause here I come," and chugged its way into his belly with a load of fire to dump.

"Open up."

Arnold opened. No problem. This was not much different

from the hospital, only now the IV tube was a bottle of Ten High, and the nurse with the white pillows for breasts had become a sweating man with a wig he had to hold tight to his head as he bent over, lest it fall off and expose the shame of baldness. Glug-glug. Stop. Arnold swallowed. The dump truck trundled, loaded with fire, burning all the way, air horn blasting.

"Just a few more, Arnie."

Arnold drank. The dump truck rolled. His stomach churned and blew smoke down his bowels. Dragons hissed in the torn lining of his belly, awakened from a long and stuporous sleep by the evil sludge being dumped on them. They got up on stinging legs and tromped through his insides, belching fire.

"Don't puke it up, Arnie, or off goes the dick. Open up now."

Glug-glug. Zoom. The truck was a high-speed racer now, negotiating those dangerous esophageal curves with deadly accuracy. The Indy 500, Indiana's only claim to legitimacy, took place in Arnold's body. The dragons screeched and stormed, enraged at being drenched, blowing their fire.

"Two more now. Just two. You're doing fine."

Glug. Glug. Glug.

Arnold swallowed. He swallowed it all. He heard the plastic rattle of the cap being rescrewed. He heard the bottle thump and roll across the floor.

Jack straightened. He turned to his father. "Fifteen minutes, Pop, and this kid'll be walking on clouds."

"Yeah? That's fifteen minutes I ain't got. I'm in my eighties, boy. Fifteen minutes is fifteen minutes away from my gold. Let me at him." He stalked over to where Arnold lay, swinging his cane. Jack pushed him away with no lack of irritation.

"Cool it, Pop. Let the damn booze work."

"Booze? Yeah!" Old Cumberland snarled at Jack, showing his lone tooth. "Now what are we supposed to drink? Water? And when the boy talks, what are we going to drink on the road? Atkinson hid the sarcophagus in Maine, I'll bet my ass on that. He was always big on spooks, him and his dumbass ideas. And Maine's got more spooks than you can shake a stick at. Christ, you can't swing a dead cat without hitting somebody who's spooked out of their mind by that crazy writer up in Bangor. Remember when we spotted Atkinson up near Jerusalem's Lot? You can bet your ass our fortune's up thataways!"

Jack regarded his father with incredulous eyes. "You dumb fuck! That town burned to the ground back in the seventies!"

"Forest fire," Alfred said. "Ten dollars says Atkinson started it to get us off his trail."

"Maybe so." Jack dug in his back pocket, and withdrew his wallet. He cracked it open. "Fuck. Three bucks." He scouted through his front pockets, and withdrew a handful of change. He counted it, squinting in the poor light. "Seventy-eight cents. You got a couple bucks?"

"What for?"

"What the hell do you think for? We can't drink the water in this town. It's probably poisoned. Everybody here's dumber than owl shit. I'd lay money there's a toxic waste dump right under the town well, or a cesspool, you can take your pick. Me, I'm not drinking anything but what that drugstore carries, and it don't sit all that well."

Nodding, grumbling, Alfred yanked his own wallet out of his baggy old man's trousers and examined its contents. He extracted three dollars, soggy and limp from sweat, and handed them over. "What are you gonna get?"

"What the fuck else? Ten High. This whole town lives on beer and Ten High. God knows if a bottle of Wild Turkey ever hit somebody's gullet, they'd keel over dead. So would I by now, probably. Can you keep an eye on the kid till I get back?"

Alfred looked over to Arnold, dead to the world on his back by the wall. His stitched and battered mouth hung open like the mouth of a corpse. A bright line of whiskey had drooled out of the corner of his lips. "You just go get the refreshments, boy. Me, I'm gonna limber up my cane till you get back." He replaced his wallet and began swinging his cane in those perfect circles, making helicopter sounds with it. Jack pocketed the money and made for the door. He opened it, letting in the screech of a million weedyard crickets, then turned.

"Don't cane him, Pop," he said darkly. "Anything but that."

"Why?"

Jack frowned. "Because . . . because it just ain't right. It'll knock the whiskey out of him, ruin the truth serum effect." This sounded pretty lame, but he seemed satisfied with it. "Just don't," he said, and left.

Alfred stared at the door for a while, making unhappy faces. The cane twirled. He sauntered over to the kid again, manag-

ing to collide with a wall that sprang out of nowhere to block
his progress. He growled at it and pushed himself away, but
still the cane spun and spun, the lion's head a treasure in its
own right, the wood some California oak implanted in it decades ago to replace whatever had been there five centuries before. A sword? A spear? A royal scepter? Nobody knew. And
Alfred Cumberland most certainly did not give a shit.

He plopped himself down on the ruined couch that was part
of the trailer's sparse furnishings, giving his cane one final spin
and thumping its tip down on the floor between Arnold's legs.
He eyed Arnold's naked penis for a second, found nothing of
interest there except the swollen purple bag below it that had
been the boy's scrotum before the cane had done its magic,
and let his eyes wander around the room. He made a face of
disgust. This was a rathouse. All of his domiciles since 1968,
when his wife, Mary, had left him for reasons he would never
fathom, had been rathouses. He had pretty much lived his life
in rathouses, even with Mary. It had been poverty without end,
but not poverty without hope. In 1932, it had been the lure of
three million dollars and a chance to kick Atkinson's butt that
had kept him going in such abysmal squalor. Now, in 1990,
with Atkinson's butt firmly kicked (so hard he had died, in
fact) there was still the lure of forty million dollars worth of
gold to keep him going in ever-increasing poverty and desperation. But like so many old people, it did not occur to him that
he had only a few years left to enjoy his riches, once he found
them. Like so many old people, he assumed that somehow,
some way, he would be able to take it with him.

And like so many old people who have sunk into delusion
and selfishness, he found that it was hard to keep his eyes open
despite the hunger for wealth that gnawed at him like a rat.

A rat in a rathouse. The joke, if Alfred had been told it,
would have escaped him entirely. He could think only of himself, and what the world owed him, and what he would do with
it once he got it.

And he did not know, as his son Jack sped drunkenly toward
the local People's Drug in a battered Dodge Dart with California plates and as his eyes fell shut and his face sagged into
an expression of stupor, that if he were to announce a desire
to become a citizen of Wabash Heights, Indiana, he would
probably be given the key to the city.

Wabash Heights was always looking for a few good men.

Mean, selfish, narrow-minded, dumbly self-satisfied, stupid, cruel. There was always room on board for a few more.

Alfred fell asleep without meaning to, and his cane slipped out of his hand.

The lion's head thumped Arnold on the chest, waking him out of the comet-shot dreamworld where Asimov and Anderson took him away and away to remote and peaceful planets, and he raised his head with a small groan, snapping his mouth shut in anticipation of more 44-D.

His 80-20 vision showed him yellow ceiling tiles, a bare bulb burning above a rickety kitchen table, paneled walls the color of dry cow pies, and an old man snoozing on a sofa with his chin on his chest. He remembered things without wanting to. The chase. The fat man and his beer and his Chihuahua who slammed the door on hope. The ride in the trunk. The cane, whack whack whack, the cane.

The cane.

He looked at his chest and saw a snarling lion's head resting sideways on his breastbone. It gleamed mellow yellow in the dead flat light. Arnold gave his belly a heave, and the cane rolled off him, thump, to the floor. Now the lion was staring at the door with its baleful golden eyes.

The old man began to snore. It was guttural, choppy slobbering. He muttered things.

Arnold stared at him for a moment, plugging himself back into reality chunk by chunk, remembering, knowing. He sat up. The entire trailer house seemed to cant sideways, as if it had been resting on the edge of a cliff and had chosen this moment to begin the plunge to the bottom. Arnold grabbed at the nubbles of the rug, engulfed in sudden panic. The trailer was rocking back and forth now; it had become Dorothy's Kansas farmhouse in the clutches of the twister. That made Arnold think of tornados, and the peculiar thirst they seemed to have for trailer courts. Over twenty tornados touched ground in Indiana every year, and while they were sometimes content to merely chew a wheat field to pieces or explode a barn, most often they would veer off toward the nearest trailer house like a bloodhound hot on the trail, and blow it to pieces, generally killing one or two people for the fun of it before sucking back up into the sky and becoming harmless dark thunderheads again.

Arnold used his left ear to listen to the wind. But there was only rain spatting down on the roof, no boom and chug of an oncoming tornado. Arnold looked around cautiously. Now the trailer was trying to spin, as if someone had parked it on a spindle instead of cement blocks. Was this concussion, then? Was there a blood clot under his skull that was, even now, leaking delusion and death into his brain?

He swallowed, tortured by fear. And with the swallow came the memory of drinking lots and lots of pickle juice, only it wasn't pickle juice at all: the bottle lay where it had come to rest against the north wall, by the door, mutely proclaiming that it was TEN HIGH in big red letters. Arnold knew about Ten High. Sometimes, when Frank was feeling particularly jolly, he would bring home a bottle from the tavern and proceed to gulp it down while watching TV. He would become glassy-eyed and sullen, sometimes jumping to his feet to holler at the set.

So this was Ten High: it made the world spin and rock. Arnold found himself grinning. Hey, this wasn't so bad, not once you got used to it. It made everything kind of . . . soft. The pain in his head and mouth and beneath his cast, the fresh stripes on his backside—they weren't so bad. Why, they were just little tickles now, little janglings of his pain receptors, as if his body were a harp and an angel were stroking him. He got to his knees, remembered that he was as good as naked, and so got to his feet and pulled his underwear up. The elastic scraped across his blistered fanny, but it didn't hurt so terribly. He bent and hoisted his pants up, becoming aware that he was stumbling around the room like a . . . well . . . like a drunk.

He giggled. What a wild and wonderful world he had slipped into. It beat the hell out of any secret hiding place, made mincemeat of tree houses. *Welcome to the domain of the drunkard,* he thought, and had to cover his mouth to keep from braying laughter. He stumbled into a wall, giggling hysterically, overcome with an urge to take a bite out of the paneling. Check it out, friends: when you drink Ten High, you fly to the sky. And to your paneling, say good-bye!

Arnold doubled over, howling helplessly. Ah, it was great, it was grand! He worked his way along the wall to the fallen bottle, picked it up, and managed to get the cap off. There were a few good drops left. He sucked them down, giggling and choking. He licked the inside of the cap clean. Then he

dropped the whole affair to the floor again and stared across
the room to the couch, where Alfred Cumberland sat snoring
at his lap. The horrible cane lay near his feet.

Arnold went over and picked it up. God, but the head was
heavy. The gold felt warm and greasy in his hand. This sucker
alone had to be worth a few thousand. Why hadn't the old man
and Jack sold it, if they were so desperate for gold?

Uh-oh. Arnold frowned. Jack. Where the heck had Jack gone
to? And if he wasn't here, what the heck was the prisoner doing
stumbling around admiring the gold and thinking of making
dinner out of the walls?

He went to the door. It was old and splintery, the victim of
previous tenants and too many summers. There was a small
window in it. Arnold went up on tiptoe and looked out. It was
dark. It came to him that maybe Jack was just around back
pissing. Drunken men seemed to have an abnormal fondness
for pissing outdoors, he knew that much from Life with Frank.

He opened the door a crack. Damp cool air drifted in, smelling of rain and wet weeds. Crickets screeched outside. Arnold
wished desperately for just one more mouthful of Ten High,
the Vick's Formula 44-D of grown-ups, and this immediately
brought the concern that he was already an alcoholic, at thirteen an alcoholic who looked like the Elephant Man. Jeez,
what a life.

He opened the door fully and stepped outside. Cement
blocks wobbled under his feet. He shut the door, shrugging to
himself. The urge to pee was upon him, but he willed it away.
He went down the three steps, leaning on the cane, which was
a little too long but made a handy walking stick. There was a
patch of gravel at the foot of the steps, and then weeds. Bulking
up to the left and right, and across the road, were the darkened
humps of more trailers. Arnold knew where he was now. This
was the Cimmaron Trailer Plaza, known to the residents of
Wabash Heights as Shitty City. It was about two miles west of
Wabash Heights proper, the dumpiest, most rat-infested area
on the planet. Arnold had heard that the mayor lived out here,
since the city only paid him three thousand a year and he was
too drunk to find real work most of the time.

Arnold took a few hesitant steps into the dark. Cool rain
misted down on him. No Jack Cumberland leapt out of the
dark; no Jack Cumberland did anything at all.

Arnold walked. He felt fine. The world twisted and rolled,

but what the hell, if he was an alcoholic he would have to get used to it.

He made it out of Shitty City without incident, and went into the woods that bordered it. He walked northeast, which was the direction of the broken-down old farm run by Norman Parker. There would be no going to Joey's tonight, no going back into that town again, not until the treasure was found and the forty million dollars safely stuck in a bank. Arnold chided himself now for having given up hope when the Cumberlands had him in their clutches. With forty million dollars, he could buy an armored limousine and hire a squad of goons to protect him. He could take his mother and his sisters and move the hell out of Indiana forever. He could even bribe a senator or congressman, a general or an admiral or something, and have them nuke Wabash Heights off the map. That would serve everybody right. It would serve them right indeed.

He walked for a long time and then found a fence, a rusting old barbed-wire job, and ducked through it. A freshly plowed and very muddy field lay before him, where the first green hints of summer wheat poked up through the earth.

He was on the Parker farm.

And in the distance, just vaguely, he could see the squat little hump that was the Parkers' house. If it had been lighter, or if the moon had been so kind as to show its face for a moment, he would have been able to see the shed where the sarcophagus . . .

. . . *coffin* . . .

. . . was buried.

He tromped off through the mud, destroying shoots of wheat, saddened to find that the fresh air and the rain and the late-night hike were sobering him up.

· 7 ·

Norman Parker

PARKER SAT INSIDE THE fallen-down shack that was his farm-house with a warm can of Steinbrau beer (a local Kroger fa-vorite—$1.89 a six-pack) in one gnarled and liver-spotted hand, his eyes fastened to the face of his ancient RCA Victor boob tube, where Eddie Albert and Eva Gabor were performing feats of comical genius on a WTHI late-night rerun of "Green Acres."

Now, Norman Parker, approaching seventy with less grace than was common and more wrinkles than were necessary, had been no fan of comedy ever since George and Gracie left the air, but by George, this "Green Acres" stuff was fabulous. Norman Parker was never one to emit so much as a chuckle in public, being the respected and sometimes feared old fart that he was, but in the privacy of his living room, late at night when no one was apt to drop by and listen at the door, he occasionally let a burp of subdued laughter rattle through his throat, whenever Eddie Albert climbed the telephone pole to answer the phone and then fell off. That was great, watching Eddie Albert all dressed in suit and tie, trying to be a farmer. The fact that his elderly tractor with its huge whirling flywheel was an exact copy of Norman Parker's own escaped him. The fact that Eva Gabor's cooking abilities rivaled his own wife's remained unknown to him. Josephine Parker had dropped dead in the kitchen one morning eight years ago, victim of a massive stroke. She had been cooking pancakes. Norman came in, stooped, shrunken, and bleary-eyed from an overdose of Stein-brau, saw her splayed across the humped and buckled linoleum tiles with her dress rucked up to her ass and her eyes staring at the kitchen table's legs, helped himself to the pancakes, then made a casual trip to town to inform the undertaker that dear

Josephine had finally kicked the bucket. Several townspeople turned out for the funeral, but Norman had sixty acres to plow that day and was in no mood to see Josephine lying around in a coffin when there were things to be done.

If he missed her, he didn't show it. Her cooking had been pure shit and she was fat. The Parkers had had no children because, as Norman liked to brag, he could never find the right wrinkle to fuck. If the truth be known, Norman Parker was a man who drank Steinbrau beer from dawn to midnight, and his pecker was as good as dead.

None of that mattered now. Josephine and her wrinkles were eight-year-old sludge in some cheap coffin. The farm still produced corn and wheat. The refrigerator still contained massive doses of cheap beer and WTHI showed "Green Acres" reruns late at night.

And if you got lucky, Eddie Albert would get a phone call and fall off that pole.

Norman Parker was not lucky tonight. That stupid pig Arnold Ziffel had won some cereal box contest and had to prove he was a human. There were to be no phone calls tonight.

"Fucking shit-ass Hollywood writers," Norman muttered into his beer can. "Wouldn't know comedy if it came up and porked 'em in the ass."

Yet he sat and suffered. When a commercial came on he got up out of his chair, groaning, and sauntered off to the kitchen, where Josephine had died, in order to procure another beer. It was at that moment, as he cranked the fridge door open and bent down into a faceful of cold and moldy air from the old Frigidaire's rotted green innards, that he heard a noise from outside, a distant but unmistakable clank.

He straightened, leaning on the refrigerator door, wobbling mysteriously back and forth in his age and his drunkenness. His creased face screwed together in a frown. There wasn't much wind tonight, despite the rain, and his farm, which carried more than a passing resemblance to a junkyard, had no business making noises of its own accord. Something, or somebody, had stumbled across a metal object in the Parker castle's sizable moat of rubble and unusable farm implements.

He waited, listening, frowning. Occasionally a whitetail deer or two would straggle onto the property if the poachers were thick out in the fields. Sometimes a raccoon or a possum would wander up to see what might be had for dinner. Norman Parker had long since given up hauling his trash to the dump, which was eight miles away. His ancient pickup truck had been acting funny lately, having a tendency to die a smoky, rattling death if it went more than a few miles from home. The trash had been piling up in the shed for years. The raccoons and possums usually nosed around for a while, sniffed out the eau de garbage drifting out of the shed, and clawed at the door. At this point Norman Parker would load up old Bertha, his trusty rusty 12-gauge shotgun, and blow the fuck out of the critter. Next day he would have coon or possum cooking in a pan on the stove.

Clank. Rustle rustle rustle.

Norman smiled to himself, still at the refrigerator, showing the blackened remnants of his teeth to the refrigerator light. Raccoon, sure it was, nosing around the shed. He let the door fall shut and shuffled off to the bedroom, where Bertha resided against the wall by the bed. He got her in his hands, found his box of shells in the top dresser drawer, cracked her open, and shoved a shell into each of her barrels. Then he proceeded on to the front door, opened it, and peered out into the night.

Cool rain spatted down on his face as he craned left to look at the shed, which stood some ten yards from the house. By squinting, he could make out the shape of the pickup truck, and various other farm objects that had died and been left in eternal disarray. The shed was a black hump, vaguely lit by the ghostly light cast by the full moon above the clouds.

No sign of movement. And no more noises, either.

Scowling, Norman went down his front steps, mentally kissing the sweet greasy taste of coon good-bye for this night. He had a flashlight somewhere in the house, but its batteries had long since oozed their strange orange-black guts out and jammed the thing forever. There was a lantern hanging in the shed, but by the time Norman got the doors unlocked and waded through the sea of garbage inside, the coon would have run away and found himself a tree. And besides, the lantern hadn't been fired up in ages, and what kerosene was left inside might well have turned to TNT by now. No sense blowing himself up for a coon dinner.

He went back up the steps, thinking of Arnold Ziffel and how stupid a Hollywood writer would have to be to believe a pig could win a cereal box contest.

Clunk!

Norman froze. Rain trickled down the back of his neck. He turned, stepped down into the mud of his front yard, and shambled off toward the shed, thinking now of robbers and the way they would steal you blind if you let them. One summer back in 1932 he and Josephine, still young and her not so fat, had decided to take a weekend off and hit the bars and motels in Indianapolis. All weekend long he had worried that somebody would come along and drive off with his tractor, maybe tow his combine or thresher away, and he would come back to his farm to find it bare. That had not happened, but something was amiss, something he couldn't quite put his finger on. Everything in the house was in its place, and the combine and thresher still stood where they ought to. But in the shed, which back then had not been a garbage dump, straw on the floor had been, well, rearranged. There were tire tracks mashed into the grass leading to the shed, for the lawn back then had been a lawn and not a mud field. Obviously someone had driven up and played with the straw. Norman had counted his tools, and they were all there. He'd inspected the padlock, and it didn't appear to have been horsed with. The only thing that really seemed odd was the shovel he kept in the shed. There was fresh dirt caked on it, and it was a brand new shovel.

"Forget it," Josephine, who would drop dead while making pancakes forty-nine years later, had said. "Nothing's missing, so forget it."

Norman did, eventually, forget it. But for years it tugged at his mind that someone had broken into his shed, dirtied his new shovel, and kicked the straw around. It never occurred to him that perhaps someone had buried something there.

He came to the shed's sagging double doors, and wiggled the padlock. It was a chunk of rust but it did the trick, and it was still in one piece. Oddly, though, it was warm, as if someone else had just been holding it. He stepped back, frowning, scratching at the wisps of gray hair his head still held claim to. His old man's bones were getting achy and he was tired of getting wet.

"Anybody out here?" he said in a voice that was not particularly loud.

Nobody answered.

"Fucking coons," he muttered, and turned away.

Clank!

He turned again. "All right," he said. "Whatever the fuck you are, you're getting off my property *now*."

He raised Bertha the shotgun over his head and let her blow. The night was lit for a fraction of a second by the orange fireball jetting out the barrel. Number 7 steel shot sailed moonward into the clouds.

Something stumbled from around the corner of the shed, some small bent thing, and headed off across the newly planted wheat field. Mud squished under its feet as it ran. Norman eyeballed it fiercely, wondering what it was, and why its head was so big and white. It had one big white arm too, which was bent like a chicken wing.

Norman's mind jumped back to a year ago. It had been on ABC, or CBS. One of them. A show about UFOs. They had shown drawings of the aliens who supposedly visited the earth on a regular basis. They had small skinny bodies and large heads. They had powers you wouldn't believe. They zipped around the universe on business no one could fathom, and for fun they kidnapped cows and sawed out their assholes. Once in a while they got hold of a human.

Norman's jaw dropped open. His bowlegs began to tremble. His mind whirled. Norman Parker was about to become famous for killing the world's first bona fide Martian. His face would be in all the papers. His story would make a book, a TV movie. Eddie Albert would play the lead role.

He levered Bertha downward, snugged her against his shoulder, and trailed the thing as it ran. He pulled the trigger, but Bertha, not your everyday modern shotgun, had two triggers, one in front, another behind. He tugged on the front one for a while as the Martian began to be swallowed up by the night. Then he cursed himself and got his shaking finger on the proper trigger. Now the Martian's large white head was the only thing visible, bobbing up and down. Norman trusted God and Bertha to direct his aim.

Norman fired.

"Yipe!" the alien said, and went face-down into the mud, ruining expensive wheat shoots.

"Gotcha!" Norman howled. Bertha had just about kicked him over backward, and his shoulder felt as if a mule had been at it, but he waved the shotgun over his head and performed victory jumping jacks anyway. When that grew tiresome, which didn't take long, Norman hurried over to the fallen Martian in order to make sure that it was dead.

It lay in the mud, chicken-wing arm splayed out, squirming and twisting. Norman's heart gave a painful thump in his chest. The alien was not dead, and aliens had powers no human could understand. He glanced fearfully up into the sky, where the alien's UFO would doubtless appear soon, bearing all sorts of death rays, but saw only thin low clouds and the white hole of the moon peeking down.

He swiveled Bertha around, taking hold of her by her twin barrels. Rain dripped off his nose. He raised her high over his head, ready to smash the Martian's oversized skull. His feet skated in the mud and he nearly fell over. A sudden jolt of pain rocketed up his left arm, seeming to blow his fingertips off, but he held on to Bertha. No alien powers were going to stop him on this mission.

The alien turned itself over. Norman saw with horror that it had a black face. Its alien eyes cracked open to slits, wetly reflecting light. Again Norman felt that jolt of power in his left arm, electricity in his bones. He took a breath against the pain and swung Bertha down with all his strength.

The alien rolled again. Bertha's wooden stock buried itself a foot deep into the mud beside its head. Norman jerked Bertha free and raised her again, wide-eyed and panting. Now there was pain in his chest, a crushing vise. The Martian rolled over and over, making sloppy sucking noises in the mud. Norman followed, swinging Bertha, chewing holes in his wheat field, always an inch or two away from that hideous head and its awesome ability to create pain.

On the tenth try he got a bit of Martian skull. The Martian cried out. Norman raised Bertha to administer the *coup de grace*, and saw with horrified disgust that the Martian's head was stuck to Bertha's butt. It hung there like a dirty deflated volleyball.

"Don't kill me!" the Martian screamed, holding its chicken-wing arm across its face.

"You speak American," Norman gasped. He jiggled Bertha to make the white thing fall away. It plopped into the mud and lay there, powerless.

"I didn't mean any harm," the alien said.

Norman snorted. "Where's your spaceship?"

"Huh?"

"Your UFO, dammit! Where'd you park it?"

Arnold White, not your ordinary Martian, got to his feet. He was a mud monster. "You shot me," he bleated. "My leg."

Norman edged closer, still keeping Bertha at the ready. He saw with a mixture of dismay and relief that it was only a kid. A kid with a cast on his arm. "What the fuck were you doing around my shed?" he demanded.

"The rain," Arnold said. He wiped mud off his face, without much effect. "I wanted to get out of the rain."

"What the hell were you doing out in the rain, anyway? It's the middle of the night."

"I'm . . . lost. Really lost."

Norman nodded. "Fine thing, kid. You scare me half to fuck cause you're lost. Half to fuck, and I mean it. You say you're lost? Goody. Keep on being lost. Just do it on somebody else's property!"

"But . . ."

"Scram!"

Norman turned away, enraged and disgusted. He propped Bertha on his shoulder, Bertha who would need an hour's worth of cleaning after this fiasco, and lifted a foot out of the muck to head back to his house.

A cold sledgehammer of pain swung out of nowhere and buried itself in his chest. He dropped Bertha with a wheeze and clutched his heart. His left arm had turned to fire. It was suddenly impossible to breathe.

"Oof," he gurgled. "Oh, oof."

"Mister?"

Norman's eyes bulged in their sockets. Eddie Albert had just fallen off the pole and landed on Norman Parker's chest, only it wasn't funny this time. Bright points of light began a shimmery dance in front of his eyes. He saw a ghost vision of Eva Gabor, and she was saying, "Olivah! Olivah! Who was that on the phone?"

"Kid," he managed to gasp. "Get me to my house."

The kid slogged over to him, limping. Norman pulled a hand away from his chest and put it on the kid's shoulder, thinking of Josephine and the sudden way she had died, and how he hadn't cared because she had been fat. "You carry all that pork around," he had said to her corpse as he helped himself to the pancakes that hadn't even begun to burn, "and you know it's

gonna catch up to you someday.'' He had only been glad she
hadn't made a hole in the floor when she fell.

They made it to the front of the shed before Norman's knees
unhinged and he dropped down like a man about to offer sup-
plication. He felt the kid try to lift him with an arm around his
waist. Distantly, the kid was saying something, but it might as
well have been Martian because Norman was in no position to
comprehend anything now but the thundering anvil in his chest
and the inability to draw a decent breath. His lips had gone
numb. Eva Gabor whispered Hungarian nothings in his ears.

His feet found themselves with no help from Norman Parker. He lurched toward his front steps, Zombie Parker now, a
blue-faced horror. He fell twice going up the steps, cracking
his shins. When his feet decided they were already in the grave,
Norman dropped down and crawled to his front door on his
hands and knees. The kid swung the screen open, and Norman
crawled onto the familiarity of his own living room carpet, an
ancient and battle-scarred purple mat purchased before the Ed-
sel was born, when the market price of wheat and corn could
make you a decent living. He bumped head-first into his easy
chair, then began a slow and laborious crawl up into it. His
heart had decided to try for two hundred beats per minute,
then two-fifty. It was an impossible rate, but a fine attempt at
record-breaking fibrillation. By the time Norman Parker had
turned himself around and was facing the television, which was
the way he had decided long ago he wanted to die, ''Green
Acres'' was almost over.

But not quite. In the olden days of sitcoms, every show had
to have a teaser and a tag. The teaser came before the first
commercial, just enough air time to sucker you into watching
the rest of the show. The tag came at the end, just before the
credits. It served to wrap things up and leave you in the mood
to stay with the same station. All very planned, crass, and
commercial. But all very normal.

And by God, Norman thought as his life ebbed from his
veins and parts of his brain began shutting down, if Eddie
Albert is gonna fall off that pole, he'd better do it quick.

Just north of Hooterville, the phone began to ring. Oliver
Douglas was in his pajamas. He climbed out the window and
started up the pole. Norman saw it through a deepening fog,
swirling mists of red and blue. He saw Oliver Douglas answer

the phone. It was the wrong number. Norman Parker grinned in anticipation, already dead from the neck down.

Oliver Douglas hung up. He started down the pole.

He made it to the ground and crawled back through the window.

He shut off the lights and went to bed.

The credits rolled.

"Cocksuckers," Norman Parker snarled, and died as unhappily as he had lived.

Arnold White stood just by the front door and stared at the second corpse he had been privileged to spend time with in the last two days. This corpse was blue. Its eyes were open. It had mud up to its knees and all over its hands. Its tongue had popped out. It seemed to be giving the television a raspberry.

He let his gaze wander away and looked down at himself. Black and shiny mud, top to bottom. His Polish sneakers were full of it. Somehow it had slithered its way under his clothes during all that crazy field-flopping. He felt ten pounds too heavy. The back of his right leg, just below the knee, ached like a knotted fist. He looked back and saw three separate rivulets of blood coursing their way out of the mud, brilliantly red against some of Indiana's finest sod. Old Parker's buckshot had caught him, but not much of it. Once again, he would survive.

He limped across the room, pausing to turn off the television, which was playing the hokey "Green Acres" theme. In the sudden and total silence he paused again, looking around, wondering if perhaps Mrs. Parker was in bed, maybe old and too deaf to hear what had been going on. If so, she would be in for a hell of a surprise in the morning. Dear Normie was feeling rather blue tonight.

He giggled in spite of himself. The Ten High was still doing a bit of its magic, turning everything funny and unreal. He wandered through the house, turning on lights, looking for Mrs. Parker. The floor of the old house creaked under his feet wherever he stepped, especially in the kitchen, where his muddy shoes left a network of tracks as he meandered around the table and saw the remnants of many meals stacked high on TV dinner tins. Flies were having a noisy feast there. The sink was full of dishes and cups, and wherever there was space empty beer cans were heaped.

He went to the refrigerator, thinking idly of food that was not weeks old, and was pleasantly surprised to find the entire Frigidaire stacked full of Steinbrau beer. He took one out and opened it. Brewed only with nature's finest ingredients, the can proclaimed, and he took it at its word. He tried a sip, grimaced, and continued his inspection of the house.

It was a rat's nest. That was okay. So was the rest of Wabash Heights, and people survived. This would make the perfect hideout. So long as Norman Parker was not missed, this would be a haven. No one would ever suspect that Arnold White was shacked up with a dead man. Why, he could stay here for weeks and weeks if he had to, maybe even take squatter's rights and live here forever. He could, in fact, smuggle Mom and Melissa and Angie out here, maybe tonight, and get them away from Frank sooner than expected. What an uproar that would cause. Frank would turn the town upside down in his rage at having lost his captives. And while Frank raged and fumed, the four of them could lead safe and simple lives in the comfort and safety of Norman Parker's farm, where Norman Parker sat eternally staring at the television with his dead eyes bulging and his tongue sticking out.

Only . . .

Dead men did strange things. Like rot. Especially in balmy springtime, where the room temperature probably hit seventy-five on a good day, especially in a beat-up shack like this. In three or four days, why, old Normie there would have maggots squirming in his hair, worms crawling out his eyeballs, and probably be swollen up like a dead cow left under the sun. That just might make this place unlivable. The flies were already bad enough.

Arnold drank and deliberated. There was a battered yellow sofa against the east wall, and he sat on it, where unfortunately he had a good sideward view of Norman Parker in all his blueness. He had died with his bony hands clutching the arms of his easy chair. The tendons there still stood out like wires under his mottled blue skin, as if he were outraged at something. Arnold decided Norman Parker had not been a nice man. Some kind of inner turmoil, it looked like. Perhaps he had led a hard life. Or perhaps he was just like everybody else in Wabash Heights, all full of meanness and cruelty.

Still, none of that mattered now. What mattered was the treasure, and how to get it. The shed was locked. The key had to be here someplace. Most likely it was hanging on a peg somewhere, or hidden in a jar, or just plain on a key chain in Norman Parker's pocket.

Which meant, natch, that somebody had to go over there and check his pockets.

Arnold took another drink of beer, staring at Norman. Norman stared at the TV. Arnold guessed he would stare at that TV for the next ten thousand years. It was beginning to get irritating.

"Hey," Arnold said, feigning casualness. "Hey, Normie."

Normie was in no mood to reply.

"Whatcha staring at so hard, Normie? TV giving you trouble? Or do your eyeballs get bad reception?"

He giggled again. The Steinbrau was doing its job. It tasted like rotten potato peels, but it was doing its job. Arnold drained the can and went in to help himself to another. The floor creaked under him. Flies buzzed. Arnold was amazed that he was not fleeing in terror from this house of the dead, but too much had happened lately. It was not the dead he had to fear, but the living.

He drank the beer standing in the kitchen, not wanting to look at any more blue corpses until the alcohol had made him immune to fear. When the beer was gone he took a few deep breaths, did some mental deep knee bends, and went back into the living room. He stalked straight over to Norman Parker, leaned over him, and wormed a hand into one of his pockets.

He came out with loose change and lint. He dropped it to the floor. Along with it went most of his nerve.

"Beer," he said into Norman Parker's face, and hustled into the kitchen. He popped a Steinbrau. He drank it down so fast it made his throat hurt.

"Keys," he said to the kitchen table, and threw the can away. It hit a pile of cans on the old wooden counter by the sink, sending them jangling to the floor. The noise seemed monstrous, loud enough to wake the dead.

"Okay," Arnold said, shaken. "Beer, then."

He opened another. The kitchen was getting fuzzy to look at. No matter. Old Normie was blue to look at, a hideous, sick, and raunchy kind of blue, not a happy Smurfy blue, not a blue-sky blue. Just dead blue.

He finished the beer. Now his stomach was swollen and hurting. He slumped against the refrigerator, looking for his courage but not finding it. He was tired, for one thing. The beer was putting him to sleep. His leg hurt and was getting blood all over the floor. His coating of body mud was drying fast and flaking off in chunks that would hit the tiles with unexpected rattly thumps. This house was creaky and spooky and inhabited by a dead man. There was a full moon out and it was the middle of the night.

"Oh, Isis," Arnold muttered. "Isis ki Osirus."

For some reason, that seemed to help. They were the magic words, the ones Atkinson had guarded for so long, for reasons Arnold might never know. They denoted treasure and riches and happiness yet to come. He pushed away from the refrigerator with fresh resolve and went back to deal with old Normie and his case of the blues.

Norman still maintained his fierce dying stare. Arnold went over to him, held his breath, bent over, and stuck his hand in the other pocket of Norman's baggy old pants. His fingers found keys.

"Isis ki Osirus," he said happily, and pulled them out.

Norman Parker breathed in his face.

Arnold pulled back. "Mama," he said simply as Norman Parker pushed himself out of his chair and wobbled to his feet. He stood staring at the television with a malignant and stupid hatred. Arnold stumbled backward, his own eyes bulging, his jaw hanging open as far as its hinges would allow.

Norman Parker stood there with his gnarly blue hands dangling, swaying on his feet like a drunk. Every ten seconds or so his chest heaved as he took a rattling breath.

"Yuh," Arnold said. "Yuh . . . yuh . . . yuh . . ."

Norman Parker's head swiveled slowly around. Arnold could hear his dead bones creak. Now he was staring at something on the wall behind Arnold. His dead eyes burned with a ghastly species of unworldly hate.

Arnold turned and bolted into the kitchen. It was all true, then, all the horror movies and horror books. There were werewolves and vampires and living corpses who feasted on hot human flesh. Norman Parker had been deader than your average doornail for the last twenty minutes. Not a breath had he breathed. Not an eye had he blinked. Now he had stood up and was staggering toward the kitchen with a dead flat gaze that made Frankenstein's monster look like an eager contestant panting to solve those mind-bogglers on the "Jeopardy" game show.

Arnold looked wildly around for a place to hide. He saw a dark space between the refrigerator and the wall, maybe eight inches wide. There was a heap of yellowed newspapers on the floor, but that was no problem. Arnold jammed himself into the space, crunching newspapers under his feet. His cast clunked against the bulky Frigidaire. He scrunched down and waited for Norman Parker's cold dead teeth to clamp down on his exposed arm and rip out a bite. He waited for a cold claw-hand to jerk him out of his hiding space and tear his arms from their sockets. He waited for Freddy and Jason and Michael and Norman Bates and Dracula and Lon Chaney and Boris Karloff and Vincent Price and Christopher Lee and Godzilla and the Blob and even Mothra, for good measure. He waited for thirty seconds with his eyes squeezed shut in fear and agony, and after those thirty seconds he opened them up and looked over to the doorway, where Norman Parker was supposed to come lurching through.

But he hadn't. And he didn't.

There was heat coming out from behind the refrigerator. It was making Arnold sweat his mud off. He pushed out of the space and darted to the sink, which was surrounded by drawers. He opened the top one on the right. Silverware in an orange plastic silverware holder. He opened the top one on the left, jangling things. Large spoons and ladles. He opened the second one down on the right, and found knives.

He pulled one out, panting, his throat dry as ash. It was a paring knife. He dropped it and tried again. This time he came out with a long skinny knife, a fillet knife for skinning those crafty bluegill the fishermen of Indiana were so proud to catch by the bucketful, the kind stepfather Frank sometimes went after with his Zebco 202, a cup of nightcrawlers, and a case of beer.

Arnold turned. There was a crazy, desperate gleam in his swollen eyes. Let the dead fucker come, go on, let him. George Romero was not directing this show. Stephen King had not written this script. The zombie in this production could be killed with a fillet knife through the heart, because monsters always had a weak point, and if the corpse of Norman Parker had a weak point, it had to be his diseased old heart.

Arnold waited, knife in fist, a kid four feet eleven inches

tall who looked, at this point, like a midget mud wrestler. He waited in the dead silence while light rain fell outside and, every ten seconds or so, Norman Parker took in a noisy lungful of air. Norman Parker was still in the living room, by the sound of it. Norman Parker might be the living dead, but he didn't seem inclined to walk much.

Arnold's tongue flicked out and licked his lips. He swallowed, thought about things, and spoke up: "I can kill you, you know."

Norman didn't disagree.

"You're supposed to be dead, you know."

Norman pondered this mystery in silence.

"Then drop dead, goddammit!"

The house rattled as if a cannonball had dropped through the roof. It felt like the famous Madrid fault 1987 earthquake, which had measured an even five on the Richter scale and given Arnold the biggest thrill of his life. Dad had been around then, and Dad had said, "It's a miracle this old shack didn't fall in on us."

"What was that?" Arnold demanded.

No reply.

A footstep? Mighty heavy footstep. Old Normie must have put on Herman Munster's shoes.

"You still in there?"

Normie wasn't saying.

"Then I'm coming for you," Arnold said, not quite believing it. The knife's wooden handle had become hot and squelchy in his fist, the mud between his fingers warm grit. He looked at the blade, long and shiny, and imagined it slipping neatly between Norman's ribs and into his heart. Those were the rules for this movie, then: the monster dies when you stab him through the heart.

Arnold believed it with most of his being. The rest told him quite placidly that he was about to be attacked and eaten by a corpse. And the worst thing was, the corpses always seemed to want to eat your face first. A day, a week from now, the cops would come out to see why Norman Parker hadn't been to town, and they would find only a cast with a broken arm in it. There would be teeth marks on it. Norman, by then swollen and dripping with rot, would lunge out and try to dine on the cops. One cop, screaming in agony, would be eaten while the other, bug-eyed and drooling, fired his revolver in a horrified frenzy. Then Norman, lurching along with one eye hanging out and maggots doing a tango in his hair, would eat the other cop. The scene would be repeated until a crusading reporter, a regular Kolchak the Night Stalker character, stumbled upon the secret of the Parker House of Horrors, and burned the place to the ground.

End of movie.

Arnold rolled his eyes. This scene had played out in a millisecond inside his head. He assumed that someday he would either be a writer of horror novels, or totally insane. There was probably not much difference.

"Coming for you," he said, raising the knife.

He took a step toward the doorway. Then another. He passed the refrigerator, pondered the necessity of having another beer before dying, and decided to forgo it. Heroes do not get their courage out of a bottle, even though Arnold had to admit that what little he had had a Steinbrau label on it.

He came to the doorway. He peeked through.

Norman Parker lay in a boneless heap on the floor in front of the TV.

"Well, I'll be," Arnold murmured. "I'll be shit on."

He tiptoed over to the body. He gazed down at the back of Norman Parker's head, where maggots neither squirmed nor tangoed. He tapped Norman with his foot.

"Mr. Parker?"

Nothing. Still blue, still dead.

Arnold shook his head. "If this doesn't beat Isis ki Osirus, I don't know what does."

Norman Parker craned his head slowly upward and fastened his bulging, hateful eyes on Arnold's face.

· 8 ·

A Brief Flashback to Shitty City

AT ABOUT THE time Arnold White was rocking and rolling in a muddy wheat field with Norman Parker wildly swinging an empty double-barrel shotgun at him, Jack Cumberland was parking his father's aged Dodge Dart in front of the trailer and waiting for the trusty slant-six to stop banging and dieseling. When the engine finally died with a defeated gasp, Jack picked up off the seat his paper bag with its load of Ten High and swung the car's door open: The hinges screeched in the dark. He slammed the door shut and made his way, stooped and hunched against the rain, up to the trailer's front steps. As a courtesy he scraped the mud off his shoes on the cement blocks, meanwhile opening the Ten High and taking a long and well-deserved swig. The paper bag crackled in his hand. He re-capped the bottle, smacking his lips, and opened the trailer door.

His father, Alfred, was snoozing on the moth-eaten couch, chin on chest as Arnold had left him. His snores filled the trailer. Jack looked around, his eyes widening. He hustled off to the kitchen. He looked under the table. He ran back through the narrow hallway to the bedrooms, snapped on the lights, and looked under beds. There was a strong stench of unwashed diapers stuck in the rugs, compliments of the last tenants, but Jack ignored it. His heart was beginning to pound loudly in his ears. His dumbfuck father had gone and let the kid escape.

"Pop!" he screamed, going back into the living room.

Pop snoozed on.

Jack grabbed him by the shoulders. "Pop! You fucking dildo! The kid's gone!"

Alfred raised his head. His eyes slid open, waxy and unfocused. He batted at Jack's arms. "Whoozat?"

"It's Jack, goddammit! Where's the fucking kid?"

"Kid?" Light came into his bleary eyes. "Why, he's on the floor just where I—"

They both looked down at the spot where Arnold was supposed to be.

Jack straightened. "Oh, ain't this fucking grand? I leave for twenty minutes and you pass out. The kid waltzes out of here like nothing happened. Forty million bucks waltzes out with him, and our last chance at the treasure." He went to the kitchen table and slammed the bottle down, his face glowing an unhealthy shade of purple under the bare bulb. Veins bulged in his neck. The phony hairs of his wig stuck out in wet spikes. He stared fiercely at his father, who was trying to get up off the couch and having a tough time of it.

"Check the back rooms," the old man wheezed. "Look under the beds."

"I already did, fucknuts! You let him go!"

"Then chase him! Follow his tracks!"

"In the fucking dark? Do I look like a bloodhound?"

Alfred made it to his feet and bared his lonesome tooth at his son. "Your fault too, big boy! You had to go marching off to get another bottle! You're such a fucking alcoholic you couldn't wait fifteen minutes without a drink! Did you bring any chicken?"

"What?"

"Some Kentucky Fried! I haven't eaten all day!"

Jack swung his arms in outraged circles. "Chicken! All you can think about is chicken! Fuck you, and fuck the chicken you rode in on!"

Alfred's face darkened. "I detect a marked lack of respect for your elders suddenly."

"Yeah? Well, detect this, Sherlock!" He flipped him the bird. "You've fucked up for the last time, old man. We almost caught Atkinson in Kansas, but you had an emphysema attack and had to go to the hospital. Atkinson got away. We almost had him in Montana, but your old car had to drop a valve and needed three days worth of fixing. Atkinson got away. We almost had him in Maine, but you threw a cigarette out the window and burned Jerusalem's Lot to the ground."

Alfred waved a hand. "Not my fault! Natural disaster! Besides, the people there were buggy. The place had me spooked. Some kid tried to bite my neck.''

''No matter. At least twenty times we had Atkinson close enough to smell, and each time you fucked it up.''

''Me, huh?'' Alfred glowered at him, his eyes bright and flickering with elemental hate. ''What about last time? Atkinson was out back on the ground with two broke legs and you decided to come in for a smoke. He crawled away. He fucking crawled away!''

''Your fault too,'' Jack roared. ''You had to pee!''

''My goddamn prostate's bigger'n a football! You know it takes me an hour to drain the old pecker!''

''If we had forty million dollars you could have the fucker bored out!''

Alfred advanced on him, shaking with rage. ''Nobody's shoving a Roto Rooter up my dick! You can suck it for all I care!''

''Sicko!'' Jack screamed. ''Pervert!''

Alfred looked around for his cane. Not seeing it, he reached out with both twisted hands and made for his son's neck. Jack punched him neatly in the face. He staggered back. Blood ran out his nose in twin streams.

He looked wonderingly at Jack. ''You hit me.''

Jack sneered. ''First time for everything, huh, Pops?''

''I'll cane you to hell for that!''

''With what, farthead? *The kid stole your precious fucking cane!''*

Alfred lunged at him. Being drunk, his aim was slightly off. He landed on the table, whose skinny legs promptly snapped. He went down in a noisy heap of wood and Formica. Jack took the opportunity to jump up and down on his back, driving his breath out in a series of startled whoops. The bottle of Ten High rolled away in its bag.

''I'll . . . kill . . . you . . .'' Jack panted, doing a pretty fair rendition of the Bristol stomp on his loving father's backside. ''You . . . stupid . . . fart . . .''

Alfred rolled over, drooling and choking. He got hold of Jack's right ankle and flipped him over backward. Jack, none too sober, thumped his head hard on the floor, rattling the trailer, while his wig sailed through the air to splat against the living room wall. It stuck to the paneling like a large misshapen tarantula. Eventually it fell off . . .

But by then Alfred had hurled himself on his son and found his hot, rain-slick throat with his old man's clawlike fingers. He pushed his thumbs hard into Jack's windpipe, enjoying the instant color change in his son's face. Jack bucked and twisted, gurgling. His shoes hammered the floor and the remnants of the table.

He reached up and took hold of Alfred's throat. He squeezed down hard, glad to hear things pop and crunch. Alfred's watery eyes bulged. His face went an ugly red. They both strangled each other for the better part of twenty seconds. Then Alfred's grip lost some of its firmness.

"Gotcha," Jack croaked, and flipped the old man away. Alfred landed on his hands and knees, retching. He saw the bottle of Ten High lying innocently in its bag on the floor, and took it by the neck. He went up on his knees, seeing Jack rise. He swung the bottle.

It caught Jack at the base of his skull with a loud, bony thump. Miraculously, it did not break. Jack cried out and rolled away, clutching his head. Alfred crawled after him, cackling madly, no stranger to seeing his son writhe in agony under the cat-o'-nine-tails of Cumberland discipline. He brought the bottle up again and smashed it across Jack's forehead.

This time it broke. Whiskey and glass shards blew out of the bag in an amber spray. The air came alive with the stench of fresh booze. Jack shot up to a sitting position with whiskey draining into his clothes and fresh red blood welling out of a gash on his forehead. He was blinking furiously.

"I ought to light your ass on fire," Alfred crowed.

Jack swung out blindly and hit him with his fist. Nose again, pure luck. Alfred saw stars, planets, and three of Jupiter's newly discovered moons. He found he was eating rug. It tasted dusty. He tried to push himself up but the exertion was too much.

"*Fucker!!!*" Jack screamed, and wrenched the remains of the bottle out of Alfred's hand. Protruding from the soggy end of the bag were two long spears of glass. He swung it up, paused only long enough to savor the hatred he was feeling and had felt for most of his life, and plunged it down. Whiskey droplets spun through the air. The glass spears buried themselves easily in old Cumberland's back. He arched up in a fishlike spasm and brayed curses.

Jack jerked the bottle free. He brought it up again, remembering childhood canings, the way his father simply would not stop even when the blood was flowing from Jack's naked ass and his throat was ragged from screaming. There had been times when his mother had dragged Alfred away from the boy, weeping hysterically. There had been times when she simply locked herself in the bathroom and threw up into the toilet.

Jack drove the shattered bottle down. It cleaved wetly into his father's back. This time a spear snapped off with a clean pinging sound, and it remained in the center of old Alfred's spine, protruding like a blood-streaked vertebra that had decided, tired of being arthritic, to pop out. Alfred's legs dropped nervelessly to the floor. Blood sprayed out his mouth. His curses became sloppy moans.

"Kill . . . you . . . ," Jack grunted, swinging the bottle and its lone remaining spear up and down. Blood welled up under Alfred's shirt and spilled down onto the rug in scarlet rivers. Alfred's breathing, never the best in the world, became labored and wheezy. His head twisted back and forth.

"Fucker," Jack whispered, and jammed the bottle spear into the back of his father's twisting neck.

Alfred relaxed. The spear had driven through his neck and punctured the sagging elephant skin of his throat, and a bit of carpet. Blood pumped out, wonderfully red, creating a pond.

Jack leaned back on his haunches, breathing hard, his head hammering. Lights shot across his vision. He remained that way, occasionally backing away from the pond of blood when it neared his knees, pondering what he had done and what repercussions it might hold for the future. The stars cleared up when his breathing had returned to normal. He felt the back of his head, and there was a fine lump there.

"The kid," he whispered, his eyes growing narrow. "That fucking kid."

He stood up and leaned over his father. The bag, wrinkled and wet, still covered the neck of the bottle. He peeled it away and observed the peculiar sight of an old man with the top half of a whiskey bottle jammed into the back of his neck, as if someone had attempted to nail him to the floor with it.

He went to the sink, got his lighter out of his pocket, and burned the bag. The whiskey helped; it was aflame in seconds. He flushed the ashes down the drain, washed his hands, and dried them on his pants.

"There are certain things," he said aloud, "that the cops must know. There are simply certain things."

He went back into the living room, steering wide of Alfred and the pond of blood he floated in, and went to the wall. He bent down and fetched up his wig. It was still wet from the rain and the sweat. He rubbed it on his pants.

"Certain things," he said quite calmly. "Certain things the cops must know."

He went to the door and pulled it open. He adjusted his wig on his head. For just a second he giggled, but only a second. His face quickly became a caricature of shock and grief.

"No kid kills my father and gets away with it," he said.

He fired up the old Dart and drove off to find the Wabash Heights police station and report this heinous crime.

Police sergeant Roy Mallone, known to his fellows on the police force as Roly-Poly Roy, was enduring another unendurable night shift at the Wabash Heights Police headquarters when the stranger in the cheap toupee staggered in and demanded vengeance for his father's murder. Roly-Poly Roy, no stranger to weird people or weird calls in the middle of the night, sat up straighter in his squeaking old roller chair, picked up a pen off the desk, and rolled it between his fingers. As the stranger ranted on and it seemed this might be no ordinary drunk with a tavern tale to tell, Roy rolled back away from his desk, opened a drawer, and withdrew a blank police report form. He sighed, rolled his eyes, and poised the pen over the paper and its many carbon forms.

"Name of complaintant?" he inquired.

"Me!" Jack Cumberland screamed at him. There was a shallow cut across his forehead that had drizzled blood in crazy zigzags down his face. He was soaking wet, and not just from the rain. If Roly-Poly Roy was any judge of character, this guy was drunk off his ass and probably in the clutches of a nasty case of delirium tremens. In his eighteen years with the force Roy had seen it all: the drunks who came bumbling in to report Martians landing in droves out in somebody's cornfield, the drunks who were dragged in screaming by some terrified friends who had also seen a large shape in the dark but couldn't be quite sure if the elephant was pink or not. There were times when a fight broke out down at the Wabash Tavern, and Roy, who weighed in at a good three-twenty and stood six feet four, would sigh, roll his eyes, and head on out to crack some heads. To be honest, eighteen years of doing this over and over had driven Roly-Poly Roy over the edge. He now kept a bottle of Ten High in the file cabinet behind the arrest forms, and during the nights he made frequent excursions to check the files. Now, at quarter till two in the a.m., he was himself, like the rest of the rat heap in his fair city, more than a little sloshed.

"Who is me?" Roy demanded.

"What?"

"You keep screaming me. Who the hell is me?"

Jack frowned. "My name?" He paused in his raving to consider it. Exactly who was he tonight, anyway? Should he be Jack Cumberland, or should he be somebody else, just for safety's sake? He looked around, thinking as fast as his spinning brain would allow. This police station was a dump. It was a cinderblock building the size, roughly, of your average outhouse. There was a one-man jail cell at the far end. Jack most certainly did not want to be incarcerated for perjury.

"Jack Cumberland," he said.

Roy dutifully wrote it down. "Nature of your complaint?"

"My father's been murdered."

"Location of incident?"

"Our trailer house. West of town."

Roy looked up at him with blandly professional eyes. "Shitty City, you mean?"

Jack shrugged. Wasn't this whole town Shitty City? "I dunno. We just moved there."

"Time the incident occurred?"

"Ten minutes ago. Maybe fifteen. This kid, see. He broke in and attacked us. He had a broken bottle, and he cut me, then stabbed my father. Four or five times, at least. In the back. God, there's blood everywhere." He feigned revulsion and shock. "It was horrible. Brutal. The crime of the century, by my reckoning."

"Sounds like it." Roy put his pen down. "Excuse me a minute, will ya? I have to file this."

"Now? What about my father?"

"You said he's dead, didn't you?"

"I did."

"Well, corpses don't walk. I'll be with you in a minute."

He disengaged his bulk from the chair, turned, and made his way to the file cabinet. He jerked a drawer open, bent over it, and fetched out his bottle of Ten High. A twinge of excitement was building in his guts, but it was muted. Somebody got killed in this town once or twice a year. The murderers generally hightailed it out of state, which was fine by Roy. It made police work a lot easier. He took six giant swallows, belched into his hand, and shoved the report into the jumble of papers inside. Then he discreetly put the bottle back. He shut the drawer, got his hat, and made his way around the desk.

"Well, let's go have a look-see."

They went outside into the rain. Jack's Dart was parked beside Wabash Heights' lone police cruiser, the motor ticking as it cooled. Roy walked toward the Dodge, skirting the blue-and-white cruiser. He opened the passenger door and plopped himself inside, making springs squeak.

"Hey," Jack said. "What about the cop car? Don't we need flashing lights or something?"

Roy's reply was muffled. "Flat tires. Punk kids do it every night."

"You didn't even look!"

"Don't need to. Old man Bateman from Bateman's comes by every morning with a fresh set."

"Huh?" Jack squatted down. All four of the cruiser's tires were flat. An ice pick was still sticking out of the side of one. He squeezed his eyes shut, shaking his head. What a town.

"Besides," Roy said as Jack got inside and started the Dodge, "you know which trailer it is. To me, they all look the same. Oughtta burn 'em, somebody should. Too many rats. And the people who live out there—niggers and white trash. If they had any sense they'd move into Wabash Heights and be respectable. It's a fine town we got here, and Shitty City's a blight on anybody's map. That Jew Murray Landsberg out of Indianapolis owns the property. Just like a kike to make the poor goys live in trailers, huh? Old Murray, he's got himself a palace somewhere. Leave it to the Jews. Me, I'll take Wabash Heights any day. Not a Jew in sight, just good hard-working people. Fine people."

"Let me guess," Jack said sourly as he backed out of the parking space and headed for home. "You were born and raised here, weren't you?"

Roy smiled. He burped, filling the car with explosive Ten High aromas. "Damn right I was," he said. "Goddamn right."

And then, to Jack's eternal dissatisfaction, he began to sing

"On the Banks of the Wabash" in a key that had not, up to then, even been discovered.

He was pouring out a cracked version of "Indiana Wants Me" when Jack pulled the Dodge, with great relief, up beside the trailer where his father lay dead. He killed the engine and waited for the car to stop bucking and heaving. Roy fumbled around with the door panel for a while before finding the handle, then levered his door open onto the night. He got out with a grunt, his wide cop's belt and holster creaking. For a moment he stood staring at the lighted windows of the trailer, thoughtfully digging his pants out of the crack of his ample ass with both hands. He sniffed his fingers, sighed, and made his way to the steps.

Jack followed with his heart thumping threadily in his chest. This was the moment of truth. It came to him like a sudden burst of cognizance that the old man was not dead at all, merely wounded, and the whole sorry jig would be up. Either that or he had managed to scrawl a dying message in his own blood before breathing his last. One way or another, old Alfred would find a way to screw things up. He always had.

Roy eased the door open. Jack peeked under his extended arm. Puddle of blood, old man in it. Bottle sticking out of the back of his neck. Nothing had changed. The old gray geezer had died, and he had not died down by the millpond.

"Foul play," Roly-Poly Roy said, nodding and frowning. "You say a kid did this?"

"Right. Knocked on the door saying he was selling magazine subscriptions. Pop let him in. He's a softie for kids working their way through school."

"I thought you said he broke in."

"Did I?"

Roy scratched his hat. "Hell if I know. Why's the table all wrecked?"

"The kid and I fought. He knocked me out with that bottle. When I came to, well, here I was. And there was Pop. Dead." He sniffed long and loud. "My poor daddy."

Roy patted his shoulder, nearly knocking him down. "Buck up there, kiddo. The old shit looks like he was on his last legs anyway." He blew an extended and noisy sigh. "Don't see no need for a coroner's inquest. Ambulance wouldn't do no good. Might get some prints off that bottle, though. I'll get in touch with the state boys as soon as we get back, get their forensic lab working on this. Did you get a good look at the kid?''

"Certainly did," Jack responded promptly. "He had on a white turban. One arm was in a cast. His teeth were all broken out. His eyes were black. He was wearing blue jeans. His name was Arnold White."

Roy gaped at him. "How the fuck did you find all that out?"

Jack took a moment to wonder about this too. "Well," he said after a pause, "I told the kid I didn't want no magazines, and he says, 'Nobody turns down Arnold White.' Then he jumped me."

"How old was he?"

Jack shrugged. "Maybe twelve."

Roy touched his forehead. "Hold on. Are you gonna tell me a twelve-year-old boy with his arm in a cast and his face all busted up managed to beat you unconscious and kill your father? That's crazy."

Jack grinned weakly while his heart blew taps inside his rib cage. "One for the books, huh? I'd say the kid was unhinged. Probably high on that PCP stuff, where you get superhuman strength. Ever heard of that?"

"Suppose I have. Most kids in Wabash Heights don't mess with the stuff, though. Too expensive. They stick to pot and booze, and God, does this place reek of booze. Must be that busted bottle. Was your old man a drinker?"

Jack snorted. "Certainly not. He had religion, may his soul rest in eternal salvation. Jehovah's Witness, that's what he was."

Roy nodded. "Yeah, we got one of them in town too. Old man Liddey. Somebody ought to crack his head, the dumbfuck." He stuck his thumbs under his belt and took one last look around. "We'll rope the place off in the morning, get the state boys down here."

"What about the kid? Are you going to put out an APB, or something? Somebody's got to find him before he kills again."

"We'll let the staters handle that. Right now, I've got files to work on. Run me back to town, eh? Your dad there's turning my stomach, no offense intended." He cocked his jaw toward the door. "Shall we?"

Jack ground his teeth in helpless frustration. "You mean to say that's it? Arnold White kills my dad, and you go back and work on your files? Can't you get a posse together, comb the fields, maybe get some dogs on the trail? By morning the kid could hitchhike his way to Albuquerque.''

"Perhaps he could," Roy said, hoping in fact that he would. "I'll radio the state police as soon as we get back, for all the good it'll do. Like as not the kid'll just go home and we'll have him. I know where he lives. I'll check in periodically.''

He went out and clumped down the steps. Jack followed, slamming the door behind himself. The fine mist of rain felt as if it was sizzling on the hot skin of his face as he walked to the car, enraged. This fat cop was an asshole. In any respectable town, this so-called Shitty City would already be crawling with cops, the FBI, SWAT teams, searchlights, bloodhounds, the works. As it was, the local law was more than slightly tanked, and anxious to get back to his bottle. Jack, no stranger to hiding bottles on the job, had seen the fat asshole take his drinks before they left. The asshole wasn't about to let a simple murder disturb his routine. And he didn't even have a usable police car, for Christ's sake. What kind of fucked-up town was this? And the state cops wouldn't do any good. They'd find no prints on the bottle, hand the body over to Jack for a burial he couldn't afford, and go on about their business.

They got in the Dart, and Jack dutifully fired it up, consoled in his misery by only one thing: at long last, the old man was dead. He had fucked things up for the last time. The fifty-fifty split of the treasure they had long ago agreed upon was null and void. That left Jack with the whole forty million to himself.

Unless he could find someone else to split it with. Someone who knew this town well enough to know where a broken-up little boy would hide from the rain and the pain.

Someone who knew the kid like his own son.

Someone like, maybe, his stepdaddy.

Jack grinned to himself as he left Shitty City's gravel drive and found US 40 East toward town.

Stepdaddy was a mean old cuss. Probably dumber than owl shit, too. But not too dumb to hand over his kid in exchange for, say, a million or so bucks in solid gold.

·9·

At the Shed

"YOU'RE DEAD!" ARNOLD screamed in Norman Parker's face.

Old Normie, never much one to oblige people in life, was quite obedient as a dead man. He promptly keeled over face-down onto his hideous purple rug. His bulging eyes stared intently into the threadbare fabric as if seeing fascinating Indiana fleas perform a floor show there.

Arnold fell back, flabbergasted, the hard-won key ring falling nervelessly from his hand to jangle on the floor, a harsh rattle in the deathly quiet. He ran his tongue over the spitless flesh of his lips, trying to swallow but not succeeding. He knew what was going on here, knew exactly what was going on. It was as clear as the image of Louis Creed standing atop the deadfall just beyond the Pet Sematary with his dead son in his arms, as clear as Jack Torrance smashing his own face in with a roque mallet in the hallway of the Overlook Hotel while performing his eerie, shuffling polka. It was as clear to the bookworm named Arnold White as anything he had ever envisioned while reading the King, even though he knew it was all fiction and none of it could ever really happen.

Yet Norman Parker was a zombie. An old and ugly zombie, but a zombie nevertheless. A blue zombie.

He wished suddenly that Stephen King would smash open the door with his fifteen-thousand-dollar Wang word processor, take a look around with mud caked on his shoes and that my-opic murderous look in his eyes and his millions sticking out of his pockets, and tell Arnold what to do next. This was a job for a pro. Arnold knew he had no business being in this story. He backed away from the body of Norman Parker and stumbled against the yellow sofa. He sat down with a whoof. *I am*

117

here, he thought with quick and stupid wonder. *I am here on a page and someone is reading me. Please God let them flip to the last page of this book and tell me if I will be sane when the story ends.*

Outside, the wind kicked up. It hooted around the gutters of Norman's crumbling farmhouse, making ghostly moans. Hard rain spatted against the windows. The refrigerator in the kitchen started up with a dreadful squeal that spoke of a desire for oil.

Then, for effect, all the lights went out. The refrigerator died with a rattle.

"Holy Isis . . ." Arnold said in that instant blackness.

He sat, wet and cold, a mudboy soiling a couch that was not in much better shape, and listened past the groan of the wind as Norman Parker got to his feet, slow and lurching, and shambled toward him. He imagined he heard that slow ten-second breathing. He seemed to see two points of light, glowing sickly yellow, the zombie eyes of Norman Parker piercing the new dark. They glimmered like twin mirrors reflecting the fires of hell. Arnold blinked, cringing, and when he looked again they were gone.

He waited, not breathing, listening, staring.

The house creaked and muttered. Shingles flapped on the roof.

The lights stuttered back to life and everything was as it had been.

"Damn books," he muttered internally. "Damn movies."

Norman Parker had not moved. Zombie or not, fiendish lover of the dark and the night, he had not moved. The wires that led from the pole out by the road to Norman's house were old and unreliable. In the wind they shorted out. It happened in Wabash Heights all the time, and it happened out here too. Sometimes it was a regular light show when it rained and the wind blew. Arnold estimated the lights had been out for thirty seconds, maybe thirty-five. In that time he had managed to imagine old Normie getting to his feet and tottering toward him, alive with the desire for hot blood to drink and warm flesh to eat. But of course he hadn't moved.

Arnold had started to get to his feet, working against the weight of his cast, when he saw something that made his heart drop down into his belly and threaten to squelch out his asshole.

There were muddy tracks on the purple rug that led from Norman's feet straight toward Arnold. They ended three feet in front of him. There they got smeary, as if he had shuffled around, knowing the lights were about to come back on, and hurried back to his proper resting place in front of the TV.

"I don't think so," Arnold whispered to himself. "I really, really don't think so."

Except, except . . .

Old Normie now had his key ring in one dead hand. The same one Arnold had . . . dropped . . . somewhere between here and there. Without moving . . .

. . . I really, really don't think so . . .

. . . old Normie had managed to retrieve his keys.

Arnold got up in a hurry. He had had enough of Norman Parker to last him a while. He marched over and snatched the key ring out of Norman's hand. There was no protest, save for the hooting wind and the patter of the rain. Moving wide of the body, Arnold went past Norman's favorite chair, in which he had died . . .

. . . I really, really don't think so . . .

. . . and went for the door.

The lights conked out again as he reached to push the screen open, where rain was blowing through in a fine cool mist and making a puddle on the carpet. He pushed it open to the squeal of a rusty overhead spring, and banged his cast on the door frame getting out.

Something banged in response behind him. Something *breathed.*

Arnold grabbed for the main door, found the edge, and swung it shut hard enough to shake the house on its crumbling foundation. He jumped down the steps, landing in mud, pinwheeling his one good arm to stay upright. The keys jingled in his hand. He found his balance, spun himself left, and ran to the shed, dodging the looming shapes of farm implements that had not seen service in four decades.

He was at the shed and had the padlock in his hand when the screen door to Norman's house squeaked open and then fell shut, slapping untidily into its frame. Unsteady footsteps clumped down the wooden stairs.

Be cool, fool, Arnold thought as he jammed key after key into the padlock. It was gritty with rust, cold as a river rock. He ducked his head down, squinting against the rain running into his eyes. There had to be thirty keys on the ring, and they smelled muskily of wet brass. His fingers were shaking, and he was thinking *if you drop these things, you are dead meat,* when a blinding flash of lightning lit the sky, turning the world into a stark and skeletal horror show. He snapped his head around and in the bright afterimage saw Norman's house quite clearly, swayback roof and sagging walls crying for paint, and there standing at the front steps was Norman, stoop-shouldered, his hands dangling beside his skinny shanks, eyes bugging out of his blue face, a bewildered zombie if ever there was one.

Arnold dropped the keys.

Sloppy footsteps started toward him, making ugly sucking noises in the mud.

He dropped to his haunches, feeling for the keys. There was mucky straw here that had been tracked out of the shed. Arnold tore up wet fistfuls of it, his breath cold and thick in his throat. The keys had dropped straight down, goddammit, and they certainly hadn't walked off. He began patting the ground with his lone usable hand and the fingers of his right that were sticking out of the cast. Something clinked, and he felt a cold steel ring that jangled when he picked it up.

Norman was pretty close now.

"You're dead!" Arnold shouted at him. "I told you to be dead!"

Lightning walked across the sky once again. It showed Norman Parker stumble to his knees. His head swiveled mindlessly back and forth. He seemed to deliberate for a moment, then pitched facedown into the mud of his yard with a meaty splat, like a wounded soldier who has finally caught the fatal bullet.

Arnold got up, his head reeling. It came back to him that he was quite drunk, and this is what drunks deserved. Too bad every alcoholic didn't have a zombie to chase him around. It would give them something else to do besides pound on their kids.

He went back to work on the keys. None of them seemed to work. Belated thunder rolled across the fields, low and rumbling. The weather was working its way eastward; already the heavy dose of rain was easing, as if the gods had decided to give Wabash Heights one last hard pissing on before heading for Indianapolis. The eastern sky flashed, spreading lightning in a quick white wave. Arnold glanced back. Norman Parker was still facedown in the mud. He had scooped handfuls of it in his latest death agony, and it had squelched between his gnarled fingers like black putty. His heels stuck straight up, his boots growing shiny green again under the rain. He still looked very much like a corpse who could get up and walk if he put his mind to it.

Arnold found a key that turned. He jerked on the padlock, which popped open with a gritty squawk. With a little fumbling he had it out of the hasp. He threw it away, pocketed the keys, and pulled on the long tang of the hasp. The right door wobbled open a few inches, scraping through the mud and straw. Hinges screeched, but only for a moment. Then the door stuck tight, its bottom edge caught in the straw and sludge. Arnold jerked it furiously, making old wood groan and crackle. The top of the door flapped back and forth, blowing out a junkyard stench of old dirt and forgotten garbage. Arnold gave up on the right door and tried the left. It was as tight as if nailed, and probably was. Norman's farm was no showcase, and when the hinges broke back in about, say, 1940 or so, he most likely just braced the thing together and clobbered it full of nails. Presto, Jethro, your shed is as good as new.

So how did he get the damn thing open? Surely he used it from time to time. From the smell coming out, he used it quite frequently as a garbage repository, for there was a mild aroma of not-too-old banana peels drifting out. Arnold decided you had to lift the door in order to get it off the ground whilst swinging it open. For a grown man, even a man Norman's age, no problem. For a kid with one arm, bad news.

He hooked the tang in the crook of his arm and pulled up, grunting. He jerked back, but by then the tang was cutting past his shirt and into his skin, cold and raspy against his tendons. He bent down and tried to worm his fingers under the edge of the door. The wood was rotted, and sloughed off in mushy chunks. He straightened again, frowning. This was stupid. He had made it through hell and high water to get to this shed, and now the door was stuck in the mud.

"Ah, Isis," he muttered, scraping at the soupy straw-and-mud mixture with his foot. "Isis ki Osirus."

The clouds parted as if on Moses' command, and a cool bright moon shone down once again, striping everything with shadows. Arnold sucked in his breath, wondering if he had indeed done that with the magic words. For the first time he could see the shed quite clearly. It was made of flimsy clapboard. What had been white paint many years ago was now sadly curled and peeling. There were indeed no hinges on the left door. And the right door was sans upper hinge, hence the sagging condition. The whole thing looked ready to collapse.

He was bending down again to stick his hand into the mud under the door when a long, guttural wheeze made him look over again at his old friend and pesky sidekick Norman. Norman had pushed himself up onto his hands. Mud dripped off his face in long strings. His head tilted upward on the hinge of his neck. His eyes opened up, and yes, yes sir, they were glowing with an unearthly yellow light, twin candles in his face. He performed a push-up and was on his knees. He lifted a green-booted foot, planted it firmly in the muck, and staggered to his feet.

Hot panic burst wildly up in Arnold's mind, and along with that the knowledge that he had to be the stupidest boy alive, because it had been clear before and was clear once again what was under way here. It was the magic words—they made the dead come back to life, three simple words that sounded Arabic or Egyptian and spoke of gods long dead. These words had only one antidote, one counter-spell. You had to convince the corpse that he was indeed quite dead again.

Arnold turned and pressed his back to the shed door, which slammed conveniently shut. His feet scooted out, and he slid down with elderly paint chips rasping through his shirt, plopping down hard enough to make his teeth click shut. He had brought Norman back to life two or three times already, and it was getting harder and harder to convince the old boy that he was maggot food and not a George Romero extra. Arnold drew a breath, determined this time to kill Norman for once and for all.

"You are dead," he said levelly as Norman advanced on him. "I command you to fall down."

Norman wavered a bit. He took a long, squeaky breath. He came at Arnold.

"Dead," Arnold shouted with rising hysteria, getting up and sidling along the shed wall. "Norman Parker, I command you to be dead and remain that way forever."

To this bit of advice Norman turned a deaf ear. He slogged toward Arnold with no regard to the antidote, no concern for the counter-spell. His boots made wet farty sounds in the mud. The lamps of his eyes seemed to glow even brighter.

"Dead!" Arnold shrieked at him, and turned to run back across that familiar wheat field to the woods beyond. He made it three steps before some large bulky object bristling with rusty spikes loomed up to block his way. Arnold knew nothing about farming, but guessed instantly that this thing had been a thresher back around the time Norman nailed the door shut. It was long and it was wide.

He skirted it, sliding and skating in the mud. Norman tromped along neatly behind him, breathing now and again through his mouthful of mud. Arnold came around the thresher, ordered his feet to obtain warp seven, and charged across the field. Something else appeared in front of him, a thing like a large white bomb lying on its side, a large white bomb covered with sores of rust. Arnold commanded his warping feet to hit the eject button, and tried to jump over the thing. With his glasses on, and with less beer in his veins, he might have made it. As it was, the tops of both feet connected solidly with the bomb, and he slapped, as Norman had slapped when he last was so kind as to obey a command, facedown into the mud.

He scrambled to his knees, hurting all over, stunned and blinking. He tried to get to his feet and something jerked him back.

A cold wet finger was stuck under his cast at the wrist, digging at the warm flesh there. Arnold let out a whoop, knowing why Norman was going for that virgin white meat, but behind him, over the bomb, he could see the skinny figure of Norman, who had just come around the thresher. His moon-shadow lurched along beside him.

Arnold ran his free hand along the bomb, which was no bomb at all but a water heater Norman had disposed of ages ago. A section of lead pipe was sticking out the top, and Arnold had managed to jam it up his cast.

Clod! his mind screamed at him. *Dumbshit!*

He wobbled his cast back and forth. Pain whomped up his arm like blasts of electricity, and he imagined freshly broken bones grinding their splintered ends against each other there. Not that it really mattered much. 'Twas a real picnic compared to being eaten alive, piece by bleeding piece, by Norman the Blue Zombie.

Arnold jerked his arm in a frenzy, amazed at the tensile strength of plaster barely one day old. The pipe dug at his flesh, cold and hard. He supposed it had carried many a gallon of hot water, this pipe had. It had served its purpose and been cast off with the water heater to die. But it had decided, perhaps under the influence of the magic words, to perform one last act. It had decided to help its former owner trap and eat a little boy.

Norman drew closer. The yellow of his eyes competed with the white of the moon. His mouth dropped open and a glop of mud fell out. His hands reached up and formed claws.

Arnold scooted backward. The water heater rolled a bit, making things inside rattle like dry gourd seeds. *Yo-ho,* Arnold thought insanely while his arm screamed pain at him. *You trashed the thing because it was full of lime.*

Norman stumbled against the water heater, his shins clunking it hollowly. He wobbled for a second, looking around with his hellish eyes, and then, slowly and terribly, he craned his head down to stare at Arnold.

"Last chance," Arnold squeaked up at him, clawing at the mud as he attempted to drag both himself and a hundred pounds of water heater across the ground. "Last chance to listen to your master."

Norman Parker bent down. His shadow bent with him. His fingers reached for Arnold's throat. His shadow fingers reached with them. His eyes shone, dull and dry and flecked with dirt, looking as big as yellow Nerf footballs. On the slow, cold outrush of his breath Arnold could smell beer and mud and bad teeth. Arnold thrashed his head back and forth, grinding mud into his ears. Cold slick hands found his throat and slid around it in a clumsy caress. Dead thumbs sought the highest portion of his windpipe, the part where one day, if he had lived long enough, an Adam's apple would have sprouted.

"You're dead!!!" Arnold screamed just as those cold, grimy thumbs began their slow and inexorable pressure.

Arnold clawed wildly at nothing. The water heater pipe held his right arm tight. He dug up handfuls of mud, much as Norman had dug up handfuls when, at last report, he had died. Arnold squeezed his eyes shut against the pain of being strangled. His hand beat against the water heater, thunking it and making its guts shed lime in dry whispers. His throat had been closed to the size of a finger, then a pin, and now, to the size of nothing at all.

His stomach ballooned up and down as his diaphragm went into frantic I-gotta-breathe spasms. Colored gnats swooped and dived inside his closed eyes. Somewhere, distantly, there began a high whine, a distant locomotive chugging its way through a crossing out west, a crossing somewhere near an oil field in Texas, Texas where Daddy went without saying good-bye.

Good-bye, Daddy, Arnold thought, and his flailing hand plopped down into the mud. His knuckles hit something hard.

There was another pipe there.

Arnold dug his fingers under it. He pulled it out.

It wasn't a pipe. It was wood.

He forced his eyes open.

Muddy, heavy on one end, nearly unrecognizable, it was old Cumberland's lion-headed cane.

Arnold let it slide through his hand. The lion's head splatted into the mud. He hefted the cane by its small end, swooped it back, and brought it down across the water heater.

From far away, past the noise of the Texas locomotive, he heard the sharp neat snap of wood. He willed his eyes to the left, and saw that he was holding a jagged stick about one foot long. He clamped his fist around it even tighter.

He brought it toward his own throat. Everything had shifted into slow motion now. He looked into Norman Parker's Nerf football eyes, and jammed the ragged end of the stick into the left one.

The yellow light went out with a thin, bubbly snap. Fluid ran down the stick, erasing the mud in lines.

Arnold rammed it deeper. It crunched against bone, and Arnold, being a boy of some intelligence, knew he had reached the back of the socket. He jammed the stick harder. There was some resistance, and then the stick slid through Norman's eye-hole as neat as you please, crunched through the mush of his brain, and bottomed out against the back of his skull.

Norman let go of Arnold's throat. He drew back. The stick pulled out of Norman's eyehole with a disgusting slurp. The secret fluids of the brain dribbled down his left cheek, looking mysteriously yellow, almost fluorescent. His heavy old man's eyelid was sunken and flappy now without its backing of eye-ball. Arnold held onto the stick, able to breathe again but not about to let the stick go, in case this last-ditch stroke of luck turned out to be a sham.

"Now leave me alone," he tried to scream, but what came out was the pinched and squeaky voice of a mouse. He swallowed, hearing strange things crunch in his throat. "Go away," he gurgled, immersed in pain. "Just go away."

Norman Parker stood over him, his legs from the knees down hidden by the water heater, above that, one lone eye gleaming yellowly. He was wobbling around like a drunk on roller skates.

The stick-through-the-eye trick seemed to have affected his balance. For all Arnold knew, that part of his brain might be part of the slimy goo stuck to the stick, which he now shook clean because part of that goo was oozing down onto his hand. Globs of brainmeat whisked through the night air, sparkling wet under the moon. They plopped down a few yards away, glowing a ghastly puke yellow.

"Go on!" Arnold shouted in his new whistly voice. "Since you won't die, then go away!"

Norman's hands dropped down to his sides. He executed a shuffling turn. He shambled away.

Arnold was struck with the sudden and inexplicable belief that he was headed for Maine. The Micmac burial ground in Ludlow, Maine. Perhaps he would drop in on Louis and Rachel Creed on the way, both of whom would certainly have no objection to having dead things around the house.

He dropped the stick and pounded his fist lightly on his forehead, amazed. Sure, Arnold, here you are on your back stuck to a water heater in the middle of the night at the edge of an Indiana wheat field, you have just avoided being strangled by a zombie, and all you can think about is the *fucking horror stories and the fucking horror books and the fucking horror movies* you have seen and read in your life, while the true horror is that you and you alone have the power to raise the dead, the power to command zombies (sort of), and the power to uncover forty million bucks worth of treasure if you can only get your *arm off this fucking water heater*!!!

He sat up. The water heater's dark innards rustled dryly.

Norman Parker was halfway past his house now, heading up the lane toward the road, stumping drunkenly on his dead legs. *That's fine,* Arnold thought. *Let him stump drunkenly all the way to town, let him stop by the Wabash Tavern for a beer. Just let him stay the hell away from me.*

He turned his attention to the pipe that was jammed up his cast. It came out of the top of the water heater, angled left and right a few times like a beginner's Tinkertoy creation, and dead-ended in plaster. Arnold angled his arm downward, pulled, and the pipe slid out as neatly as the stick had slid out of Norman's eye. Arnold knew then why so many people were found dead in piles by exit doors after a fire in a theater or crowded restaurant. In their panic they couldn't remember how to open a door. If the thing said push they pulled, and if it said pull they pushed. Anything to get away from the heat and the capering, flaming madman called death. In his panic, Arnold had misread the sign, which said, simply, "Angle arm downward and pull free."

He got up. His knees creaked. His back popped. Pain needled him from a dozen interesting directions, mostly from under his cast. The fall over the water heater had trebled his headache, and now he had a sore throat to boot.

And the door, yeah, the shed door, it was still there, stuck, with no one around to open it.

He stepped wide over the water heater and walked toward the shed. It occurred to him that he could call out to Norman and order him back, have him open the shed door and then send him back on his way to Maine. The old cane-in-the-eye trick seemed to have tamed him remarkably, but no, there was no way of being sure. It would be best to let him go his own way.

Whichever way that was. Wabash Heights, most likely. That lay east, toward Maine. At his bedraggled rate, he would stagger into town around dawn, much to the amazement of the locals, perhaps make himself a sign that said "Maine or Bust" and hitch himself a ride. Arnold didn't really give much of a shit . . .

Except . . .

A dead blue Norman Parker hobbling through town might stir some interest. It might get people interested in finding out just how Norman had turned so blue, and why he was walking around with one eye poked out and a hitchhiker's sign in his muddy blue hands. Nobody would be able to figure out why he was headed for Maine (current spook headquarters of the world), but they would want to know what had happened to him.

Which would bring them out here, to the farm. To the farm, the shed, and Arnold.

Arnold hurried himself up. The moon burned down with flat dead light, shimmering on the mud and glistening in the puddles, cold and accusing. The breeze had died when the clouds disappeared and above the slip and plop of his own footsteps Arnold could hear Norman's boots crunching over wet gravel as he went up the lane on his senseless mission.

He would be in town around dawn. Nah, maybe he would just head straight ahead and disappear into the woods beyond Route 40. Hell, he might open a fruit stand on the highway and peddle melons. Who could know?

Arnold considered it one more time. Call him back, get the

door open, perhaps even make Norman do the digging? Risk being strangled again by those wet and raspy hands? The stick was back in the dark somewhere. The shotgun (which Arnold assumed had to be empty; it had, after all, been fired twice and then become a club) was lost out here somewhere, too, dropped by a feeble and dying Norman, who had no idea at the time just how bursting with youthful energy he still was.

Risk it, or not?

Arnold stopped by the thresher, watching the shadowed shape of the zombie he had created as it walked away, a mud creature, as Arnold was, stalking in the moonlight past the skeletal maples that lined the lane, with its zombie shadow keeping time beside it. Why had it (him) tried to kill him (Arnold)? Why would a zombie turn on the human that had brought it back to life?

And then, like a ghost image floating just this side of his vision, Arnold saw Atkinson lying on his crisp white hospital sheets, his hands pedaling the air, his lungs wheezing and gurgling as they prepared to breathe their last.

Isis ki Osirus. Don't say it too often.

Of course. The trick, the trouble, the double entendre. The monkey's paw syndrome. You get three wishes, Bud, and them three wishes is two too many. Anything used can be abused. Ask any junkie who swore he'd shoot himself up once, just once, just that one time to see how it felt. Ask him ten years down the road, when he's sold his soul to the devil and is dying in a gutter just south of Times Square, down where the rats dine on winos' ears and junkies' eyes while they sleep. You can use it, Bud old Bud, but you can't abuse it.

Guck. Arnold shuddered in the cold. Norman Parker was no longer his business. Any attempt to deal with him now could only lead to further disaster. And besides, he was already close to the end of the lane and almost on Route 40, wherever that would lead him.

Arnold went around the thresher and came to the shed. He pulled on the door, and it gave its customary few inches before accepting the law of gravity and digging itself obediently into the earth. Arnold bent down, got a handful of edge, and lifted. Perhaps lighter on a hot July day, the wood was now water-soaked and in no mood to be hoisted. Arnold grunted, breathing hard against the wood, which smelled dead and rotten, gourmet fare for the termites and wood beetles when they awakened from their winter slumber. He slammed it shut again and went to the task of scraping the heap of mud it had dug away with his foot. He opened it again, scooping a fresh heap, where dead straw stuck out like soggy wires. He scraped it away and pulled some more. The door wobbled, as it had wobbled before, digging in deeper. He decided the damn thing would dig itself all the way to China if given the chance. He pushed it shut.

So close. So damn close, yet so far away.

Something popped mutedly off to his left, and he looked over. The lights had come back on in the Parker house, harsh white squares speckled with leftover rain. The line leading from the pole to the house hung leisurely, drooping as everything here drooped, still swaying a bit. It cast a long stripe of shadow on the gray-white ground, crossing a rectangle of light spilling out onto the mud from the single window on the north side of the house. Arnold frowned, thinking of houses with windows, barns with windows, sheds with windows . . . wasn't there a law that said every building had to have a window or two?

He walked around the shed, toward the house, where it was lighter. Dead wet weeds tugged at his knees, and old beer cans clanked underfoot. The shed wall was at his right, blank, blistered, peeling, windowless. He crossed its fifteen-foot length and peeked around the other side.

There was a window in the back wall. It only stood about four feet off the ground, and it was big enough for two kids to crawl through. Arnold went to it, smiling. Someone had even been so nice as to bust out the glass. He went up on tiptoe and looked inside. Ghostly slats of moonlight pierced the blackness inside, courtesy of the shed's ruined roof. Beer cans winked secretively; glass twinkled. And the stench was so fine as to drop a fly in midair. Arnold pulled his head out, making faces, aware that he was due for many hours of breathing that stink, but willing to bear it.

Now he just needed three things. A chair to stand on, a light to see with, and a shovel to dig with. Once uncovered, there would be the matter of transporting the sarcophagus to Terre Haute, where one or two shops dealt in coins and silver and gold. Or perhaps a smelt, where the thing could be melted down to ingots. Or maybe even the Swope art gallery, which would surely pay a handsome fee for an actual sarcophagus . . .

. . . coffin??? . . .

. . . an actual relic stolen from Egypt in 1932.

Arnold went back to the house, thinking of King Tut and the fabulous sarcophagus *he* had been entombed in. Solid gold, top to bottom, its lid made in the shape of its inhabitant and bearing a likeness of his royal face. Had there been jewels in it, ruby eyes or something like that? Arnold thought so. Cumberland had let it slip that this was a sarcophagus of a treasure, no bag of pirate's doubloons, no crate of gold bars. To Arnold, it didn't matter what it was. It was forty million dollars, and with that much money a person could work magic. A person could get out of Wabash Heights forever. A person could put his mother and sisters in a mansion fit for King Tut himself, a mansion located in Texas, convenient to the oil wells and the father who had left and would surely come back when he saw the fortune his son had made.

He decided, as he went up the front steps with a final glance back to the lane, that he would sell the ruby eyes for enough cash to hire a truck. A wrecker, probably. Something to get the thing out of the ground with. He would bribe the driver to keep his mouth shut. Two ruby eyes, sure, they would bring a small fortune.

There was only the small matter of time. Norman Parker of Blue Zombie fame either would or would not be in Wabash Heights by morning. If he wasn't, Arnold had all the time in the world to do his secret things. If he was, well, the Parker dump would be crawling with cops and interested persons shortly after sunup. Possibly WTHI would be there with their ActionCam, filming the whole thing.

He went into the house, got a chair out of the kitchen, and was dragging it past the refrigerator when he saw a greasy box of Blue Diamond wooden matches parked at the back edge of the stove. He picked it up and stuck it inside his shirt. Feeling suitably equipped, he dragged the chair outside. He propped it beneath the shed's window.

The smell came at him, thick and nauseating. He mentally clamped his nostrils shut, swung his cast through, instructed his feet to perform a short launch, and pushed himself inside, expecting to land on dirt or straw or even a broken bottle, which would add to the fun. Instead he fell into a mountain of mushy trash bags that had not been tied shut. Things belched out, clattering. Fresh stink billowed up, enveloping him in nasty fog. He battled his way free, knocking things aside, got the matches out, and lit one, not expecting to be surprised if the shed and its load of garbage gas exploded like a bomb.

The match showed him many things in its yellow, flickering light. A sea of trash bags, some black, some brown, some white. Shed walls that had never seen paint and had become a dusty gray with age. Ancient shelves piled with rusty paint cans, hand tools, leather objects, and gardening implements—you name it and Norman had it in here, none of it looking usable or remotely modern. There were bent and rusty nails driven into the walls here and there, from which hung more appropriate things. Norman owned a pickax. Norman owned a hoe. Norman owned a shovel, and Norman even owned a lantern.

For Arnold, it was a gravedigger's paradise.

He rocked himself up onto his feet and made for the lantern. Halfway there, pitching and swaying on the trash bags, his fingers got stung by the match and he let it drop. He got another one going, held it overhead, and waded to where the lantern hung. He got it off its nail and leaned against the wall, holding it by its rusty hoop handle. He shook it and heard liquid slosh inside. No expert on lanterns made in the Roaring Twenties, he took three minutes and fourteen matches to figure it out. It had knobs and levers, none of which felt like turning very easily and each of which crunched in protest when asked. Rust sifted off like fine sand.

It only took two matches to get the wick afire, once Arnold figured out how to get the glass up. White light filled the shed. Arnold lowered the glass, hooked the hoop back over the nail, and set the box of matches on a shelf. He rubbed his hands on his shirt.

"No time to waste," he whispered, and went at it.

Someone strolling by outside, perhaps a hobo or chicken thief or late-night deer poacher, might have seen light streaming out of the shed's solitary window. That someone, curious, might have wandered up and taken a peek inside.

He would have gotten a faceful of trash bag. They were getting tossed out the window in a frenzy.

Arnold was cleaning up.

· 10 ·

A Grave Subject

MORNING CAME TO Wabash Heights, and by then, Arnold had managed to dig through three feet of dirt that decades of shed-protected dryness had turned to hard-packed dust. His only problem, aside from working the shovel with one hand, enduring the first grating hangover of his life, and staying alive surrounded by a fog of years-old garbage stench, was knowing where to dig. The shed was fifteen feet long by about ten feet wide. He had started in the middle, dead center, the lantern throwing cold flat light across the straw-littered earth and reflecting balefully off the remaining trash bags Arnold had left along the edges. Uncountable beer cans shone like eyes in the dim corners; Arnold's shadow kept him company until sunup, a twisted thing with a shadow spade in its shadow hands. Once, around four o'clock, a mouse had darted out of its hiding place without warning and shot like a bullet across Arnold's vision. He had jumped back with a cry, dropping the shovel and nearly tripping over his own feet. The mouse flew into a new hiding place that was apparently better than the old one. From then on the only sound had been the shovel crunching through dead earth, and Arnold's steady breathing as he worked.

His intention had been to dig an exploratory hole straight down, but the hole widened of its own accord as powdery dirt cascaded in. Now, with the morning sun well up in the sky and heat beginning already to sink through the shed's flimsy walls and roof, Arnold, standing in the hole up to his shoulders and wondering without much interest if he could possibly crawl out, drove the shovel tiredly down for the billionth time, and it struck something with a muted *thunk*. Something hard, but vaguely springy.

His heart jumped to a higher gear. He scraped at the hardness, standing on the slope of the hole with his sneakers full of dirt, his cast held behind him for balance. Sweat stood out on his face in a network of beads, and he paused to dab at them with a sleeve. The shovel had grated across something hard and flat. Something was buried here.

Well of course something's buried here, you buttwipe. Why do you think you're standing in this hole? Get busy before Norman Parker makes it to town.

He used the shovel to fling more dirt out, creating a dust storm. His fingers ached from holding the shovel one-handed, and he doubted if he would ever be able to unclench that fist again. His shoulder throbbed like a big extra heartbeat. He had a feeling that from this night of dust and digging his nose was packed with boogers the size and color of rotten peanuts. Who cared? With forty million in the bank he could hire a butler to ream his nose with pipe cleaners ten times a day.

Soon the shovel was thumping more and more against the hard thing. With a groan of relief Arnold heaved Norman Parker's battered old shovel out of the hole and let it balance on the edge. He went down on his knees, forced his hand to open (the tendons seemed to have turned to hot wires), and brushed the loose dirt away from what he had uncovered.

Something stabbed his index finger and he jerked away, stifling a yelp. He stood up and held his hand to the light.

There was a long splinter of wood sticking out of his finger at the crease of the knuckle.

He pulled it out with his teeth. *There is danger in grave robbing,* he thought sagely, and spat it out. Sometimes, the grave fights back.

He went back down on his knees and pressed his face close to the wood. It smelled like dirt, old dirt that had not been exposed to fresh air since, say, 1932 or so. More carefully now, he brushed the dirt aside, making a large circle. It was not a single board, he discovered, but a series of rough-hewn and poorly fitting slats. His heart pulsed in his throat. The light from the lantern cut deep into the conical hole, but not deep enough, and the sunlight coming through the window wasn't doing the job, either. It was too dark to see.

But so what? he thought, wild with anticipation. *Atkinson said they put it in a crate and stamped it with the words "ma-*

chine parts.'' There is no mystery here, no reason to see. Just dig, for God's sake.

He eyed the handle of the shovel, flexing his hand, grimacing. His mouth was dry and lined with dust. He needed to pee. He had not tasted food for hours, days maybe, and his left arm, the good one, felt as heavy as his right. The digging had barely begun, and he had been at it all night. In better light he would be able to see four blisters on his hand, one of them already popped and ready to bleed. He was, he realized, in no shape to go on without taking a break.

He crawled out of the hole, pulling down handfuls of dirt and pushing little avalanches with his feet. What had been uncovered got covered again. He came fully out into the light, back into the warm stink of garbage. He went over to the wall and unhooked the lantern, then carried it to the edge of the hole, which looked like a fresh bomb crater. He held it overhead and looked into his creation.

Your basic hole. He smirked to himself, not knowing what he had expected in the first place, and set the lantern down. The light stuttered and flashed, and now he noticed that it was hissing in a strange way. Well, it had served him through the night and could run out of gas if it wanted to. But first . . .

He picked up the shovel and stuck it down the hole. He scraped on those slats again until the blade was rasping against clean wood. He hauled the shovel out and tossed it aside, aware now more than ever that his hand was blistered beyond repair.

He held the lantern up again. Its light was dying, and fast. He thrust it over the hole. He saw old wood the color of dirt. And faintly, in ink that had been dry for fifty-eight years, these letters:

ACHI
RTS

His mouth was suddenly dry, utterly spitless. His lips were pasted to the stubs of his teeth, his tongue super-glued to the roof of his mouth. *Fill in the missing letters, Arnold old chum. See if you can solve the puzzle. You are not surprised, remember that. You dug all night for this moment and you are not surprised, but your heart is beating so fast it just might fail you, you are about to wet your pants, and if anyone ever de-*

served to scream for sheer joy, it is you. achi rts. machi arts.
machine parts. Just like the old man said.

The lantern died. Arnold set it down, shaking at the knees,
quaking all over. His mouth split open in a grin that threatened
to tear his stitches apart.

achi rts. Mumbo jumbo, just like the magic words, but
mumbo jumbo full of power. Inside this crate was treasure
beyond belief, a treasure that meant more than money or power
or, for that matter, fame.

It meant an escape from Wabash Heights, and the chance to
find a father who had disappeared but forgot to say good-bye.

Arnold went to the window, walking, in his own way, like
a zombie. He climbed through without being aware of it. He
walked under a brilliant April sun to the house, and went inside
to find a bathroom and a bite to eat.

There was a lot left to be done, and not much time to do it.

Jack Cumberland was jerked out of a troubled drunkard's doze
by the sound of two car doors slamming. He pushed himself
up onto his hands automatically, disoriented, wondering where
in the hell all the light was coming from. He had spent most
of his adult life waking up in unfamiliar places, so the sensation
was not particularly disturbing. He sat up and bumped his left
shoulder against something. His mind told him it was a steering wheel, and then he knew.

The Dodge. He had dropped that asshole of a cop off and
come back to the trailer to wait for the state cops, but the
thought of cooling his heels in the vicinity of a corpse was too
much even for him. He had opted to wait in the car. Sometime
in the night he had keeled over and slept in a faceful of old
foam rubber.

He rubbed his face with his hands now, wishing for a couple
of oversized C-clamps to screw onto his head to hold his splitting skull together. Squinting, he saw that a nice new Chevy
was parked beside the Dodge, and that two nice-looking men
in nice suits had gotten out and were looking around with cal-
culated disdain. One of them saw Jack and bent down to peck
on the window.

Jack got out to the unbearable screech of dying door hinges.
He inhaled a chestful of fresh spring air. It was nauseating. He
saw his wig lying on the seat and hurried to reach back in for
it. When it was on his head and seemed liable to stay there,

he pulled himself back out. He slammed the door and a charge of dynamite exploded in his head, making his eyes water. He knew he was not a very pretty sight, but then, the grieving relatives of murder victims were not supposed to be. He hurried around the car to greet the pecking man.

"Jack Cumberland," he said, aware that tears actually were running down his cheeks from this ungodly sunlight. It was perfect.

The man eyed him coldly. "You associated with this?"

Jack pointed to the trailer. "My father. Last night. What took you guys so long?"

"Just got the call," the man said. He was wearing a white polyester tie that seemed to glow under the sun, adding to Jack's misery. His partner, toting a large black bag that reminded Jack of a doctor's kit, was examining the ground as if looking for a likely cigarette butt to smoke. "Besides, it's a half hour from Terre Haute." He cocked his head toward the trailer. "Is the body still in there? That the trailer?"

Jack nodded. "Yeah, nobody's touched him. See, this kid broke in last night and—"

The cop waved a hand. "Your local man gave us the details." He pulled a small notebook out of an interior pocket and flipped it open. "Positive ID as Arnold White, local teenager. Scuffled with you, knocked you out with a whiskey bottle, and stabbed your father with the broken bottle." He stared at Jack and the crusted lines of dried blood on his face. Jack avoided his eyes, those damned cop's eyes that seemed to bore right through you and see the inside of your soul. "Pretty big kid, this White boy?"

"Big? Yeah, well, average. What are you going to do with him if you, uh, catch him?"

The cop shrugged. "Send him through the courts, what else? He's a juvenile; he'll do some time. If you're hoping for the death penalty, you can forget it. I hate to be blunt, but the law's the law. Myself, the way crime's been going, I'd fry them from age eight on up, the little bastards."

"Will I be able to see him? Talk to him?"

"And wring his little neck when nobody's looking? I doubt that."

He flipped his notebook shut and made it vanish inside his coat. "If you're thinking of revenge, I'd forget it. From this moment on, it's a matter for the law to handle, like it or not. Do you understand me?''

"Sure." Jack raised his hands defensively. "I'd just like to tell the boy that I, that I . . ."

The cop frowned. "That you what?"

"That I forgive him."

His jaw dropped. "You what?"

"I . . . forgive him. I'm a, um, Jehovah's Witness. Devoutly so. We don't believe in, ah, vengeance. Forgiveness, that's the key. The key to heaven.''

The cop scraped at the gravel beneath his shoes with a toe, looking suddenly uncomfortable. "Yeah. Well, we'll let the juvenile authorities decide on that.''

"I'd like to see him as soon as you catch him.''

"Out of my hands. He'll need a lawyer, they might set bail if the case is weaker than we think, the court might order you to stay away from him if his lawyer thinks it's detrimental, the kid might simply refuse, shit, a thousand things could screw it up. The law doesn't work like a Perry Mason show.''

"But I really need to talk to him. To, um, ease my soul.''

The cop's toe had dug a hole. He began to fill it up, fidgeting under his suit. His partner continued to study the ground, looking like an utter moron. "Out of my hands, sorry to say. You check with us periodically, and we'll let you know what develops. Okeydokey?''

"Sure,'' Jack said sourly. He gestured toward the trailer. "All right, let me show you what the little—I mean, the poor misguided lad did inside.''

This time the cop raised his hands. "No, you've done your part. We can't have civilian intrusion on the crime scene. You go make whatever arrangements people of your, ah, faith, have to make. I'll let the Wabash Heights force know when you can send someone out for the body, assuming the coroner doesn't need it.''

The cop hustled away, obviously glad to be done with anyone remotely smelling of Jehovah's Witnesses before he got handed a tract and a speech, probably about to have a good chuckle with his partner once they got inside the trailer. They went inside and slammed the door, leaving Jack alone in the sunlight wondering if he had goofed things up for good. If the law got hold of the brat and convicted him, it might be years before Jack had the chance to get his hands on him. And now that the fog of whiskey was lifting from his brain, Jack was able to see what a spot he had put himself in. Little Arnie had quite a tale to tell—that he'd been chased in the night, that he'd been caught on somebody's front porch pounding on the door screaming for help, that he'd been caned by old Alfred—and then the law would be asking Jack a lot of questions he didn't feel like answering.

He turned and leaned against the Dodge. After a moment he rested his forehead on the roof, eyes closed against the light and the demons of anxiety that were pitchforking his brain. Why hadn't he just buried the old man out back somewhere, thrown him in a ditch, burned him up inside the trailer, or any of the thousands of interesting things one can do with a corpse? Why in the fuck had he called the cops? What had he been thinking?

He clutched his head with his hands, one small part of his mind assuming that if the cops inside happened to peek out a window and see him this way it would be excused as a sign of grieving, while the rest of his mind screamed accusations at him. The story of Arnold breaking in (or had he been peddling magazines? Jack no longer recalled with clarity) was as thin as water; the kid was a runt and had a broken arm. It wouldn't take the police long to find the seams in Jack's hastily sewn story and rip them apart. Out would tumble Jack the Murderer, Jack the Father Killer, Jack the Abductor of Little Boys. The treasure would be useless because its owner would be attending an indoor barbecue at the penitentiary, featuring the guest of honor, Jack, doing the twenty-five-hundred-volt boogie while sitting in a chair.

Oh, yeah. He had fucked things up good this time. Inherited trait from father Alfred. Genetic defect. Call it what you want, Dad had given him the ability to do one thing over and over again, and do it well: fuck up.

It came to him that he should run, hightail it out of this screwball state, get a new identity, trade in the curly wig for something less incriminating. He had been thinking of becoming a blond anyway, so perhaps now was the time for it.

But the treasure, the ever-beckoning treasure, it was close. Arnie knew where it was. Arnie was probably there right now digging it up, or else on his way to wherever it was. Even if the cops found him, he would have the sense to keep his mouth shut about it. Even if he was convicted of murder, a possibility

Jack now found absurd, he would be out of juvenile detention in a few years, and still the treasure would be there, waiting as patiently as it had waited these last fifty-eight.

Jack raised his head and willed his eyes open. He was staring into the underbelly of his wig. He knocked it back in place with an inward snarl. All his life he had sought this treasure. Now he was thirty-seven and could smell gold on the air, gold so close you could reach out and touch it, but just beyond that, out there where vision ended and imagination took over, hung the specter of the electric chair. It was enough to drive a man insane. A lesser man's nuts and bolts would come unscrewed, and he would fall apart like a dismantled robot, right here on the gravel outside a trailer that might bring four hundred bucks on the open market if you could find a handy blind man with the brain of a monkey and money to burn.

Jack rapped his forehead with his knuckles. Money. What a swell thought to have. He was currently broke, with no hope of income. There was no time to find a job, nothing to live on before the first paycheck came if he did get work. He hadn't eaten since the day before yesterday. Forty million bucks lay out there for the taking, and the rightful inheritor was too broke to eat, and even worse, too broke to drink. It was astounding, unbelievable, maddening.

''That fucking kid,'' he growled, mentally checking his nuts and bolts for signs of looseness. Sure enough, there were a few that had managed to unthread themselves and were poking out dangerously. He was coming apart. If he ever found that kid, he would tear him limb from limb and use his bones to bolt himself back together. It was his only hope.

He hurried around the Dodge, remembering something that had occurred to him last night. He knew where the kid lived. It was his remaining card, and he would play it well. He would strike a deal with Arnie's ferocious stepfather, and together they would find the little shithead. But time was running out.

He got the car started and drove to town. With any luck the ferocious stepfather would be home this fine Friday, and the deal could be struck . . .

. . . only the stepfather wasn't home, which was on par with Jack's luck these last thirty-eight years. He found himself staring through a fly-specked screen door at a wispy, timid woman wearing a colorless blouse and ragtag jeans. The stench of old bacon grease drifted through the door with the slow outpour of heat; housetosis it had once been called in an old TV commercial, and this shack had it bad. Still, it made Jack's foodless stomach jump.

"Know where I might find him?" he asked as casually as he could.

"He's at work," the little woman said. She looked shell-shocked and waxy. Apparently life with father was no trip to Disney World.

"Where might that be?" Jack asked.

She looked perplexed. "I don't know if he'd like me telling you."

"Hey, no problem," Jack said sprightly. "He knows me. We've met before, see, and he said to look him up whenever I wanted to. We have mutual business."

She stared at his face. *God,* he thought suddenly, *I look like shit. There's blood on my face and I haven't seen the inside of a bathtub in weeks. I probably smell like a whiskey jug from last night's festivities. If not for this wig, she would find me revolting.*

"Hyman and Sons Body Shop," she said after some hesitation. "But he's in a pretty foul mood. He was in a fight last night."

Don't I know it, Jack thought. *You brained him with a skillet while I watched through the window. You're pretty tough for a scrawny little bird. Nothing like* my *mom, the simpering hag.*

"Okay," he said, putting on a grin. "I think I saw the place in town. Main Street, right? Go left at the tavern?"

She nodded. From the depths of the house came the sound of a baby squalling. She turned and prepared to shut the door.

"Just a sec," Jack said. "Is there any chance that little Arnold is home?"

She jerked back, smudgy brown eyes widening. "Arnold?" she squeaked. "No. Why? Are you a . . . are you with the police?"

Jack attached his best con-man smile to his face while his mind, used to lying but not particularly good at it, churned up various falsehoods, examined them, and selected the best possibilities. It was a process that took two seconds. "Of course not. I was involved in an automobile accident two nights ago, and was in the hospital." He touched the cut on his forehead. "Short coma. No insurance, so they threw me out when I woke

up. Didn't even clean me up. I was in the same room as little
Arnold, and we quickly became friends. I promised to visit
him."

He beamed at her while she pondered the logic of this. "You
made friends while you were in a coma?" she said, frowning.

Oopsy-daisy. Chalk one up to Daddy's DNA. "I had short
terms of sanity," Jack bleated lamely. "Anyway, where is little
Arnie?"

To his surprise, the woman began to cry, and he knew his
lie had been swallowed hook, line, sinker, fishing pole, and
tackle box. It filled him with tremendous glee. "Oh," she
moaned, "Roy Mallone was here this morning. He said Arnold
murdered an old man out in Shitty—out in the trailer park. But
he was supposed to go to Joey's, I told Roy that, I told him
Arnold had no business being that far from town, and he said
the state police were looking for him. I don't know what I'm
going to do—the police can't find him, I can't find him, he's
so broken and hurting, and I can't, I can't do *anything*!"

Jack watched her cry. She blended in well with the baby's
background vocals. The stink of bacon was overpowering.

"Know anyplace he might hole up if he were in a jam?"
Jack asked, tired of this. "Any special hideout? Tree house?
Cave?"

She shrugged helplessly while tears dripped off her chin. "I
just can't imagine. He's always been so *good*. How could he
be in such a *mess*?"

'Cause he fucked with me, *lady,* Jack thought savagely, nail-
ing his smile in place before it could be lost forever. "I'll tell
you what," he said. "I've got a few days off. I'll look for
Arnold. I used to be a private eye after I left the CIA. If anybody can locate him, it's me."

"Will you?" she said, her face twisted with an odd mix of
joy and desperation that Jack found weirdly attractive. *Clean
this lady up, brush her hair, toss on some makeup, and she'd
be a looker,* he guessed.

"You bet," he said.

She zipped out of sight. Jack stared at the vacant spot where
she had stood, his jaw hinging slowly open. What the fuck had
he done wrong? Alakazam, alakazoom, the lady who was here
is no longer in the room. He mashed his nose against the
screen, looking around. Crappy furniture, baby toys in disarray, an ironing board with a torn cover, a television soundlessly

showing a rerun of "Gilligan's Island." No lady. Had she seen through Jack's lies and gone off to fetch a shotgun? To call the cops? What?

He was just about ready to get the hell away when she reappeared. She opened the screen door and handed Jack the fattest paperback, book he had ever seen. It weighed nearly a pound. "I saved for weeks," she said. "When you find him, give him this. Tell him Mommy bought it for his birthday, but now, well, now . . ."

She cranked on the tears again. Jack backed away, almost beginning to be affected by the palpable aura of misery that hung around this house. The place reeked of bacon and bad fortune. He backed off the porch, glad to be going, went across a muddy square of lawn, and got in his car. He tossed the book on the seat, started the Dodge, and headed down Kentucky Street toward Main Street, aka US 40, also aka Maplewood Avenue. He turned left at the Wabash Tavern, thinking of the lady and the beast she had married, and wished he had a dollar in his pocket so he could stop in and have a beer. Anything to wash away the sour taste building in his mouth. In order to get Arnold, he would have to strike a deal with the beast. At this moment he would prefer to kill him. But the gold awaited, and the key to it was working at a place called Hyman and Sons Body Shop . . .

. . . which he found six blocks west of the tavern. It was a rusty Quonset hut surrounded by a moat of smashed cars. Jack pulled in beside a rusty old Chrysler that had, for reasons of its own, no doors. He got out, mentally preparing himself for what had to be done, and wended his way between the wrecks to the open double doors of Hyman and Sons fine establishment. It was nicely dim inside, but hot. Four or five cars in various states of exhaustion were scattered about. Someone was pounding on something to his left; to his right hung a huge vinyl curtain that was splotched with more shades of paint than Jack knew existed. A shadow was moving around behind it using a sprayer, and the tang of fresh paint was thick in the air.

He stood for a minute, letting his eyes adjust, nearly cringing every time the invisible someone to his left walloped metal with a hammer. Then, adding to the noise, someone at the far end fired up a pneumatic sander and started shooting a fan of sparks across the floor. Jack's dental fillings began to ache. This place was the portal to hangover hell, and with typical Wabash Heights hospitality, he was being ignored.

He went to the vinyl curtain and looked for an opening. Failing in that, he lifted it up and stuck his head inside.

A man wearing a gas mask whirled. He waved his sprayer at Jack, shouting something muffled. Jack caught "the fuck out you dumb fuck" before making a hasty retreat. Finally someone in tattered gray overalls ambled up with all the enthusiasm of a man walking a gangplank, poked a filterless cigarette between his lips, and said, "Whaddya want?"

"Need to talk to Mr. White."

The man got out a lighter. He looked over both shoulders. Jack wondered if the idiot was actually going to strike it, because the paint fumes were thick enough to swim on. Regardless, the man struck it. Jack awaited the explosion with weary regret. What a way to exit the planet.

Nothing exploded. The man in the overalls took a deep drag, blew smoke in Jack's face, and said, "Ain't no Mr. White here."

Jack frowned. White was Arnold's last name. What had that dumb bitch at the hospital said the stepfather's name was? Wargle? Wopple? Whipple?

"How about Whipple?"

"Weasel?"

"No, Whipple."

"Weasel Whipple."

"Who Whipple?"

"Who's on first?" the man said, and abruptly screamed laughter in Jack's face. "What's on second? Haaaaaahhhhhh!"

Jack staggered back. This was more than God had intended any drinking man to endure. "Just point him out, huh?"

"Over there making noise," the man said, pointing with a thumb to Jack's left. "He's in one foul mood today, though. Fouler than usual, if that's possible. Somebody nailed him with a baseball bat last night. Fucker's head looks like a hand grenade went off inside it. Approach at your own risk, if you get me."

"You're got," Jack said.

"Me, I'm gonna go take a break. The fumes in here are frying my lungs out."

He walked past Jack into the sunshine, trailing blue smoke. Jack shook his head, wondering how the fates had ever brought

him to this turd of a burg. Then he made a quick review of
some basic karate techniques, decided a good old Three
Stooges boing to the eyeballs would suffice if things got out of
hand, and went over to confront Weasel Whipple.

Weasel was squatted beside the right front fender of a weather-
beaten red Pinto. His back was to Jack. He had one arm inside
the wheel well. With the other he was beating the fender, giant
flathead hammer in one huge fist blurring in the air. Jack could
count at least five hairless lumps on his head that had scabbed
over. There were dried lines of blood on his neck. The little
lady had done a nice job on him. Miracle he had woke up this
morning. No miracle that he did not recall what had happened.

"Excuse me," Jack shouted.

He went on hammering. Jack came closer, ready to dodge
back if it was a trick. Then he noticed Weasel's ears. Small
white sticks were poking out of them. The old Q-Tip number.
Jack himself had used it before when employed at noisy jobs.
It didn't work very well, but it kept your brains from leaking
out your ears.

He tapped Weasel on the shoulder. Weasel slumped forward
onto his knees and hung his head. His arm dropped out of the
wheel well. He was holding a fist-size piece of steel in his left
hand. "What now?" he grunted.

"We got business to discuss," Jack said.

Weasel turned his head. One big eyeball came into view. It
was as red as the Pinto. It swiveled sideways and fastened itself
on Jack.

"You again," he breathed.

He got up fast for a man his size. The hammer was swooping
through the air like a battle-ax before Jack had time to realize
it was there. His left arm jerked up in instinctual reflex, and
the hammer's wooden handle smashed into his wrist. He
lurched backward, howling in pain and thankfulness that the
hammer had not connected with his skull, because if it had,
he would now be quite dead. As it was, his wrist was merely
ruined.

"Ow!" he screamed. "Ow, shit! You broke my wrist!"

"Gonna break more than that," Weasel snarled, and swung
the hammer again.

Jack decided karate and the Three Stooges could go to hell.
He turned and ran. Weasel's heavy boots crunched over dirty
cement as he gave chase. Jack barreled straight into the smok-

ing man, sending him sprawling across the hood of a car. His cigarette, a good hearty Camel, flipped up like a tiny white baton, spinning end-for-end. This was not noticed by Jack, neither this, nor the fact that the cigarette, when it came down, came down in his hair. He was intent on regaining his balance and putting distance between himself and the raving lunatic who was Arnold White's stepfather. He dodged between two wrecked cars, leaving a strip of his pants and a chunk of skin on a piece of wrinkled metal. He heard the hammer crash down on something behind him. Weasel was growling like a bear and, to Jack's way of thinking, probably drooling like one as well. He was in no mood to look back. He saw his familiar Dodge Dart and made for it, praying that the battery was just simmering with electrical charge and would start the trusty slant-six in a heartbeat, because Weasel was only a heartbeat away and time was at a premium here.

He made it to the Dodge and hauled the door open with his heart thundering in his head and his left wrist engulfed in pain. He flung the door just as Weasel flew up to greet it. The collision was both noisy and helpful. The door slammed shut hard enough to shatter the glass into pebbles that belched across the seat like a cartload of sparkling diamonds. Weasel rebounded, his arms pinwheeling, and fell across the trunk of a blue Datsun that was born too early to know its real name was Nissan. He dropped the chunk of steel beside the left rear wheel. Jack hustled over and picked it up. It was roughly the shape of a small anvil. When Jack straightened again, Weasel was back on his feet and ready for center-ring action, the main attraction.

He swung the hammer. Jack's karate skills sprang to immediate life. He raised the piece of steel and glanced the blow away. Weasel swung again, grunting. The hammer swooshed. Jack put the piece of steel in its path. They thunked together, spitting sparks. The impact sent a jolt of heavy lightning down Jack's arm, but steel against steel beat the hell out of anything else currently available.

"Lucky fucker," Weasel roared, hauling back.

Conk! The bones of Jack's forearm sang like a tuning fork, but still, it beat the hell out of the alternatives.

"I just want to talk," Jack panted while Weasel raised the hammer again.

"Talk to this," he sneered, and swung.

Conk!

"It's worth money to you!"

Weasel hesitated with the hammer raised over his head, the thick wooden handle gripped in both sweaty fists. "What kind of money can a fucking orderly offer me?"

"I'm not an orderly. I'm an entrepreneur."

"As if I speak French, you asshole." He swung the hammer. Jack deflected it. Sparks flew. He noticed with mild alarm that a small crowd had gathered at the entrance to Hyman and Sons and was watching the show. That was not good. This was private stuff.

"I need to find Arnold," Jack said as Weasel raised the hammer. It flashed in the sunlight.

"Find him and fuck him," Weasel said, and swung.

Conk!

"Look, this could go on all day. It's worth a lot of money to you."

Weasel squinted at him, breathing hard, sudden interest flaring in his deep-set black eyes. "How much is a lot?"

Jack kept an eye on the hammer as he wiped sweat from his forehead. The sun seemed extraordinarily hot today. "We can't talk here. Too many ears." He dropped his voice a notch. "But I guarantee I can make you richer than you've ever dreamed. Richer than you'd ever believe."

Weasel lowered the hammer. "It better be good. Five o'clock tonight, Wabash Tavern. Meet me there."

"Okay." He nodded toward the hammer. "You done with that? This chunk of metal's getting heavy."

Weasel laid the hammer on the trunk of the Datsun. "Don't need it anymore."

Jack grinned. "You trust me, then?"

"Nah." Weasel grinned back at him. "Your hair's on fire."

Jack showed the crowd at Hyman and Sons some interesting dances as he bade farewell to his flaming wig, and stomped it to death.

· 11 ·

Second Thoughts

ARNOLD WANDERED AROUND the inside of the Parker house with a turkey pastrami sandwich in one hand and a glass of water waiting for him by the sink, wondering idly why Norman Parker would be a fan of turkey pastrami when he seemed to be more of a meatloaf kind of guy. The stuff was coated with sandy pepper granules and after a few bites heated up the mouth quite nicely; probably it went well with beer. Arnold, looking in the refrigerator, had toyed with the idea of drinking one, but after some deliberation decided his drinking days were over. Liquor was some kind of double-action poison: it flew you off to a place that was good and clean and wholesome for a few hours, then crash-landed you on a parched desert to crawl around until you either died or went mad from the pain. It was something he could do without.

The house was still cool from the night, but that wouldn't last long. Sunlight streamed through the slits in Norman's venetian blinds, casting horizontal bars the color of butter across the kitchen linoleum and the awful purple rug with its maze of muddy footprints. Arnold tried not to look down at them as he paced round, eating his sandwich, especially the big ones that dead-ended a few feet from the sofa. If the power hadn't come back on when it had last night, if it had stayed out just a few seconds longer, those glowing yellow eyes would have loomed closer and closer and those cold dead hands would have been around his throat. There would have been no lion-headed cane to save him.

He wandered into the bedroom, brushing the back of his hand across his throat. It felt swollen, and was probably bruised, which was no biggie, because now it matched his

147

face. He saw that Norman's dresser was thick with dust and useless bric-a-brac, littered with a few coins and a half-eaten pack of Tums. There was a photograph in a chipped gold frame propped behind some beer cans. Arnold pushed the cans aside and looked at it. It was a black-and-white portrait of a fat lady smiling uncomfortably into a camera that had been consigned to the rustpile before Arnold was born. There was an old-fashioned hat on her head. Some crude genius had drawn a mustache and goatee on the glass with a pen. *Say hello to Mrs. Parker about twenty years ago,* Arnold thought, and wondered for a moment if she might show up today. He believed not. If memory served him right, she had died ages ago.

He went out, frowning. Sure, she had died ages ago, but Normie had died last night and come back to life. It didn't make sense. "Isis ki Osirus" were powerful words, but for all he knew, they might be Arabic for "please pass the potatoes." Did they mean Arnold had the power to go to the nearest grave-yard and raise the dead? He doubted it. Elsewise, the Egyptians would be having a massive population explosion because whenever somebody died, the grieving relatives would please-pass-the-potatoes him back to life. Egypt was no Fantasy Island, he knew, and it certainly wasn't teeming with walking corpses. There had to be some other reason for Norman's deviant behavior.

He finished the sandwich, fanned his mouth, and made for the kitchen, not able to figure it out. In any event, it had not worked out well. God knew where the famous Blue Zombie was now. With any luck he had staggered across the highway into the woods, and fallen into one of the many ponds that were in the area, compliments of Peabody Coal and lots of 1950s strip-mining activity. Or with better luck, he had stepped in front of a semi doing sixty-five and was now a colorful hood ornament. There was no way of knowing.

He checked the clock on the kitchen wall. Ten after ten. Lots of digging to do, no time to waste. He put the glass in the litter of dirty plates in the sink, rinsed his fingers, and dried his hand on his pants. Big mistake—his blue jeans had become brown jeans. His blisters jabbed him like deep bee stings as he flexed his hand, looking at it. Without a glove that hand would be bleeding soon. And he had endured just about enough pain lately to make the prospect seem particularly uninviting.

He went back into the bedroom and searched the drawers

for gloves. Pants, underwear, socks, shirts, a tattered copy of some magazine called *Cavalier* with the pages stuck together—no gloves. Norman was a tough old bird. By the feel of his raspy hands on Arnold's throat last night, he had never worn a glove in his life.

Band-Aids, then. Arnold went into the living room, still flexing his hand, not wanting to continue this without some kind of protection. His head was splitting, his face and throat ached, his arm inside the cast put out a thick, grinding pain that seemed likely never to go away, and his shins still hurt from the collision with the water heater. Worst of all were the remains of his front teeth, a constant agony. He paused in front of the blank TV to assess, for the first time, the extent of the damage. Six uppers gone, six lowers. An even match. Some of the stubs were pointy and threatened to slice his probing tongue. You're talking hundreds of dollars worth of dental work, he thought. Hundreds of dollars Frank would never pay. With the forty million, though, the finest dentists in the world would flock to Arnold's doorstep. Might be he would be the first millionaire in the world to have an in-house dentist. The thought almost made him giggle.

He went into the bathroom. A stink to rival the filthiest outhouse greeted him, decades-old pee rotting on the floor. He saw with disgust that Norman was one of those old-timers who liked to put his used toilet paper in the trash instead of flushing it. Septic tank problems, no doubt. The little metal trash can beside the toilet was overflowing with wads of brown-smeared paper. Hordes of flies were fattening themselves on it, buzzing furiously. Arnold ceased breathing and opened the medicine cabinet. A rusty tin of Band-Aids was on the third shelf. He snatched it out and hurried back into the living room, slamming the door. He plopped himself down in the chair in front of the television and took a grateful breath. He had gotten the box open and was sorting through the various sizes inside when it occurred to him that Norman had died in this very chair.

He jumped out of it as if catapulted, almost crashing into the TV. He reached down and turned it on, suddenly needing something pleasant to break the silence of this haunted house, living voices to quiet those of the dead. The old RCA took a while to warm up, but by then Arnold was on the sofa (which held memories of its own) and trying to wrap his blisters.

A commercial blared, cajoling listeners to dial a toll-free

number to get more information about an exercise machine that would firm up their tummies and turn that disgusting flab into useful muscle. Working with his teeth and the fingers sticking out of his cast, he was ministering to the third blister when the WTHI newsbreak came on at ten-fifteen.

Arnold tuned it out. He had no interest in world affairs, most certainly no interest whatever in what went on in the Wabash Valley. It wasn't until he heard the name Alfred Cumberland that his ears came fully awake and his head snapped up.

The announcer looked fine, a prim little man in a suit pronouncing Arnold's death sentence in his best TV voice. Arnold stared at him with a Band-Aid hanging out of his mouth and his blackened eyes flaring with alarm.

". . . dead of multiple stab wounds, was identified by his son late last night, who was present during the attack and tried, but failed, to ward off the assailant. He was able to give positive identification of the alleged murderer to local police, however, and both state and local authorities are now looking for the suspect, a thirteen-year-old resident of Wabash Heights who is believed to have fled on foot. Again, Alfred T. Cumberland of Wabash Heights, dead at the age of eighty-two. A look at local weather after this brief message from Terre Haute Farm Implements."

The TV started showing tractors. Arnold shot to his feet while the Band-Aid fluttered to the floor. "I didn't kill him," he said to the RCA, dumbfounded. "He fell asweep."

This lispy bit of news did nothing to the progress of the tractor commercial, which announced that financing was available to qualified buyers.

"He just . . . he just fell asweep!" Arnold shouted. He knew that he was being as stupid as Elmer Fudd shouting down the rabbit hole, for Elmer Fudd would never catch that wascally wabbit and Arnold White would never convince a TV that he was innocent.

His mind raced in crazy circles while his heart speeded up to keep pace. His mouth was suddenly drier than it had been before he drank the water. He would have to go back to town immediately, of course, hitch a ride or walk, it didn't matter; get his ass to the police station and straighten this matter out. He still had Norman Parker's keys and might find a vehicle parked outside somewhere amongst the junk, might even be able to teach himself to drive, anything to get there quick and tell the cops he was innocent. Nobody had stabbed the old man, Jack hadn't even been there when Arnold left, there hadn't been any stabbing going on, a lot of caning, yes, but you can't stab a man with a cane . . .

except old Norman Parker, yes, you can stab a man with a cane, Arnold, because you did it yourself just last night, right through the eyeball, pop, zoom, right to the moon, yellow goo on the stick, phosphorescent brains flipping through the air, the police would certainly never believe that, and they won't believe you didn't stab Cumberland the same way, and either way, by the way, your ass is grass!!!

He nearly wept with despair while the TV talked optimistically about today's weather. He lurched over and shut it off. Thirty seconds ago he had been a kid bloated with happiness at the treasure he had discovered. Now he was a deflated balloon. No amount of money could save him. Forty million in gold couldn't be spent behind bars.

He flopped down in Norman's death chair, no longer worried about spooks or the secretive silence that filled the house. He was a wanted boy, a fugitive. His picture might be tacked to the wall of the post office downtown. The people of Wabash Heights, always on the lookout for quick cash, would be beating the woods and fields for him, deer rifles in hand, itching to gun down Wabash Heights' newest star, the Elephant Boy with the price on his head. They had done the same thing a year or two ago when Richard Carter, the Terre Haute teenager who killed his mother and father in a fit of drug-induced rage, was purported to be in the area. Coon hunting had been abandoned in favor of Carter hunting. A citizens' posse was formed. The reward was upped and upped until it reached the astronomical sum of five hundred dollars. This sent droves of Wabash Heights' respectable citizens, the drunks and the child abusers and the welfare shysters, into a delirium of Carter fever. When the news came out that Carter was apprehended clear up in Chicago, the whole town had been in mourning for a week. No quick five hundred to be made. No panicky, helpless, hopeless kid to gun down. No more blood sport for the good and kind people of this saintly town; once again they were reduced to bagging only deer, raccoon, possums, and squirrels, all deadly enemies of mankind and friends of the skillet.

Arnold shoved the Carter incident from his mind and concentrated on his own predicament. Things looked pretty crappy, but only because things were. He couldn't go back to Wabash Heights, and with Norman Parker stumbling around, it was only a matter of time before he drifted instinctually into town, and then the town would come to Arnold. It flitted through his mind briefly that he should load up Norman's shotgun, wait for the cops, and go down fighting. But that would be stupid, senseless. No one would ever know the truth, and more shame would be heaped on the tatters of his family. He wondered what his dad would do in this predicament, but his dad would never be in this predicament because his dad did not have Frank Whipple to get him into impossible messes; his dad had left and allowed Frank Whipple to be his replacement. He never wrote, he never called; he didn't care and maybe he never had.

Yet Arnold remembered the times before Dad left, the before times, he was beginning to call them in his mind, the before times when Dad was there at the breakfast table spooning down Lucky Charms with his right hand while pressing an open paperback to the table with his left, occasionally glancing up with a dazed and mystified look, entranced by the wonders of what he was reading, and surely then he was not thinking of leaving. Sometimes reality would come back to him and he would admonish Arnold and Melissa to hurry up to school, then go back to his book, unaware that he was about to be late for work. He would be wearing his dark slacks and a white shirt with a Kroger nametag pinned to the pocket. John White, the nametag said, no more, no less. John White who worked as a checker and secretly dreamed of other things. Arnold had been lulled to sleep since birth by the muffled clacking of Dad's old Remington typewriter, which he kept in the bedroom on a TV tray. After supper he would carry his chair into the bedroom, and the door would be shut. Soon, Arnold would hear a sheet of paper being ratcheted into the machine, and then the clacking would start, coming in bursts like hesitant machine-gun fire. Arnold had accepted this behavior as normal for any father, but when he was seven he had gotten old enough to be curious, and asked Mom what Dad was doing. Business, she would say, and it was let go at that.

Arnold felt hot tears sting his eyes as these memories resurfaced. Dad would hammer away at the Remington from suppertime to bedtime, pausing long enough to come in and tuck Arnold and Melissa into bed and give them a goodnight kiss, his slender hands putting off the odor of the groceries and produce he had handled during the day, but his eyes would be faraway, dazed and mystified, as if the Remington had stolen his soul and would not let it go until the night's business was finished. Back he would go into the bedroom, sometimes muttering things to himself, and Arnold would fall asleep with the typewriter machine-gunning well into the night. Next morning there would be Dad, ready for breakfast but weary and beat-looking, paperback in hand, and the ritual perpetuated itself.

Two years ago Arnold had been sick with stomach flu. Mom had gone to the Laundromat; Angie wasn't born yet and Melissa was in second grade. Dad was at work. A bug of curiosity had appeared out of nowhere while Arnold watched television, urging him to go into the bedroom and do some snooping. He hadn't known was he was looking for, or what he would find. He looked through the dresser drawers, feeling sly and vaguely guilty. He found clothes. He looked under the bed, hoping a few early Christmas presents would be stashed there, but there were only dustballs. It's spring, he reminded himself, but went to the closet and snooped through it anyway. Below the hanging clothes were several cardboard boxes. Two of them were stuffed with used baby clothes, awaiting the birth of Angie. The third one was huge and had a lid that could be pulled off. The top and sides were stamped with a smiling celery-man, his green feet standing on the words "California's Finest." Arnold pulled the lid off and found a thick stack of brown envelopes inside. He opened one, frowning, and slid a thin sheaf of typewritten pages out.

It was a brief story of some sort. A small slip of paper was fastened to the top with a paper clip. It informed someone named "Contributor" that the story didn't meet current editorial needs, but thanks, anyway.

Below the stack of envelopes was a frazzled pile of unbound papers almost a foot deep. Arnold scrabbled through them with his fingers, puzzled, then decided they must be book manuscripts, unpublished novels, maybe. He was turning his attention back to the little story when the front door banged open and Mom was back, grunting under her freight of laundry. Arnold jammed the story back into its envelope and shoved it in the box, then shut the closet door and scurried out. But he had seen enough, and he knew what this typewriter business was all about.

Dad was trying to be a writer.

The following winter Arnold happened to be on his bed plowing through an ancient Spiderman comic while Mom and the girls were out, when Dad shuffled past in the hallway with the celery box in his arms. He looked strange, somehow grim before he passed beyond Arnold's sight. The back door squealed open and banged shut. Arnold waited several minutes, wondering, his comic forgotten. Where could Dad be taking his box of stories, the things he had spent so many evenings writing?

Arnold slipped out of bed and padded down the cold bare floor. He eased the door open and stepped out into the chilly November night. Cold wind gusted at his pajamas and lifted his hair. He saw his father standing by the trash barrel at the edge of the alley. Flames were dancing out of the can, a circle of orange fire that the wind pulled strongly to the left. Dad was feeding papers one at a time into the fire, his face clearly visible in the light from the flames. He looked old and shrunken, though he was only thirty-five.

Arnold slunk back inside, uneasy about snooping, aware that the strange backyard ritual was an affair between his father and his own failed creations, those stories that had been born in a decrepit Remington typewriter and had never found a home in print. Arnold snapped off the bedroom light and fell into a light and troubled sleep while Dad burned the work of years.

The next day, John White left home for work, and never came back. Mom got a postcard from Texas eight days later that showed oil rigs thrusting up from barren desert into a flawless blue sky. It didn't say much. There was no return address.

These bitter memories went through Arnold's mind like a slow unwinding of a movie too often seen to make sense anymore. Dad had wanted to be a writer, but it had only helped drive him away.

"I liked you as a checker," Arnold whispered, aware now that tears were running freely down his cheeks and dripping on his lap. He understood that desperate need to get away. His dream had been to find gold and ransom himself and his mother and sisters from the fate Dad had left them to. He understood the power of a dream, and that understanding was this: that the dream only has power when it comes true. A failed dream is a burden.

He got up out of the chair, wiping his face with his hand. Forty million in gold, but it might as well be lead. He had to run. He would never get anywhere on foot. Tack up another post office poster: Arnold White, wanted for car theft. Or truck theft. Whatever Norman Parker had here that could be driven to Texas.

He went outside, pulling Norman's bundle of keys from his pocket. There was an ancient green pickup truck parked in the weeds beside the lane. He walked to it with a regretful glance back at the shed. All that digging. All that useless digging.

The truck didn't look promising. Large flaking letters on the grille proclaimed that it was an ORD. Rust had dined on the fenders for uncountable years, exposing tires that were utterly bald. The sides of the bed were shot full of jagged holes. The door handle was missing. Arnold stood on the running board, reached inside, and found the door lever. It came up with a metal groan, and the door popped reluctantly open.

He sat inside behind the huge steering wheel. The truck stank of age and dust and spilled beer, a smell not unlike stepfather Frank's old Malibu. Arnold supposed he would have to get used to it; Texas was a mighty long way away. He sorted through the keys, trying several that looked likely, finally finding one that turned. The faded red needles of the gauges in the dash crawled slowly to new positions. The fuel gauge climbed to the one-quarter mark and stayed there. Arnold stared at it with dismay.

Okay, bright eyes, how are you going to buy gas? How many tankfuls will it take to get to Texas? And where in Texas, by the by? Where had that postcard been postmarked? Austin? Dallas? Hole-in-the-Wall?

He turned the key back off, watching dispiritedly as the gauges sank back to home position. He had no money for gas, and to be brutally honest, he didn't know how to drive. The truck had a stick shift poking up through the floor. On the well-worn black knob were traces of a shift pattern that resembled an H. He tried the clutch and found he could sink it, with a little strain, almost to the floor. Okay, a little time, a little trial and error, and he could teach himself to drive. But he could not teach the truck to run without gas.

He rested his aching head on the big black button in the center of the steering wheel, staring down at his dirty sneakers. His mashed toes throbbed from the single push he had given the clutch; how many pushes would it take to get this old buggy to Texas? It was hopeless. He was a squirrel in a wheel, running steadily toward nowhere. He pressed his eyes shut, wishing for an escape but seeing no way out. He might as well sit here sunk in misery until the town came after him, just keep his eyes closed and drift off to sleep for the first time in over thirty hours, blotting out the light and the hurt and the failure. Just to sleep, and perhaps never open his eyes again.

Eyes.

He sat up straight, staring through the cracked windshield but seeing nothing. His face was like that of a battered prizefighter who has kissed the canvas over and over but finally spots an opening in his opponent's defense.

Eyes.

He had fancied that the sarcophagus had ruby eyes. Ruby eyes the size of golf balls. Rubies that big would fetch a hefty dollar or two at a jewelry store in Terre Haute. If he could uncover the crate and get the lid off, he could get the rubies (or emeralds . . . sapphires . . . *diamonds*???) off the sarcophagus and sell them for cash. Hundreds of dollars. Thousands. Enough to gas up a fleet of trucks. Enough to sleep in the finest Holiday Inns between here and Texas. Enough, when he got there, to hire a Texas detective to find Dad.

He pushed the door open and hopped down into the weeds, feeling fifty pounds lighter without that burden of failure on his shoulders. There was hope after all, and the hope was not all that slim. He would have to work hard, and he would have to work fast. He slammed the door, causing rust to sift off the truck like sand, and jogged across the yard to the shed. The old glee was back, the old pirate's sense of mission. He still had a treasure to uncover.

As Arnold wriggled through the shed window, a man named Bart Raymond was about to break the county record for the biggest largemouth bass ever caught in local waters. He had been fishing since daybreak this Friday morning in his trusty aluminum Jon boat, a ten-foot job he had picked up used two years before for the sensible price of seventy-five dollars. The trolling motor had been a tad more, but it was a Johnson and guaranteed for three years. He had even changed the metal propellor to a clear plastic one that was supposedly invisible to fish. The battery was a Sears Diehard, sixty-month guarantee, and boy, did she power that Johnson like a champ. His fishing pole was the best graphite Shakespeare had to offer, his reel a top-of-the-line Daiwa. For today's fishing Bart had selected from his monster tackle box a large spinner, to which he attached a strip of pork rind, a combo guaranteed to sing a siren song to big bass and tickle their taste buds as well.

It was twenty after ten when the monster struck. Bart, a big man with a scraggly Wabash Heights beard, lifted his greasy baseball cap off his head and resettled it, mentally counting to three, a habit he had developed to keep from setting the hook too fast. He didn't want the bass that was jiggling his line to swallow the bait, but he didn't want to make him spit it out either. It was all in the timing. He gripped the pole with both hands and gave it a tremendous upward heave, rocking the boat and making water slosh against its sides.

Bingo. The bass turned around and poured on the throttle, pulling line out of the Daiwa while the drag, perfectly adjusted of course, shrieked like a tiny motor gone berserk. Bart let the fish run, edging it to the left to keep it away from the stumps and fallen trees by the shore of this pond, where it might circle back and hopelessly tangle the line. That would be a crying shame, because Bart knew by the protest of his drag that this baby was a beauty. Big enough, maybe, for Don Marston, the local taxidermist, to stuff and mount.

The drag shut up suddenly. The line went loose. Bart cranked the reel for dear life, needing to keep things snug while the bass played the old bass trick of shooting under the boat, where the line could get hooked on the propellor or shaft, and then Bart would have to cut it, which would make him highly unhappy. Not that the spinner or the pork rind was worth that much; it was the thought of telling this tale tonight at the Wabash Tavern and having it have a sad ending that made Bart's heart beat loudly in his chest and thump in his ears like quick drumbeats. If there was one thing men in Wabash Heights took pride in more than their jobs, it was their hunting and fishing skills. If this bass turned out to be the monster Bart imagined it to be, and if he landed it, he would have a glorious story to tell for years to come, and tell it he would, for if there is one thing a fisherman loves more than fishing, it is talking, and Bart was no exception.

The bass turned tail again and ran. Bart let it, knowing it would have to blow off a lot of steam before this battle ended.

It doubled back. Bart cranked in a frenzy, no longer sitting but half-standing, making the boat rock dangerously. Something crashed in the woods off to the right, just past the shoreline, but Bart gave it no heed. His pole suddenly bent in an upside-down U as the bass went bottomward. This he fought against, because the pond was shallow and the bottom was thick with tangled growth. The bass obliged him by shooting to the surface, where it jumped two feet into the air, flapping, its jaws wide, head jerking back and forth as it tried to dislodge the hook. Bart's eyes nearly fell out of his head. The damn thing had to be two feet long, shimmering green and black and white under the sun, nested in glistening water drops. Bart cranked the Daiwa, panting. There was a cooler full of beer in the front of the boat, and he wished he could call time-out for a minute and recharge his alcohol batteries, but the battle was on and could not be interrupted, even for beer.

He fought the fish for six minutes, sweating, grinning, gasping for air. The thing in the woods came noisily out of the brush and stood at the shore. Bart chanced a glance toward it. Just a man, somebody here to watch the show. He turned his attention back to the business at hand. The fish was tiring, no longer pulling against the drag but keeping the line taut. Bart reeled it slowly in, ready for anything. When it came close to the boat, a ripple on the troubled surface of the water, Bart reached down and got his net in hand. He only hoped it was big enough.

It was. The bass let itself be scooped up, performing one last flopping fit when Bart laid it on the bottom of the boat. Then it lay there on its side, gills opening and closing like heartbeats, mouth yawing open, lidless eyes staring into the sun.

Bart set his pole down. His hands were shaking. He tried to swallow and found that his throat had closed up. He thought for a moment that his heart was going to shut down on him and leave him here dead with the county's biggest bass in his boat, but his ticker kept on ticking, and after a bit he was able to lean forward and pull his cooler close. He pulled a Falls City out of the ice water inside and popped it open. It hit his dry mouth like a slug of arctic cold, too tasty and refreshing for words.

Bart hoisted the can high, saluting the man on the shore.

"Got him!" he shouted, pointing at the bass. "Biggest fucker I've ever seen!"

The man stood there, slump shouldered, wobbling on his feet. He didn't wave.

Bart reached back and grasped the trolling motor's handle. He clicked it on and steered toward shore, his lips skinned back in a grin that would not go away. He would tell this man, in minute detail, everything that had happened in the last eight minutes, so that the particulars would be clear in his mind when this story took twenty minutes to tell tonight at the tavern. The story would begin, as all fish stories must, with Bart waking up with a funny feeling that today would be the Big Day.

As he drew closer, Bart recognized the man on shore. It was Norman Parker, the old coot who lived just west of town. He looked ragged-out, or drunk, probably both. What remained of his gray hair stuck out of his head like broken spokes. His hands dangled at his knees. Something yellow had dribbled down the side of his face, as if he had mis-aimed the bottle and squirted himself with rotten mustard.

Bart drove the Jon boat onto shore, lifting the Johnson expertly before it could bottom out. He looked up at Norman, who was staring across the pond.

"What the fuck happened to your eye?" Bart asked with alarm, his grin fading.

Norman shuffled around to face him. The sun was a blinding halo behind his head. Now he looked like a dark autumn scarecrow hanging from a nail, weary and drooped from the summer.

"Norman?"

Bart got out of the boat, stepping over the fish and the cooler. He stepped into the mud at the bank, careful with his beer, and dragged the boat a few feet inland. The bass decided it had rested long enough and began to flop.

When he turned Norman was shuffling around again. His boots slurped in the mud. His arms were coming up like a sleepwalker's.

"What's with you?" Bart asked, stepping closer, squinting. As far as last words go, these were not about to win Bart any county records. Norman lunged forward and hooked his fingers into Bart's neck. Cold raspy thumbs crushed his windpipe shut. Bart dropped his beer. White foam coughed out, sparkling and hissing on the mud and sloshing across Norman's green rubber boots. Bart's hands shot up and seized Norman's skinny forearms, but by then Norman had lifted him a foot off the ground.

Bart's eyeballs bulged. The portion of his face visible above his beard flushed a fabulous purple. His expression was that of a man undergoing major surgery without benefit of anaesthetic. He jiggled and flopped, not unlike the bass that was dying in his boat. One swinging foot hit Norman squarely in the crotch, but Bart was not aware of it, which was okay, since it didn't matter anyway. Norman's sex life (which consisted of a subscription to *Cavalier* and weekly chokings of his aged chicken) had died the night before, along with Norman.

Bart expired three minutes later with his eyes open. So did the fish.

Norman dropped him and staggered off into the woods, headed, roughly, in the direction of Wabash Heights and, possibly, Bangor, Maine.

· 12 ·

Talking Turkey

JACK CUMBERLAND WAS waiting at the Wabash Tavern while the clock ticked on toward five, sitting at the bar with his chin in his cupped hands and his ass on the squeaking round bar stool, doing absolutely nothing but killing that old enemy of the unemployed, time. The Budweiser clock with its plastic Clydesdales tromping off toward nowhere reminded him of just how dismally slow time can pass when you are hungry and thirsty and out of money; it was made doubly excruciating because he did not know if this Weasel Whipple character would show up wanting to talk turkey or engage in some more fisticuffs. Hell, the dude might come in with a pack of his buddies, all toting ax handles. He might even come in with a gun.

Jack had spent the day in the Wabash Heights city park after the noisy meeting with Whipple, sitting unhappily on the soggy remains of a park bench watching the weeds grow, checking his watch again and again. His stomach had been a mournful knot in his belly that felt like it had been washed in kerosene, tumble dried in a furnace, and hung up in a shooting gallery. The taste in his mouth was like warm chrome. Usually in lean times like this he would buy himself a pack of Marlboro reds and smoke his hunger away, though he was not a smoker by habit, but right now the times were so damned lean that he'd had to forgo even that miserable pleasure. After an hour or two, when the bars of shade cast by the swing set were at their shortest, he had pulled a handful of weeds out of the damp ground, plucked their leaves and thistles, and tried chewing them. As a result, his teeth, which had not encountered a brush in weeks, were now flecked with bits of green, as if he had

161

gargled a handful of chopped chives. And from sitting in the sun all day, his scalp had turned an unlovely pink. In spots it was blistered, not from the sun but from his final duel with his wig.

Shortly before four he had gotten tired of doing nothing in the park, and decided to do it at the tavern, which at least offered shade. He had begged the bartender for a beer or a bottle, inventing the lie that he was new in town, employed at the mine, and wishing to establish credit, but the bartender had looked him over with a practiced eye and decided he was not worth the risk. What he got was a complimentary glass of water. It had nearly choked him. Liquor bottles gleamed on their shelves, rich and mellow, begging to be drunk. There was a giant jar of beer sausages sitting atop the long beer cooler, a plastic jar of Frito Lay jerky strips, some pickled eggs, some olives packed with pearl onions. Jack stared at them, drooling, then back to the bottles, drooling some more. There was even a cardboard placard stapled full of aspirin, Bufferin, Anacin, and Alka-Seltzer in little paper sleeves propped within hand's reach, which could end the crushing headache Jack was enduring and lessen the pain in his left wrist, which had now puffed itself to the size of a bicep. When the bartender asked him if he'd like another glass of water, Jack told him to shove it where the sun never shined. For this the TV got turned off, but it was showing "Jeopardy" anyway and Jack could accept the punishment.

Five o'clock came and drifted away. No Whipple. The bar, which had been deserted, began to fill up, to Jack's annoyance. Everyone was in high spirits, whooping and shouting, unaware and not about to care what Jack Cumberland was feeling like, which was pure shit. Money flew. Beer bottles clinked. Liquor gurgled over ice. The TV came back on, now presenting the weather, which predicted another load of rain tonight, sorry about that, folks. The jukebox clanked alive and blasted out country music. Jack moved to the farthest end of the bar, near the pinball machine and pool table, both of which sported signs saying they were out of order. Perched in the far corner, by the restroom door, was a battered vending machine that offered assorted chips and candy bars, and Jack's hand went into his pocket for the tenth time to rummage for change that was not there.

Five-fifteen came and went. Jack's despair rose around him

like foul water, threatening to drown him. The fucker Whipple wasn't going to show up. It was getting pretty obvious. The door kept banging open, grinning fools kept coming in blinking and staring in the semidark, but none of the fools were Whipple. Jack reviewed his options as they currently stood, and found that they stunk. He would have to go back to Whipple's house, this time not to politely interrogate the lady of the house, but to face the savage madman she was married to. There would probably be another fight, and Jack was feeling too weak and unsteady to face that particular boogeyman again.

He decided to wait until six. Maybe Whipple got hung up on the job. He watched without interest as a skinny man in some kind of uniform ambled past, opened the vending machine, and began to inventory its contents, jotting things on a pad. With greater interest Jack watched him go back outside, leaving the machine door wide open. Racks of chips sat exposed in colorful symmetry—Fritos, Doritos, Indian Corn Chips, Cheetos, even pretzels and popcorn. His stomach cramped at the thought of something salty and solid. He waited, staring at the vending machine, mesmerized, his jaws aching. The damn thing was sitting right beside the pisser door. Someone could just walk right past, snap out a hand, and borrow an item or two. Jack had been quick enough to ward off an attack with a hammer. Shouldn't he be quick enough for this?

He took a quick inventory of his own, studying people. They were all engaged in boisterous talk. The bartender was rushing around handing out drinks. The guy in uniform was out getting supplies from a van Jack could clearly see through the small window set in the door.

He slid off his stool, eyes darting, suddenly a portrait of criminal intent. He did not have to piss, though his face could stand washing. He started for the rest room when somebody breezed past, pushing him aside. Growling, Jack sat back down and waited. His wrist, which he assumed was either broken or brutally sprained, yammered pain at him in speedy pulse beats. After a minute the man came out, zipping up, chuckling to himself at some inner joke, and dove back into the crowd.

Jack hurried to the rest room before some other joker's bladder could sound the gong. He pulled the door open, glancing back, then over at the food. He thought he could smell it, and it was a sweet smell indeed. He snaked a hand out and pinched two bags of Doritos Cool Ranch together. They popped out of the wire spiral as easy as you please.

"Hey!" somebody shouted.

Jack's heart dived into his shoes. The skinny man in uniform was at the far side of the bar with a cardboard box parked on his shoulder, elbowing people aside with his free arm like a man fighting his way through a thick Indiana cornfield. He was staring at Jack.

"You there!"

Jack looked stupidly over to his own hand, where the two purloined items hung looking blue and white and accusing. State's exhibit A, your Honor: two fifty-cent bags of Doritos, stolen out of an unsecured Rowe vending machine by the defendant in a most vile and heinous way, a crime witnessed by over thirty persons. We recommend the maximum sentence allowable under Indiana law, and that sentence is . . .

Silence. The jukebox shut down as if on command. The television faded to black as some desperate WTWO technician tried to figure out which switch he had hit with his elbow. The crowd turned its collective face toward the back of the bar and Jack. Quiet had descended like a black sheet.

"Fucking thief!" the skinny man bellowed, breaking through, nearly falling and spilling his box of various goodies across the buckled wooden floor. "Get your paws out of that machine!"

Jack withdrew his paw. Miraculously the chips came with it, as if some survival instinct was in command of his fingers and would not let go of today's Minimum Daily Requirement. He held the bags out, tweezed between two fingers, and made motions as if to give them back.

The man, who according to the name tag on his uniform went by the name of Jed Heathrow, snatched the bags away, his face a caricature of a snarling bull terrier. Jack realized he had done the unforgivable: he had fucked with somebody's job. If the vending machine didn't match inventory, this skinny, wasted-looking chap might get fired. And if there was one thing held in high esteem in this corny town, it was a man's job. Woe to the unemployed; they might as well nail their balls to a stump and jump off.

"Look here," Jack said, "I'm sorry. I slipped on the wet floor and my hand fell into your machine. I believe I even sprained it."

Jed Heathrow regarded his puffed wrist. "It was your other

hand, stranger, and the floor ain't all that wet.'' He snatched the chips away and dropped them into the box.

"Simple mistake," Jack said.

Jed looked at him, his sunken eyes gleaming with fury. "Who you trying to fuck with, Bozo? This is my last stop, and you want to go and fuck me up."

Jack flinched with surprise. He could kill this ninety-eight-pound weakling with a single stroke. But he realized the crowd was pressing closer, all eyes beady with eagerness, and each set of eyes represented someone this skinny jerkoff knew. Mr. Vending Machine had probably grown up with these hillbillies, gone to school with them the required eight years, landed himself the enviable job of stuffing junk food into metal coin thieves, and considered himself one of the town's leading citizens. Might even be, for all Jack knew.

"Knock his block off," someone goaded, and the rest grunted approval.

"Waste him, Jed. Nobody knows who he is anyway."

"I'd kill the dumbfuck if he touched my potato chips."

"I'll drink to that."

Incredibly, they all tipped their drinks in unison, like performers in a well-rehearsed stage show. Their eyes seemed to shine like a horde of alley cats' eyes in the dark. They armed beer off their lips and beards.

Jed put his box on the floor, squatting slowly, his eyes never leaving Jack's. The television flashed to life, but the bartender had turned the sound off to watch a better show.

Jed stepped forward. His fist shot out. Jack blocked it without thinking, catching it in his bad hand. Pain bolted up his arm from his wrist in a searing flash, igniting the short fuse that led to Jack's anger control center. Rage broke like an acid bubble in his brain. He was out of money and he was starving. His liver was screaming for alcohol. He had not slept for nights uncounted, and Weasel Whipple was not a man of his word. That, and this ratpack was out for his skin for the crime of filching two handfuls of chips.

He hit Jed Heathrow in the mouth, able to feel his skinny lips splay against his teeth as they split neatly open. Suddenly blood was streaming down Jed's chin. He staggered backward and fell across the pool table, kicking and screeching, his over-large brown pants flapping against his shins.

Jack looked from man to man, his own lips drawn up in an unhappy snarl. ''Who's dumb enough to be next?'' he shouted.

They all volunteered. A human tidal wave moved toward Jack, tromping the box of precious goodies and really spoiling Jed's inventory. Jack backed against the rest room door, assessing his chances and finding them remarkably dismal. With karate he could pretty much handle four at once, but thirty? Even Bruce Lee would opt for a machine gun at this point.

He pushed back into the door and scuttled into the rest room, where the stench of fresh piss mingled with the stench of old. He slammed the door shut and leaned against it, propping one foot against the toilet, making a wedge out of himself. Bodies leaned against the door, making it amazingly heavy. Jack strained and groaned. It was getting noisy outside as the mob spirit took over. Someone thunked a beer bottle against the door, rapping it three times before it shattered. The toilet gave against its mushy moorings a bit. Jack crushed his shoulder into the door with new vigor, wondering just how long he could keep this up, estimating he had about thirty seconds before the door came open or the toilet broke completely free.

He was off by ten on the short side. The door moved inexorably open. Hands reached in and scrabbled at his face, seeking purchase in his hair but finding no hair to purchase. He bit at the big dirty fingers poking him. Someone yelped curses, more hands came in, then arms, then a shoulder.

Jack jumped back. The door fell completely open and six men tumbled in. Jack climbed this writhing mountain of humanity, seeing his opening, but the opening was quickly blocked by waving fists. He got punched in the nose and fell backward off the mountain, which was getting to its feet.

And then hands were having at him, were all over him, big hairy hands smelling of cigarette smoke and spilled beer. He snapped his eyes shut and covered his face with his arms, a tactic in karate known as giving up. Feet kicked his shins and stomped his toes. Fists rained like hail. Someone grabbed his left hand and wrenched it round and round, cackling gleefully at the funny grinding noise it made. Jack whooped and screamed, trying to move away but colliding with bodies and walls. He felt himself being lifted. His screams took on a sudden echoing quality, as if a pail had been put over his head.

He realized he was upside-down. He opened his eyes and saw a world gone white. He accepted without enthusiasm the fact that he was being stuck head-first into the rest room's lone toilet. Hands were clamped around his legs like iron bands.

"Heave-ho!" someone shouted.

Jack had time to take a snatch of breath before he was dunked. He was rammed vigorously up and down, in the water, out of the water. It went on and on, a small eternity for Jack Cumberland, the Human Plunger. He was remotely aware that the hands were leaving his legs one by one, aware that it had grown quiet on the upstroke. The last set of hands left his ankles and his knees crashed to the floor, the rim of the toilet butting him across the stomach. He jerked his head out of the foamy water, gasping and blowing. A big hand slapped down on his back just below his neck, got a fistful of his soggy shirt, and hoisted him to his feet.

He swiveled to his head and was looking into the sneering, grease-smudged face of Weasel Whipple.

"Guess I got here just in time," he said. "Man, but do you make friends fast."

Jack pulled away, adjusting himself. He saw that the doorway was still crammed full of men, and recoiled.

Weasel eyed them with a hatred that made Jack's heart falter. "I told you fuckers to beat it," he growled. "This guy's with me."

They turned away, the mob breaking apart like a pile of leaves under a persistent wind. They went back to the bar and their tables, muttering things. Weasel leaned out the door. "Mike! Throw me a bar towel!"

Distantly: "I don't want no piss all over my towels."

"Just throw me one, goddammit!"

One was thrown. Weasel snatched it out of the air and threw it in Jack's face. "Payday," he grunted. "The banks stay open till six, but you gotta stand in line." He watched Jack dry off. "You'll never know how much I liked what I just seen, big shot. And it's gonna happen all over again if you're playing me for a fool."

Jack sopped the foam off his shirt, then dried his hands. "It's no joke, Whipple. This is serious business."

Weasel took a noisy breath through his mouth. "We'll see about that. Come on, let's get a drink. I can't talk without a beer in my hand."

"Wait." Jack dropped the towel on the floor, glad to be rid

of it. "This is very private stuff. There's too many people here."

Weasel eyed him with weary contempt. "Nothing in this town is private. By tomorrow morning everybody and their grandma'll be talking about your trip down the plumbing. They'll be laughing at you behind your back. Come on, I'll protect your ass."

He went out. Jack followed, crunching over brown shards of glass, wanting desperately not to be here anymore. The men in the bar watched him slink through their midst as Weasel heaved people aside to make way, snickering into their hands or brazenly baring their teeth at him. Jack felt like the poor humiliated simp in high school who invariably got de-pantsed during P.E. or had his jockstrap run up the flagpole. He had been as effectively neutered as if they had jerked down his pants and snipped his balls off with wire cutters. He decided that when the forty million was his, he would buy this town and have it bulldozed to the ground, the remains sown with salt. Still some evil fog would hang over the area, though, the crazy swamp gas that turned everyone here into a moron. Perchance the place would have to be nuked.

Weasel came to his favorite bar stool, which was occupied. Weasel leaned down and barked something in the man's ear. He got up fast and found himself a table. Weasel sat down. Jack stood behind him, feeling more and more like a kid, which wasn't fair, because he could kick any man's ass here, including Weasel's.

Weasel turned in his stool. "Sit yourself down." He indicated the stool to his left, where someone sat hunched over a bottle of beer. With a sigh, Jack prodded the man on the shoulder. The man turned. Jack felt his DNA twitch; somehow he had fucked up again.

It was Jed Heathrow. The blood was just starting to dry on his chin. Their eyes met and locked.

Everything got quiet again. Jack felt himself slipping sideways through time, entering the land of déjà-vu. This meeting had happened before.

"What?" Jed snapped. His split lips were swollen and going purple.

"Could I borrow your seat?"

"You thieving cocksucker," Jed hissed, eyes blazing. Tough-acting little bastard, Jack had to admit. But it was easy to act tough when you had thirty guys on your team, which Jed still did. People were already starting to get to their feet. Jed hopped off his stool and put his little fists up. The appetizing scent of beer blew out with his breath. "Try that fancy karate trick again, mister. Just try it."

Jack backed off, but the mob was forming again, leaves magically turning themselves into a pile. He swallowed and heard an audible click in his throat, like a revolver being cocked in preparation for another shoot-out at the Not-so-OK Corral.

Jed swung, but this time it was Weasel's hand that snapped out and caught his fist. He crunched it counterclockwise and Jed dropped immediately to his knees.

Weasel stood up. "You fuckers back off, or I tear the runt's hand off. Me and my bald pal here, we got business to discuss. He's gonna make me a millionaire." He grinned at his townsmen.

Heads swiveled in the crowd. Uneasy laughter broke out. *No,* Jack thought, *no, no, no. This is private, you dumbass.*

Weasel let Jed go, simultaneously handing him his beer. Jed scurried away, red-faced, talking to himself in wounded and indignant tones. He sat down at a table by the jukebox.

"So," Jack said, sitting down beside Weasel. He took a breath, feeling nauseous and faint, and waited for the hum of conversation to build to the point where it might mask his words. "Now the whole town knows."

"The town doesn't know shit. Mike!"

Mike Taraday, busy at the other end, waved a hand that said hold on a sec.

"We need to find Arnold," Jack said, pressing his face as close to Weasel's ear as he dared. The man had monstrous BO. "He has information."

Weasel put a hand over Jack's face and pushed him away. "Ease up, baldy. You smell like you got crotch rot. Mike!"

Mike waved.

"Listen," Jack said in a half-whisper. "We have got to find that boy."

"And I have got to find a beer. Mike!"

Jack sat and simmered, his hands clenched into fists on the edge of the bar. Years and years he had waited, and this baboon was making him wait some more. He ground his teeth until the fabled Mike came over.

"Look, Weasel," Mike said, folding his arms, "your tab's higher'n the moon. No pay, no drink. Old man Liddey read me the riot act this morning."

"Fuck you, and fuck Liddey," Weasel snapped. He aimed a thumb at Jack. "Baldy here's picking up the tab tonight. Right, fearless furless?"

Jack made a variety of helpless faces. Mike laughed. "Your buddy is stone cold broke, Wease. He's been drinking water since four."

Weasel looked at Jack with narrow eyes, a pretty fair Clint Eastwood imitation. "You mean to tell me," he said, "that you're gonna make me rich, but you happen to be broke? How dumb do you think I am?"

Pretty dumb, Jack thought, but shoved it back inside himself and dug through his luggage of lies, looking for something that might fit, yet be subdued and in good taste. All he dredged up was a toothful smile.

"Ah, fuck," Weasel growled, and dug out his wallet. He produced a twenty and a five, and shoved them across the bar to Mike. "Put twenty on my tab, and use the fiver for a City. Good enough?"

Mike scooped it up. "Better than getting shit on, I guess. You want to buy your buddy here a beer? He looks like he needs one."

Weasel snorted and shoved his wallet back in his pocket. "Give me two seconds, and I'll answer that." He turned to Jack. "Convince me, Cue Ball."

Jack tried to wet his lips, pondering, but his mouth had gone as dry as ashes from the almost second encounter with Jed Heathrow and his pals. He needed a beer the way your average drowning man needs air; his whole body was shrieking for it. He cupped his hands around his mouth (his left wrist was mercifully numb now) and leaned sideways to whisper.

"What say?" Weasel asked, frowning.

Jack whispered again.

Weasel jerked away, his face drawn up in an almost comical mask of disbelief. "Buried treasure?" he nearly screamed.

Jack's head shrank down between his hunched shoulders. He saw heads turn, Jed Heathrow's among them. The noise level had dropped a good twenty decibels.

Weasel slammed a fist down on the bar, causing ashtrays to jangle. "*One* Falls City, Mike. Keep 'em coming."

"Want a jar of olives?" Mike asked sweetly.

"Up your ass, fuckface. One beer."

Mike went away, grinning. Jack's heart plummeted into his

shoes again. Death from exposure to sobriety was imminent, but it would be preluded by another nasty fight, this one with his new business associate. Lord, but this was a mean town full of mean people. He dropped his head wearily into his hands, waiting for what had to come. He could hear Weasel breathing hard through his nose. He was drumming his fingers slowly on the bar, tapping out a countdown.

The fingers stopped. So did the breathing. Jack started to slide off the stool, his elbows scraping across the bar, too tired and sick to raise his head.

"What kind of buried treasure?" Weasel asked casually, lighting a cigarette.

Jack looked up. "Sarcophagus," he muttered.

"I told you I don't speak French, skinhead. Lay it out in plain American."

"Egyptian mummy coffin. Solid gold."

"Solid gold!"

Help me, Jesus, Jack thought, wanting to bang his head down on the bar until consciousness fled. Instead he nodded, aware that a dozen people were craning around to look at him.

"What's it worth?"

"Couple million."

"A couple fucking million? Dollars?"

"Please don't scream," Jack begged. "In the name of God, don't scream."

"Hangover, huh? Tell me about it. Where's this solid gold at?"

"Nobody knows. Except Arnold, your kid."

"He's not my kid. How come he knows?"

"Somebody told him in the hospital."

Weasel hammered the bar again. "Sure! Yeah! That's why you were there! That's why you tried to kidnap him! Now I get it!"

I'll bet you do, Jack thought miserably. *I'll bet you just fucking do, along with everybody else here.* "We need to find Arnie, and fast. He may be headed out of state."

Weasel laughed. "The little shit's home, probably with his nose stuck in a book."

Mike came over with a beer and change. Weasel scooted a dollar back to him. "Liquidate my friend here, Mikey boy. He's parched."

Mike shrugged and trotted off. Jack felt a great surge of relief. For a crazy instant he almost wept; for a beer, he was willing to spill his guts in front of thirty strangers. For a ter-

rifying moment he feared he might be an alcoholic, but the
knowledge that he would be able to quit as soon as this nightmare was over squelched it.

"We drink our beers, then we go roust the kid," Weasel
said. "I'll squeeze the truth out of the little bastard. That is,
if there's any truth to squeeze. Like I said, if you're jerking
me around, you're dead meat. Plus you owe me ninety cents."

Jack nodded, staring at the bartender named Mike as he
dredged a Falls City out of the big aluminum cooler, hypno-
tized by the simple ritual of popping the cap on the long-neck
bottle. He watched it come toward him as if experiencing a
pleasant dream. Presently it was sitting in front of him, paid
for, brown as a mule's ear, a haze of moisture building on its
sides, and his hand reached out and took it. Then it was at his
lips, and in his haste to swallow it all at once a stream ran
down his chin and dripped on the bar.

"Ready?" Weasel asked, pushing away. His beer was already gone, though Jack had not seen him drink it. Inhaler,
this guy.

Jack shook his head, back to reality now, waving a hand that
indicated he could not quite speak yet. His stomach was opening like a flower, but his esophagus had become a frozen pipe.
He pounded his chest with a fist, and the ice melted. "Wait.
Arnie's not at home."

"Bullshit."

"I checked. Your old lady sent him away."

Weasel looked genuinely perplexed. "What the fuck for?
When?"

"Last night, after she beaned you with a skillet."

Weasel's hand snapped up. He felt the goose eggs on his
head. "She did this to me? That puny cunt?"

That puny cunt, Jack thought, *is better than you've ever
deserved.* "She certainly did. You were pounding on Arnie
again."

"Zat so?" Weasel smiled a dark and ugly smile. "Wish I
could remember that." He began slapping his right fist into
his open left palm. "Wait till I get home. I'll mutilate the
bitch. She'll bleed a little, and then she'll tell me where
the brat went."

"She doesn't know," Jack said. "I already talked to her." He
did not feel comfortable with the thought that he had sicced the
mad dog on the poor lady, but then, life was tough in general,

and everybody had their problems. Right now, more than anything else, he was concerned about getting his hands on one of the liquor bottles sitting on the shelves above the cooler.

Weasel glared at him. "What are you, a detective or something? Who told you you could talk to my old lady?"

"Take it easy," Jack said, seeing the storm clouds brewing on the greasy expanse of Weasel's brow. "I've been chasing this matter most of my life, and I've found that a little honey works better than vinegar sometimes. I told her I was a friend of Arnie's, and she really doesn't know where he is. She sent him to some kid named Joey's house last night, but he never got there. Even the cops don't know where he's at."

"Cops? Why should they give a shit?"

"Ah." Jack smiled, feeling the upper hand shift to him at last. "It's quite a tale, but I do talk better with a beer in my hand. Give me a bottle of good hooch, and I just can't shut up."

"Mmm." Weasel mulled it over. He got his wallet out and found another twenty. "Remember," he said, flapping Andrew Jackson in front of Jack's face, "you jerk me around, you die. Anybody ever tell you your head looks like a bowling ball without the holes?"

"Many times," Jack replied evenly.

"Well, it'll have some holes if this is all a pile of shit. Mike!" Mike found the time to come over.

"Bottle of Ten High for piss-breath here. Get me one too."

Mike winked at Jack. "Going treasure hunting, are we? It's going to rain tonight, boys. Better wear your rubbers."

Weasel grabbed for the front of his shirt, but missed. "I'll wear my rubber after you pull it out of your ass, barkeep. Just get us two bottles, and keep your mouth shut."

Mike grinned, safe behind the bar. "Two bottles of everybody's favorite, and a jar of olives. With onions, natch."

Weasel lunged again, but Mike was already walking away. "Faggot," Weasel grunted, and sat back down. He turned to Jack. "Okay, Mr. Clean, you've got your bottle. What's this about cops?"

"Well," Jack said, "it seems Arnold killed a man last night."

Weasel's jaw fell open. In the black recesses of his eyes Jack could see mental gears trying to mesh with this new and ill-fitting bit of information. Then he laughed. "You're fucked in the head. That little shit couldn't pull a cat's tail."

"Think so, huh? Then why are the state cops after him?"

"Says who?"

"Ever heard of Roy Mallone?"

"Roly-Poly? He's no state cop."

"No, but he radioed them this morning. I was there when they came to examine the body. Truth is, the man who Arnie killed was my father. He was stabbed."

Weasel examined this news with a look of stupid befuddlement, looking to Jack like a man in the last stages of Alzheimer's Disease asked to recall his own name: his bushy eyebrows were drawn together in a single furry line, his eyes were glassy and somewhat crossed, and he was sucking his teeth as if they had developed a new and interesting flavor. Suddenly he stood up on the lower chrome rung of his stool and began waving his arms.

No no no, Jack thought. *No more announcements.*

"Hey," Weasel barked. "Anybody here heard about one of my rugrats killing somebody? Skinhead here claims Arnold killed his daddy."

There was a general shaking of heads. Weasel plopped back down, no longer befuddled, his teeth bared.

"Your luck just ran out, Chrome-Dome. I'm going to go show the old lady which side of the skillet is which, and then I'm coming back for a chunk of your ass. You had me going for a minute, and I'll admit it was more interesting than sitting here watching the boob tube, so I'm giving you the chance to clear out before I really lose my temper."

He crushed his cigarette into an ashtray, put the twenty back in his wallet, and stood up.

Jack grabbed his arm. "Wait. I can prove it. Come with me out to the trailer park, and I'll show you. There's blood everywhere. The cops have probably roped the place off. Or we could go to the police station and talk to the fat man."

Weasel jerked free, opening his mouth to say things Jack felt sure would be less than complimentary, but Mike the bartender strode up just then and thumped two bottles of Ten High onto the bar. "I heard about the murder," he said, and aimed his eyes at Jack. "Your name Cumberland?"

"It is," Jack said.

"Can't remember the first name of the old fart who bought the farm, but I remember the last. Cumberland. TV said some Wabash Heights kid had been identified as the killer. The state boys are out hunting for him." He looked at Weasel. "Look, like your boy is taking after his new daddy, Wease. Didn't you knife a man in Terre Haute a couple years ago? In the back?"

Weasel ignored him. "Your name's Cumberland?" he asked Jack. "Your old man really got killed?"

"That's what I've been trying to tell you."

"And Arnold did it? How do they know that?"

Jack put on a smile that was a mixture of bereavement and strange triumph. "I saw him with these two eyes, my friend."

Weasel sat down. He looked perplexed and oddly proud, like a father whose fat, wimpy son has just slammed a home run into the Little League bleachers. Dreamily, he hauled out his wallet and paid for the whiskey.

"Two million in solid gold, huh? And Arnold knows where it's at?"

"That's the gist of it."

"And all we have to do is find him?"

"Simple as that."

"And we split it fifty-fifty? A million apiece?"

"Cross my heart and hope to fart."

Weasel unscrewed the cap off his whiskey. His hands were trembling visibly. Jack watched with utter fascination as he slurped down a quarter of the bottle. Jack did likewise, blessing the gods of alcohol for smiling down upon him from their hidden places in the skies. But he was not very happy when Weasel climbed atop his bar stool and shouted for everyone's attention, which he quickly got.

"To all the fuckers of this shithole tavern who have laughed at me," he brayed, wobbling and lurching heavily on his precarious perch, "I have but one final word before becoming a millionaire." He slammed his bottle down beside Jack's elbow and straightened again. Jack saw him fumble with his belt, and closed his eyes. Private business? It was all very public now. Like Weasel had said, by tomorrow morning everybody and their grandma would be talking about this. Especially because, because . . .

Jack opened his eyes, hoping not to see what he knew he would see.

Weasel had dropped his pants and was mooning every face in sight.

· 13 ·

The Gleam of Gold

BY FIVE-THIRTY, roughly the same time Jack Cumberland was enduring utter humiliation in the Wabash Tavern's rest room, Arnold White was done digging. And it was a good thing too: his left hand had cracked open in five or more places, first smearing the shovel handle with blister water, then blood, making it greasy and hard to manage. The turkey pastrami sandwich he had eaten seven hours before had deserted his stomach, leaving behind a gnawing ulcerous pain, compliments of the pepper and his damaged stomach lining. His head thudded with sickening regularity, and his broken arm, which he had pressed into service when the ordeal of lifting the shovel single-handedly had become too great a burden to bear, felt infected and inflamed. He imagined gangrene crawling through his flesh there like some loathsome green mold, and fancied at times that he could smell it, the cold, carrion scent of decay emanating from the tubular ends of the cast. But it was just the garbage, Norman Parker's fly-infested bequeathment to the world he had departed and re-entered so many times.

The hole had wound up being cruelly huge because of the powdery condition of the dirt. It was, when Arnold at last heaved the shovel aside and stood gasping on the crate he had fully exposed, some six feet wide and ten feet long, the sides sloping outward, the edges piled high with hillocks of dirt. He thought briefly of the books he had read about the first world war, where the soldiers of both sides had dug over fourteen hundred miles of trenches in which to fight and die. He could not imagine such a labor, yet his own great-grandfather had fought in the Great War and survived it, according to the tales

176

John Arnold White had told. What grandpa remembered the most, Dad had said, was all that damned digging.

But it was over now, the war and the digging. The crate and its phony words "machine parts" lay exposed to the light for the first time in over five decades. Victory had been achieved at great cost. The bottom end had been the hardest, the part where the crate pointed east. There the dirt had been hardpan, like thick fudge. It didn't take a genius to see that the shed's decrepit roof had been leaking over that spot for years uncountable. The crate itself was stained a dark, rotten brown there, the slats of the lid warped and hilly. It was on this side, where the soil was too damp to crumble, that Arnold crawled out of his hole now without fear that precious loads of dirt would tumble back down onto the crate.

He flopped face-down onto one of the mountains he had created, puffing dust out in lazy clouds. The heat in the shed had climbed around noon to a point Arnold assumed was suitable for baking cookies. He had abandoned his shirt some unknown time ago, used it for a sweat rag until it was drenched, and tossed it away. His eyes had become owl's eyes from so many hours in this semidark, and the thought that he had once needed a lantern for this work seemed preposterous. Yet he knew that night would be falling again in two or three hours, and his owl's eyes would become blind again. Time, unusually precious ever since this ordeal began, was at a premium now. He had to have the ruby eyes, cash them in, and be on the road before Norman Parker made it to Wabash Heights (or Bangor, or wherever zombies felt compelled to go when they were minus an eye).

He pushed himself up with dirt raining off his face like powder. He was able to get to his knees, where he remained for a tick of time, swaying, wishing the court dentist would make a quick appearance and knock out the remains of his thundering teeth. Ah, fantasies, wishes. His own father had wished for a once-upon-a-time escape from poverty and Wabash Heights, and gotten cold rejection slips for his years of labor. Arnold realized with a quick stroke of insight why his father had kept his mad ambition so secret: the people of Wabash Heights would have crucified him if they found out. He would have become an instant joke, the grocery store checker who thought he could write. The townspeople, smug and secure in their death-defying jobs as robotic factory workers or truck drivers or coal miners, would fear for their egos if John A. White actually made it. They would be unmasked as the hopeless fugitives from success they actually were. Therefore the enemy and his dream would have to be tromped underfoot, ridiculed, exposed, before he could do the damage he unwittingly and so innocently sought.

Ancient history, Arnold thought, trying to dismiss it from his mind. As ancient as the war where the trenches were dug by the believers of victory, but where, in the end, someone had to lose and someone had to win. The winners went home to cheering crowds, the losers to glum ones, but when all was said and done the dead were still dead and the world still spun without caring. The survivors, Arnold had read, were known as the "Lost Generation." They had fought the war to the end, but left their souls behind.

Like Dad. Somewhere along the line, shell-shocked, out of hope, and terrified in a war started by his own ambition, he had called it quits. The war was over, the war was lost. The dead that littered the battlefield were not bodies but his stories and books, and instead of being buried they had been burned in a trash barrel.

You think too much, Arnold—know that? You have been on your knees for the better part of two seconds, and you have thought far too much. Get up and get busy.

Arnold got to his feet, favoring the left foot, the one loving Frank had crushed in the door of his car at the hospital parking lot so many ages ago. He tried to push away, for the moment, all thoughts of his dad and the wonderful historical metaphors that thinking about him produced. Too many history books, too many wonderings about his dad and the ghost he had become, that was the cause of this. Mental meanderings were becoming increasingly useless; perhaps Dad had peppered his books and stories with too many of them, and that was why his manuscripts stunk. Or, just perhaps, his manuscripts had not stunk until they were burned. Dad had not been a dumb man; he was deft with phrases, he delighted in language, he read more books than any man should have to.

Forget it! Start looking around!

He began to scour the shed for a crowbar, a length of pipe, a hammer to pry boards up with. That was then and this was now, to paraphrase a title from a movie, and Arnold had little time for the then of things. This was now, indeed it was, and now was growing short.

There was a pick hanging on the wall beneath the shelf where Arnold had found the lantern. He unhooked it from its nails, amazed and dismayed by the weight of the thing, and dragged it to the edge of the hole. He climbed down and pulled it in after him. Its previous owner had seen fit to leave it out in the rain more than a few times, like everything else around here, and the business end of it was pocked with rust. Arnold pecked tentatively at the springy wood of the crate, not wanting to smash through and perforate whatever was inside, but the slats were old and hard and the blunt end of the pick boinged against them without effect.

Arnold swung harder, lifting the pick about chest high. This time there was a gritty crunch, and he had to work to get the pick out of the hole he had created. He set the pick aside and went on his knees to look. He stuck his eye to the hole and stared inside.

Black.

He put his nose to it and sniffed. Nothing. At least nothing that could compete with the crusty smell of old dirt and garbage.

All right, then, we makes us a bigger hole, he thought, got up, and went at it, chipping pieces away like a careful sculptor. It got old quick—*gonna take all night this way,* his mind sang out—so he snugged the end of the pick into the opening and pried a whole slat up. Nails screeched, banshee screams in the quiet. Arnold set the pick aside again and wrestled the slat up until the nails at the end popped free with a final grumble. He tossed the board away, and it banged against the side of the shed before flipping down onto the garbage bags. The resident mouse, startled, let out a squeak.

Arnold looked at the long black stripe he had made in the crate. The old excitement came back, the exhilarating boy-on-wild-adventure enthusiasm. Here was gold, folks, the metal that drove men mad. He dropped to his knees with blood pulsing loudly in his ears. The moment of triumph.

The gold looked funny. The gold didn't look like gold at all. It looked more like old burlap bags. The smell drifting up was that of musty canvas, somebody's old tennis shoes. Memory came back to him then, old Atkinson gasping his last, believing Arnold to be an Arab and divulging his secret. *We snuck it*

past the port authority's noses in a crate marked machine parts.
What he had failed to mention was that they had wrapped it in
burlap first.

Arnold put a hand inside and got a fistful of burlap. He
pulled. The burlap, having rested so comfortably for fifty-seven
years, did not yield to this intrusion. The sarcophagus was
wrapped, Arnold realized, not just covered. The covering was
pinned under the weight of unguessable pounds of gold, probably wrapped in twine.

Groaning, he took the pick in his bleeding hand again and
began to pry the rest of the slats away.

A man named Spack Laird, grumpy from a hard day driving
a heister at the Anaconda steel mill in Terre Haute, tromped
wearily into the Wabash Tavern at 6:15, a dirty white hard hat
on his head, his pudgy face dark with diesel soot, and saw his
brother-in-law Jed Heathrow at a table by the jukebox. Behind
Spack walked Jimmy Hallis, a feeble young man who had recently amazed everyone in town by marrying Spack's little sister Agnes. Ten years ago Jed Heathrow had married Spack's
elder sister Gertrude, to the same kind of amazement. The
Lairds were a notoriously strange and ugly family, and the
century-old rumors of incest and inbreeding had never completely died out.

The two men elbowed their way to where Jed was sitting,
and joined him at the table. Spack eyed the jukebox hatefully
as he sat down, knowing that at any moment it would start
blasting noise. He opened his mouth to say something nasty
about it, but Jed shushed him by waving his hands, then pointed
to the bar. Spack turned, frowning. The bar was jammed, typical Friday evening stuff. He turned back, and noticed that Jed
had dry blood smeared all over his mouth. Curiosity overpow-
ered him. "What's up?" he whispered.

"Weasel," Jed whispered back, still pointing. "Him and
that bald asshole. Tried to punch me out. They've got a line
on some buried treasure."

Spack rolled his eyes. He'd spent ten hours going deaf in a
factory whose thundering machinery made more noise than
a screaming jet, and now he had to listen to fairy tales in a
tavern. Sometimes he wondered if everybody in this town
wasn't nuts. "Mike!" he called out. "Over here!"

Mike glanced up from whatever he was doing. His eyes found Spack's, and he cocked his head.

"Need a Bud," Spack shouted. "Nah, make it three."

Mike nodded. Spack focused his attention on the two idiots he was unfortunate enough to be related to, Jimmy and Jed, who were useful to him only as a boost for his considerable ego. They admired and respected him and his hardhat and his union wages. They even listened with real admiration to his endless tales of the wonderful world of heister driving. Village idiots, no doubt about it, but they did form the core of the Spack Laird fan club, which surely had, to Spack's strange way of thinking, branches worldwide.

But now they were staring not at Spack with the usual fawning humility he imagined, but at that big creep Weasel Whipple and some other dude with not much hair and a lot of blisters on his scalp. Spack glanced at Weasel and the bald guy, annoyed, and overheard Weasel say something about a million dollars apiece.

"What's going on?" Spack said to Jed. "Did some lucky fucker win the lottery over in Illinois again?" He assumed that this would turn the heads of his two in-laws, and start another heated discussion about whether Indiana ought to have its own lottery or not. He knew that both were against one, believing that somewhere in the Bible it was prohibited by God or Jesus or one of the other holy dudes. Spack enjoyed demolishing their puny arguments with his knowledge of economics, which he had supposedly learned in a match cover correspondence course. Amazingly, he claimed to have taken correspondence courses on every subject that ever came up while the beer flowed. He was aware, in the dimmest parts of his brain, that if he wasn't proving his superiority around these two, a funny feeling twisted his guts up and made him sweat. The Laird reputation was a heavy burden.

Jed leaned closer to him, ignoring the lottery issue. "Check this out, Spack. That bald guy's a detective of some kind. He knows where there's gold buried around here. Him and Weasel are striking a deal."

Spack lifted his hard hat and wiped his forehead with his arm. The jukebox was making tiny crackling noises, preparing, he knew, to blast out enough decibels of country music to rip his gray Anaconda overalls from his body. "Say what?" he asked, scooting his chair away from the dangerous, multicolored machine. He jerked two cigarettes out of the pack in his pocket, tore the filters free, and stuck them in his ears.

"Shhh," said Jimmy Hallis, the man who had married all three hundred pounds of Spack's sister Agnes. He pressed a dirty finger to his lips. "They said Weasel's kid Arnold knows where it's at."

"Where what's at?"

"The gold," Jimmy said, leaning close enough for Spack to see the deep, dirt-filled pores on his nose. Jimmy worked at McCauley's on the other end of town, running a drill press in the machine shop. Spack happened to know that the bathtub in the hovel Jimmy called his home over on Walnut Street had been plugged up for eight months, and in those eight months he had not touched a bar of soap. "Looks like it's finders keepers, Spack," he said.

Spack was about to snarl something malicious when Mike rushed over and set three Buds on the table. "Two-seventy, Spack."

Spack threw three dollars at him. His brothers-in-law ignored this generosity entirely, looking past him like kids engrossed in a good cartoon. Spack looked up at Mike. "Are these fuckers on drugs, Mikey?"

Mike shrugged, grinning. "Gold fever, I'd say. A lot of ears around here have gotten mighty big all of a sudden. It seems Weasel and his buddy have a track on a golden coffin."

"A what?"

"That's what I picked up. Mummy coffin, one of those King Tut jobs. The bald guy's spent his whole life looking for it. Could be close by, according to him. Could be in another state. Supposedly Weasel's stepkid Arnold knows where it's at."

Jimmy Hallis frowned, and turned to look up at him. "That don't make no sense, Mike. If he knows where the thing's at, why don't Weasel know? Or at least pound it out of the runt?"

"God," Spack blurted as Mike walked away without answering, "you guys are so dumb it's embarrassing. There ain't no mummies left anymore. King Tut was the last one, and they cut him up to see what mummies used to eat. Put his turds under a microscope, they did, and found petrified corn and some pollen. I wrote a report on it once in college. Mummy kings ate corn and flowers."

They stared at him blankly for a moment. Then their eyes and attention drifted back to the bar and the talk of gold. "You guys are fucked in the head,'' Spack growled, and sucked at his beer. The jukebox roared alive, too loud for anyone to actually understand what song it might be playing, sitting this close. Spack looked for a better table, saw an empty one across the hazy room, and was about to nudge Jed and Jimmy when four men trooped over and sat down at it. He mouthed curses at them. The tavern was becoming as full as a cattle chute on slaughter day. Spack slammed his beer down and shouted at Jimmy and Jed. ''Somebody ought to feed a grenade to that fucking noise box! I wanna tell you about what happened at work today!''

Jimmy nodded dreamily. Jed ignored him entirely, too busy stretching his neck toward Weasel and his preposterous business. His Bud was untouched. Spack picked it up and wagged it in front of his face. ''Hey! Earth to Jed. Come in, Jed.''

Jed blinked. His eyes found a new focus. ''What say?''

''You can't even hear what they're saying no more,'' Spack shouted in his face. He jabbed Jed's beer at him. ''Drink up. I wanna tell you what happened at work today. See, they hired this big colored dude and told me I had to show him the ropes, how to run his heister, which dock he loads at, all that stuff. One of those equal opportunity deals, this boy was—you know how *that* goes. Anyhow, I says to him, I says . . . Jed?''

Jed's attention had flagged. Greed had turned his head again. Spack knew he might as well have been talking to the howling jukebox. And Jimmy's jaw was hanging open, revealing a mouthful of blackened teeth as he stared at Weasel's back. His beer hadn't been touched, either. Spack put Jed's beer bottle down. A scary feeling was hatching inside him, that ugly old feeling that he got when no one was admiring him for his high-paying job, his new Ford truck with its white capper-top, his hard hat, or his nonexistent correspondence course education.

He knew he had to think fast. These brothers-by-marriage of his had a severe case of gold fever, just like Mike had diagnosed. He had to counteract the disease before his ego went totally flat.

Something popped into his mind with the force of a searing flash bulb. Was it good enough? Maybe.

''You want treasure?'' he said, so softly that it was almost to himself. ''A real live buried treasure?''

Jimmy aimed an ear toward him. ''What's that?'' he asked,

raising his eyebrows but still looking toward the bar. "What say?"

"Treasure," Spack said loudly. He leaned back in his chair and folded his hands atop the expanse of his belly.

Jimmy poked Jed in the side with his elbow. Jed let out a whoof and glanced at him crossly. Jimmy cocked his jaw toward Spack.

At last he had their attention. And to be perfectly honest he really *did* know where a treasure was buried. He had, in fact, seen it with his own two eyes when he was a child years ago. Yet he had, until now, not thought of it again.

"What treasure?" Jed asked. "Another mummy coffin?"

"Yeah," Jimmy said, his pimply face shining and greasy in the flashing colorful strobe of the damned jukebox. "You know about another treasure?"

Spack grinned at them, grateful to feel his fear dwindle away to nothing. "Does the date 1932 mean anything to you gents?" he asked them.

He leaned forward again, pleased by their mystified faces. They were so engrossed in what he had to say that when Weasel and his bald pal left, each with a bottle of whiskey in his hand, neither Jimmy nor Jed even noticed.

A few minutes later, the three of them left, too.

It took Arnold twenty minutes to free the top of the crate from its piecemeal lid. He threw the pick out of the hole with what had to be the last of his energy and stood on his prize with his breath running hotly in and out of his lungs. Sweat dripped off him, staining the burlap. Beneath his feet were strange lumps and irregularities; this was no ordinary flattop coffin. He dropped down to his knees and knocked on it. It was like thumping a slab of rock. Arnold grinned. Solid gold, baby, a coffin fit for a king. So what better way to send the king off to his eternal rest than with a handsome set of ruby eyes?

He crawled across the lid, feeling the odd lumps and curvatures beneath his hand. The whole thing had been secured with ten strands of thick twine, which Arnold had snapped with the pick. Still the burlap held, though, tucked securely underneath. With a knife he could have made short work of it, but there was no knife and his only object was the eyes, those marvelous glittering eyes that signaled money and gas and a trip to Texas.

He came to the end of the coffin . . .

. . . *it's a* sarcophagus, *Arnold old chap, no run-of-the-mill pine box, but a real* sarcophagus *from Egypt, the land of gold, Pharaohs, the Nile, Boris Karloff and Peter Lorre, the Mummy, the Return of the Mummy, the Mummy's Revenge, the Mummy's Bride, I was a Teenage Mummy* . . .

. . . *Knock off the bullshit, Arnold* . . .

. . . *the mummy shambling through the moonlight with one arm outstretched and one dead foot dragging, heavy-lidded eyes dull with hate, lips shriveled and gray and cracked, driven by ancient gods and incantations, somehow fueled by tea leaves and tannin, seeking his mindless revenge* . . .

. . . *KNOCK IT OFF, ARNOLD, YOU'RE STARTING TO SCARE YOURSELF* . . .

. . . *the Mummy's Hand, the Monkey's Paw, the Blob, Frankenstein, Dracula, Michael Landon in a high school gymnasium, Louis Creed in the Micmac burying ground* . . .

Arnold gripped his forehead with his bloody hand. Thank you, Hollywood, he thought, thank you, Bram Stoker, thank you, Mary Shelley, and all the people who have helped make this nightmare possible, but thank you most of all, Mr. King, for turning me, your average kid, into a frightened and babbling idiot.

He clawed at the area where the eyes had to be, shoving all imagined terrors from his mind. The sarcophagus of King Tut had toured the world and not once was a paying customer attacked and strangled by the good and kindly King.

The burlap came up in tiny twisted tufts, bits of curly fiber in Arnold's aching fingers. It was like trying to tear a sack of grain open without first finding a seam. He swung his casted arm down, got two handfuls of burlap, and jerked in a frenzy, eyes closed from the effort of it.

Riiiiiippp!

He fell over backward, knocking his head neatly against forty million dollars. He scrambled upright again, throwing aside two weightless swatches of burlap, and stared down at the holes he had made.

In the late evening sunlight, solid gold gleamed up at him, spotless and mellow, flashing in the light. The two holes almost seemed to be staring at him. *What took you so long, Arnold my chum? Here I have lain since 1932, and before that I rested for five centuries in a land you will never see, formed*

*by hands long since gone to dust. How do I look? Tarnished,
am I? Not on your life. I am eternal, unchanging, immortal.
Touch me, and know my power.*

Arnold touched it. It was cold. There seemed to be—seemed
to be, but maybe not—just the slightest hint of vibration beneath his fingertips. A hum, like a wire carrying a lethal but
protected dose of electricity. Arnold dismissed this, though,
because he was trembling with relief and a giddiness that felt
like approaching insanity. He stood up, breathing raggedly
through his mouth, not aware that his wounded teeth were filling his head with pain. Two evenings before he had been a
helpless rag doll under the swooping fists of Frank Whipple,
Master of Disaster. Now he was rich.

But the gold would belong to someone else soon. It was the
ruby eyes he was after, the rubies of his salvation, like Dorothy
in Oz who merely had to tap her ruby heels together three times
for the magic to occur.

He ripped the burlap away, exposing the golden face of the
nameless inhabitant of this memorial. The face was gigantic,
flawlessly molded, but it was not the face of a man staring up
at Arnold in the fading light. Arnold jerked back with new
horror blossoming in his brain like an ugly flower.

It was the face of a jackal, turned sideways to profile its long
tubular snout and sharp teeth. Its ears were long and pointy.
The lone eye was small and almond-shaped, and it most certainly was not a ruby.

Arnold tore the rest of the burlap away, working his way
down to the end, jittering near the edge of panic. Once again
he had relied on the insight of a thirteen year old, who saw a
sarcophagus as something embedded with jewels the way a
good Toll House cookie was embedded with chocolate chips,
and once again he was crushingly disappointed.

It was gold, all right. Top to bottom, it was gold. In huge
bas-relief, as if something inside had tried to push its way up
through the lid, was the form of a man, right down to the
sandaled feet, a man with that peculiar and creepy jackal's
head. He was wearing a short pleated skirt. There was a necklace around his neck and rings on his fingers, but the jewels
were molds of jewels, not real at all.

A treasure hunter would have fallen dead of a massive cor-
onary on the spot. A grizzled old prospector would have turned
cartwheels at the sight of all this gold. Arnold, on the other

hand, pressed his dirty, tired and aching arm across his eyes, and wept. All his hurts roared back at him—the broken bones, the teeth, the bruises, and the blisters. Junk, all of them, pieces of junk accumulated on this trash-strewn road called life, a road he had walked for only thirteen years, stumbling, falling, hurting. Trash and junk, scars and hurts. It had to be a Wabash Heights version of a stroll down the yellow brick road, only this road ended not at Oz, but inside the ruined shed of a dead man whose only legacy was trash and junk.

There were no rubies. Nothing but a golden lid that weighed far more than lead, and was just as useless to the boy who had worked so hard to discover it.

He let himself collapse against the wall of the hole it had taken sixteen hours to dig. He mashed his face into the dirt, shaking with despair, wishing he could eat a hole through the cool soil, tunnel through it like a mole, and live the rest of his life safe underground. Underground, where the dead rested in absolute peace, where worms crawled in damp blackness with no need to see the light. There was peace underground, safe haven, eternal rest.

The light was fading. Arnold breathed the gritty air, electric with hurt, knowing that at last he was drowsing toward sleep despite the thousand things trying to stab him awake. Part of his mind became unplugged, detaching him from the things that were too full of pain to bear, and he heard his father's voice, a distant and weary voice, and behind that, droning on and on, the sound of typewriter keys clacking uselessly against paper.

He came out of his drowse some minutes later—the light coming through the shed's window was not appreciably darker—because the mouse of the house had decided it was quiet enough at last to go snooping for a snack and had caused a beer can to clank. Arnold opened his eyes. They burned in their sockets like old coals, making him blink. A few seconds of sleep in forty-eight hours—welcome to treasure hunting in Indiana, Gentle Reader. He pushed himself back up on his knees and regarded the ageless jackal-man, frozen in gold. His mind dredged up a bit of Egyptology from a previously forgotten history lesson a few years ago, Mr. Bender's class, fifth grade. Mr. Bender had used a slide projector to show the pyramids and some of the ancient buildings that still stood. It was inter-

esting stuff. All the old temples had carved walls, every inch
covered with hieroglyphics and skirted men carved in weird
poses. Even the huge thick columns that supported the struc-
tures were etched with pictures. "This one," Mr. Bender had
said, making the slide projector click, "shows the royal name
of Toot-an-ka-mun. Notice that it is circled. The names of the
royal Pharaohs were always circled to show that they were both
rulers, and gods."

Click.

"Here we see the royal king Toot-an-ka-mun after his death.
Notice that his body is surrounded by priests. The sticks in
their hands are incense, thought to please the gods."

Click.

"Here is the highest priest of all, the royal embalmer, whose
task it was to preserve the body for its eternal voyage through
the afterlife. Notice he has the head of a jackal. This half-man,
half-jackal is common to all burial sites, and demonstrates a
belief that persisted for centuries that the jackal was a creature
of mystical powers. No evidence has been found, of course, to
prove that such a jackal-man ever existed."

A pause. A twitter of halfhearted laughter. When Mr. Bender
paused, it meant you'd better admire his humor.

Click.

"Here is the Great Pyramid, the last remaining wonder of
the seven wonders of the world. Notice that, mighty though it
is, time and weather have taken . . ."

Arnold clicked him off. *Whoop-dee-do,* he thought. *Pre-haps
I am standing on the sarcophagus of an actual jackal-man.
Pre-haps I can bring him back to life. Pre-haps I do not give
a shit.*

He was starting to climb out of the hole when a sudden
thought made him stop, consider, and slide back down.

The lid showed a jackal-man wearing a necklace and many
rings. Was this not supposed to be a representation of the actual inhabitant, one Egyptian jackal-man, name as yet unknown? Could not a determined boy pry the lid up and do a
little . . .

. . . *urk!* . . .

. . . grave-robbing? Peel the rings off those dead fingers, lift
the necklace over that head? A head that, to Arnold and any
passerby still possessed of his marbles, was not a jackal's head
at all but the shriveled, sunken-eyed mummification of a for-

mer high priest who had not plied his trade in five centuries. Options were at a premium here, and all had evaporated for the moment. Why not pry the damned lid up and perform a little heist on the corpse?

Arnold reached up and grabbed the pick before the scattered smidgens of fright building in his belly could assemble themselves into a good solid fear. Uncovering buried coffins was one thing, but opening them up and peering inside, well, that was gruesome. It was Frankenstein material.

He chipped away a portion of the side of the crate, which was made of heavier wood than the top and did not surrender easily. With his hands he scooped the dirt and wood shards aside and, by feeling down the side of the sarcophagus, found a lip of sorts. Sidling around, he got off the lid and squatted in the dirt of his overlarge hole. *Open sesame*, he thought, and tried to lift the lid with his fingertips wedged under the narrow lip.

It was a joke, requiring a pause and a twitter of laughter from the class. Here is Arnold trying to lift a two- or three-hundred-pound slab of gold with one hand, the myopic and bruised eighth wonder of the world. Not for his strength do we wonder at him, class, but for his stupidity. Arnold, go stand in the corner.

He stood up, slump-shouldered, dazed by his own inanity. Option number last had taken a quick hike. He got the pick and stuck one pointy end under the lip. He strained against the handle, but it was like pushing on a tree. Man, but those Egyptians had been fond of heavy things in the olden days. Pyramids, statues the size of the Eiffel Tower, engraved columns big enough to hide a bus behind. Where had they gotten so much energy?

He shoved the pick aside and sat cross-legged in the dirt, thinking of drills, hammers, chisels, dynamite. This whole adventure was starting to stink as bad as Normie's old garbage.

Normie. There was an idea. Normie had gained a lot of strength after his heart attack. Normie was a regular Arnold Schwarzenegger as a dead man. But unfortunately Normie was a real bear in his new role as a zombie, not one prone to following orders. Anyway, he had to be miles from here by now, and if Arnold did manage to find him and coax him into coming back, what guarantee was there he would be so kind as to lift this lid? More than likely he would throttle Arnold and gnaw on his bones.

Arnold put his elbow on his knee and dropped his head onto his hand. Here was a dilemma to puzzle Einstein. How does a thirteen-year-old kid lift a slab of gold as heavy as your average Volkswagen? There was almost nothing to grab onto from the outside. Maybe if he was inside and had a scissors jack he could raise the thing, but that left the pesky problem of how to get inside. Besides, this coffin was occupied. Atkinson had said so.

He'll do as you want.

Arnold raised his head, his thoughts suddenly speeding up. The answer had been in the back of his mind, perhaps from the beginning, biding its time, waiting to pop out and yell "Surprise!"

He grinned wide enough to make his stitched lips hurt.

"Okay," he said aloud, touching his tongue to his stitches, tasting briny blood. He bent over and shouted at the seam of the coffin hard enough to blow a puff of dust.

"Isis ki Osirus!"

Time ticked. Arnold waited, bent forward like an Indian awaiting his turn at the peace pipe, and in that silently ticking time he heard the sounds of nothing.

Soundproof coffin? Or nobody at home? He'll do as you want, sure, but what if he's not in the mood?

"Raise the lid," he shouted.

Nothing. Arnold drummed his fingers on his knee.

"Push on it!"

It seemed then that something crackled inside, the sound of a piece of paper being wadded up, but the mouse had squawked to life at Arnold's shout and was burrowing through things.

And then the lid moved. Slightly sideways, slightly up. Metal grated against metal. A long sliver of yellow light shafted out of the coffin, making Arnold's dirty knees shine.

His lungs suddenly needed more air than they could get. He scuttled backward, moving up the side of the hole, pushing waves of dirt that washed against the open rim of the coffin and spilled inside. Breathing out with the broadening slat of light was a smell that made Norman's garbage bags seem perfumed; it was the smell of dead wet leaves, bitter dust, and rotten meat. Particularly rotten meat, a stench like old chicken guts and potatoes gone to black mush.

The lid crept up. Arnold stared at the light, squinting, his face drawn up with muddled hope and terror. He could see an arm, then another. They bulged with layers of dirty gauze, some of which had split with age and were coming unraveled. The lid was a foot above the coffin now, tilted against its base.

Arnold made himself move back down, wanting to see the hands and the rings he imagined to be there, and the necklace, doubtless solid gold and peppered with rubies. The light was blinding. He stuck his head as close as he dared, breathing through his mouth against the stink.

The light was coming from the mummy's eyes, blazing like search lamps, nothing like Norman Parker and his feeble headlights. Arnold stared at the face of the mummy . . .

. . . mummy? Who's kidding who? That's not a mummy, it's a jackal, it's just like the carving on the lid, the god of embalming himself, we have here a jackal-man, the immortal god who dug the guts out of a hundred Pharaohs and pickled them in herbs . . .

Its head was not wrapped. The ears were furry and pointed. Its muzzle had dropped open some ages ago and its horrible canine teeth were yellow tusks. Nestled in its mouth was the dried brown slab of a tongue.

It turned its jackal head with a papery crunch and stared at Arnold. The lid wobbled. Arnold tore his eyes from that unbelievable animal face and saw that the jackal's right arm, quite a human arm, was crumbling. Chunks of gauze and dried meat were flaking off like pieces of old plaster from an ancient statue.

The mummy (jackal?) was disintegrating.

"Push the lid off!" Arnold squeaked through a throat that was as dry as the mummy's dirty linen.

The mummy's right arm had flaked off to a black stalk of bone. The lid dipped. There was a dry snap, old Egyptian bone breaking, and the lid crashed down, leaving an opening some three inches wide along the side. Yellow light beamed out of it.

"Open it!" Arnold screamed. "Open it!"

The lid wobbled. It threatened to slide back into place.

"Stop," Arnold said, seeing his chances vanish. The mummy was too weak. The mummy needed some work before it could function properly. Tea bags and tanning, Atkinson had said, and you can bet he knew what he was talking about.

"Be dead," Arnold groaned.

The light faded away. The open wedge between lid and coffin went black.

Arnold sat in miserable silence for a long time then.

· 14 ·

Driver's Ed

THE OLD ORD, crusty and rotting to pieces, started with the first turn of the key, as if the weird humming power of the sarcophagus was strong enough even to keep dead machinery running. The motor continued to run, after a fashion, chugging and popping like a tired tractor, jiggling Arnold on the ruined seat. He eased the clutch out with his aching foot, expecting motion of some sort, but the truck still sat in the weeds, bouncing and farting, the clutch's greaseless throw-out bearing howling metallically.

He fumbled with knobs, finding one that made the headlights pop on. In the half hour he had spent sitting in the hole with his dazed thoughts careening and colliding in his head, a new night had drowsed across the sky, blotting out the last of the day's light. Rain clouds, predicted by the somewhat apologetic WTWO weatherman hours before on the Wabash Tavern television, had slid in from the west in a dreary wave, building their anvil shapes and obscuring the night's stars. The air smelled heavy with approaching rain. It made little difference to Arnold, except that he had left his shirt in the shed and the temperature was falling into the sixties. His molars were chattering, but not from the cold.

He had never driven a car in his life. Sure, once in a while, when he was little, his dad would let him sit on his lap and steer, but back then, Dad was doing the footwork, and his car had been an automatic. This goofy ORD had three pedals sticking up from the floor, all of them wearing rubber pads that had been worn to the metal in spots. Arnold had enough sense to know what they were for, but to operate all three at once, plus steer this beast, plus *shift* in the process? It seemed like a task for an octopus.

And that gas gauge, that pesky gas gauge. Its faded orange needle stuck to the one-quarter mark as if glued there. Was it broken? Was this old tub running on fumes already?

Arnold mashed the clutch to the floor again, got the gearshift knob in his fingers, pulled it left, and pushed it up. Gears crunched tiredly into place, rattling his arm and making his broken bones sing. He gave gas. The motor roared out of control, blue steam clouds of exhaust blowing out of a pipe that had not been partnered with a muffler since 1967. Arnold let the clutch out. The ORD jumped, spurting clots of mud and weeds from the rear tires. Arnold was under way.

He was under way, in fact, toward Norman's front door. The scenery through the starry windshield was wild and bouncy, the headlights cutting crazy circles through the dark. He spun the way-too-big steering wheel hard to the right, not familiar with power steering but realizing that this tired bird did not have it. He managed to miss the house, and ran instead into a tree.

Everything got quiet pretty fast. The headlights faded to a dismal yellow. Leaf buds from the startled tree chattered down on the roof.

I don't think we want to do that again, Arnold thought. There was a fresh bump on his forehead where it had met the wheel. He got ORD going again, tried a variety of gears, and found one that would back him up. The tires spun out in the half-dried mud, but the truck crawled far enough away from the tree to get a fresh start.

This time he worked the steering wheel all the way to the right before starting out. He tried a gear and dumped the clutch. Mud flew in chunks. ORD rattled forward, its probing headlights finding the lane, and Arnold was pleased to be actually driving in a straight line. Without his glasses everything was green and brown fuzz, but 80-20 is not blindness and he kept to the road well enough. With the motor roaring and the speedometer showing a good fifteen miles per, he lumbered down the lane and came to US 40.

He put both feet down, one on the clutch, the other on the brake. Both mushed all the way to the floor. ORD bounced merrily along, threatening to carry him across the highway, the median strip, the westbound lane, and dump him into the woods beyond. He worked the gearshift like mad, decided it was not the thing to do, and pumped the brake. The master cylinder, familiar with this routine, pumped brake fluid to the wheels, and they squeaked to a stop.

Arnold breathed again. The nose of the truck was halfway across the southernmost strip of highway, the lane headed east, Arnold's intended direction. He cranked the monster steering wheel some more, found that good and familiar first gear, made the motor to blast, and peeled out in a fresh spray of mud. ORD lurched onto the asphalt, floor full of beer cans rattling, bits of grit from the ruined roof lining sifting down yellow dust. Arnold got the truck in the right-hand lane and headed for Wabash Heights at the breakneck speed of fifteen miles an hour.

Sitting in the hole while darkness fell, he and his tired brain had discovered yet another option. And that option was in town, right on Main Street, US 40, Maplewood Avenue, call it what you want.

Arnold White, runaway child, suspected murderer, boy on the run, bait for every cop in the state and treasure hunter in town, was about to add a new chapter to his career of crime.

He was about to become a thief.

Weasel and his new friend Jack were putting on a bad performance of I am a Bereaved Parent about that time.

Weasel had been unaware, until now, of just how little he knew of his stepson, where he went, what he did. His role in this charade was growing increasingly poor, first of all because he was not a bereaved parent, and second of all because he was beginning to think it was a stupid waste of time. Not to mention money. He had dumped about a quarter of his paycheck on beer and booze for his new partner Baldy and himself, not to mention the twenty on his tab at the tavern, that rotten stinkhole where forty-cent beer went for ninety and old man Liddey went to church three times a week in an obscure trailer house in Terre Haute, where inflamed evangelists of the Jehovah's Witness persuasion filled his mind with shit and emptied his wallet of money. As his wristwatch ticked on toward eight and he began to run out of places to knock on doors . . .

. . . *"My stepson Arnold White is missing, ma'am. Is he here?"* . . .

. . . *"Sorry, I'm afraid I don't know any Arnold White."*
. . . Weasel began to think that all of this was a stupid sham and Chrome-Dome the treasure hunter was a nut.

But a lot of what he said clicked. Arnold was wanted for murder. Mike Taraday had confirmed that. Baldy's father had been the victim. Mike had verified that too.

But how in the fuck did that tie in with a mummy's coffin?

He was waiting in his not-too-trusty Malibu at 1298 Forest Street, sucking on his bottle of Ten High and passing time while the Cue Ball asked the lady of the house (all the men in town had managed to escape to the tavern of their choice) if she had seen Arnold. Cue Ball was Uncle Jack. Weasel was Weasel. Thirty houses in a row without results, and both were getting tired of the hunt.

Jack stumped down the sidewalk, opened the door, and slumped into the Malibu. He reached for his bottle on the floor, unscrewed the cap, and drank. Weasel eyed him, Weasel a ghost-face against the lights from the dash, with black marbles for eyes.

"Lemme guess," he said. "Ain't seen Arnie in months."

Jack nodded. "Do you keep that kid tied up or something?"

"His fucking books keep him tied up. That dumb fuck has read everything from Winnie the Poop to Moby Dick. Maybe he's at the library. If they've got that new book from that famous horror fucker, you can bet on it."

Jack checked his own watch, a nice digital affair that glowed in the dark. "Probably closed. I think the kid's hitchhiking out of state."

Weasel drank again, disgusted. Right now he could be home pounding the old lady silly for bopping him with that skillet. But no, Skinhead wouldn't hear of it. "I talked to her and she don't know," he kept saying as the liquor worked on Weasel's mind and the hate that festered there grew hotter. "Besides, if you kill your wife you won't be in on the treasure."

Weasel capped his bottle and drove. The crumbling and hilly streets of Wabash Heights bounced under the shine of his lone headlight, brick streets humped into earthquake shapes, most of them, the rest gravel lanes full of watery, bottomless holes that could tear the underside off your car in a heartbeat. In his state of mild rage and approaching drunkenness, he did not notice that the headlights of several cars were bobbing in his rearview mirror, had, in fact, been dogging him all evening.

"Where now?" Jack asked.

"One more place. The old lady used to try and peddle Avon there. That was after her old man split. She needed the dough."

They drove right, left, right again. Weasel stopped the car. The cars behind him stopped at discreet distances.

"Your turn, Baldy."

"The name's Jack, you know, and it's not my turn."

"Fine, Jack-off, go pound on the door while I piss. Then we call it quits."

Weasel noticed that Jack was rubbing his head with his hands. He was beginning to think Jack had jumped the fence at the Katherine Hamilton mental health center in Terre Haute, and made his way to Wabash Heights, where most insane people tended to wind up. It was a puzzle that fit together pretty well. Crazy Kate's, as the locals called it, was the only funny farm in miles. So this house-to-house search for a kid who could be anywhere was insane, too.

Jack walked up to the house and made small talk with the woman who came to the door, while Weasel stood beside his car and unloaded his bladder. This street was Blakely Avenue, one of the ritzier neighborhoods. It was here that the bank clerks and bill collectors lived, as well as those lucky few who worked in Terre Haute at real jobs. That fat shit Spack Laird happened to live just up the street a bit, him and his fancy new truck, and Weasel aimed a squirt in the direction of his darkened house just for the hell of it. A bit farther was Harley Gimbel's house, he of the hateful stares and floozy wife, who had witnessed Weasel's battle with the onion and nearly laughed himself into apoplexy. Weasel squirted him too, still determined to someday ram his pecker up Harley's wife and give her a squirt or two of a different sort.

He was reassembling his pants when he noticed all the cars parked along the road behind him. They hadn't been there when he drove this way. He could see heads inside, and the flash of beer bottles being tipped.

"Dipshits," he muttered, and got back in his car. Half the town was on his tail, seemingly. Big deal. They were wasting gas and time.

Jack came back, looking sour. He dropped onto the passenger's seat and rubbed his head some more.

"Headache, Copper-top?"

"Yeah. You sure this is the last place Arnie might be?"

"Can't be sure of anything. Except that we're being followed."

"Huh?" Jack turned in his seat. He squinted through the rectangle of plastic that was taped there in lieu of a rear window. His face fell together in an expression of total defeat. "Fine," he groaned. "A posse."

"Just the usual assholes looking for an easy buck." Weasel started the car. "I'm headed back to the tavern. Want me to drop you off at Kate's?"

"Whose?"

"Nothing." Weasel drove. Lights flashed on behind him. In a way, it was gratifying. These worms had laughed themselves silly when he had an onion stuck up his nose. Now they were the dupes. It wasn't much of a payback, but it was a start.

"Let's hit the country roads," Jack said. "Roads Arnie's familiar with, the ones he'd stick to. We'll start at the trailer court. We could cover hundreds of miles by morning, and lose these assholes."

Weasel turned his head to give him a couple eyeballs full of contempt. "I hate to break this to you, furless, but I'm headed back to the tavern. You can shove your mummy coffin up your ass. My bottle's almost empty and I need a better buzz. Remember, I got business with the old lady tonight, and it's gonna be a special treat. Gonna cook her supper, I am, cook it in a big iron skillet."

Jack rubbed his head again. There was no headache there—in truth he was feeling quite human again, thanks to the Ten High and its amazing rejuvenating powers—but his head felt cool and naked without its protection of wig. What really hurt was the knowledge, growing over the last hour or so, that this Weasel character knew no more about Arnie than the man in the moon. Yet without him—if Jack were dumped, passed off as a crackpot—there would be no more liquor and no more hope. Financially, Jack's last legs had waltzed off about the time Arnold stole Pop's gold-headed cane, which would have brought a hundred or two at a hock shop, and without it Jack could quite easily starve in this heartless burg. The best he could hope for would be a night in jail and a free meal, but for that he would have to commit a crime of sorts, and the only sort of crime he felt like committing now was throttling Arnold White.

"There *is* a sarcophagus," he said as Weasel turned left

onto some nameless potholed street. "Mummy coffin," he hastened to add before his moronic partner could defame the French language again.

"I've seen pictures of them. Never seen one in Indiana, though."

"I believe it is here, though. The man who stole it was born and raised in Wabash Heights and spent his last days here. Does the name Atkinson ring a bell?" He looked hopefully at Weasel, whose deep-set eyes registered nothing but reflected dash lights, hate, and the glaze of whiskey.

"No bells," Weasel grunted.

"My father and him went to Egypt in 1932. Partners, they were, and it was the Depression. Atkinson had a college degree of some sort, probably phony, history or the like. He was admitted as an archaeologist. My dad went along. They tromped the Valley of the Dead for eight months, looking for undiscovered tombs. The pyramids had already been looted, the temples scrapped for building blocks. But the Valley of the Dead, the Egyptians had a fear of it. You get me?"

Weasel rolled down his window and tossed his empty bottle out. It crashed noisily against the passing curb.

"They bribed some old geezer with booze and got him to tell them where an unopened tomb might be. The tomb of Ktis, he called it. They dug for two weeks before finding it, only it wasn't your average tomb. You said you've seen pictures. King Tut was laid out like a—well, like a king—gold everywhere, a full-size boat for the journey to heaven, urns full of rubies, billions of bucks worth of loot. But this Ktis, he'd been stuck away without much in the way of finery. It's as if the ancients just wanted him put someplace where he'd be forgotten. The old man said he wasn't even a man, but not a god, either. See, the Egyptians believed . . ."

"Make your point," Weasel snapped. "You've got thirty seconds."

"Ktis," Jack went on. "It's not a king's name, not a god's name. It's not even a name. It's a . . . thing."

"Twenty seconds."

"Ktis was sealed in a golden coffin. Dad and Atkinson hauled it out of the Valley of the Dead, who knows how. Dragged it with mules, stole a truck, carried it by hand, the old man's story always varied. Point is, they got it out. Then Atkinson turned traitor. He threw my dad overboard at the port. He hid the . . . the mummy coffin . . . somewhere in the U.S. He always believed that this Ktis wasn't really dead. He claimed that with the help of the old Egyptian, he made it get up and walk one night. He was nuts, of course, but the fact remains that there is a golden coffin worth fo— *burp!* Jeez, excuse me . . . worth two million dollars hidden somewhere, probably close by. Arnold knows where. We melt it down, and half is yours. One million bucks.''

''Do me a favor,'' Weasel said, very matter-of-factly.

Jack frowned. ''Sure. What?''

''Hand me your bottle.''

Jack shrugged to himself, hoisting the bottle to the weak light. It was as good as gone anyway, less than an inch of amber heaven left inside. He handed it over.

Weasel pulled over to the curb. The cavalcade of cars behind them did likewise.

He gripped the bottle by the neck, unscrewed the lid, and drained it into the hole of his beard where his mouth was. Then, swinging suddenly, he smashed it across the dashboard. Glass exploded in a noisy rain of shards. Jack shrank back, his hand fumbling for the door handle.

Weasel pressed the broken remains of the bottle to Jack's neck, flooding Jack with memories of his own betrayal and the power of glass spears to puncture and cut and kill.

''Swear it's true,'' Weasel snarled.

Jack gulped. Three points of glass were puncturing the skin of his neck like thick hypodermic needles. He felt hot blood trickle into his collar. Oh, how he had underestimated this maniac, this beater of kids and fender dents. His hand clawed the door, trying to find a handle that seemed to have disappeared.

''I've cut better than you,'' Weasel hissed at him.

Jack, unable to find the door handle, found his voice instead, but it had become strangely squeaky, a fair rendition of Mickey Mouse. ''It's all true. On my mother's grave, it's true.''

''Describe Crazy Kate's.''

Bewilderment filled Jack's mind. What had he said?

''It's a brick building beside a hospital,'' Weasel shouted. ''What's the name of the hospital?''

Jack clenched his eyes shut, knowing now that the bottle of booze had driven this Weasel insane.

''What's the name of the hospital?''

"County General!" Jack screamed. "Holy Mary's! Saint Elsewhere! What the fuck does this have to do with anything?"

Weasel grinned. He eased back and tossed the broken bottle neck onto the backseat. His hand smashed the gearshift lever into drive and the car peeled away from the curb.

"We'll have us a drink," he said. "Get us a couple more bottles, search those roads. Sound good?"

Jack clutched his neck. Blood slicked his fingers. Faintness washed over him in warm splashes. "What in the fuck," he said. He swallowed. "What in the fuck was *that*?"

"Crazy Kate's is next to Union Hospital," Weasel replied. "I spent ten days there in the de-tox ward myself, not the crazy-house part. Guess you've never been there, huh? Never . . . escaped?"

Jack sat mute, grim-faced with shock. He had indeed never, and he never would.

During the two-mile trip to town, Arnold discovered he could get the old truck up to thirty by horsing with the gearshift and the clutch. Once he had dumped it into some unmentionable gear where the engine loaded down and threatened to quit, backfiring like a cannon and wheezing like an iron lung with a bad valve, but a little crunching and maneuvering of the shift lever put the ORD in a better frame of mind and made the roadside scenery wash past in a satisfying blur. He was in second gear without knowing it, but it was good enough.

Occasionally a car would flash past, a Friday-night party car weaving drunkenly on the pavement, finding the shoulder in a tornado of dust and mud, lurching back to center, its taillights melting into the nest of house and streetlights ahead that were the outskirts of Wabash Heights. Arnold passed a familiar green sign that read WABASH HEIGHTS THE FRIENDLY CITY, over which some wiseacre had spray-painted in drippy phosphorescent orange the more official slogan of the town, DEADSVILLE. He slowed down to the required twenty-five and made himself sit higher in the seat, hoping to pass himself off as a sixteen year old who knew damn good and well what he was doing. This was for the cops' benefit. For his own benefit, he was scared to death.

He bounced over the double set of railroad tracks that greeted every visitor to this fair city, and cruised up to the first stoplight, pumping the brakes until they squealed alive. The truck shuddered to a jerky stop, idling more roughly now, talking shop with itself and deciding whether to live or die. Arnold thought of gasoline, and the crummy position he would be in if this old turd gasped its last here in the middle of the road.

A car pulled up beside him, its radio blasting country loud enough to drown the ORD's coughing attempt to live. Arnold chanced a glance over. Teenagers swilling beer. There was a girl in the middle. Her skirt was tugged up to her waist and the driver had a hand in her panties. They were laughing and screeching. The light went green, and the car roared off with the hurt squeal of roasting rubber, leaving Arnold in a cloud of blue. He turned his eyes back to the road and let the clutch out. ORD's motor mumbled a sorry and somewhat apologetic good-bye, and died.

Glassy panic charged up Arnold's throat as he fumbled for the key ring. He got it in his shaking hand and gave it a turn. ORD chugged. ORD belched. ORD hissed and gurgled like a dying dragon. The headlights dimmed to a lackluster orange, then went out.

Quiet filled the world, save for the tinkling of the keys and the sound of blood pulsing in Arnold's eardrums. ORD was really dead. All the gauges had fallen to new positions, except for that damned lying gas gauge that still read one-quarter. Arnold pumped the accelerator, remembering that once his father had told him never to do that because you'll flood the engine, only now it didn't seem to matter because you could flood this engine until it begged to be loaded on Noah's Ark, since it wasn't even turning over.

Arnold sat while the light turned red again. He sat while it turned green. A few cars came and went, all of them finding the left lane as if sensing that the guy up here with no taillights was in trouble and Friday night was no night to be playing Samaritan.

Arnold decided that now would be a swell time for a good little cry. ORD had been his last hope, and ORD had seemed to be in relatively fine shape back at Norman's. It had started on the first try. How could a battery go so totally dead so totally fast? He knew nothing about car batteries, nothing about cars, most especially nothing about ORDs. The vague notions he did have about cars hinged on a book he had read, but it had been a horror story and not exactly Compton's Complete Car Guide. It had been about this old wreck, and this teenaged kid who fell in love with it, only this car was, well, haunted, and if you pushed it backward, it fixed itself. Some punks smashed it up, and the kid, the kid whose name had been, had been . . .

. . . *Arnold?!!!* . . .

. . . Arnie Cunningham, he had pushed it backward all night and made it whole again.

The stoplight flashed a bleary red, its lens seeming to signal an end to everything. Arnold was not a character out of a Stephen King novel and ORD was no Christine. If good old Stevie had decided to name his book ORD instead of Christine, then Arnold would now know what to do, because Stevie would have told him in the book. Stevie would have said, "In order to make ORD run again, our hero Arnie did not push her backward, no he did not, instead he recited the magic words, and ORD came back to life."

Arnold shrugged. It sure as hell was worth a try.

"Isis ki Osirus," he said without much hope, and turned the key.

It was unfortunate that he had not depressed the clutch first, because ORD roared like a lion who had stepped into a spring-steel trap, and lunged forward, rear tires chattering in a mad blur, belching tornadoes of tire smoke. Arnold was thrown backward into the seat, losing his grip on everything and getting his naked back poked by seat springs. Maplewood Avenue angled a bit left here, but ORD didn't care. There was a telephone pole up ahead, but ORD didn't care. ORD was an ORD on a mission. As Arnold grappled wildly against the G-forces for a hold on the steering wheel, ORD crunched into the telephone pole, throwing Arnold face-first through the gigantic hoop of the wheel and conking his head on the dashboard.

ORD groaned, seemingly outraged by this setback. The rear end bounced up and down as if on a trampoline. The telephone pole, perhaps weakened by previous encounters with drivers a bit too glassy-eyed to negotiate the curve, canted forward like a slow tree falling. Wires were pulled taut as the pole held on for dear life. ORD began to crawl up it.

Arnold kicked about for the clutch, found it, and mashed it down. His head was still stuck in the steering wheel, but he was aware that the truck was beginning to roll backward. There was a giant metallic screech. The motor screamed even though his foot was nowhere near the pedal.

"Back off!" Arnold shouted, feeling like a goofy version of Charlie McGee trying to rein in her firestarting powers. "Back off, dammit!"

The truck thumped down hard, bumping Arnold's head again, and the motor droned down to a merciful idle. He disengaged himself from the steering wheel, straightened, and saw that ORD's front bumper had chewed a stripe up the pole some four feet high, dug itself into the wood as the truck fell back, got hung up, and now adorned the pole like a grinning chrome mouth. Bright chunks of spark were falling off the overstretched wires above, ticking on the truck's roof and sputtering on the sidewalk.

He snapped his head around, trying to look in all directions at once. No one was coming. No one had seen.

He found reverse fast. Norman Parker's snow tires howled. Still no one was coming, no one had seen. He crammed the gearshift into the handiest available gear, which happened to be fourth, and popped the clutch.

The motor clunked. And quit.

Arnold ground his teeth, not caring if they hurt. "I said back off, not fucking die off," he muttered, and turned the key, careful this time to push the clutch in first. The motor screamed alive, six aged pistons going berserk at once and not seeming to like it. Arnold's eardrums squealed. "Slow down," he shouted above the racket.

ORD settled down. Arnold found first, babied the clutch out, and got under way again, emerging from a dense cloud of ORD-manufactured smoke into the cleaner dark of late evening, where storm clouds in the west promised rain soon, and lots of it.

· 15 ·

Spack, Jimmy, Jed

THE THREE OF them tromped back into the tavern just after eight o'clock, Spack, Jimmy, and Jed, three middle-aged men in various stages of physical disrepair caused by too many cigarettes and too many years' partnership with the bottle. Jimmy, tagging along at the rear, was carrying a huge and dripping glob of mud in his hands. Jed's brown work uniform was a sculpture of black mud from his feet to his knees. Only Spack seemed unmuddied: his gray Anaconda overalls were filthy with simple industrial grease and soot, the same things he carried with him every day. A smug grin pulled his face into a cruel, piglike leer when the dim tavern lights hit his face. He was a man in charge of his own fortune.

Most of the patrons of the estimable joint had gradually drifted back as the evening droned on, Spack noticed as he searched through the smoke for an open table. He decided they were doubtlessly tired of chasing Weasel's prehistoric Malibu on its fruitless trip up and down Wabash Heights' ruined streets. Well, it served them right. Mummy coffin indeed.

There was only one table left, and no stools at all at the bar. The table was the same one he had left to get away from the thundering tones of a jukebox whose volume control had been forged in Hell. Fortunately for the moment, it was running on idle, demonic lights flashing, monster speakers humming slightly with controlled power. His grin gone, Spack dumped himself into a chair and waited for Jed to park his skinny ass. While Jimmy Hallis waddled over with the pile of goop, Spack waved a hand at Mike. Mike, along with everybody else, was watching Jimmy with an expression of raw bewilderment. Spack noticed that flaky bum Weasel Whipple and his pal still

at the bar. They each had a fresh bottle of prime Ten-High
parked in front of their faces, the idiots. Spack would show
them what a real treasure looked like.

"Just slop it all down," he said to Jimmy, and Jimmy did
just that. Mud shot to the table's corners in wet ropes, splat-
tering onto the floor. Harley Gimbel's wife May was heading
for the jukebox behind the table, quarters clinking in one hand,
bottle of Falls City firmly in the other. She stopped and stared
at the mess.

"Birthday cake, Spack?" she said, and shrieked with laughter.

"Hey, Spack," someone shouted, and he looked around for
a face. "I heard the Lairds were shit eaters, but I never seen
a turd *that* big before!"

He snarled something ugly; the heckler could have been anybody, maybe even that baboon Weasel. He turned gruffly on
Jimmy. "Dig the fucking jar out, Hallis," he growled. May
walked off, cackling like a drunken hen, and fed quarters into
the jukebox. For the first time in his life, Spack was glad of
it. This pack of losers wouldn't be able to hear Jimmy and
Jed's screams of surprise when the treasure was exposed. Buried in that heap of mud was something that might be worth
more money than Jed made in a year filling vending machines,
more than Jimmy made in two years drilling holes in metal at
McCauley's. It might even be more than Spack made in six
months behind the wheel of his heister. Not a million bucks
like the fabled mummy coffin, for sure, but a hefty hunk of
change.

Jimmy was going at it, trying to wipe the mud from the core
of the mudpile and expose the mayonnaise jar that had been
nothing but a cold lump in the dark when they unearthed it out
by Chicker's Pond, near the sorry lane that called itself the
Wabash Heights airstrip. Spack considered it a feat of genius
that he had been able to find it after all these years. How old
had he been back then? Eight? Nine?

"Got the lid," Jimmy said. He made faces, trying to un-
screw it. The jug spun in his muddy hands. There was even a
bit of label left on the glass, the logo of some forgotten company that had made mayonnaise in the early forties. Jimmy
grunted and chewed his tongue as he worked.

"Ah, hand me the goddamn thing," Spack snorted, and
Jimmy gave it to him. The lid was sandpapery with rust under

his soft, fat hand, but he managed to work it loose. The jar itself seemed too heavy to contain what it did, which should have been mostly just air. The years had apparently allowed the thing to fill with groundwater. Well, he wondered, so what?

He laid the lid on the table, and stuck his hand into the black water inside the jar. His heart was pounding. Both Jed and Jimmy were bent forward in their chairs, jaws almost resting on the tabletop, eyes bright with expectation. Foul-smelling water sloshed into the mud on the table. The jukebox roared alive. Johnny Cash screamed something unmelodic and off-key.

"Got it," Spack said, and have it he did. He held it up.

"A coin," Jimmy breathed.

"A nickel," Jed wondered.

"A wet nickel," Jimmy said.

"A rusty nickel," Jed said.

They were right. Spack examined the coin, turning it in his fingers, frowning. May Gimbel sauntered up behind him and stuck her face over his shoulder. Cheap perfume danced in the atmosphere around her. "What's that?" she wanted to know.

"A coin," Jimmy muttered.

"A nickel," Jed grumbled.

She giggled. "Lot of muddy work for a nickel, wouldn't you say, Spacko? How old is it?"

He peered at it hard, trying not to breathe with her around. "Nineteen thirty-two," he told her, still frowning. "I buried it when I was a kid. Found it somewhere. It used to be real shiny and new, kinda. Should be worth a lot now."

"I hate to say this," she said, but said it anyway: "It's awfully corroded."

"She's right," Jimmy and Jed said in unison. "Corroded."

Spack stood up suddenly. His chair fell over backward and skidded to the jukebox. May Gimbel blundered off, cackling again. "Hey," he shouted above the music. "Anybody know what a nineteen-thirty-two nickel might bring? A corroded one?"

"I'll give ya four cents," someone shouted back. Spack didn't know who, but put him on his shit list anyway.

"Anybody here collect coins?" he bellowed at the crowd. "Anybody?"

He was being ignored. He almost sat down before remembering that his chair had fallen away, and straightened again.

"There's a coin shop in Terre Haute," he said to Jimmy and Jed, who were looking somewhat deflated. He could feel their doubts gnawing at his ego. He had put himself on the line with this treasure business, and God help him if they told him in Terre Haute that it wasn't worth a small fortune. He looked at his watch. Eight-thirty, but the coin shop probably stayed open till nine. They would have to make tracks.

He got his wallet out and peeled three dollars from the sheaf inside. "Head for the truck," he ordered. "We can make Terre Haute before the hour's up. Jimmy, scrape some of this mess up. You help him, Jed. I'll grab some beer for the road. I gotta hit the men's room too."

He hurried to the bar, let Mike know he needed three to go, and charged into the rest room. He did his business, and hurried out. In his state of agitation, he failed to look where he was going. He ran into what seemed like a fleshy brick wall charging in the other direction. Being fleshy himself, he rebounded, nearly losing his hard hat. When he got his balance back and looked up, he saw the bearded and malevolent face of Weasel Whipple.

"Watch where the fuck you're headed," Weasel snarled, showing lots of yellow teeth.

Spack opened his mouth. He did not know Weasel much better than anyone else in town, but he knew he was one mean SOB. He decided tonight was not the night to fuck with him. "Sorry," he said. "Accident.'

Weasel's beady black eyes looked him up and down. "You're that big shit from Terre Haute."

Spack spread his hands. "Just me, partner."

"I'm not your partner."

"Well then," Spack said, "acquaintance."

"Not even that," Weasel said. His eyes shifted to the rest room door, which was just being closed by someone else. "Now I missed my turn, fatboy. You got eyes in that fat head?"

"Now, look," Spack said.

Weasel reached out with one big paw and snatched Spack's hard hat off his head. He plopped it down on his own. It balanced there, looking eight sizes too small. "Now I'm the big shit, huh? Huh?"

Spack's eyes grew narrow. God, what a day. "You'd best give that back," he said, but the tone of his voice did not convince even himself.

"Make me," Weasel said thickly.

Spack pressed his eyes shut. This couldn't be happening, not today, not now. A challenge to fight in the Wabash Tavern was as mighty and as sacred as a challenge to duel had been in the South before the war. He could not back down. He only wished Jimmy and Jed would look over, because between the three of them they might stomp this fat shitter.

Weasel hauled a fist back. Spack watched in fascination, thinking of dentures and how much they might cost, and if the old nickel would bring in enough cash to pay for them. But then a hand came from behind Weasel and closed over that big fist, stopping its forward motion.

Weasel spun around. Spack saw a bald guy, the same bald guy who had fascinated Jimmy and Jed so. There was dried blood in three thick lines on his neck. "No time for this bullshit," the bald guy said. "We came here for a reload and a piss, not fun and games."

Weasel shook his hand away. "Cue Ball," he said, "I think I'm gonna kill you."

Spack ducked past them, no longer caring if his precious hard hat wound up on Weasel's head, the head of Jesus himself, or as a birdbath. He threw three dollars at Mike Taraday, who had a small brown bag waiting, grabbed it up, and elbowed his way out. Fresh air greeted him, as well as his truck. He hustled inside and tossed the bag on Jed's lap. Five seconds later he was on Maplewood headed west, the engine purring steadily, the automatic transmission shifting like silk.

"Where's your hat?" Jimmy asked, leaning over and looking concerned. Jed dug in the bag and handed him a beer.

"Forgot and left it on the bar," Spack said.

Jimmy's Budweiser opened with a hiss. "Better go back."

Spack shook his head. "They're free. No biggie."

"Free? Wow!"

Jesus help us, Spack thought, and roared through town as fast as he dared roar. The stoplight that bordered the city limit turned green just as he prepared to run it red. He saw without concern that some poor dumb bastard in an ancient pickup was broke down there, the driver a small hunched figure probably cranking the key on a dead battery. Screw him, screw them, screw the world. Spack had a small fortune in his pocket— hopefully. He glanced over and saw that Jed was handing him a beer, already open. Spack took it with shaking fingers and slugged it down gratefully, blinking away the pain it caused in his throat. Lord, but did that Wabash have cold beer. But could he ever go there again with the half-human Bigfoot named Whipple after his ass? He doubted it.

Maplewood Avenue magically became US 40, a straight stretch toward darkness, deep woods, and Terre Haute. Spack made himself stop drinking, wanting to save some, but a glance at the bottle showed him it was as good as gone already. He tipped it back, draining it all the way, his eyes closed in appreciation to God for making beer, and that bald guy for stopping Weasel. The truck swerved toward the gravel shoulder a bit, but Spack was aware of it, and was easing the steering wheel back to the left when Jimmy and Jed screamed in a strange and frightening unison:

"Look out!!!"

Spack looked back down to the road, the beer bottle still idiotically stuck to his lips. In the crisp glare of his Ford F-250 headlights he saw some kind of tall brown creature . . .

. . . *Bigfoot?* . . .

. . . lurching toward the truck. It was less than ten feet away. Spack stared at it as his headlights bored holes in the dark, waiting for his foot to come up to the brake, waiting for his hand to jerk the steering wheel hard to the left and possibly send the truck into a hopeless spin or a flip-over, waiting for anything to happen but what really did.

Before he hit it, he knew it was a man. He saw the shape of its head, the slope of its shoulders, even the dark holes of its eyes. He was dimly aware that his tires were screeching on the road as his foot finally got into the act, but it was far too late. The truck thumped as if someone had swung a wet two-by-four into the grille, and then the man bounced up like a bent and misshapen ogre springing out of the dark, his arms flailing, and plowed head-first through the windshield. Glass sprayed through the cab, peppering Spack's face like buckshot, and still the tires screeched and screeched. Jed Heathrow let out a groan, then screamed in a cracked high voice. The strange pedestrian's head had rammed him in the chest.

By Spack's estimation it was about four hours until the truck finally stopped and the scenery outside ceased to be a crazy blur, though in truth it was more like four seconds. A pebble of windshield glass had struck one of his bulging eyeballs during the ordeal, and pain was knifing through his head. He

looked around with one eye squeezed shut and saw that the
Ford had come to rest crosswise on the highway.

"Get him offa me!" Jed screamed, squirming away. The
newly killed man's head had slid down onto Jed's lap, and Jed
seemed most anxious to get out from underneath it. Spack saw
some kind of yellowish fluid smear itself across the seat as Jed
scooted over toward Jimmy, crunching him against the door.

"Better move fast," Jimmy said, his voice hollow. "This is
drunk driving. You'll be in the slammer for ten years."

That ended any hesitation Spack felt about this situation. He
threw the Ford into reverse and made rubber melt. Then he
was in drive again and headed west, the crime of hit-and-run
now added to his roster of strange things done while drunk,
hoping to God no one would see that a man's legs were sticking
out of the windshield. The steering wheel felt greasy in his
hands, and he realized he had crushed his beer bottle with his
hand in his terror. Shards of brown glass twinkled on his lap,
were, in fact, still stuck in his hand. He pulled them out with
his teeth as he drove, his mind a hurricane of confusion. Cool
wind blasted through the remains of the windshield as he
brought the truck up to fifty, then sixty, then seventy.

"You better dump this guy," Jimmy said. "A cop might go
by."

Just then the guy pushed himself up on his hands. He craned
his head around with his thin gray hair blowing across his face.

Jed screamed again. When he was done he said, "It's Norman Parker! You ain't kilt him after all!"

Norman Parker? Spack wondered stupidly. *Why would that
old shit be out on the road?*

"Hospital," Jed said. "Turn around."

Spack, too shocked to think straight, prepared to do as he
was told, but Jimmy Hallis was waving his hands and his beer
bottle.

"Fuck, no! Then it'll be drunk driving for sure. Spack'll
get a breath test. Just dump him. And Jesus, slow down! You're
doing ninety!"

Spack slowed down. His thoughts played tag with each other,
never connecting.

Jed, still mashed against Jimmy, shook his head. "Somebody might go by and see us! Speed up!"

Spack speeded up. Meanwhile Norman Parker inspected the
inside of the truck with his remaining eye swiveling and glow-

ing mustard running out of his eyehole. Spack cringed, ready
to throw up now.

"Go left here!" Jimmy suddenly shouted. "Take the lane!"

Spack hit the brakes with both feet, adorning the asphalt
with more expensive tire rubber. He spun the wheel left,
crossed the median, and found himself cruising down a gravel
lane.

"Stop at his house," Jimmy commanded.

Spack turned into Norman's muddy yard. The lights were
on in the house. His headlights threw long spiky shadows behind Norman's assemblage of dead farm machinery.

"Kill the motor. And for God's sake, turn your headlights
off."

Spack did as ordered. His hand was bleeding down his arm.
Norman wobbled around beside him. How had the old fart
survived a cruncher like that?

"Okay," Jimmy said, "everybody out."

They fell out of the truck, and huddled in the damp breeze.

"He needs a hospital," Jed whimpered, staring at the odd
sight of Norman's uselessly pedaling legs poking out the windshield.

"No chance of that," Jimmy said. "Besides, he's as good
as dead. Spack? You still alive?"

Spack answered by leaning down beside the front tire and
throwing up a great blot of beer and old lunch.

"Come on," Jimmy said, tugging at Jed's sleeve. "Hop on
up. We'll pull the fucker out." He clambered onto the hood
while Spack dry-heaved onto the mud and Jed stood shivering.

"I ain't touching him," Jed said.

"Puss-face. I'm getting my share of that nickel if it kills
me." Jimmy grabbed his feet and hauled him out. Norman's
neck got hung up on a shard of windshield. Jimmy grunted,
his knees bonging on the hood and making large dimples in
the metal.

"You're cutting his head off," Jed moaned.

"BFD." Jimmy yanked harder. Glass sliced deep into Norman Parker's neck. His head tilted oddly backward. Jed recoiled, expecting a spray of blood, but there was none. In the
dim light he could see that the glass had sliced Norman's neck
nearly in two. The back of his head was between his shoulder
blades. Jed covered his eyes, wishing he could cover his ears

against that sound, that sound like a freshly killed chicken getting a leg torn off. Tendons popped and snapped.

"That did it," Jimmy said, breathing hard. He rolled Norman off the hood, who thumped to the mud at Jed's feet.

Spack straightened, looking green even in the miserable light from the house windows. "What now?" he croaked.

"We toss the fucker in the pickup and sink him in a pond somewhere," Jimmy said. He looked down at Spack. "Can you still drive?"

Spack squeezed his throat with his uninjured hand, shaking his head. "Ain't got no cement blocks, Jim. The body will bloat; then it'll float. We'll have to bury him."

"Makes no difference to me." Jimmy jumped off the hood and hurried around to the back of the truck. He opened the capper lid. "Got a shovel in here?"

"Uh-uh."

"Fuck." He slammed the lid down. "Parker's bound to have one. You got a flashlight?"

"No."

"Swell." He looked at the house, then squinted at the shed. "I'll get us one. Can you drive this buggy through the mud? We'll bury him so far out nobody'll ever find 'im."

"Don't know."

Growling, Jimmy hurried off toward the shed, skating in the mud and dodging huge hunks of debris. He fumbled at the crack of the double doors, found the hasp open, and pulled. The door wobbled. Familiar with sagging carpentry, he lifted the door a few easy inches off the ground and pulled it open. The solid stench of garbage and rot came out, smells Jimmy was also familiar with.

He dug in his pocket and got his lighter out. He lit it and stepped inside.

A few seconds passed. Back at the truck, Jed Heathrow clutched himself with his arms and wished he had brought a coat.

Spack Laird squeezed his punctured hand and blinked his aching eye.

It was Jimmy's sudden, wild scream that sent them running to the shed, cold breeze, punctured hand, and aching eyeball forgotten.

● ● ●

Ten minutes later:

Jed. This lighter's getting hot. You sure that lantern's dead?

Jimmy. Yeah. Spack, try lifting this side.

Spack. Oof. It's just too heavy. We need a hoist or something.

Jimmy. Jed, loan us a hand.

Jed. What about light?

Spack. Fuck light. Get down in this hole and help us lift.

Jed. Weighs a ton. We need a hoist or something.

Spack. He's right. Where can we get one?

Jimmy. Over at work. McCauley's. They've got one.

Spack. You got a key for the place?

Jimmy. No, but since I won't be needing to work there anymore, we'll just bust in. Deal?

Spack, Jimmy, Jed: three grinning men climbing out of a hole they had no right to be in, a hole it had taken Arnold White sixteen hours to dig.

Spack, Jimmy, Jed: three of the happiest men currently on the planet, heading for the truck and Wabash Heights and riches beyond any man's dream.

Spack, Jimmy, Jed: thirsty.

· 16 ·

In Town

ARNOLD MADE IT halfway through Wabash Heights and was
sitting at a red light at the intersection of Maplewood and Kentucky with the motor, new and improved by the Egyptian
please-pass-the-potatoes method, idling at high speed, when
the blue and white WHPD police cruiser pulled up behind him
and sat waiting for him to make one false move.

His heart, which seemed to have taken up permanent residence in his throat, pulsed thickly in his neck, making his
eardrums bulge. The ORD's rearview mirror was cracked and
yellow, but it was still a mirror, and it didn't lie. He could
even see the pale face of the cop behind the wheel. He was
puffing on a cigarette and flipping the ashes out the side window. Arnold stared at him with sick fascination, this hunter of
killers and car thieves. He saw him reach across the seat, produce a small bottle of whiskey, and guzzle some down. He
screwed the cap back on and made the bottle disappear. And
then he honked.

Arnold's heart squirted up into his brain, thumping loudly
there, making thought impossible. His vision seemed to fail
him for a moment, going double, then completely black. He
blinked and it was back, but the cop was still there, the car
seeming to crouch low for the kill, a bizarre blue-and-white
panther. A panther that could really lean on that horn, because
the cop was doing it again.

Arnold's eyes moved over to the stoplight. It was green.
Arnold gaped at it, numb with relief. The cop simply wanted
him to move his ass.

He dumped the clutch and ORD kicked the bucket.

"No, oh no," Arnold wheezed, reaching for the keys. He

turned the bulky ring and the truck began to grind and grind, the headlights dimming as they had dimmed before, at the stoplight where a nearby telephone pole now had a rusty chrome smile four feet wide. Had the cop seen that yet? Would he recognize it as belonging to this truck? Would ORD ever start, and would the cop ever stop honking?

The engine stopped turning at all. The lights went out. The stoplight turned red.

"Ooohhh," Arnold moaned, because now the cop was done honking and was opening his door, putting his feet tiredly on the pavement, and when he saw the thirteen-year-old driver of this buggy he would first shit a brick and then, having finished that painful task, make an arrest. Even if Arnold's poster hadn't made it to the post offices of the world yet, this local boy would know the scoop. Now he was leaning out of the car, now he was straightening up, now he was slamming his door, now he was adjusting his hat, and now, with his cigarette poked between his lips, he was ambling toward ORD and Arnold.

Arnold bent over and pretended to be hunting for wires under the dash. Unwanted sweat popped out on his forehead and upper lip. *You better think up something better than this,* his mind taunted him. He wasn't wearing a shirt and the temperature was diving into the low sixties. That wouldn't make sense to the cop. He was too short to be driving and was skinnier than the wimp getting sand kicked in his face in a Charles Atlas ad. There were bruises up and down his ribs and back from the recent pounding administered by Stepfather Dearest. His hair was caked with mud and his jeans were a mosaic pattern of dry mud cracks, like a dead river bottom. What we have here, Officer, is a Suspicious Person.

The cop pecked on the glass, using, Arnold had no doubt, the butt of his revolver. Arnold waved a hand in the air, indicating that the cop should not worry, should go on about his business, take a hike, get screwed. Anything but open the door.

But he did open the door. ORD's hinges screeched like crusty mausoleum doors, like the hinges of a coffin lid being pried up after dirty centuries in darkness. Arnold wagged the wires under the dash, hoping for a spark that would show he was no stranger to this truck and its weird ways. The shift lever was a cold bar digging against his shoulder.

"Dead battery, eh?" the cop asked mildly.

Arnold made his voice low. "Yup."

"Well, you're gonna have to push her out of the way. Traffic's piling up."

A lone car honked. Then another. The drunks were out in force tonight.

"Well?" the cop asked.

Arnold let go of the handful of wires. The jig was up. So he sat up.

"Hey!!!" the cop bellowed in his ear, nearly knocking him over. Arnold turned his head to face his accuser. His weary neck bones crunched, the way, he assumed, they would crunch when they hung him at the gallows.

The cop was gone. Arnold was staring at a blank building across the street. He leaned out and looked back. The cop was charging down Maplewood Avenue, his holster flapping. *"Hey you punks!"* he was screaming. *"Stop! Stop!"*

Arnold frowned. A group of kids were scattering over the street, laughing and howling. Distantly, over their noise, something was hissing.

Arnold looked at the cop car. There was an ice pick sticking out of the side of the rear tire, which was developing a bad case of flatfoot.

He looked forward again. The light turned green.

Time to pass the potatoes.

"Isis ki Osirus," he said, and ORD began to jigger forward, once again in some impossible gear, but she was moving and that was what counted. Buildings were sliding past once more. Arnold shut the door with a screeching bang and puttered down the street like a dowdy old man on a Sunday cruise, wondering what the hell had happened to the power of the magic, because mighty ORD was sounding mighty pitiful. He pressed the clutch and found second. Not much better. He gave gas. It helped, but not much. The headlights were stuttering on and off. The motor belched and farted. Arnold bounced around helplessly. It was like riding a four-wheeled pogo stick.

He made it one block, then another. The next one was Clark Street, and it was there that he needed to go left. The light was red when he got to it, but he lurched through anyway, straining against the old steering wheel, trying to make sense of things through the flash pops of the headlights. He needed to get to Don Marston's shop, and it was here somewhere, and if only he had his glasses he could make out the faces of the houses. Don Marston kept his taxidermy shop in his garage, which bordered an alley behind his house. Once, years ago, Dad had brought him here to pick up a finished fish for one of Dad's friends, and yes, it had been Clark Street, but which house number? Which alley?

Arnold took a wild guess and swung right into a gravel alley barely wider than the truck. It looked vaguely familiar. Most of the garages here opened on the alley; most of them looked to be on the verge of collapse. Don Marston's was not, Arnold remembered that much. It was a big double-wide with the windows boarded up against that occasional demoralized hunter who would steal a deer head rather than admit defeat for the season. It was brown, too. Brown with a white roof.

ORD emitted one last agonized wheeze and died forever. Arnold passed the potatoes a few times, getting a dim orange glimmer from the headlights.

Don't say it too often. Anything used too much loses its effect.

He got out. The breeze caught him and he began to shiver. The garages here were all swayback ruins, built in the days when skinny Model Ts would fit quite nicely, no longer able to hold any but the smallest of the small imported cars. Since nobody in Wabash Heights was about to drive a car put together by some baby-eating Kraut or Pearl Harbor–bombing Jap, the garages became, as Norman Parker's shed had, storage huts for junk, while the giant Chevys and Buicks rusted out front.

Except Don Marston's garage. It was his place of business, the place where paying customers came with cash and dead wildlife in hand. It was presentable, and Arnold remembered that it smelled funny inside, kind of like the way the inside of the sarcophagus had smelled, old meat and funny chemicals, the smell of mummified animals and mummified mummies.

Arnold walked. *Mummy?* he wondered. *Had that thing been a mummy?* Well, sure it was, all wrapped up in gauze like that, but that weird head, that animal's head. Jackal's head. It was no ordinary mummy. It was, without a doubt, a monster of some sort, some creepy mythical thing on the order of unicorns and flying horses. Only this thing *did* exist, or at least had existed, centuries ago. Passing the potatoes to it made it come alive, but it was a weak brand of alive. It even had a broken arm now, thanks to Arnold and his frenzy to get the sarcophagus open. Bad mistake, that had been. Tea bags and tannin, Atkinson had said. The monster needed tea bags and tannin.

Deep in thought, Arnold almost walked past a really nice boarded-up double garage without noticing. When he did notice, he stopped, not wondering at his luck or his fabulous memory, not even wondering if Don Marston had inside what he needed. He was just cold and wanted to get somewhere where it was warm.

Memory again: the door was around the side. Mr. Marston only opened the big overheads when he was spray-painting fish, and you could be sure they were locked tonight. So Arnold walked around to the side, stopping to pick up a rock with which to smash some glass and break some plywood apart.

He didn't need it. Light was spilling out from the crack under the door. He tested the knob and found it unlocked. He pressed himself against the side of the building, glad for the warmth coming off the siding but not glad about anything else. A radio was playing inside. Someone was moving around.

He knew then he should have brought the lion head from the cane. That sucker was solid gold. Mr. Marston would part with a little tannin for solid gold.

What now? he wondered tiredly. Hide and wait until Mr. Marston closed up his shop, whenever that might be, then break in? Or walk home and get some tea bags out of the rusty cannister Mom kept by the refrigerator? That would take an hour, maybe. By then old Marston would be gone. Wouldn't he?

Arnold rested his forehead on his open hand, the hand that had dug for so long that even the Band-Aids had disintegrated, slumped against the garage with his ruined teeth chattering and his legs shaking. Nothing was making sense anymore. He needed a bed and some sleep. He needed food and maybe even a drink of water. He needed Dad to come and tuck him in then wander back to the Remington clack-clacker and produce some more trash barrel fodder. He needed a time machine to take him away and away from this endless misery.

The door opened soundlessly, and Don Marston backed out carrying two large white plastic buckets. He saw Arnold and shrank back.

"What the hell are you?" he wheezed. His buckets clunked against his shins.

Arnold looked up at him. "I don't know," he said, and then he dropped to his knees on the damp ground, fell forward onto his face, and sobbed into the grass that smelled sourly of springtimes come and gone, come and gone forever.

● ● ●

"Tammim?" Don Marston said. "You mean tannin?"

Arnold nodded. He was slouched in a lawn chair Marston kept for customers in his workshop, drinking Lipton Cup-o'-Soup from a mug. Marston was sitting on a high wooden stool at his workbench, the heels of his loafers hooked over the rungs, a pair of Ben Franklin glasses perched on the end of his nose. He was smiling at Arnold with grandfatherly concern. Arnold remembered now why everybody called him old Don Marston. He was old.

Twenty minutes had passed since Marston put his buckets down and helped Arnold into the garage, muttering and murmuring to himself. He had put him in the chair and hustled away. Some time later he came back with the soup, instant mushroom soup, and Arnold, never a fan of the spore, found himself burning his mouth in his eagerness to get it all down.

"What do you need it for?" Marston asked him now. Around him the pegboard walls were adorned with the resplendency of his peculiar trade: immobile deer heads that sprouted from polished plaques; a variety of fish doing imitation flops, their dead skins shiny with varnish; in this corner, a mallard roosting on a tree branch; in that one, a raccoon on a table, pretending to bite into a walnut. On the east wall, draped from metal pegs, hung a dozen skins turned inside out, all of them putrid yellow and looking brittle. And overhead, balanced on the rafters, were innumerable sets of sawed-off antlers. Here was Wabash Heights' collective hobby under one roof: the killing and mummification of living things.

Arnold looked up from his cup. "I've got a dead animal I want to . . . keep."

"What . . . your dog died? Look, Arnold, it isn't a good idea to—"

"Mo—I meam, no . . . dog," Arnold said. This lisp was driving him batty. The soup simmered in his stomach, smooth and mellow, but jeez, did it make his teeth scream. No pepper in this stuff to fry his stomach, though, uh-uh. Norman Parker could shove his turkey pastrami up his dead ass.

"What, then?"

"This, um, this dwied up squiwwel I found."

"Dried up?"

"Fwom the sun. You mo. Mummified."

Marston nodded slowly. "Seems to me he would have rotted."

"Found him in the basement," Arnold added hastily.

"Sunshine in your basement, eh?"

Arnold looked back to his cup. He drank in silence. There was a clock on the wall, and it ticked in this stillness full of lies.

"It's like this," Marston said after a minute. "To perform taxidermy, you have to get the animal while he's fresh. Not a season goes by I don't get some dumbass in here who's hung his deer in a warm garage for two weeks and then decides he wants it mounted. Can't be done. The smell alone is enough to kill even an old nose like mine." He adjusted his Ben Franks higher. "Anyway, this animal of yours has to be dead no longer than ten days, tops, unless you've kept him frozen. Even then there's a chance the hair will fall out while it's soaking."

"In tammim," Arnold said.

"In this stuff." Marston got off his stool and bent under his workbench. He came up with what looked like a white bleach jug. He spun it so Arnold could see the label. "Contro-Tan, they call it, which I guess means controlled tanning. Doesn't matter. Main ingredient is tannin, along with a lot of other happy horseshit that costs me a fortune."

"How much?"

"What, for this jug? Thirty dollars. Fancy that."

Arnold fancied it while his heart sank. Why hadn't he brought the lion's head?

"Main thing is this," Marston went on, putting the jug down and moving to the skins hanging from their pegs. He unhooked one and held it horizontally with one hand. It stayed that way, looking like a folded yellow umbrella. Marston rapped it with a fingernail. "Hard as a board, huh? This skin's been worked, so that's no problem. I just soak it in water, then I put the old Contro-Tan to it. The water makes it soft. The tannin makes it firm. Does that make sense?"

Arnold nodded. "So you meed to soak it in watew fiwst."

"Bingo. Get it just wet enough, then throw the tannin on. I use a paint brush." He put the skin back. "Your dead squirrel, though, that's another story. Chances are his insides are gassy and he'll just blow up."

Arnold drank. No chance of the mummy—the monster—blowing up. Falling to pieces was more likely.

Marston ambled back over to his stool. Once more he looked Arnold over. "Did they get the license number off the car that hit you? Or was it a semi truck?"

Arnold almost smiled. "Nah. I fell down the basement steps."

"Oh, yeah, falling. I gotta watch that. Rusty hips, you know. I'm near seventy, maybe past it by now. How's your dad?"

Arnold jerked, nearly dumping mushroom soup down his chest. "Huh?"

"John. I remember him. Remember you, too. Wasn't it a month or so ago you both came in here to pick up a fish for somebody?"

"Two years ago," Arnold said.

"Ah." Marston stroked the top of his gray head with the flat of his hand. "Guess I work too many hours. Being self-employed sucks, don't let them lie to you, and days pass like the wind. Still checking groceries, is he?"

"Mo."

"Laid off, huh? Ain't this town a bitch. Weren't for the taverns, well, I guess she'd just blow away. Not that anybody'd notice." He put his wrinkled hands together and sighed. "I remember the old days, the clay factory days. Amitex plant down south employed hundreds, made glazed brick. But who needs glazed brick nowadays? Nobody around here. Is your dad still writing?"

This time Arnold did spill a dollop down his chest. "What?"

"Writing." Marston made scribbling motions. "Stories, books, stuff like that. Seems like a few months ago a couple of guys were in here bringing some deer—or was it fish—who knows? Some time ago, we'll say, these two rowdies were in here, and they started telling me about Mr. Famous Author. I says, who's that? And they says, that John White down from the grocery store. Laughing, they were, saying he was crackers and the whole town knew it. Myself, I felt for him. Being self-employed sucks, don't let them lie to you, and if writing a book is anything like filling out deer tags, I'd hate to try it. 'Specially not for a living. Did anything ever come of it?"

Arnold scraped soup off his chest with a finger. Did anything ever come of it? You bet. Dad standing outside in the wind-blown dark with his face twisted and pitiful, orange flames dancing out of the trash barrel, words going up in smoke. Dad leaving.

New tears tried to seep into Arnold's eyes. The whole town knew it, eh? Maybe Dad had showed a particularly good story or book to a friend, someone he trusted, and presto, the whole town knew it, probably passed the manuscript from hand to hand and roared. What a chuckle. A Famous Author from Wabash Heights? Let's try putting a man on Mars first.

"Mo," he said simply.

"Perhaps it's best. I went solo in this taxidermy business back in the early forties—or was it the thirties? Dunno. Anyhow, you should have heard them howl when I quit the brick plant to do this thing. You're gonna starve, they told me. You ain't got the talent, they told me. And then, when I started making a buck or two here and there, they said I was just too lazy to work a real job. Said I was using taxidermy as an excuse to sit on my ass and do nothing. This went on for years while I built the business, and I tell you now I was ready to head out of this state forever, only I'd sold my car to put food on the table and wasn't about to walk. So I had to keep on plugging, keep on plugging, and ignore all the laughs and the jokes and the cruel things people would say. Worst part was, after a while I *was* starving. And I do spend most of my day sitting on my ass. But I work while I'm doing it, and I do it twelve to sixteen hours a day, and that's what these people could never understand. Why, one time a man I considered to be a friend came flat out and told me if I didn't go look for a job he was gonna haul me out himself and force me to. Needless to say, I hid out till he got off *that* kick."

Arnold stared at him, gritting his remaining teeth together so hard that the pain became exquisite. He shut his eyes to push the tears away, and the time machine he had wished for was there, only it had taken him back to the night when the cold November wind had been ripping at his pajamas as he stood on the back steps and watched his father's hopes turn to ash in the bottom of a barrel.

He opened his eyes and the image was gone. In its place was Don Marston sitting on a stool fiddling with his glasses. He was wiping a finger behind each lens, leaving damp smears on the bags of his eyes. Arnold realized the old man was getting misty. Had the ordeal hurt him that bad, so bad the memory of it could make him weep now, forty years later?

Marston sniffed. "Damned chemicals. So what's your pop doing with himself, if he ain't writing or grocery checking?"

"Went to Texas," Arnold mumbled.

"Oh. I see. Looking for work, I guess. Gonna pick the family up, is he?"

Arnold stared into his cup without answering. The soup was almost gone, but now his stomach hurt again, and there was no pepper to blame.

Marston frowned. "This squirrel of yours, he's pretty special, isn't he?"

Arnold nodded. Another lie to add atop all the others. Who cared?

Marston bent under the bench again. He came up with a fresh jug of Contro-Tan. "I'm gonna give you this, Arnold, because I think it'll do you more good than me. You've got a tough row to hoe, by the looks of it. I'll even throw in a paint brush. But I want to tell you a story first."

Arnold glanced at the clock, beginning to fidget. Marston wagged a finger. "Only take a second, and I want you to know you're the only human who's ever heard this tale, though God knows I've told it to these walls again and again when it's late and dark and nobody's here." He set the jug on the bench beside the other one. "One evening after I'd been at this taxidermy stuff for three years and not making a dime, I went to where I was living then, and there was a note on the door that said the rent was three months overdue and I was to be out by the morrow. The year before I'd sold my car to keep going, but was I ever broke. The bills were all overdue. I was a laughingstock to everybody in this town, and because of that I wasn't getting their business. Oh, a fish here, a deer there, just enough to keep beans in the skillet every other day or so. But that night I'd been at the Wabash Tavern, which existed then as it does now, hoping somebody'd buy me a beer so's I could forget my troubles. Nobody would. I was told several times that if I wasn't such a lazy ass I could buy my own beer. I realized I was practically a beggar then, that I'd turned out just as everyone had predicted. Yet I'd been practicing and practicing on roadkilled game, perfecting my art, working my fingers to the bone and my brain to the point of insanity."

He dug his fingers under his glasses again. "Damned chemicals. See, Arnold, this night I went home and I sat on the blanket that was my bed—I'd sold it too—and I decided I was done for. I'd given it my best shot but it just wasn't working out. Instead of making my dream come true, I'd watched it turn to ashes. But I couldn't go back to the factory, 'cause I'd be a laughingstock and Mr. I-told-you-so for the rest of my life. The hurt was so deep it was like I'd been gutted with a dull knife. So I opened the baking stove and I stuck my head inside, and I reached up that old-fashioned thing and turned the gas on. Back then you needed to light it with a match, see, but I had no need of matches 'cause I hadn't seen food in two days. Anyhow, I started breathing real deep, hoping that gas would work quick and painless, and I must have stayed that way for fifteen minutes, bawling like a baby there on my knees with my head stuck in that old white stove, and then it came to me that I wasn't dead. In fact, I couldn't even smell no gas."

He smiled grimly. "They'd shut me off, Arnold. My gas, I mean. I couldn't pay the bill, so they shut me off. I realized this and got up, and after a minute of staring at that dead stove I started to giggle, then I was chuckling, then I was laughing like a hyena. I laughed myself purple. I was so poor I couldn't even afford to kill myself. And then I decided that no town was gonna beat me, 'cause I had a *dream*, and dreams don't die unless you let them. I went back to the shop, which was my momma's back porch, and I begged some butcher paper from her—she'd just about disowned me by then—and I started making advertising posters. I must have made a hundred. Then I stuck them up all over town, hitchhiked to Terre Haute, and stuck them up in that fair city. Next thing you know, business started to trickle my way. After a few years people began to see that I was making a handsome living, and they started getting chummy all of a sudden. It made me sick to my stomach, those two-faced bastards, but time heals that. And to this day, one of my fish hangs in the Wabash Tavern, though I swore to God then and I do now that I will never set foot in that place again. It's a magnet for every lowlife scum in town."

He opened a drawer and took out a paintbrush. He brought it and the jug over to Arnold and set them by his feet. "You pay me when you can, Arnold. Now go fix up your squirrel."

Arnold stood up. His throat felt tight and hot. "Thamk you," he said, handed the empty cup over, stuck the paintbrush in his pocket, and picked up the jug with his good hand. He went for the door. Cold wind gusted in when he opened it. A thought struck him, and he pressed the door shut. "Do you have any tea bags, Mr. Mawston?"

"Tea bags?" Marston shrugged, looking at him curiously.

"I suppose everybody keeps some tucked away someplace. Why?"

"My mom sent me over to get some."

Marston folded his arms. "Well. I guess I've heard stranger things, but then again, maybe not. Does Lipton suit your taste?"

"Egyptian would be better."

"Well, that old Lipton is just full of teas from around the globe, don't let them lie to you. Step aside and I'll be right back."

He went out with Arnold's cup dangling from a finger. A few minutes later he was back with a handful of tea bags. He jammed them in Arnold's back pocket. "All set now? You come and see me again, will you? I get mighty tired of getting my ears talked off by these buttholes who come in bragging about how they bagged the big one when all they've got in the trunk is a button buck with antlers no bigger than your little toe, and I'd like to know how things turn out with your dad."

"Okay," Arnold said, opened the door, then reconsidered and shut it once more. Mr. Marston had been more than kind, and this was going to stretch things, but it had to be done. "Could you drive me someplace?" he asked.

"Would if I could," Marston answered promptly, "only they took my license away 'cause of my eyes. Too many years staring at close-up work did me in." He touched his glasses. "Even with these Coke bottles I'm lucky to see three feet."

Arnold's heart sank, but only a little. He had received more good will in the last half hour than he deserved, since he had come here to rob the old man in the first place. He wiggled the fingers sticking out of his cast as a gesture of good-bye.

"One last thing, Arnold," Marston said before he could go.

Arnold shuffled around.

"They don't always turn the gas off, you know."

Arnold shook his head. He was still shaking it as he went out, still shaking it as he went up the alley past the corpse of ORD and found the street.

· 17 ·

Spilling the Beans

"Fuck," Jimmy Hallis panted. "This ain't working. The block's falling apart."

"Smash it again," Spack said. "She'll bust."

Jimmy hoisted the cement block overhead, a block that would have been handy as the eternal anchor for Norman Parker at the bottom of a strip mine, if they'd had it before. Jimmy had found it nearby, but it was performing badly as a lock-smasher. They were at the back door of McCauley Machine & Welding, Jimmy Hallis's place of employment up until tonight, where inside there sat, begging to be stolen, a large tripodal contraption that could hoist four tons. McCauley's, definitely no Anaconda factory, was a ramshackle wooden building with a tin roof on the top and a cement floor on the bottom. Like Hyman & Sons Body Shop, where Weasel worked, McCauley's was surrounded by a moat, not of wrecked cars but of junked machinery and bulging crates of metal parts that someone in this world had once found useful, but no longer. McCauley's four employees worked these parts into something an obscure tractor factory in Fort Wayne had use for, and in this way McCauley's survived.

Jimmy smashed the block down onto the big padlock that held the door shut. There was an explosion of cement dust. The block fell to pieces. Jimmy jumped back, howling through his teeth, rubbing his hands.

"Well, shit," Spack said. "Jed, find some kind of pry bar."

"Where? I can't see my hand in front of my face."

"Jimmy? Where's a bar?"

"Don't know. Most of the shit back here's stripped bolts and old crane parts."

"Well, fuck."

They stood in the dark while the wind snatched at their clothes.

"This is gonna be bad," Spack said after a while. "But I guess I gotta."

He found his way through the darkness to his truck, which he had backed close to the building, and opened the driver's door. He leaned inside and reached under the seat. He pulled out a large army surplus holster and snapped it open. The butt of an army surplus .45 gleamed under the dome light. This was Niggerchaser, his helping hand in case the colored population of Terre Haute ever woke from their complacent doze and went rioting. He kept it packed with seven hot rounds of SilverTip hollow-point bullets, guaranteed to drop the biggest rioter in his tracks. He slid it out of the holster and walked back to where Jed and Jimmy stood.

"Whatcha got?" Jed asked.

Spack pulled the slide back and let it snap forward with a click. "Answer your question, does it?"

Jimmy and Jed backed away. Spack felt the outlines of the padlock, located the center, and positioned Niggerchaser's big barrel on it. He stuck a finger in his left ear, grinning. God, the years he had waited to shoot this thing. Too bad the target was only a rusty old lock.

Boom!

The padlock had apparently never heard of the name Masterlock, because it shattered in pieces to the ground. Spack felt for what was left and discovered that only the U portion had survived. He tugged it out of the hasp and threw it away.

"Inwards, men," he said, swinging the door, keeping his pistol ready and feeling very military. The acrid smell of gun smoke was pleasant and thick. "Grab the hoist."

Jimmy and Jed hurried in. Jed immediately tripped over something and fell down. "Turn on the lights, will ya?" he said, sounding hurt.

"No, dumbass," Spack growled. "Jimmy, hold his hand or something. I'll stand watch."

Jed got up, and he and Jimmy slunk through the dark hand-in-hand while Spack waited at the door. Spack heard things rattle and clank, then the fleshy thud of Jed falling again. Curses, mutters, growls. Spack wished a colored security guard would jump out of the dark so he could gun him down. No white jury in Wabash Heights would convict him, that was for sure.

Now a chain rattled. Jimmy and Jed grunted. Something metal crunched across the floor. Pretty soon they were at the door, breathing hard.

"Will it fit?" Spack asked, squinting uselessly to see it.

"Lemme fold the legs," Jimmy whispered, and things clanked some more. "Okay, Jed, tip it."

Jed grunted. They carried the thing out the door with a long chain dragging behind. Jed stepped on it and fell again. This time he hollered.

"Shut up!" Spack hissed at him. "Want somebody to hear?"

They loaded the hoist into the truck. Spack put his pistol back under the seat, started the Ford's mighty motor, and drove into the night, crazy for joy, crazy for money, crazy for more beer.

"This is fucking insane!" Jack Cumberland shouted. It was okay to shout, because he and Weasel were still at the Wabash Tavern and everyone else was shouting, too. The Budweiser clock was pushing ten, the Clydesdales still marching to no-where. Just like Weasel, but he was doing it on his ass.

"Mike!" Weasel shouted. "Two more!"

Mike Taraday was running himself to death, as was usual for payday. He waved to signal he had gotten the message. Cigarette smoke was so thick he looked like a man in a fog. The jukebox roared full steam.

"We got things to do!" Jack shouted. "We got to find the kid!"

Weasel looked at him. His eyes had become black glass. His face was puffy and red, his beard wet with spilled beer, the idiotic undersized hard hat balanced on his huge head. He had become an obscene parody of some kind of working-man's Santa Claus, and was just about as useful. After the brief en-counter with Spack Laird he had not killed Jack as promised, merely sat at the bar and proceeded to get sloshed. Jack guessed he was trying to drench the heat of his anger in cold Falls City, but time, well, she was a-wasting.

"Free, ain't it?" Weasel snorted.

"Yeah, fine, I appreciate the generosity. One more beer and we go."

"The night is young. Some prime pussy in here, too." Wea-

sel looked around. He tried to stick his cigarette in his mouth
and missed. "Blowing my whole paycheck," he muttered,
stabbing himself around the lips. "Whole frigging thing."

"Then quit. Let's go before you're too drunk to drive."

"You drive, then. I'll point the way."

Jack ground his teeth. His world, ever on the verge of ca-
tastrophe, was collapsing around him again. He doubted that
having Weasel was even necessary anymore. But he had money
and Jack did not.

The beers came. Jack eyed them without much enthusiasm
while Weasel paid. His gut was swollen with beer and liquor.
His head was reeling with it. Arnold White was probably admiring a golden sarcophagus about now, perhaps soberly hack-
sawing it into salable ingots. The thought made Jack's heart
falter.

"I'm going," he said. "Loan me ten bucks for gas."

Weasel chuckled drunkenly. "You ain't leaving without me,
and I ain't giving you a fucking dime. Drink your beer."

Groaning inside, Jack drank. The door far off to his right
flew open, and three more customers tromped in, mashing
themselves into the crowd. Jack recognized one of them as the
beefy man Weasel had tried to fight, the guy with the hard hat.
In his mind's eye Jack could see it all in colorful VistaVision:
Weasel looks over, sees the man, they fight, the cops come,
people get arrested, shit generally gets flung against the fan.
And Jack loses his Sugar Daddy and spends the next two weeks
dying of alcohol starvation.

He looked quickly back down to his beer. He noticed that
Weasel was looking in the direction of the door. His eyebrows
had drawn together in a single furry line.

"So," he breathed, and pushed himself to his feet.

Jack sprang up and waded through the crowd. He got to
Spack and his buddies while they were still surveying the place
for a likely place to sit. They looked extraordinarily cheerful.
"Hey!" he shouted, and they looked at him. "You'd better get
out of here!"

Spack turned his nose up. "Who's gonna make us?"

Jack felt hot breath on the back of his head. "I am," Weasel
bellowed behind him.

Spack's eyes moved to focus on Weasel. His face seemed to
sag in on itself. It was clear to Jack that the idiot had forgotten
that he was Weasel's pick of the day. But to his surprise, instead

of turning green and bolting for the door, he brightened, then sneered.

"We're gonna buy this place, big man. And we're gonna buy Hyman's shop. You're gonna be out of a job and out of a tavern. I think we'll even buy this town and have you thrown out. Right, boys?"

The other two grinned.

Weasel threw Jack aside, slamming him into the jukebox, which skipped across the record and ruined a really nice Merle Haggard song. While the needle bounced and the music stuttered, Weasel screamed: "Union-wage fucker!" He launched himself at Spack.

Jack regained his feet while World War Three erupted beside him. *What was this talk about buying things all of a sudden?* he wondered. *Even union wages can't purchase a town.*

Fists flew, connecting mostly with air. Weasel was too drunk to fight. Jimmy Hallis had gotten hold of Weasel's beard and dragged his face down low enough for Spack to pound on it. The undersized hard hat hit the floor and rolled away. Jed was busy kicking his shins. Jack jumped at the skinny man and pulled him away.

"What's all this talk about buying the town?" he screamed in his ear.

Jed tried to hit him. Jack ducked. Jed spun in a circle and fell against the jukebox. Merle Haggard upped and ooped like a man trying to sing into a bad microphone. People were starting to stare.

"Answer my question," Jack snarled, cocking a fist back.

Jed righted himself, cringing. He stuck out his tongue. "Finders keepers, baldy. You're fucked."

Jack felt his strength melt away. Finders keepers? Holy, holy shit. They had found little Arnie and the sarcophagus while he and that dildo Weasel sat here soaking up cheap beer.

He was barely aware that Jed was hitting him in the face. He backed away, tasting salty things and the vile elixir of his own failure. "Where is it?" he shrieked, his voice a crazy falsetto. "Where?"

Jed hit him once more, knocking him to the floor, then went to work stomping Weasel's toes. Jack sat in utter despair with blood dripping out of his nose. Half of Pop's life wasted in a futile search. His own life wasted. All hope gone. Three goons with the collective intelligence of a flea had done what decades of scouring the country had not. Pop had given his life in this quest. Jack had given his liver, if nothing else. And all for naught. Unless . . .

He leaned over and grabbed Weasel by the legs. He jerked them out from under him. Weasel went down like a falling bomb, giving the floor a shake.

"You guys better run," Jack shouted. "I know karate."

They stood panting and blowing while Weasel writhed on the floor. Then Jed said, "He ain't lying, Spack. I seen his tricks. Anyways, we got work to do."

Spack dropped his fists. "Okay. We'll celebrate later."

They went out. Jack let go of Weasel and crawled to the door before it could fall shut. He saw them get into a red-and-white Ford truck with a white cap over the bed. The headlights popped on and it backed into the street, then headed west on Main, burning rubber.

He got to his feet, digging in his pants for his car keys. Neither God in his heaven nor the devil in his hell could stop him from following that truck. Only Weasel, who had found his own feet and had now become a 240-pound torpedo. He plowed into Jack and Jack plowed into the door. Both fell out onto the sidewalk, Weasel rolling drunkenly to plop down in the gutter while Jack squirmed around trying to find his breath and figure out who had set off the nuclear explosion behind him. He got to his knees and begged his lungs to start pumping again before he died.

Weasel got up. He staggered over and aided Jack's quest for life by clamping his hands around his throat and strangling him.

"Urk," Jack said. "Urgle-awk."

The doorway jammed with people. They laughed and laughed, a sound that took on, as Jack passed into the never-never land of asphyxiation, a bizarre echoing quality, reminding him of that gray area just beyond the rim of sleep where voices whisper and shadowy figures prance. He saw spots and swooping stars. Weasel's face was a hairy white moon swimming in the forefront of his vision.

His left hand came up of its own accord, the hand with the swollen wrist. It aimed itself somewhere in the vicinity of Weasel's beard. It shot out. Dull pain crawled up to his elbow, but the moon was falling back, the stars fading. Voices shouted encouragement while others screamed dismay.

Weasel had landed on his butt. He went for Jack again.

"The gold," Jack croaked, rocking on his knees. "They found it. Have to follow."

Weasel, also on his knees now, was getting ready for a good old-fashioned fist to the chops. He hesitated. "Huh?"

"The fat guy and his pals. They found it."

"Says who?"

"The skinny guy."

"The vending guy? He told you?"

Jack nodded, massaging his throat. Weasel lunged for him again, but this time his big hands went under Jack's arms and pushed him upright. Then Weasel stood up.

"Your car this time, Jack. And for Christ's sake hurry up."

They staggered off to Jack's Dodge.

A minute later the bar began to empty out.

"I think we're being tailed," Jimmy said as Spack ran the last stoplight in town.

"Yeah?" Spack looked at his big side mirror. There was a trail of headlights a mile long behind him, about four blocks back. He gripped the steering wheel harder. "Okay, who blabbed?"

Jed sat, tight-lipped.

"Well, we'll lose the bastards." He mashed the accelerator to the floor and turned off the headlights. Rain began to splatter against the black windshield.

"Whoa," Jimmy said. "I can't see shit."

"You don't need to see. I drive this road to work and back five times a week, remember? I know it by heart." He checked the rearview mirror. The procession was falling back. He clicked on the dome light briefly and found he had reached seventy-five. Woe to any cop who dared try and stop him tonight. Niggerchaser's barrel was still warm, and with all that gold you could buy your way out of prison and into Rio.

"Coming up, I think," Jimmy said after a minute.

"Yeah, yeah." Spack reluctantly let off the gas and hit the brakes, fervently hating brake lights and the man who had invented them. But the cars behind had fallen back a good mile, and here was Norman Parker's lane already. He turned hard left, got off the brake, and gave gas. The truck bounced down the lane, throwing gravel and a bit of dust. The rain would dampen that soon enough. He swung into Norman's muddy yard and killed the engine.

"Out. Quick."

They got out and slammed the doors. Jimmy and Jed pulled the hoist from the truck and began to grunt their way to the shed. Spack watched the highway. The first car went past. Thirty seconds later the rest began zipping by, following their blind leader. Spack smiled. You don't drive a heister for twenty years without learning a trick or two.

He ran over and opened the shed door. The left part was stuck fast. With a heave he peeled it away from its ancient nails and let it slap into the mud. Jimmy and Jed waddled in. He heard the hoist thump heavily to the ground inside as they dropped it.

"Light," Jimmy said. "I gotta set this up."

Jed produced light. Jimmy did one of the few things he knew how to do, working feverishly to extend the hoist's legs in the dancing yellow light from Jed's Bic. Metal clicked into place. Spack watched the thing unfold to become a three-legged octopus with metal plates for feet and a series of pulleys for a head.

"Okay," Jimmy said. "Spack, help me lift it up. Two feet on this side, one on the other."

Spack hurried over. "You mean tip it?"

"Of course I mean tip it."

They lifted the top. The hoist balanced on two legs, the third sticking over the grave.

"Okay, let her drop."

They let her drop. Jimmy worked with the chain, resetting it on its pulleys. Jed began to moan that his lighter was getting hot.

"Just another minute." Jimmy jumped down into the hole. The chain, which Spack now saw had three ends equipped with adjustable hooks, ratcheted loudly. Things clicked. Jimmy climbed out.

"All set."

Jed lit a cigarette from his overheated lighter. His hands were jittering. Then he let it go out, and they were in darkness save for the bobbing orange tip of his Marlboro.

"God, for a flashlight," Jimmy panted, and began hauling on the chain. He went at it for a full minute, pulling up the slack. When it was tight he began to grunt. "Fucker weighs a bit," he said. "Should have brought the spare pulleys."

"Yeah, and it's just the lid," Spack replied. "The real meat's underneath."

"That'll take some work. How we going to carry this to the truck?"

"Elbow grease, I guess. How heavy is it?"

"Hard to tell. I got three pulleys and it's no picnic. Four hundred pounds, easy."

"We'll manage it. Might have to go get those pulleys for the bottom part, though. Wish you'd thought of it before."

"Haste makes waste."

The lid made a scraping noise. Spack stared down at nothing. "Light it, Jed."

Jed made fire. Spack saw that the feet of the hoist had dug themselves deep into the hillocks surrounding the hole, but had now bottomed out and were putting the action where it belonged. The lid swayed from the triple chains, inching upward, scraping dirt from the rough sides of the hole. Jimmy smelled like a gym sock full of spoiled tuna fish, but Spack didn't mind. The man was a hell of a worker.

In four minutes, most of it spent in darkness while Jed's lighter cooled, the lid was raised to waist level. Spack noticed a new smell. Something rotten. Well, he reasoned, what could you expect from a coffin, even a fancy one like this? Roses? And it had to be at least a hundred years old.

He ran back to his truck and backed it to the shed, avoiding the brakes whenever possible. The tailgate was already open, and it was only as he got out and went around it to go into the building, and stepped on something squishy underfoot, that he remembered Norman. Spack jumped back with a cry of disgust; the corpse had blown a bubbly sigh when Spack had stepped on its stomach. When this was done, Spack vowed, he would toss the good Mr. Parker in that mummy hole and there he could rest forever. But when the old fart wound up missing, the cops might scout the place. A pesky matter to be dealt with, but later. First, the gold.

Jed was on his knees at the edge of the hole, his lighter held low into it. He was gaping at whatever was inside. Jimmy knelt beside him and stuck his head down. *Jesus,* Spack thought, *if that lid lets go your head's going to be a pancake.*

"Holy fuck," Jimmy whispered. "Spack, take a gander at *this*."

Spack went on his knees in the soft dirt and took the offered gander. He had to blink three times before he could believe what he was seeing under that guttering yellow light. "It's a wolfman," he said when he could find his voice. "Just like on the lid."

Jimmy nodded his sweaty head. "Look at the tuskers on that fucker. Hate to have *him* chewing on my ass."

"A mummy of some kind," Jed said gravely. "One of his arms is busted off."

"No kidding."

They stared at each other. Finally Spack said, "Anybody give a shit?"

Nobody did.

"So let's get the lid in the truck. I'll take one side alone. You two weenies take the other. Just don't fall in, or you'll land on Jaws there." He laughed and got into position. It was going to be tough and the footing was lousy, but for this kind of loot he would do jumping jacks barefoot on broken glass. He wrapped his fingers around the lip. It was better than an inch thick and seemed to be putting out some kind of inaudible hum, making his fingers tingle. The strain on the chains, Spack decided. "Okay, Jed, pocket the lighter and lift. We have to come clean away from these hooks, or the whole mess is going to fall in sideways and smash Lon Chaney down there." He laughed again. "Ready?"

It became dark. Things jingled in Jed's pocket. "Ready."

Spack lifted. His feet skidded in the dirt, then held. It was tremendously heavy, but it was liftable. He batted the chain aside with an elbow and heard the others do the same. "Clear?"

"Clear."

They shuffled sideways. Jed wheezed like the chronic smoker he was. Jimmy's BO swirled with the air currents wafting through the open front of the shed. It took time, but no one gave up and no one fell. One of Jed's skinny shanks bumped the open tailgate of the truck, and he let his end of the lid rest on it with a groan of relief.

"Okay, Jimmy," Spack said. "Shove it on in. Jed, give us light."

They slid it in. It fit perfectly. Spack turned his face up to the rain, glad for the coolness on his face. His heart was thudding a little too heavily for his taste. He wondered if an angry God would strike him dead of a heart attack right now for killing Norman Parker and hauling off his secret. Not too keen on religion, Spack nevertheless had a healthy respect for spooks. He pulled the nickel out of his pocket and tossed it to the sky. A small token, something to atone for his little transgression here. A finger of lightning zapped through the dense clouds overhead. Spack ducked back inside the shed with a squawk.

"Now the hard part," he said loudly, his voice jittery. "Jimmy, will those chains reach?"

"Ought to, yeah."

"Then let's do it."

Jimmy stuck his hands in his pockets, staring down in the hole. "Uh, Spack?"

"Yeah?"

"What about creepo down there? Do I have to crawl all over him?" He made a face. "I get queasy."

"Oh." Spack thought about it. Creepo did indeed present an imposing image. He looked as if he would be seven feet tall if somebody stood him up, but that would be difficult because Norman's leaky roof had let rainwater and snow-melt soak the bottom end of the coffin, and Creepo's feet had toe bones sticking out of the brown and soggy wrappings. That would account for the stink. "Jed, hold that light closer. I'm going to see how heavy our pal is."

He slid down into the hole and put a foot on each thick edge of the coffin. Bending down, he was able to get his hands under the thing's arms. This was grave robbing of the weirdest sort, and for a wild second he had a mental image of this thing snarling to life and lunging up to tear out his throat. The feeling passed soon enough, but not completely.

He lifted, then chuckled nervously. "Light as a bag of feathers," he called out, and tossed Creepo out to land at Jimmy's feet. Jimmy jumped back with a cry of disgust. The broken-off arm sailed out next. Jimmy kicked it away and it rolled under the truck.

"Your turn, Jed," Spack said, smiling up at him. "Throw our monster-man outside someplace. He stinks."

Jed grumbled for a while, but then his lighter became too hot to keep his thumb on. He pocketed it and took hold of the mummy by one stiff leg. He pulled it out into the rain, grumbling, and dragged it into the weeds beside the shed. "Yuck," he muttered, dusting off his hands. They felt dirty, almost alive with dirt. He scrubbed his palms on his uniform pants, grimacing, but the strange feeling persisted.

"Light," Jimmy said when Jed walked back inside. He and Spack had exchanged places, Jimmy in the grave, Spack out. Jed flicked on the lighter, burning his thumb in the process but not really caring. His hands felt funny.

Jimmy was reeling the chain down when Spack noticed light outside. He hurried to the doorway.

A car was coming down the lane. A short distance behind it was the entire posse, a cavalcade of cars, twenty or thirty at least, containing every human being the Wabash Tavern had to offer except Mike Taraday, who was watching television and enjoying the quiet.

· 18 ·

Arnold Laid Low

HE STAYED WITH the darkened back streets of Wabash Heights
until the streets tapered off to gravel roads that went in a crazy
network of directions: this one led north to Coal Creek; this
one led west a while then curved south and dead-ended in a
farmer's field. The only direct route to Norman Parker's house
was US 40, and this was a road Arnold most decidedly did not
want to take.

He passed the last building in town, a boarded-up warehouse
that had, once upon a time, kept bagged soybeans out of the
rain until they piled up sufficiently high to warrant trucking
them to Indianapolis. The slow death of local mom-and-pop
farming had spelled a lingering and miserable end to the warehouse. Broken glass crunched dirtily underfoot as Arnold
passed. Ivy had crawled up the eroded brick walls in mysterious green bunches. It rustled impatient secrets in the growing
wind. Arnold shivered, not for the first time.

He wished he had asked Don Marston for a shirt or jacket,
but by now they would have been soaked anyway. The rain, a
gentle patter at first, had progressed to what the locals liked to
call a fine April shower, something to bless the already muddy
fields with extra water; who could know when a nasty drought
might come along and kill every standing plant in the county?
Indiana farmers knew nothing of irrigation—the water either fell
from the sky or it didn't. And now, just after planting season, no
farmer in his right mind would object to this little storm.

Arnold looked at the western sky before he left Wabash
Heights proper and entered the dense woods that bordered the
highway. Above the treetops the horizon was a dead black
curve, the sky overhead seeming low enough to reach up and

touch. Rain washed out of it in a steady downpour, cold drops
that ran down Arnold's chest and back in little rivers and
dripped from his eyebrows. The heat that Marston's Cup-o'-
Soup had implanted in his belly was gone. A tasteless acid
burning was all that was left.

The woods closed over him, tangled Indiana woods full of
maples and elms and scruffy saplings. Last year's briars still
stuck up like bizarre clots of giant's hair, grown in disarray
and presenting, at times, impenetrable fences. Arnold stayed
close to the border of the highway, gauging his direction by the
lights from an occasional passing car. At one point an entire
procession of cars went by, maybe twenty or thirty, and Arnold
could only guess that it was a funeral. The headlights threw
stark black shadows behind the trees, shadows that swung in a
half-circle as the cars rushed past. He was in a forest of sun-
dials, frozen in a squat so that no one would see him as anything more than a stray dog or a deer looking for a spot to bed
down out of the rain.

Then the cars were gone. Arnold went forward again. The
jug of Contro-Tan had magically added weight to itself and
now was a good thirty pounds, and was growing heavier with
each passing minute. His fingers ached from clutching it, and
for a trial he switch it to the other hand. Instant pain groaned
alive under his cast, and he hastily switched hands again. Mr.
Broken Arm had had enough torture and would take no more.
He held it up as a shield against low-hanging branches and the
sharp sticks that could poke you a good one in the eye, and
walked, skating and sliding in the spongy mulch of leaves and
sod underfoot. In this manner he made his way the two miles
to Norman's house. It took an hour. ORD would have made
the trip in five minutes, probably with the heater blasting if
Arnold could have found the right switches, but ORD was presently and forever dead.

He stopped at the turnoff, looking left and right for approaching cars, cops on the prowl, the citizen's posse he so
dreaded. There were no cars coming from either direction. He
darted down the weeded embankment and crouched in the
drainage ditch there. Cool water surfed over his shoes, making
them white again. Lightning slashed across the western sky,
turning the world into a harshly brilliant snapshot; in that moment he saw that Norman Parker's house was surrounded by
cars and people.

Belated thunder boomed in the distance. Arnold stood up with the snapshot image of his last hopes forever gone printed on the black field of his vision. His body felt as if some secret inner layer, some fine thin crystal that encased his flesh just beneath the skin, had suddenly shattered and fallen to pieces in his shoes. For a long tick of time he stood, unaware that perhaps cars were coming and perhaps not, unaware that cold raindrops the size of dimes were splatting against his face, aware only that his famous final option had been a hopeless sham like all the others. He had worked and suffered, and the town had won again.

He staggered up the slippery incline of the ditch, the gallon of Contro-Tan dangling from his nerveless fingers, his feet skidding now and again on the long, wet weeds. He fell down and landed hard on the elbow of his cast, but the pain, if it came at all, did not reach his brain. He stood up mechanically and found the gravel beside the road. It crunched under the soles of his cheap K-Mart sneakers. Then he was on pavement, lurching across the highway much as Norman Parker had lurched the night before on his mindless quest to find a route to Maine.

He reached the lane. Lightning popped, and thunder walked the western sky on huge monster's feet. The flash burst of light showed it all. The cars were parked helter-skelter in the lane, in Norman's front yard, by the shed, wherever space had been found. Flashlights bobbed and winked in the dark. Voices floated out of the rain, men in a state of high excitement. Some of them were fighting. Most were crowded at the shed's doorway, which had been ripped fully open and gaped like a large square mouth. A dozen flashlights were aimed inside it.

Arnold walked past two men who were throwing wild, drunken punches at each other. They were screaming something about "Mine! Mine!" There to the left, at the foot of Norman's front steps, three men were rolling in the mud, fists flying, mud being flung in big blotches against Norman's house and the surrounding cars. They kicked and screeched. Arnold walked past them with the shattered remains of his soul still in his shoes. He was ignored. The people in the shed were shouting at each other. Arnold went around the back of the shed, pausing to peek in the window. He was staring down at the hole his left hand and sixteen hours of hell had dug. The golden lid was gone. The monster was gone. Three chains hanging from some tripodal contraption were being hooked under the

base of the crate by some dark shape while another held a
lighter overhead despite the flashlights.

And there, arguing fiercely with a beefy-looking man, was
dear stepfather Frank, he of the big fists and the onion-in-the-
nose fame.

Arnold waded through the ocean of trash bags he had thrown
out the window the night before, and made his way around the
shed. Fury burned in his brain at this absurd outrage. He
tripped over something and went sprawling in the rain-soaked
weeds. A weak twinge of lightning ignited the sky for a brief
moment, and he saw that the monster had been thrown beside
the shed as if it were just another pile of garbage. His fury
brightened, blotting out reason. He got up and skirted the shed,
coming fully into the light.

"It's mine," he said through a throat that felt full of wool
and hair. "All mine."

He was ignored some more. Men stood around the grave,
shouting advice to the man inside it. Frittering helplessly about
was Jack Cumberland, whose long, thin face showed a mixture
of fabulous joy and unbearable worry. Somewhere along the line
he had given up his wig. Flashlights reflected off the wet skin of
his head. The smell in the shed was more exhaled beer fumes
than garbage. All that was familiar had now become strange.

"Mine," Arnold barked, being elbowed back and forth as
a new fight broke out beside him. He was knocked to his knees.
A flashlight fell into the mud and straw beside him. He picked
it up and aimed it at Cumberland.

"You can't have it," he shouted, and Cumberland turned to
look at him, squinting. Then recognition charged across his
features, changing him into the sly and malevolent ogre he had
been when he stuck a knife in Atkinson's eye.

"You," he said huskily, then grinned. He sidestepped and
tugged on the back of Weasel's shirt. Weasel had a hand around
the beefy man's neck and was about to blast him through the shed
wall and into the next century, but this made him hesitate and
turn. His eyes fell immediately upon Arnold.

"Well," he said, letting the beefy man go. "If it ain't the
runt." He grinned a wicked and brown-toothed grin. "I ought to
thank you, leech. You made me the richest man in the state."

"No!" the beefy man screamed. "We found it first!"

"First this, union-boy." Frank slammed a fist squarely into
his nose. He flew backward and bonged against the wall, then

performed a slow slide downward into the garbage bags with his booted feet sticking out. Blood sprayed out of his nose and mashed upper lip. His eyes snapped shut and his head fell sideways in a classic drunkard's pass-out pose. A mouse squeezed its way out of the mashed bags and bulleted around the shed in a frenzy of terror.

A skinny man wearing a brown and tan uniform had put his lighter away and begun reeling in the hoist's chain. The man in the hole scurried around checking his connections. Screaming bedlam continued outside as every drunk in town made his claim and found it contested. Gold fever hung in the air like a pestilent gas, turning former drinking buddies into slavering animals. Arnold was aware that behind him, beside him, in front of him, the face of Wabash Heights was peeling away its shoddy mask to expose the mutated horror that lay beneath. For a brief second his mind jumped back to a better day, the day Dad got hold of a copy of a book called *Night Shift*. The man from Maine had been a short-story writer as well as a novelist. One of the stories was called "The Boogeyman" and had pitched Arnold into such a state of dread that he could barely sleep for three nights running. In the story a man tells a psychiatrist of the strange way his three children were killed in their sleep, and that always the kids' closet door was open just a crack, and when he looked inside, the remnants of the stink of old seaweed were all he could find. The man tells his tale, leaves the doctor's office, then comes back to mention one more thing. The doctor is gone, but the closet door in his office is open . . . just a crack. And then he shambles out, no longer wearing his doctor-mask; he is the boogeyman himself, and he reaches out with his spade-claw hands, and . . .

Arnold shut the vision down. What was happening here was similar, if not worse. There were possibly forty people outside, maybe more. They were carpenters and plumbers and handymen and trash haulers and factory robots, but now their masks were down and they were the boogeyman, all of them, not boogeymen out for blood but for gold, instant riches, anything to prove they were a cut above the norm, better than the average in a town where the average was so low that no scientist could chart it and a computer would blow up if it tried. The Naked City was battling itself for a piece of the pie it did not deserve and would not have.

"Atkinson gave it to me!" Arnold screamed, hoping that his

own mask was not peeling away to reveal anything more than a scared kid who had always tried to do his best. The mask he was wearing now was one of rabid determination. Atkinson *had* given the sarcophagus to him, and the magic that lay inside. It was his. This shrieking mob had no right to it, no understanding of it.

Cumberland looked at Weasel, who was examining his fist with drunken pride. "You know what?" he said.

Weasel looked up. "What?"

"That kid of yours is getting on my nerves."

"So? Knock his ass out."

"He killed my dad, you know."

"Knock him out twice, then." He looked at Arnold with his sunken eyes. "Is there a price on the little rat's head yet?"

Cumberland shrugged. "Might be."

"I don't suppose it compares to our little treasure here, though."

"I doubt that."

Weasel stared down into the hole. "Two million bucks. Imagine me in a Cadillac. With a nigger shofer. Imagine me rubbing elbows with the mayor. Imagine me getting rid of the ratty bitch I married while she was pining away for her old man. Catch that, Arnie? You can kiss your free meals good-bye."

Arnold stared into the mindless evil mask of Weasel's face, feeling his stitched lips draw apart in a snarl. This human pile of puke had turned an empty and devastated family into a wasteland of fear and bottomless misery. In his boundless stupidity he believed he had done them a favor. Now that he believed himself rich, it was time to cast the ruins aside and move in at the Ritz.

Arnold hurled himself at Weasel, his feet sinking deep in the piles of cast-off earth that had cost so many hours of sweat and pain, his heels kicking sprays of it behind him. He hauled back with his cast in the two seconds it took to cross the shed, and slammed Weasel in the side with it. There was a bright and nearly unbearable explosion of pain under the plaster, but Weasel was falling, no, *reeling*, his face a new mask of stupid surprise. His feet skidded on the soft earth surrounding the hole, and he fell noisily inside, knocking the chains away that Jimmy Hallis had spent so long putting into position. He fell into the sarcophagus with a loud whoof and a yelp of pain.

Cumberland looked at Arnold, his face taut with a strange
mixture of apprehension and admiration. He glanced down in
the hole, where Weasel was struggling to sit up. "If I was you,
kid," he said, "I'd get the fuck out of here *fast*."

Weasel's head and shoulders popped up. Flashlight beams
tossed crazy multiple shadows behind him. Arnold dropped the
flashlight and picked up a trash bag. He threw it in his face. It
was like throwing a feather at a mad dog. Weasel scrambled
out of the hole with the chains clanking noisily around his
shoulders and Jimmy Hallis cursing. He charged at Arnold like
a runaway locomotive, both hands bunched into fists the size
of canned hams. Arnold picked up another trash bag, and the
bottom fell out, spilling piles of garbage and beer cans across
the ground. He found he now had a limp plastic whip in his
hand. He lashed out with it, spraying smelly liquid droplets of
filth across Weasel's face. It made him pause long enough to
wipe his eyes. When he opened them again, they were bright
with elemental hate.

"Now . . . you . . . die," he grunted, and swung one of
his Hormel-sized, hammy fists. Arnold held the jug of Contro-
Tan in front of his face as a last protective reaction.

Nothing happened. The shouting outside went on as usual.
Chains clanked as they were reattached. Someone grunted and
strained.

Arnold lowered the jug. Weasel and Jack Cumberland were
hand in hand, performing some kind of strenuous waltz. Weasel towered over Jack by at least eight inches and had to out-
weigh him by sixty pounds, but somehow Jack was doing things
to Weasel's hands or fingers that made him weak. Grimacing,
Weasel sank to his knees, his face a rictus of pain. He tried to
bite Jack's stomach.

"Get outta here," Jack groaned.

Arnold shook his head. There was no outta here to get to.
The treasure was his.

"It's your funeral, then," Jack said, and let Weasel go.

Weasel lumbered drunkenly to his feet, flexing his fingers. He
curled them into fists and swung at Jack. The punch was expertly
blocked. Weasel swung again, and Jack ducked. Weasel spun in
a circle and fell down, throwing up a cloud of dust. He got to his
hands and knees and stayed that way for a while, wobbling, blink-

ing the dirt out of his eyes. Then he looked up at Jack. "One of these days, Chrome-dome. One of these days."

He got up and came at Arnold. He grabbed him by the cast and hauled him outside. Arnold kicked and screeched while pain shot through his broken arm in hot, jagged splinters. Cold rain pelted him. People wrestled and shouted all around him. Weasel dragged him to one of the cars and threw him up against it. Arnold struggled to see in the dark, to make out which direction those fists would come from. Weasel was a huge black shadow, a dark monstrosity with flashlights dancing behind him. Arnold squinted, his mouth hanging slack, his tongue unconsciously pressed to the broken remnants of his front teeth to protect them from the cold.

"This is for not telling me about the gold," Weasel said, and an instant later his right fist drove itself under the shelf of Arnold's jaw, slamming his mouth shut and knocking his head backward into the car's window. Glass broke with a dull crunch. Arnold howled while blood filled his mouth. The tip of his tongue felt as if it had been laid on a post and mashed with a hammer. He felt a warm sliver of something floating in the pool of blood inside his mouth, and realized with sickened horror that he had bitten off the end of his tongue. He leaned forward and spat the chunk of tongue and a great blot of blood onto the mud.

Weasel grabbed him by the hair and pulled his head close. "I ain't as dumb as you think, boy. You found that gold first and that means it belongs to me. See, you're a minor and I'm a major. Dig it? Hah! So now, just in case you decide to run away again, I'm gonna do this."

He bent down and pulled one of Arnold's legs out from under him. Arnold grappled for a handhold on the car, but it was all smooth metal and easy curves. He plopped down on his butt, losing his jug of Contro-Tan and jarring his teeth again. Weasel had Arnold's skinny left leg in both hands. Arnold sensed that he was squatting down. He felt his calf being pressed against Weasel's thigh.

Weasel grunted. Knowledge roared into Arnold's brain like a swift mental tornado, and along with it, a new and unfamiliar pain. He screamed, but the world was already filled with screams and one more didn't seem to matter. There was a heavy wet snap, followed by a brilliant firework of agony.

"One down," Weasel said casually, and picked up Arnold's other leg. He brought it down across his thigh like a man breaking sticks for a campfire. There was that same heavy, muted snap, the same firework of pain. Arnold's screams became sloppy gurgles.

Weasel opened the car's door and tossed him inside. "Let's see you walk away on *them* stilts," he said, blowing the stench of whiskey and beer in Arnold's face. Under the harsh yellow glare of the dome light he looked cunning and insane. Arnold looked down at his legs and saw that he had developed new joints between his ankles and his knees. His sneakers were pointing in crazy, useless directions. He felt his own sanity waver on the edge of some horrible abyss, an endless drop-off into a black and bottomless pit.

Weasel slammed the door and walked away, knocking people aside.

Arnold rested his head on the back of the seat, panting, feeling alternating rushes of heat and cold race up and down his body. This was death, then, the feeling people got just before they died. He had been raked over the coals so many times that the coals had grown cold and his heart was tired of pumping blood through the ruined mess of his body. It was time to call it quits. His father had tried to make something out of himself and been ruined by the ordeal; Arnold had done no more and no less. His dad knew when to call it quits and had fled from the horror of this town and its mindless inhabitants. Arnold was too broken to do anything more than he had already done. He sat in Jack Cumberland's Dodge and waited for the end, occasionally leaning forward to spit a mouthful of salty blood on the floor. When he lost enough blood he would lose consciousness, choke on his own blood, and that would put an end to this.

He sat and waited, shivering. Pain racked him from all angles, top to bottom, side to side. His head began to feel too heavy, so he let himself fall sideways across the seat. *Rest in peace, Arnold,* he thought, and shut his eyes.

Something was digging at his arm. It felt like a brick, its sharp corners cutting into his skin. With effort he raised himself up on his elbow and felt the seat for the thing that was tormenting him even in this, his hour of death. What he found was a fat paperback book, the fattest he had ever seen. He held it up and in the stuttering light of a dozen aimless flash-lights saw in big silver letters the words

STEPHEN KING

Below that, harder to see in this crazy light, a single word—

IT

There was a picture of a sewer grating with some green claw-fingers sticking out of it. Arnold's heart jumped. He knew what this book was about, vaguely: Danny Heathrow had already read it and told him it was absolute dynamite. Something about a group of kids who battle this incredible monster that could be any monster you want: a vampire, a werewolf, a Creature from the Black Lagoon. Even a mummy, if that's what you happened to fear the most. Whatever scared you the worst, that's what you got. And these kids beat it, at least for a while. Even when it looked hopeless and impossible, they beat it.

They didn't give up. In the world of Stephen King, the heroes never gave up.

Arnold clutched the book to his chest. If his own heart was failing, then let this be his new one. His legs were gone, but this book would be his crutch. His tongue had no tip, so let this book be his mouth.

He sat up fully and opened the door. Rain fell in steady big drops. Still the men outside were pounding each other silly as they laid claim to this or that part of the sarcophagus, this or that many pounds of it once it was melted down. Arnold fell out of the car, careful not to let the book land in the mud. His freshly broken legs howled; this kind of pain would take some getting used to. He searched for the jug of tannin, finally finding it a few feet under the car. With the book in one hand and the jug of Contro-Tan in the other, he dragged himself toward the shed on his elbows, digging twin shallow trenches in the mud, moving through a churning sea of legs and boots. He was stomped on time after time, kicked this way and that, but as usual, ignored. He came to the side of the shed and was pulling himself through cold wet weeds. Then his hand fell upon the soggy arm of the monster.

He made himself sit up. The paintbrush was still in his

pocket, caked now with mud. No matter. He set the book carefully in the weeds and unscrewed the cap of the jug, wishing for more lightning or a flashlight or anything that would help him see, but none came. He doused the monster with a big dollop of the tannin and began to paint it. The chemical smelled like turpentine and old leather. When he had finished with the front side and the jug seemed half-empty, he sidled backward and turned the monster over. It was heavy with water, smelling more and more like spoiled meat, especially around the feet. Arnold sensed that something was wrong there. He ran a hand over one of the monster's feet and found it disgustingly mushy. Worst of all, bones were sticking out.

The monster had rotten feet. *Well,* Arnold thought, *nobody's perfect.* He continued to paint until the tannin was gone, then tossed the jug aside. Through the wall of the shed he could hear the sound of a chain steadily clanking. They were hoisting the bottom of the coffin out. Fine, let them. Less work for Arnold White.

He got the tea bags out of his back pocket. They had fallen apart, and he had a handful of tea and bits of soggy paper. For lack of a better idea, he stuffed the wad into the monster's open mouth, hating the raspy feel of its canine tongue, ready to cringe back if that mouth should close.

It didn't. In fact, nothing happened. Arnold didn't expect it to, since working with mummies is tricky stuff, even for the experts. He picked up the book, noticing sadly that it was wet and beginning to swell. He scooted backward a few feet, acutely aware of the way Norman Parker had behaved when the magic words roused him from the peace of his death. His only hope was that the monster was in a kindlier frame of mind.

"Okay, mongster," he said, and blinked in surprise. Mongster? Just how much of his tongue had he bitten off? He spat blood on the weeds and tried again.

"Ready, mongster?"

Well, okay. Before we had a lisp, and now we've got a speech impediment. Before we had two good legs and now we have none, so why bitch about the little things when the big things are so bad? Arnold took a breath, exhaled, took another one. It was now or never.

He clutched the book tightly against his heart and said, "Isis ki Osirus."

Things began to happen then, but not quite like Arnold expected.

· 19 ·

Mongster

THE LAMPS OF HIS EYES.

It was part of the title of an old science fiction short story
or novella Arnold had read not long ago, and it popped into
his mind now as the animal eyes of Mongster flew open,
splashing the side of the shed with yellow light. Mongster was
lying on his back with his face turned slightly away from Arnold. Arnold both saw and heard his long jackal's snout snap
shut as he came alive. With horrid slowness, he turned his head
to stare at his master, blinding him with the lamps of his eyes.

Master? Arnold thought wildly as the twin cones of light
settled on his face. *Am I its master? Or is this a rerun of the
Norman Parker Blue Zombie fiasco?*

Mongster stared at him. Arnold stared back with his blood
pumping thickly in his veins, blood suddenly turned to sludge
by those eyes. What could he read in them? Hate? Compassion? Or a simple and mindless desire to kill? He tried to
swallow, but his throat had become a clenched fist. If this
thing, this Mongster, chose to attack, Arnold's only weapon
was a sticky paintbrush. Flight was impossible. His screams
would only mingle with the others that were filling the night
and Norman Parker's mighty estate.

"I am your master," Arnold squeaked at the jackal-man
"You must obey my every command."

Mongster stared at him, as unmoving now as a taxidermist's
trophy. It came to Arnold that if Don Marston would put a
yellow bug-proof porch light inside the head of one of his deer
the light shining through the glass eyes would look just like
this. Was Mongster an empty shell, a stuffed animal? Or was
it really life that was blazing out of those eyes?

250

"First command," Arnold said, beginning to breathe a little easier now. "You will, under no circumstances, try to eat me. Also, no strangling. Got it?"

Mongster stared through the lamps of his eyes.

Arnold decided all was well and good so far. "Now, get up."

Mongster sat up. His waterlogged body squished, as if it were full of worms. Rain pattered on his head and dripped off the tips of his ears and snout. He scuffled his feet, found his balance, and rocked forward to stand up, his left arm held out, his broken right one a wet stump below the elbow, where a jagged chunk of bone protruded through the doughy meat inside. His wrappings hung in tatters. The years had not been kind to him, Arnold decided. Four or five centuries underground had to be tough. From his broken arm the cloth had unwound itself in a listless spiral that tickled the ground. Worst of all, centuries of lying on his back had eroded the gauze on his buttocks and shoulder blades to the thickness of tissue paper; even now the rain was dissolving it. Mongster was becoming bare-assed.

Arnold shrugged to himself. Hollywood had no idea what a decent mummy ought to look like. This critter was shriveled like a prune; the Hollywood jobs were always large hulking monsters with bodybuilder's physiques under neat and tidy (if a bit dusty) wrappings. Mongster was an understuffed scarecrow. But he would have to do.

The noise of the chain inside the shed stopped. There was a period of quiet. Arnold could picture it easily enough: the bottom of the sarcophagus was out of the hole and people were admiring it. He dragged himself over to Mongster and tugged on his leg.

"Make them go away, Mongster," he said. "Scare the piss out of them."

Mongster lifted a leg and took a step. Swaying drunkenly, he took another. Something snapped, a recently familiar sound that was for all the world like a wet twig breaking, and Mongster crashed over on his face. He lay in the weeds, continuing to mimic walking like a fallen wind-up toy. Arnold rolled his eyes. What a rip-off for a mummy. If he had bought this thing at a store, he would return it and demand his money back.

"Stop walking," he said, and Mongster was still. Arnold reached out with his good hand, found a leg, and worked his

way down to the foot. The front half of it was broken off, held
to the rest by the rotten remains of its wrapping. Arnold tore
the chunk off; the gauze ripped with greasy, sickening ease.
He tossed the chunk away and wiped his hand through the
weeds. The smell was really bad now. So was the situation.
Mongster couldn't walk. How do you scare forty people away
with a mummy who keels over every second step?

A thought struck him, and he got busy untying the laces of
one of his Polish sneakers. Pain surged up his leg and nested
itself in the splintered bones of his new joint, but he clamped
his jaws shut against it and got a shoe off. He opened it as
wide as possible and jammed it over the remains of Mongster's
foot. In life, Mongster had had big feet, but no more. Something had shriveled them. Arnold got his other shoe off and
tried to put it over Mongster's other foot. The naked toe bones
scraped his hand like claws, making gooseflesh ripple across
his back. This foot was too big; the shoe wouldn't fit.

He sat straighter and thought about things. The swelling paperback was still mashed to his chest, pressed there now by
his cast. A warm library smell drifted out of it. Mongster's
eyes blazed through the weeds, throwing weird shadows on the
shed wall. It was getting noisy inside there again; fresh fights
were breaking out. Pretty soon they would have the sarcophagus loaded and be gone.

Arnold made a grimace of disgust, swore to God he would
not puke no matter what, and began breaking Mongster's toes
off, one by one. Chunks of slimy meat stuck to his hand as he
peeled Mongster's size twelves down to sixes. The bones broke
at first as easily as wet chalk, then became more stubborn,
more like wood. Arnold broke these too. He rubbed the foot
in the weeds, satisfied that he had done pretty good work for
an amateur, and stuck his shoe over it. It was a tight fit, but
Mongster didn't seem to mind. Arnold set the book aside and
tied the laces of both shoes extra tight.

"Okay," he said, breathing hard and picking up the book
again for good luck. "Go get 'em."

Mongster began to propel himself to nowhere again, his
knees and elbows thumping the ground. Arnold began to think
of his Mongster as somewhat of a dummy.

"Get up first, okay? Like, on your feet?"

Mongster did a one-handed push-up, got to his knees, then
to his feet. His new shoes squeaked in the weeds as he fough

for balance; he seemed dizzy. Arnold wiped the rain out of his eyes, disgusted again. Hell, even Norman had been better at the zombie game than this clown. But then, Norman hadn't been lying around for five thousand years and was in better practice. Mongster should have come with an instruction book.

"Step into the light and scare people," he said evenly. "Can you do that?"

Mongster nodded. He shambled away and disappeared around the front corner of the shed.

Nothing happened. People grunted and strained, obviously trying to lift the coffin and get it into a truck. Arnold held his breath, waiting for that first scream of terror, the mad flight toward cars and safety.

Five seconds passed. Then ten. Arnold ticked off the time with his inner clock. Soon somebody with a flashlight would have to chance its beam across the jackal-faced monster, and then, oh man, watch out.

Fifteen seconds. Twenty. Arnold was panting. Were they so damned busy loading the coffin that they couldn't see or smell the sneaker-footed mummy who had lurched into the shed? Where was the terror, where were the screams? Where, for that matter, was Mongster?

Arnold dragged himself through the slick weeds to the edge of the shed with his broken legs shrieking. He peered inside.

Six men were on each side of the sarcophagus, groaning and sweating. The chains hung empty over the hole; they had made it halfway to the truck. Weasel was directing operations while Jack Cumberland stood wringing his hands. The shed was jammed with people, all of them aiming their flashlights at the operation in progress. Dirty gold gleamed. And there, standing in the dark among them and towering a foot taller than any of them, stood Mongster, watching the entire affair.

Arnold let his head sink miserably to the ground. It was never this way in the books or in the movies. There should have been an explosion of pandemonium when the mummy went in. People should have gotten cornered and hideously strangled by the relentless mummy, whose only desire was to kill. Stupid Hollywood. They had faked everybody out. Lon Chaney, Boris Karloff, Christopher Lee, Vincent Price—actors, all of them. And the writers, the Stephen Kings and the Ray Bradburys and the E. A. Poes—mythmakers, the whole pack of them. Here in this unknown town in Indiana was the world's

first and only actual monster, a mummy with the head of a
jackal and the body of a man, a dead thing come back to life
after centuries in the grave. But nobody was noticing, because
here, where illiteracy was prized almost as much as hunting
prowess, nobody believed.

Arnold rolled onto his back in the wet cold weeds and lifted
the paperback to where the light from the shed could catch it.
Was it lies? Could a man become rich and famous and make
TV commercials for credit cards when he was nothing but a
professional liar? Is that what Dad had striven for? To become
a well-paid and respected liar? Or was there truth behind the
lies, more truth than anyone could guess?

He raised the book to the sky while tears slid down his
temples into his ears, hot in comparison to the cold rain that
battered his face. The book was still swelling, becoming almost too huge to hold. Arnold flipped it open, half expecting
a garbage dump of lies to fall out. Instead he saw words on
paper. Nothing more, nothing less. Words on paper. The truth
behind the fiction was that there was fiction behind the truth.

Truth. Fiction. Lies. *Dad.*

White shirt with a Kroger nametag.

The Remington had stolen his soul.

Clack-clack.

He burned the work of years.

Clack-clack.

They don't always turn the gas off.

Clack-clack.

One man's words on paper, printed and reprinted a million
times for eyes hungry for lies. Another man's words clack-
clacked onto paper a single time, destined for the bottom of a
fiery trash barrel. Why? Why?

Arnold clenched his eyes shut. The urge to throw the book
away was coming over him, becoming almost unbearable. He
had no idea how it had gotten into Jack Cumberland's car. He
did not care. He only knew that it was getting so heavy it was
hard to hold up anymore. His mouth was full of blood again,
and he wanted to spit it into those pages full of lies. Only . . .

It had been Dad's dream to be a writer. A writer of fiction.
Perhaps the noblest profession in the world, perhaps the hardest. Dad had wanted it so badly he worked at it for years, but
in the end he went to Texas, where they always turn the gas
off.

Arnold threw the book as hard as he could. It arced in the air and landed on the shed's roof with a wet, flat thump. At the same instant a blue-white lightning bolt zagged out of the black sky from the east and touched the roof. Arnold felt every hair on his body go erect. There was a curious smell, like methane. Then the roof exploded, blasting fireworks into the sky. Arnold rolled away from the shed, his legs thumping and twisting at odd angles. Men began to scream. Something thumped down hard on his chest, warm and smoking. He picked it up and looked at it under this new orange light from the flames of the burning shed.

It was the book. A little blackened around the edges but still by Stephen King and still *It*.

Arnold grinned while new tears streamed down his face and filled the cups of his ears. There were no lies in the world his father had tried so desperately to enter. It was all truth, after all. To be a good liar, perhaps you had to be a good truth-teller first.

He rolled over once and went up on his elbows. The dregs of Wabash Heights were streaming out of the roofless shed, some of them batting at the flaming hair on their heads. It was purely satisfying mayhem. One of the shed's walls leaned dangerously inward, bristling with fire. Mongster walked out from behind it, smoking but too wet to be aflame.

"Scare them!" Arnold screamed. "Make some noise!"

The men had clotted near one of Norman Parker's maple trees to check themselves over and watch the shed burn. A few were moving their cars to safer positions. Mongster shambled toward the men by the tree. Arnold saw his head tilt back like a wolf about to bay at the moon. When he howled, it was a ghastly, dry-throated cough. Tea blew out of his mouth like a cloud of gnats. He chewed, making vulpine faces of disgust. Arnold sighed. So much for Lipton. It wasn't Egyptian after all.

"Frig!" Arnold screamed at him, hammering the ground with the book that most certainly had better monsters than Mongster sandwiched in its soggy pages. "Do *something* scary!"

Mongster waved his arm-and-a-half and hopped around as if attempting jumping jacks, looking like a weary referee calling a halt to the game. Nobody noticed him; they were busy speculating whether Spack Laird, who had just stumbled out of the

shed, would get his truck moved in time before the gas tank
blew up and melted all the gold inside. Someone was hopping
around and howling about having smashed his finger when they
put the coffin in the truck. Somebody told him to quit belly-
aching; they began to fight. Spack got his truck started and
drove as far as he could before the cars in the lane blocked
him.

Arnold dragged himself through the weeds and mud, dodging debris and smoldering chunks of the roof, his mind reeling
with the memories of what he had endured to unearth the sarcophagus and bring the mummy back to life. Nobody noticed
him. He saw Jack Cumberland and loving stepfather Frank
hurrying to follow Spack. They began shouting at each other
about who got what first and who had rights to this and that.
But they had no rights, none of them. It all belonged to Arnold.

It took him a full minute to drag himself to where Mongster
stood performing his useless aerobics. The shed behind him
was a pyre of bright yellow flame; there were muted explosions
as cast-off aerosol cans overheated. Sparks billowed up into the
starless sky, forming spiral patterns. Everyone stared at the
blaze, mesmerized as all men are by the sight of something
burning. Arnold heard somebody joke that if he'd a-knowed
they was gonna have a campfire, he'd a-brought some weenies.
This brought a round of nervous laughter.

Arnold reached out and grabbed Mongster's bobbing ankle.
Mongster, busy doing the two-step, ignored him. Arnold got
jittered up and down, making his broken legs scream. "Stop
moving!" he shouted, and Mongster did. He craned his head
slowly around and looked down at Arnold.

"Kill," Arnold said into those lamps.

Mongster lurched away with mud and bits of straw stuck to
his sneakers, his headlights boring twin pencil-beams into the
dark. He came to the group under the tree and grabbed the
first available man by the throat. Arnold grinned, staring with
avid fascination. Here was Hollywood, folks. Here was the
mummy in action, doing what all good mummies were brought
up to do: strangle people with one hand.

And Mongster was real good at it, after all. He hoisted the
man by the throat two feet off the ground. The man pedaled
his legs and gobbled. He managed to kick someone, and that
someone turned around to complain, and at that moment two
or three others turned to see who was making all the turkey

noises. For a long moment they were silent, digesting what their drunken eyes were offering up, and then, finally, the pandemonium Arnold had tried so hard to instigate was under way.

"Holy shit!" someone screamed in a high falsetto of terror. *"What the fuck is that?"*

Heads turned. There was a communal gasp. Mongster dropped the man and grabbed another. This one he tossed remarkably high up into the tree, rattling the branches and making tiny leaves sift down. It didn't fit the Hollywood script, Arnold had to admit, but it was effective. The man in the tree tumbled down, bouncing off branches, and thudded into the crowd. There was a general shift of position as the mob turned itself to run. One man stood petrified, staring up at the seven-foot apparition of what appeared to be a long-snouted dog on top and a hospital burn victim from the neck down. Mongster deviated from the script once more and jabbed the man in the eyes with two fingers, Three Stooges style. He flipped him overhead this way, making Arnold wince and the man die.

The crowd was dissipating like a colony of ants under siege. Feet slopped through the mud. Car doors opened and shut. Motors started. Headlights flared alive. Horns honked and people screamed at each other to get that fucking heap out of my way. There were several noisy fender-benders, but no one seemed inclined to stop and wait for the law. Those who found themselves suddenly without rides scrambled atop the nearest moving vehicle and hung there like clinging bats. Mongster went for the slowest of them, killing one man by crushing his face with a mighty squeeze of his pass-the-potatoes–powered hand. Another slipped and fell while Mongster stalked him. He lay on his back, gibbering useless prayers. Mongster put a sneaker on his chest and pulled his left arm off. Blood, looking oily black in the firelight, shot out as if from a hydrant. Mongster tossed the arm away and unscrewed the other one, though Arnold doubted that it was necessary. This short bit of carnage was actually more than he had intended. He raised himself higher and took a breath to shout.

Only now Mongster was stalking Weasel, who had flattened himself against the side of Spack Laird's truck and developed eyes that were not deep-set and beady but huge and bulging. Jack Cumberland was beside him, looking positively aghast. Behind the wheel Spack Laird was all eyeballs. Mongster ambled toward them with agonizing but effective Hollywood slowness, one arm outstretched, fingers cupped for a good throat-hold. Rain sheeted down, sparkling like orange diamonds in the fiery light and hissing in the wreckage of the shed. Jack Cumberland's mouth fell open and he shouted.

"It was true!"

Nobody seemed to know what he meant, but Mongster turned slightly and went for him. Arnold squinted, wishing desperately for his glasses so that these fuzzy figures would be clear in this, their last moments on earth.

But . . .

Jack Cumberland had stopped his father from caning Arnold, maybe even killed the old man to make him quit; it was hard to remember. And he had stopped Weasel from attacking Arnold's young self, for a while. If he had a heart, it was a small one, but somewhere in his chest a thing was beating, somewhere under that bald skin was a brain that had feelings for a little kid who was out of hope.

Mongster came at Jack and slid his soggy fingers around his throat. Weasel turned and ran around the truck.

"Stop!" Arnold shouted. "I command you!"

Mongster stopped. Jack slid away from his grasp with his face pulled up in a grimace of horror and disgust.

"You'd better run now!" Arnold screamed at him. "You'd better run so far away you can't find your way back!"

Jack's face screwed up. "But it's mine," he protested. "All my life, it's been mine."

"It was your dad's," Arnold said. "And I didn't kill him. You know what that means."

Jack stared at him with rain dripping off his eyebrows. Meanwhile Spack started his truck and roared off, tossing from his tires two fountains of mud that splatted against Jack's legs. The logjam in the lane was clearing; everybody was headed back to Wabash Heights as fast as their ancient cars and balding tires would carry them. Mongster had become no more than a posed wax figure in a museum of elderly horrors.

"All my life," Jack squeaked. He was actually crying.

"Go," Arnold said.

Jack gave Mongster a last look, then performed a shuffling turn and walked to the lane. He stopped there and turned again. "Arnie?"

Arnold watched him.

"They stole it, you know. The town stole it. They stole it from me and from you. It belongs to Wabash Heights now."

"Just go," Arnold said, and watched him turn again and walk up the lane. When he came to the highway he went left, toward Terre Haute and away from Wabash Heights. A burst of lightning showed him, a slump-shouldered figure walking with his head bent to the rain. Then it was dark again and he was taken by the night.

Arnold turned his eyes toward Mongster. "Come here," he said, and Mongster turned around.

· 20 ·

Showdown

IT WAS A lousy way to travel but the only means available; Arnold tried to be understanding about the situation but found it difficult. For diversion, as he bounced along with his broken legs thrumming like overworked guitar strings and his poor eyesight bouncing in time to Mongster's steps, Arnold thought of a new title to add to all of those Groovy Golden Oldies in the Hollywood library of ancient horror films. He had already reviewed your basic *The Mummy*, then *The Mummy's Return*, and *The Mummy's Revenge* and, of course, *The Mummy's Hand*, but now there was a follow-up to all of these classics: *The Mummy's Back*.

He decided it wouldn't work: too ambiguous. People would expect to see a movie about the mummy coming back. That's not what it meant. Perhaps a better title would be *I Was a Teenage Mummy-Driver*. Yeah. That sounded better.

Mongster was tooling along at a good clip: Arnold's K-Mart sneakers splashed a steady drumbeat in the puddles beside US 40 with Mongster's size-6 feet firmly inside them. Arnold had his good arm clamped around Mongster's neck and his bad arm, in its cast, slung around his neck on the other side; it was a backward bear hug. A new thought struck Arnold as the interminable two miles were eaten up: *I Rode Piggyback on a Mummy*. Might attract an audience. Might not. People were pretty well sated on mummies these days.

Mongster plodded along with his burden of Arnold while the rain hammered down in monster drops and lightning crossed the sky in jagged white monster streaks; tonight was to be the night of the monsters. Armed with a crumbling mummy and a paperback book that was swollen like an exploded loaf of bread, Arnold was going to face the town of monsters and get his gold back. No one would dare cross the mummy; no one would dare cross its master. It was a law of some kind: when the mummy says jump, you jumps.

Unless, of course, you happen to be a monster of some sort yourself. And Wabash Heights had no lack of *them*. Thugs, idiots, wife beaters, child abusers, men who went out of their way to hit a squirrel on the road, men who hit and hurt and maimed and killed for the fun of it: proud men, all of them, fine, upstanding members of a community of monsters, all of them with jobs a starving migrant would sneer at, all of them so full of self-importance and ego that they would drive away a tall and thin bookworm of a man because he dreamed of being the writer instead of the reader in a town where no one could read.

They don't always turn the gas off.

Arnold hung on as Mongster crossed the railroad tracks and entered the muddy hole that called itself Wabash Heights. Arnold looked with sickened eyes at its hilly potholed streets and the red-and-green glare of its three traffic lights. No, they don't always turn the gas off, but plenty of them would be quite happy to turn it on. The whole crew from Norman Parker's house would be in one place right now, the place Don Marston had called a magnet for every scum in town. They would either be fighting it out for a piece of that mighty golden pie in the back of Spack Laird's truck, or, having settled that, be inside drinking to their good fortune while waiting for someone to go fetch a hacksaw. The small matter of a few dead men strewn across Norman Parker's yard would be told to the police at a later date, as soon as the treasure was divided and securely hidden. Where they would lay the blame Arnold could not guess. Not even a dope like Roly-Poly Roy would believe any of this mummy crap.

Nevertheless, Arnold rode the mummy into town much the way he had ridden ORD into town, and it was about now, at the first stoplight, that Mongster began to have motor troubles. The steady splash-splash of his strides became erratic; as they passed beside the bent telephone pole where a rusty chrome bumper was still embedded in the chewed-up wood, Mongster missed a beat and nearly fell down. One of Arnold's shoeless feet touched down on the sidewalk, bending his leg at a terrible angle. He turned his scream into a gargle; now was no time to be attracting attention . . .

. . . *as if riding a jackal-headed mummy into town isn't enough* . . .

. . . when there was so much left to be done.

"Cang you make it, Mongster?" he said into Mongster's furry right ear. He got no response, but Mongster was going fairly slow, doing one of those funny-looking fast-walks that is an obscure sport in the Olympics. When Mongster had picked Arnold up and settled him on his back at Norman's, he began running like Jesse Owens chasing Hitler; this new pace was a good indicator that the gas gauge was nearing the fabled one-quarter mark. And there were six blocks left to go: one-half mile. If Mongster broke down, there was nothing left.

They made it one more block; Arnold thanked the gods of Egypt that the streets were dead. A bad thought hit him then: all this rain was washing the Contro-Tan off of Mongster. Did that mean he was becoming waterlogged? Or was he stiffening up? At any rate, something was happening, because halfway down the next block Mongster slowed to a walk and his furry head began to droop. Arnold switched the ten-pound paperback to his bad hand and held his good hand in front of Mongster's eyes. He saw two pale circles of yellow on his palm. Mongster was dimming.

His walk became a shuffle. Arnold held on with his arms aching and his legs dangling, knowing that any second now a car was going to pass by and somebody was going to get curious, maybe get out into the rain and have a little look-see at this weird apparition of a boy trying to strangle a mummy from behind. He glanced back, scrubbing his nose across the furriness of Mongster's head and getting a fresh reminder of that smell of turpentine and old leather, the smell of the tannin that was so quickly washing away. No cars were coming—*we'll thank Egypt for that too*—but Mongster was starting to lurch like a dying man.

Arnold frowned to himself. ORD had acted just like this. So full of power at Norman Parker's, but losing it every inch closer to town. It had to be the sarcophagus. He remembered that odd tingling hum he had felt when he touched it; the thing was electric in some way. But the sarcophagus was in the back of a pickup truck now, just four blocks from here, so that power should be making Mongster stronger instead of weaker. So why had he slowed down to an old man's creep?

Arnold pulled himself up higher and spoke into Mongster's ear. "Isis ki Osirus, old buddy."

Mongster's headlights flared, splashing yellow reflections off the wet sidewalk. Arnold had time to get a handhold on the rotten wrappings of Mongster's chest before he charged forward as if a starter's pistol had been fired at the local mummy Race-a-Thon. A block flew past. Another. Then . . .

ORD again. Chugga-chugga-chugga. Pop bang boom. Mongster slowed to a weary shuffle. Even his pointy ears began to wilt.

Arnold's arms were lead weights shot full of poison darts, but he would not let go, could not let go. He jacked himself up higher and told Mongster to pass the potatoes, and quick.

Mongster jogged for a while. The Wabash Tavern was only half a block ahead, its tiny neon sign proclaiming simply BEER in dismal flickering purple, when he slowed to a walk again. Arnold was ready to weep with frustration. The sarcophagus was close, parked just ahead, there could be no doubt. After hauling the thing out of the ground the men would be powerfully thirsty, and here was where they would stop. What was blocking the magic power? The steel bed of the truck? That simple?

Well, whatever. Mongster was dying. He shambled along like an old lady on her last legs, his arm-and-a-half dangling limply. His body seemed to be a burlap bag full of seaweed, slowly collapsing. His five-thousand-year-old joints creaked like a clockwork of tired hinges oiled with dust. Arnold hooked his thighs around Mongster's hips and begged him to pass the potatoes to everyone from here to China.

He speeded up a bit. The BEER sign passed overhead. Hating it, Arnold told Mongster to stop at the door. Here was where things got tricky. D-Day, you might say. One deflating mummy and a wet kid with all his parts busted invading the beaches of the Wabash Tavern against uncountable enemy forces. Worst of all, perhaps, was the sign on the door proclaiming you had to be twenty-one to enter. Arnold was underage, and Mongster had no ID. The thought made Arnold cackle madly, and he wondered if all the impossible things that had been happening lately had finally driven him insane after all.

He peeked into the tavern through the window set in the door. Music was thundering inside. The place was packed. Everyone was in high humor; apparently the agreement had been reached and everyone was satisfied they were getting a piece of gold out of the deal. Without doubt Frank got the lion's share, but a man who has zoomed from poverty to unbelievable riches overnight can afford to be generous—even a man like Weasel. The seedy customers of the Wabash Tavern had probably decided he was the best buddy they'd ever had.

Arnold put his lips to Mongster's cold droopy ear. "Go in," he whispered.

Mongster hesitated, seeming to gather his energy, and walked into the door. Unfortunately it swung outward instead of inward, and once again, as Mongster walked to nowhere with his new shoes squeaking on the sidewalk, Arnold wondered how much brain matter was left in his doggy head.

"Stop walking. Back up. Reach for the knob. Open the door."

Mongster found the knob and proceeded to jerk on it. Arnold raised his hand and pressed it to Mongster's wet and furry forehead. No fever. The poor thing had simply been born stupid. "Turn the knob first."

The knob turned. Mongster shuffled backward, opening the door and letting out a blast of music and smoke.

"Now go in," Arnold said, and in they went. Mongster conked his head on the door frame and slipped on the wet floor. Arnold held on tight while the door swung shut behind him and Mongster performed a slow, drunken boogie-woogie to find his balance. People looked over. There was a series of shouts. Everybody looked over. Arnold hitched himself up higher. "I control the mummy," he shouted, hoping Mongster was putting on a wicked snarl. "And we want our coffin back!"

They stared at him in stunned surprise. Someone dropped a bottle of beer and it burst like a small bomb. A girl standing by the roaring jukebox in a silver blouse and pink high heels dropped her handful of quarters. They bounced and rolled on the floor. The bartender gaped at Mongster with eyes as big as the pickled eggs in the jar beside him. Weasel, sitting at the bar beside a man wearing a white hard hat, turned and eyed Arnold with his usual festering hatred.

"I mean it!" Arnold shouted.

Things waited on hold. The girl dug her fingers into her

cheeks and stumbled away, landing in the lap of the man wearing the hard hat. His beer spilled across the bar. Johnny Cash sang out of tune while rain drummed on the roof and dripped through the cracks in the ceiling.

"Well?" Arnold screeched.

Thunder boomed outside. Johnny Cash came to the end of his song. Mongster's legs were getting wobbly; Arnold hoped nobody would notice. He had opened his mouth to shout again when Weasel, the town's newest Citizen of the Year, stood up.

"Who's gonna make us?" he said flatly. "You and that sack of bones? Who's inside that costume?"

The man in the hard hat, Spack Laird, tugged on Weasel's sleeve. He whispered something to him. Weasel frowned and said, "Inside the coffin? You sure?"

Spack nodded hugely, as did Jed Heathrow and Jimmy Hallis.

Weasel sneered at Arnold. "Frank Whipple ain't scared of no man, living or dead. Not even a wolfman." He advanced on Arnold with his work boots thumping on the wooden floor, cocked a fist back, and hit Mongster on the snout. Mongster swayed a bit. One yellowed canine tooth dropped to the floor with a dull click. Weasel howled and rubbed his fist.

Arnold grinned a wicked grin at him. "All I have to do is say the word, and he'll rip your throat out, *Dad*. Would you like that, *Dad*?"

Weasel darkened. "You're gonna regret the day you were born, kid," he said, and punched Mongster in the stomach. Air and a cloud of Lipton tea whoofed out of Mongster's mouth. He rocked backward and nearly fell over.

"Looks like your mummy pal can't take much, kid. Especially not when it's forty against one. Right, men?"

There were a few grunts of approval. Most just stared, no doubt recalling the recent mayhem at Norman Parker's, when Mongster's batteries were still charged and he could toss a man into a tree with one hand. Arnold decided they needed some convincing; he only hoped Mongster was up to it. He put his mouth to his ear and shouted.

"Isis ki Osirus, Mongster! Kill him!"

Mongster jerked. Arnold had the feeling that this was the last pass-the-potatoes he would ever respond to; he was almost as dead as ORD. But his remaining hand did come up too fast for Weasel to stop it, and his soggy gray fingers clamped hard around Weasel's throat. He lifted the big man a few inches off the ground. Weasel's hands clawed at Mongster's wrist, tearing pieces of gauze and cheesy flesh away. His face became a dowdy purple while he tap-danced in the air.

The gentlemen and ladies of the Wabash Tavern rose in unison and scrambled for the door, pushing past Weasel, Mongster, and Arnold. Their feet were like drumming thunder. Arnold and his hostages were pummeled and pushed, but Mongster held on, and still Weasel danced while his eyes bugged out and his lips drew back in an involuntary grimace.

"Weasel," Arnold remarked before he realized the enormity of his mistake, "you need to see a dentist. Plus I'd get rid of the beard. And by the by, I hate you."

Weasel's eyes rolled up to show nothing but whites. His boots twitched feebly.

Arnold heard cars gunned to life outside, and then he knew. They were escaping with the sarcophagus.

"Mongster, quick!" he screamed. "Go outside!"

Mongster shuffled stiffly backward, still holding Weasel by the throat.

"Drop him, turn, and run!"

Mongster dropped him in a heap. He turned. Moving agonizingly slowly, he came to the door and thumped into it. There he walked like a defective robot, sneakers skidding in the puddle by the door.

"The knob," Arnold moaned. "Turn it and push."

Mongster did. The door wafted open. The night outside was ablaze with headlights and taillights, thick with the smell of exhaust. Everybody was getting away. Arnold spotted the red-and-white truck off to the right. The man in the hard hat was hurrying toward it, tailed by two others. Arnold recognized the one in the uniform as Danny Heathrow's father, a notorious drunk in a town of notorious drunks. "Chase them," Arnold shouted, and forgetting his broken legs for the moment, tried to goad Mongster on by jabbing him with invisible spurs. Pain spurted up his splintered bones. The man in the hard hat had almost made it to the truck. Mongster slogged gamely forward with the last of his energy.

Arnold and Mongster were ten yards from the truck when the dome light came on. Spack Laird had opened the door. Arnold watched all hope vanish as he leaned inside. Mongster was staggering, thudding into the brick wall of the tavern, careening away to stumble over the curb. He had lost all sense of direction. His legs scissored and wobbled.

"Come on," Arnold groaned in his droopy ear. "Please help me."

Mongster dropped to his knees. Arnold's legs got newly bent, and he screamed. He saw Spack Laird fumbling with something inside the truck. A door behind Arnold blew open and crashed shut. He looked back and in the misty glare of the streetlight at the corner saw Weasel Whipple stumble out of the tavern. He was holding his throat and doing a lot of spitting. Lightning flashed; he looked over and his black-button eyes met Arnold's wide and terrified ones. He turned and came at him in a shambling run.

Spack Laird came out of the truck. He propped his hands together on the top of the roof. Lightning snapped silently overhead. Spack had a gun. Thunder followed in an immediate crash. The gun, Niggerchaser by name, boomed. Sparks jumped off the sidewalk beside Arnold as a SilverTip hollow-point bullet burned across the cement and ricocheted to the sky with a high squeal.

Arnold tightened his bear hug on Mongster; Mongster was dying and so was he. The gun boomed again, fire jetting out the barrel like an orange flower. A piece of Mongster's left side blew apart in a spray of rotten gauze and moist flesh. The stench of death blew out with it, innards that should have been dust five thousand years before but had been preserved by a magic long forgotten. Weasel's boots splashed through puddles. He was close now, breathing hard, grunting with each step. He was death, doom, and destruction in one compact form, the epitome of an evil that had begun with the dawn of man and would never see an end as long as man existed: a man full of strength and stupidity and hate.

Lightning cracked the sky again. Arnold saw the barrel of the pistol aimed at his face; reflexively he brought up a hand to shield it. The gun boomed, and something smashed against Arnold's nose hard enough to make him see stars. He opened his eyes and realized that his hand was holding the swollen paperback copy of *It*. Smoke was boiling out of the sodden pages; they had taken the impact of a huge bullet and stopped it. Arnold turned it over. Dead center was a hole the size of a dime. That bullet had been meant for him. Words had stopped it. Not lies on pages, but real words with real form. Somewhere inside these magic pages a flattened bullet was sizzling where it should have been sizzling in Arnold's brain.

He grinned. The magic did exist. ORD had died and Mongster was rapidly croaking, but the words lived eternally, mummified on paper for all time.

Weasel was close. Spack was preparing to shoot again.

Arnold raised the paperback to the sky. Rain splattered his face, but he was grinning still with his broken teeth and his face smashed and bloated, grinning because he knew his father, his *real* father, had not labored in vain.

"I believe!" he screamed at the black and rain-soaked sky. "Isis ki Osirus, *I believe*!"

A straight bolt of lightning burped down from the sky, white as paper against clouds that were dark as ink. It arced down to the lightning rod of pages Arnold held in his hand. For a megasecond his hand was enveloped in blue light; traceries of it spiraled down his arm and enveloped him and Mongster. Arnold shrieked with joy and wonder, pierced by a thousand needles of electric fire. Thunder crashed immediately, walloping him with its huge concussion. Then the night was black again save for the dismal glow of the streetlight at the intersection of Maplewood and Kentucky, site of the Wabash Tavern.

Mongster rose up as if injected with adrenaline; Arnold barely had time to catch hold. Mongster turned as Weasel lunged at them, his gray mummy's arm blurring. To Arnold's knowledge no karate had existed in ancient Egypt, but Mongster knew it well enough. The edge of his smoldering hand cracked across the side of Weasel's head, splitting his skull. His brains splattered out and then the body of Weasel Whipple splashed down and stayed dead forever.

Spack Laird fired again while Jimmy Hallis and Jed Heathrow cowered behind the truck. The bullet struck Mongster squarely in the chest, but Mongster was recharged by the power of faith and did not care. Arnold tore his eyes away from the sight of his brainless stepfather and dared to sneak a look over Mongster's shoulder.

Spack was aiming again. Jed Heathrow and Jimmy Hallis had popped up beside him, their eyes huge as they gaped at the ruined corpse that had been Weasel. One of them wobbled, looking ready to faint, and bumped against Spack, spoiling his aim. He turned and snarled something. Arnold noticed a curious yellow glare reflecting off his face; Jed Heathrow suddenly screamed and began to wave his arms in large circles. Arnold pulled himself higher to see.

The palms of Jed's hands had turned the color of mustard, and were throwing searchlight beams in wild patterns across the wet sides of the tavern and the puddled street as he screeched and danced. Wisps of yellow smoke formed rings in the air around him and his whirring arms. Then his arms snapped out straight and he lurched stiff-leggedly toward Spack as if pulled by wires.

Spack staggered backward, his eyes huge in their sockets. Unnatural, blinding light splashed his face, painting stark shadows across his piglike features. Jed stalked him, his own face wide with horror. His glowing hands jerked apart, then clapped shut against Spack's fat neck.

Jed lifted him off the ground and strangled him, howling frantic apologies. Something cracked, something bony in Spack's neck. Blood squirted out of his ears. His teeth were clenched together, his eyes screwed tight in a horrible grimace of agony. His face became dark, then black. Arnold screeched in horrified wonder, too full of awe and revulsion to look away.

Niggerchaser boomed. A chunk the size and shape of a boxing glove exploded out of Jed's back. He crumpled, and fell together with Spack. Jimmy Hallis caught a spray of Jed's blood and guts, and the bullet as well. He dropped like a sack of bones, looking sad and puzzled.

Mongster walked past the truck. Arnold swallowed, not wanting to see any more, afraid of what he might find at this new angle, but he *did* look, and saw that Jed's yellow hands had not died with him, but had crawled upward and were tearing the flesh from Spack's dead face. Blood ran into the swollen gutter in multiple streams, where a white hard hat had rolled to a stop and was acting as a small dam.

"No more," Arnold whispered, and clenched his eyes shut. He heard the hands flop down onto the street.

Mongster hesitated; Arnold opened his eyes again, thinking the power was growing weak, but Mongster's headlights were pushing two steady cones of light through the dark. He was waiting for orders.

"Take me home," Arnold said, and as Mongster began to jog along he felt that lone cold hand come up under his bottom to help hold him up. Arnold smiled a troubled smile, resting his cheek against Mongster's fuzzy neck, dazed and exhausted.

Mongster stopped at Arnold's house, but by then Arnold had drifted off, tugged into a bouncy half-sleep by the powers that decreed young boys must sleep every two or three days no matter what. It was the sudden lack of motion that awakened him; for a moment he was in a dreamworld where dead people walked and Frank Whipple died and stayed dead.

He came fully awake and realized it was all true. That was all right. He had Mongster and the book, and with Mongster and the book he could face both the past and the future. He was shivering, and the aching need to be clean and sleep in a warm bed was overpowering. He told Mongster to take him up the steps to the front door, and Mongster did. He thought that it might be too much of a shock for Mom and the girls to open the door on this apparition of a delapidated jackal-headed mummy, so he had Mongster set him in front of the door. Mongster was no nurse, and certainly no doctor, because in the process of getting him off his back he managed to bend Arnold's ruined legs in a dozen different excruciating directions. But he did get him down, and Arnold looked up at him with the affection he had previously given pets, before Frank Whipple showed up and forbade any goddamn dogs or cats in his house. *His* house. What a laugh.

"Listen to me," Arnold said, and Mongster bent low. "I want you to find my dad. Stay away from roads and people. Travel at night. Bring my dad back even if you have to hog-tie him. Understand?"

Mongster straightened. His jackal head nodded.

"Bring him here. Don't hurt him, you know, but force him. I'll explain it to him when you bring him back. God, but I wish you could talk."

Mongster snapped his jaws open and shut a few times. The brown slab of his tongue was dusted with bits of tea. God only knew if real Egyptian tea would unlock his vocal cords. Lipton hadn't.

"Go on, then," Arnold said. "Isis ki Osirus."

Mongster stared at him. The glare of his eyes did not change; he was beyond passing the potatoes. The power of the book had usurped it. He turned away and went down the steps. Arnold saw him go left at the sidewalk, which meant he was heading west, before the night made him vanish. Oh yeah, west, you bet. Texas bound, Texas or bust. Dad coming home to riches beyond comprehension. Screw the book publishers.

the magazines, the whole heartless business that had rejected him for so many heartbreaking years. With forty million bucks, Dad could buy a publishing house and make himself the biggest author in the country. But hopefully his heart was strong, because when Mongster tracked him down to whatever motel or boarding house he lived in, it might be heart attack city for John Arnold White.

Arnold banged on the door. He guessed it was ten or eleven o'clock, maybe twelve. He heard footsteps thump inside. The lock clunked and the door swung open a few inches. Missy peered through the crack, searching the night and proving it was earlier than he thought, unless today was Friday or Saturday and she got to stay up until stepshit got home. And just what day was it, anyway?

"Down here, dope," Arnold said.

Missy looked down at the bloody and broken specter of her brother, and, just like he figured she would, she screamed.

· 21 ·

Dad

SIX WEEKS LATER Mongster came back with Arnold's father in
a 1988 Olds Cutlass, which Dad had purchased with the fabulous amount of money he had made working in the oil fields
of Texas. He walked in the door looking suntanned and lean
and wearing a ridiculous Stetson, and there sat Arnold watching television with both of his casted legs propped on a foot-
stool. It was a Saturday. They looked at each other for a long
moment, and then John Arnold White ran over and hugged his
son while Mongster stood by in his worn-out sneakers, looking
tired and pretty well ragged-out. Arnold told Mongster to take
a break because he certainly deserved it, and Mongster keeled
over dead, never to rise again.

   This is the way the story should have ended. John Arnold
White would have written it this way, and for this reason it
probably would have been rejected, because horror novels in
general are supposed to have a sad or creepy ending, something to give the reader one last scare or drag a tear out of his
eyes before he tosses the book across the room and wonder
why he bothers with this preposterous tripe. In truth this book
was not rejected, because it was written by a better writer than
John Arnold White, and because it is a true story. You will
understand this better when you read the epilogue, which is
coming up.

   What really happened is that when Melissa screamed i
brought Arnold's mother, Karen, running. She hurled the door
fully open, looked down at the broken remains of her son, and
burst into tears of gladness and sorrow. As gently as she could
she dragged him inside to the familiar smell of bacon grease
and home. She ran to the phone and snatched up the receiver

intending to call an ambulance, but discovered that sometime during the day the phone company had discontinued service due to nonpayment. So, in a way, Don Marston was right: occasionally they turn the utilities off at just the wrong time, or the right time, depending on which side of the fence you happen to be on.

Karen Whipple (now a widow but not knowing it) frittered about while Melissa asked an endless stream of questions Arnold was too tired to deal with. The baby was mercifully asleep in her crib and did not add to the mayhem. All Arnold wanted to do was crawl into bed and forget the whole nightmare, but the sarcophagus was in the back of a truck that could be hotwired by anybody in town and driven off into oblivion. Arnold told Melissa to call not an ambulance but the cops, because he had had a story to tell and had the broken bones to prove that what he said was true. If there was any doubt, he would bring Jed's tainted hands back to life again and show Roly-Poly Roy Mallone what passing the potatoes in the vicinity of that sarcophagus could do. Such a demonstration would be proof of ownership, and if necessary Arnold could have the body of Atkinson taken out of the morgue cooler or dug up from his grave, point to his punctured eyeball, and tell what had happened. Atkinson had given the sarcophagus to him.

Karen told Melissa to get a couple pillows and a blanket, which she did. Arnold's head was gently raised, the pillows shoved under it, and his head lowered with the loving touch only a mother could give. Then she settled the blanket over his shivering body and tucked it up tight.

"Missy," she said, "I want you to go knock on doors until somebody lets you in to use the phone. I know it won't be easy in this neighborhood, and you'll get soaking wet, but we need an ambulance."

"Cops," Arnold croaked. "Cops."

"Okay, the cops, then. Do it."

Melissa nodded and ran outside, in her agitation slamming the door hard enough to rattle the walls. The baby woke up after all and began to howl.

Karen, kneeling beside Arnold, ignored the squalling. She turned Arnold's head and looked into his eyes. "Now you tell me what's been going on, young man. There have been cops here; people are saying you're wanted for murder. A man who said he was a friend of yours from the hospital was here, and

I gave him a book for you.'' She indicated the lump under the blanket that was the huge bullet-holed paperback. "I see you got it. Where have you been, and what happened to your poor legs?''

Arnold took a breath. Where to begin? Where to end? Would she believe in Mongster? Would she think he was delirious?

He shrugged to himself, and told it all. It only took a few minutes, though Arnold could scarcely believe that the last three days could be encapsulated in a three-minute oration. He ended up by telling her how Mongster had dropped him off at the door.

She nodded. She frowned. She felt his forehead, then nodded again. "My poor baby,'' she said.

Arnold started up on his elbows. "But Mom! It's really true!''

She kept nodding, which was getting irritating.

"Honest!''

Nod nod nod.

"Really!''

Nod. "So where is this Mongster now?'' Nod.

"I sent him away.'' Arnold smiled, glad to be at the best part of all. "To find Dad. I told him to find Dad and bring him back.''

She quit nodding. A barrage of emotions crossed her thin face, ending up with an untidy mixture of apprehension and doubt. "This Mongster does everything you tell him to? Everything?''

Now Arnold nodded.

Karen stood up and began to pace the living room. Arnold felt sullen and mistreated. He had presented her with a cake worth forty million dollars and frosted it with the news that Dad was coming back. She should be mad with joy, but she wasn't.

Melissa burst through the door a short while later, dripping wet. She scrubbed an arm across her eyes. "Found one, but the cop said it would be a while. I asked him why, and he said something big had happened down at the Wabash Tavern.'' She looked around, puzzled. "Is that okay?''

Karen stopped pacing. She looked down at Arnold. "Mongster?''

"I didn't lie.''

Something kicked the door. Melissa turned to open it.

"Don't!" Karen shouted.

Arnold scowled. "That dumb Mongster. I should have known he was to stupid to—"

"Make him go away!" Karen screamed.

"He won't hurt us," Arnold said. "Anyway, I forgot to tell him where Texas is."

The door was hit again. Arnold heard the distinct squeak of his wet sneaker against the wood. What a monster. How the hell would he ever get to Texas? Perhaps if he were equipped with a map . . .

"No!" Karen shrieked as Melissa put her hand on the door-knob. "Don't open that door!"

Arnold managed to sit up. "What are you so scared of, Mom? I rode on his back all the way from the Parker place. He looks ugly, but he's nice. Not real smart, I'll give you that, but nice. Okay?"

Her nods had become violent head shakes, making her hair whip back and forth across her face. "Arnold, I . . . I think you know your dad read a lot of books and things."

Arnold nodded.

"You probably know he was trying to be a writer."

"Yeah. So?"

"And he always gave you the books and stories he liked, so you could read them. John and I talked about it a lot. He was giving you the books so you would learn to love them the way he did. He hoped you'd try to be a writer someday yourself, and he wished you more luck than he ever had at it."

The door thumped again.

"So?" Arnold said, growing impatient. "I'll write a book about Mongster someday. Now, if somebody would just open that door."

"NO!"

Arnold's jaw dropped. "Huh?"

Karen stared at him fiercely. "There was no trip to Texas. No oil rigs. There was a note pinned to his shirt. I bought the postcard at a curio shop in Terre Haute. His instructions were explicit. There's no shame in leaving town for a better job. But there's terrible shame in killing yourself. He didn't want to suffer that final indignity. So I lied for him."

Arnold's eyes were growing hot, filling with angry tears. "You mean you let him stick his head in the oven? You stood and watched and didn't turn the gas off?"

"No. He hung himself in the closet with his belt."

The door boomed. Arnold felt himself spinning down into some kind of shell-shocked hell. Hung himself in the closet? Hung himself in the closet?

"I buried him in the backyard. It wasn't deep. I took the plates off the car and ditched it in the woods. Your Mongster isn't as stupid as you think." She was crying now, too. Melissa, not following any of this, was staring at them both as if they had flipped out. Her hand was still on the knob. Mongster kicked again. *Of course he kicks,* Arnold thought dismally. *His hand and broken-off arm are holding what is left of my dad.*

Arnold turned his eyes to Missy, determined to look past the door and greet his father face-to-face. "Open it," he whispered.

She pulled the door open. The black stench of wet dirt blew in with the wind. Arnold studied the pitiful thing Mongster held in his arms while Melissa turned and ran past him, shrieking, into the depths of the house. A hot Indiana summer and a wet Indiana winter had not done Dad any good. Cleaned up a bit, he could pass for one of those hanging skeletons in an anatomy class. As it was, he was a thing made of mud and bones. His skeletal jaw was cranked open in an eternal scream of despair.

Arnold scrabbled forward and got hold of the edge of the door. "Take him back," he told Mongster through a throat that was tight and aching. "Take him back where you found him, then go guard the sarcophagus."

Mongster nodded. He backed up a step, and one of Dad's skeleton arms swung downward with a moist, bony creak. Arnold stared at the dirty bones of the fingers that had clack-clacked a zillion words into the abyss of rejection.

He slammed the door and fell back, listening to his sister's screams and the baby's cries and his mother's sobs until it all blended together into one cacophony that carried him off to the black painless nothingness of sleep.

• Epilogue •

Summer/Central Texas/1994

ARNOLD SAT AND stared at the grinning teeth of Dad's old Remington, the famous clack-clack machine that had killed him. Arnold could afford a brand new Wang word processor if he wanted it, but here in this dimly lit den in his new house he had decided the Remington would sit until the time was right for it to speak again. And now the time had come.

After a bit, he slid a piece of paper out of the ream beside the typewriter and stuck it behind the platen, which had changed with age from a mildly firm rubber tube to a piece of stone. It didn't make any difference. What Arnold had in mind to do had to be done on this machine, the typewriter that had murdered his father. He ratcheted the platen until the paper appeared in front, holding the rusty chrome bar with its three ossified rollers out until the paper was behind it. Then he let it slap into place.

And did nothing.

Minutes ticked past; he stared at that ugly blank sheet and thought of the monstrous burden he had inside himself of words that must somehow make their way onto the paper in coherent form. He had just turned eighteen and knew he was too young to ever write anything publishable, but it was a heritage passed down to him and one he had to fulfill. His only solace in this hopeless endeavor was the knowledge that S. E. Hinton had published her first book when she was seventeen, that great story about Soda Pop and Pony Boy, the kids from the wrong side of the tracks with hearts of gold.

He drummed his fingers on the metal sides of the typewriter, wracked with memories and words that were begging to tumble out. He thought of the past. Puberty had dropped on him like a bomb when he turned fourteen; in the year after leaving Wa-

277

bash Heights he grew four inches. He filled out, changing from hopelessly skinny to mean and lean. He was on the wrestling team in junior high school at Medfield Junior High here in Medfield, Texas, on the outskirts of Dallas. Basketball and football were out of the question because of his meager weight, but he toyed with the idea of taking up track. Once upon a time he had ridden on a mummy's back and faced the hatred of a mean little town's filthiest citizens, and beaten them. He could still recall with great clarity the phone call he had made from the hospital to Indiana State University's archaeology department. The dope he had talked to, some guy who called himself Professor Randall, had actually laughed when Arnold told him he had an Egyptian sarcophagus that ought to be returned to its home, but the dope came anyway and almost shit his pants when he saw what was in the back of Spack Laird's truck. For propriety's sake Arnold had removed his shoes from Mongster and told him to lie down and be a good dead mummy before the dope professor showed up, but Roly-Poly Roy had never been the same afterward: Mongster had menaced him all night while he tried to make sense out of the mess at the tavern.

Arnold had been in the hospital while the cops sorted out the bodies and tried to decipher the reasons for this carnage. They heard tales of a wolfman wrapped in muddy bandages; they heard tales of a weird mummy that had been punched in the snout by a man named Weasel. None of it made sense. Jack Cumberland got arrested shoplifting a tin of Spam and a case of beer at a Kroger store in Terre Haute; he became agitated while in custody, screaming that he had killed his father because the old man had defective DNA, and was eventually committed to the Katherine Hamilton mental health facility, the Crazy Kate's Weasel had believed he originated from in the first place. Arnold assumed he was still there.

The dope Professor Randall from ISU had contacted the State Department, who in turn contacted the Egyptian Embassy, who in turn contacted the American University in Cairo, who in turn contacted someone else, who then contacted someone else, and blah, and blah, and blah. It took five weeks for the Egyptian authorities to show up at the Wabash Heights police station and haul the sarcophagus off. It took another twelve weeks for the reward for recovered or stolen artifacts to be processed. Because the sarcophagus was so huge and the bizarre mummy inside so rare, Arnold got his picture in the Terre Haute paper as he was handed the check for $250,000 by a short, swarthy man who seemed to believe himself to be of some importance in Egyptian archaeological matters. Maybe he was. At least the check didn't bounce.

Arnold pulled his eyes away from the blank page now, and stared out the window to his left. Neat suburban houses, all in a row. People cut their grass here. They even watered it. They were affable and friendly and, perhaps best of all, Mom had a boyfriend who lived two houses away and actually did work the oil fields, but as an executive with Exxon.

He looked back at the blank page. A story was boiling inside him, a story that was screaming to be told. On the other side of the typewriter was a stack of hardcover books: *It*, *Misery*, and *The Tommyknockers*. Atop this pile was a charred paperback with waffly pages and a hole in its center. The bullet was still inside, and would stay there. It was Arnold's only remaining proof that those incredible three days had actually happened. There were nights when he woke up with a scream trying to burst through his throat; other nights he woke up weeping because Mongster was gone. It sickened him to think that he might have been dissected by scientists in Egypt. Mongster was no genius, but he was the best friend a scared and broken boy could have.

It was *his* story that boiled inside Arnold. It had to be told.

He ratcheted the paper a few more times and wrote.

MONGSTER
by Arnold White

Fine. What a great start. Memories boiled in his mind, in his gut. How could he ever put them down on paper, and if he *did* succeed in that, who would ever publish it? The name John Arnold White had been imprinted on countless short stories and novels, and all of them got rejected. Every editor in New York probably knew the name by heart. If Arnold did finish this book, the first editor who got it would probably lean over to the guy at the next desk and say something like "Hey, Ralph, here's another one from that John White guy, only now he's pawning himself off as Arnold White, so what say we nail his manuscript to the rest room wall and give it the treatment it deserves?" Haw haw haw.

Arnold ripped the paper out of the typewriter and crushed it into a ball. He dropped it into the neat little wicker wastebasket beside the desk. He leaned his chin on his fist and stared at the typewriter. As Stephen King had said so often in *Misery*, the damned thing seemed to be grinning. Hell, this one was talking. *Your dad failed and so will you. All you can churn out of me is unpublishable garbage. Your name alone is enough to make editors cringe.*

All right then, fine. Arnold put a fresh sheet of paper in, centered it, and wrote.

MONGSTER
by Stephen King

He grinned. This looked mighty fine. Imagine the editor who opened this little masterpiece and saw who wrote it. It would be published overnight. It would sell billions. Only . . . Stephen King might get mad. He might not like having his name taken in vain. From what Arnold had read of him, he seemed to be a nice enough guy, but he was big and Arnold was small, and he might just fly all the way to Texas from Maine and beat Arnold up. Weirder shit happened in the world.

He tore the paper out and made it vanish into the wicker wastebasket. His chin went back onto his fist.

He couldn't be Arnold White. He couldn't be Stephen King. He could be anybody he wanted to be, but he didn't know who.

The story boiled inside him. Boiled.

He slipped another sheet of paper in and positioned it. He licked his lips. Boil. Boyle. That would be appropriate. And how about Randall, that dope ISU prof who had laughed? It was generic enough.

Arnold gnawed his lower lip and wrote:

MONGSTER
by Randall Boyll

Damn, damn, he had messed it up. Arnold was a typist of the two-finger school, and one of his two fingers had missed the e in Boyle. Now it was Boyll, and when you stuck that together with Randall, it sure made a lot of l's.

But it would fool the editors. Wouldn't it?

He ratcheted the page a few lines more and commenced to make the keys go clack.